CASPIAN SEA

KINGDOM
OF
MEDIA

KINGDOM
OF
BACTRIA

KINGDOM
OF
ELAM

ZAGROS
MOUNTAINS

FAILAKA
ISLAND

Babylonia

COSTANZA CASATI

Babylonia

Signed Edition
July 2024

PENGUIN MICHAEL JOSEPH

UK | USA | Canada | Ireland | Australia
India | New Zealand | South Africa

Penguin Michael Joseph is part of the Penguin Random House group of companies
whose addresses can be found at global.penguinrandomhouse.com

First published by Penguin Michael Joseph, 2024
001
Copyright © Costanza Casati, 2024

The moral right of the author has been asserted

Set in Sabon LT
Typeset by Couper Street Type Co.
Printed in Great Britain by Clays Ltd, Elcograf S.p.A.

The authorized representative in the EEA is Penguin Random House Ireland,
Morrison Chambers, 32 Nassau Street, Dublin D02 YH68

A CIP catalogue record for this book is available from the British Library

HARDBACK ISBN: 978–0–241–60963–7
TRADE PAPERBACK ISBN: 978–0–241–60964–4

www.greenpenguin.co.uk

For my grandfather,
who brings so much light,
and my grandmothers,
who are looking at me from above.
I know you are proud of me.

Author's note

Babylonia – not to be confused with Babylon, which is a city in this novel – across the centuries has become the embodiment of lust, excess and dissolute power. It refers to the world of Ancient Mesopotamia, 'the land between the two rivers'. This is a glimpse into that world.

Cast of Characters

IN EBER-NARI:

Semiramis: an orphan adopted by a shepherd. Also known as **Sammuramat**
Amon: Semiramis' brother
Simmas: Amon's real father and Semiramis' adoptive one, the chief shepherd of the village of Mari
Derceto: Semiramis' mother
Baaz: a blacksmith's son
Ninurta: a soldier

IN KALHU:

Ninus, also known by his royal name **Shamshi-Adad the Fifth**: King of Assyria, second son of King Shalmaneser, grandson of King Ashurnasirpal
Assur, also known by his royal name **Assur-danin**: brother of Ninus, firstborn son of King Shalmaneser, grandson of King Ashurnasirpal
Nisat: daughter of a cupbearer, wife of two kings – King Ashurnasirpal and then King Shalmaneser – mother of Ninus and Assur
Onnes: governor of Eber-Nari, close friend and confidant of Ninus
Sosanê: Ninus' daughter
Ribat: a slave in Onnes' palace
Ana: a slave in Onnes' palace
Zamena: a slave in Onnes' palace
Sasi: eunuch from the Phoenician city of Tyre, Spymaster and member of the king's council
Ilu: commander-in-chief of the Assyrian army, governor of the Bit-Adini, close friend of Shalmaneser and member of the king's council
Bel and Sargon: Ilu's sons
Marduk: prince of Babylon
Taria: princess of Urartu, hostage of Assyria
Bârû: a seer and priest
Dayyan-Assur: Shalmaneser's second in command, killed by Assur during the civil war

Assyrian Deities

Adad – lord of storms, of tempests with thunder and of kindly rain. He is often depicted standing upon his bull, holding a lightning in his hand

Anu – father of the gods, god of heaven. He is part of the first triad of the great gods (Anu, Enlil, Ea) who, between them, exercise supremacy over the three elements: air, earth, water

Ashnan – goddess of grain

Aya – goddess of dawn

Ea – god of water, wisdom and magic and inventor of the human culture. In Sumerian he is known as Enki. He is represented by the symbol of a monster with the body of a fish and the forequarters of a goat

Enlil – god of the earth

Ereshkigal – Ishtar's sister, ruler of the Underworld, wife of Nergal

Gula – goddess of healing

Ishtar – goddess of war, fertility and love. She always carries her bow and quiver, and sheaves of weapons spring from her shoulders.

Nabu – god of scribes, literacy and wisdom

Nergal – god of death and the plague

Ninurta – god of war

Nusku – god of fire and light

Shamash – the sun god, presiding over law and justice. His animal is the lion, and his emblem the solar disc

Sin – god of the moon, who governs the passing of the months by his waxing and waning. He is part of the second triad of the great gods, with his two children: Shamash the sun and Ishtar the planet Venus. His animal is a dragon, and his emblem the disc of the moon

Shala – 'lady of the ear of grain', goddess of nature

Tašmetu – Nabu's consort goddess

Tiamat – primordial goddess of the sea, symbol of the chaos of creation. From her slain body, the storm-god **Marduk** forms the heavens and the earth

A Note on Ghosts and Spirits

Both Assyrian and Babylonian religion were profoundly influenced by a belief in the existence of spirits, which perpetually surrounded mankind. The good spirits were heavily outnumbered by the bad ones, who surrounded their victims by every side, lying in wait for them day and night. Some of the evil spirits were ghosts: of those whose lives had been unhappy, those who had been betrayed or whose death was violent, or unjust.

A Neo-Assyrian Glossary

Apkallu – a demi-god protecting humans from evil spirits

Ashakku – demon responsible for spreading illnesses

Asû – a physician, different from an *āšipu*, who is an exorcist or ritual healer. While both physician and healer specialize in treating signs of sickness, the profession of the *asû* focuses more on surgical interventions and the knowledge of medicinal substances. A ritual healer is more interested in spiritual techniques

Bârû – a priest and diviner

Eber-Nari: term established during the Neo-Assyrian Empire (911 – 605 BC) in reference to its Levantine colonies

Gala: priests who work and pray in Ishtar's temples. They often adopt female names and characters

Kadee – a rich and buttery pastry

Lamassu – magical stone guardians in the form of colossal human-headed winged bulls and lions

Šarratu – a queen, a woman who rules in her own right

Sēgallu – literally 'woman of the palace', a term for Assyrian consorts

Turtanu – Assyrian general appointed by the king to lead the army. In the novel, the title belongs to Ilu

Ziggurat – pyramidal stepped temple tower built in Ancient Mesopotamia

Babylonian Calendar

SEASON		MONTH NAME	PRESIDING DEITY	GREGORIAN EQUIVALENT
Spring	1	Month of beginning and of happiness	Enlil	Mar/April
	2	Month of the blossoming and of love	Ea	Apr/May
	3	Month of building	Sin	May/Jun
Summer	4	Month of harvesting	Tammuz	Jun/Jul
	5	Month of ripening of fruits	Shamash	Jul/Aug
	6	Month of sprinkling of seeds	Ishtar	Aug/Sep
Autumn	7	Month of beginning (i.e. the start of the second half-year) / month of giving	Anu	Sep/Oct
	8	Month of awakening of buried seeds	Marduk	Oct/Nov
	9	Month of conceiving	Nergal	Nov/Dec
Winter	10	Month of resting, 'Muddy Month'	Papsukkal	Dec/Jan
	11	Month of flooding	Adad	Jan/Feb
	12	Month of evil spirits	Erra	Feb/Mar

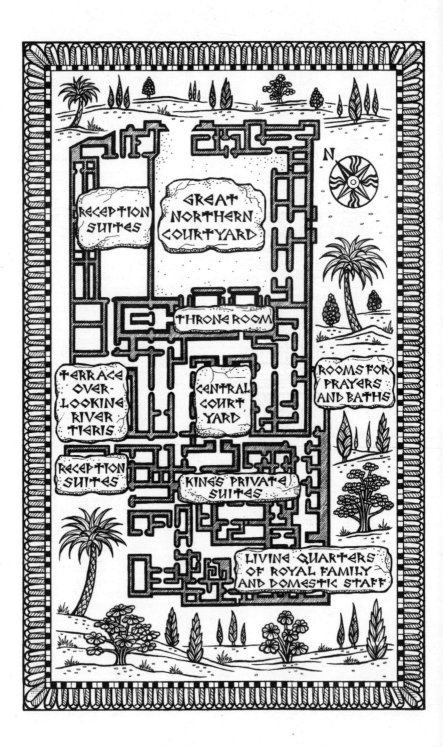

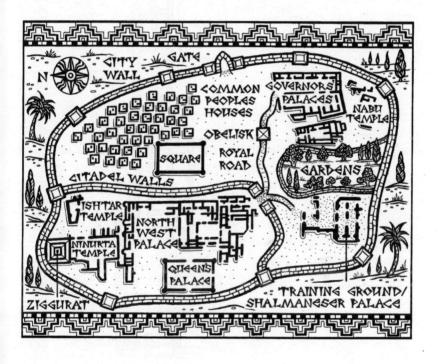

Prologue

She kills her lover on the altar of a foreign goddess.

It is the month of beginning and the valley is flat and green. The sanctuary stands in the darkening sky, with no attendants in sight. Derceto walks past the temple's columns. In her arms, her baby stares with eyes as big and bright as moons. *Don't worry*, Derceto thinks. *It will be over soon.*

She finds him in the main chamber, his body shrouded in shadows. The muscles in his shoulders tense as he polishes the altar with loving care, as if it were a woman he had under his hands, not a piece of stone.

He turns when he hears her. His expression is torn between panic and pity. She can't help but remember the wonder his eyes held the first time he saw her. *Is this all you feel for me now?* she wants to ask. Instead, she holds the baby towards him. 'This is your child.'

'You can't do this, Derceto,' he says. 'You can't haunt me. You must live without me.'

I can't. She knows she is weak. All her life she has walked in the darkness, fearing every shadow, every spirit. He was her only light, until he pushed her away and her world grew cold again. Somehow she can't find the light within herself.

'Don't you want to hold your child?' She is aware of the desperation in her voice, but it doesn't matter. There is no dignity left in her.

He blinks. 'That is no child of mine.'

Suddenly she is furious, her pulse throbbing. *You won't leave us behind.* She walks closer until their faces are only inches apart. He tries to push her back, but she shoves the baby into his arms. He takes her, despite himself, wincing when the baby starts to cry. For a moment his face softens, a glimpse of affection.

Derceto takes a knife out of her vest – the one she found outside the temple, used by votaries to sacrifice pigs and doves. He doesn't have time to react. She stabs the blade into his chest, and they cry out in unison, as if both were wounded. Blood flows between them, wetting his white tunic and her dark dress. The knife stands in his chest, like an evil limb.

He looks at the blade in shock. 'This is my goddess punishing me,' he whispers.

'No,' Derceto says. 'This is *me* punishing you.'

Her tears fall on his cheeks. He stretches one shaking hand towards her, touches her hair before burying his face in it. The memory is like a burning brand pushed through Derceto's head. She welcomes it. She wants to remember there was a time when she thought she could be happy. And she wants to remember how she lost it all.

*

The first thing he had ever said to her was, 'Your hair is made of waves so dark they seem cut from the night sky.'

Men had often told her she was beautiful, but their words were empty, spoken to please themselves and their pride. He seemed to speak from the heart. He wasn't interested in her reaction: he spoke as if he felt the need to say what he thought. That was why she didn't walk away from him.

Outside the sanctuary, he was cleaning the statue of a woman, naked except for a tunic draped across her hips, so detailed and beautiful it was hard to believe it was made of stone. Behind him, a temple with columns like long, pale legs.

'Did you sculpt this?' Derceto asked, for she had never seen such a beautiful statue.

'I did.'

His gift is a wonder, she thought, *almost equal to a god*. 'What is your name?'

He nodded to the statue, whose face was unreadable. 'If I tell you, my goddess will punish me.'

'And what is her name?'

'The Greeks call her Aphrodite. She is the goddess of love.'

'Surely she will forgive you, then,' Derceto said, and she kissed him. He didn't pull back but kept a hand on the statue, as if to anchor himself. *That is how I want to be touched*, she thought. *As if I am a rock in someone else's world, not just a twig carried by the current.*

She started walking to the temple every evening, passing the marshes and small villages clustered on the banks of the river. There were other sanctuaries on the way, where travellers worshipped the animal-headed gods from Egypt, or the deities Derceto had known all her life: fierce Ishtar, crafty Ea, shining Anu.

They spent night after night together by a lake near the city of Ascalon, where silver fish gleamed beneath the surface as if the water was filled with gems. She confided in him that her family was dead, and all that was left for her was a hut at the edge of her village, where she treated fevers and illnesses with herbs and amulets. He didn't tell her much, just listened, but she didn't mind. Every part of his body, every bit of his skin, was hers. There are different ways to know a person. Sometimes if you know the body you know the soul.

He left her every morning at dawn, back to the smooth halls of his temple, and she went back to her village, the promise of the next night like a heart inside her, keeping her alive.

But happiness is a liar, for it makes us believe it will last for ever, when it never does.

The goddess Aphrodite didn't forgive, and her lover was a coward. When Derceto told him of the child growing inside her, of *his* child, he betrayed her. He slithered off to his temple, desperate to win back the love of his goddess. Derceto wept and cried and pleaded, but the votaries of the sanctuary sent her away. She returned to her village with madness in her eyes and grief in her heart, but even they rejected her: a pregnant woman without a husband was only a stain.

And so Derceto was alone again.

*

Outside the sanctuary the sun has sunk, and the world has gone cold. Derceto's arms are bare, the wind pressing against her skin like a blade. Desert nights are unforgiving, and so are the gods to those who insult them.

The baby in her arms stares at her resentfully. As if she knows what her mother is about to do. *You'd do the same, if you were me*, Derceto thinks.

The lake rests under the darkening sky. The wind carries the gods' whispers. Derceto's head throbs as she tries to lull the baby. She is an angry child, carrying her mother's sorrow inside her. And why shouldn't she? This world has no mercy for people like them.

The water below her looks like a pool of tears. Derceto settles the baby on a rock before tying one end of a thick rope around her own ankle, the other to the heaviest stone she can find.

All her life she has been afraid. Now she will finally rest. She takes a deep breath, then pushes the stone into the lake. The rope stretches and pulls, dragging Derceto with it. The impact of the water shocks her, and instinctively she tries to swim up.

The last thing she wonders, before her body stops fighting and her lungs fill with water, is what kind of woman her daughter will become, if she lives.

BOOK I

823 BC

The hammer shatters glass but forges steel.
Assyrian proverb

I.

Which Hand Would You Like to Lose?

*Land of Eber-Nari, western province
of the Assyrian empire*

Semiramis crouches behind a thornbush, her hand on a small knife, her breath held. A few feet from her a man is dying. Two arrows deep into his calf, his face is purple with the effort of keeping silent.

Semiramis watches as he crawls down the slope towards a patch of trees, a swarm of flies trailing eagerly behind him. She has been watching since the soldiers shot him down on the road lined with cliffs and rock walls. They hid between the boulders, tunics the colour of dust and faces covered with mud. When he was close enough, their arrows flew down on him like rain. The man kept riding, two arrows piercing his leg, until a third hit his horse and they both fell, raising a cloud of dust. The horse made a desperate cry before it stilled, blood leaking thick and dark. The soldiers climbed down the cliff quickly, like lizards, but the man was gone, half running, half dragging himself on the slope.

She understands his desperate will to live. It is the way of her people. Death is hopeless, colourless, and to die is to travel to the land of no return. She has seen that land from afar: it waits for her every time her father strikes her, when her head pounds and blood trickles across her face. There is a moment when she thinks it is over, when she sees herself from above, her arms lifted, begging. *Get up*, her father always says, daring her, and she always does, before he walks away, and the dogs come to lick her wounds.

No matter how many times she is hit, she knows she can't die. Death makes men prisoners. The house of dust, they call it, where

3

commoners sit with kings in the darkness, clay for food, and wings to cover themselves and their shame. No Assyrian enters the house of his own free will.

The sun is setting, orange and angry. The man has stopped crawling and is lying on his stomach. Above him the rocks are sharp against the bleeding sky, below him the placid sound of the river. The soldiers' voices have quieted – they must have gone in the wrong direction, scavenging the cliffs.

Semiramis places her knife in the pouch around her waist before moving forward, careful not to let her foot slip down the slope. The man twitches. One, two, three steps and she is close enough to smell him. His scent is strange – there is no trace of animals, no whiff of the desert, just a feeble hint of rotten flowers. *Is this how the rich smell?* she wonders.

Slowly, he turns and stares at her. His armour is bronze, inlaid with silver pieces. He has tears in his eyes, golden circlets in his ears and rings in his oiled hair.

'You have been following me,' he whispers. 'Help me.'

The day's shadows are long, painting the land in dark strokes. There is no sign of the soldiers, no sound except the flowing water of the river in the distance. She should leave him here and run home before it is too late. But all her life, ever since she was old enough to walk, she has always gone where trouble is.

'I can take you down to the river,' she says. 'It will carry you east, to the heart of Assyria.' He stares at her, eyes shiny with pain, and nods. 'But I'll take these in exchange,' she adds, touching the rings in his hair.

The man looks shocked. Thieves lose a hand if they are caught; the code sanctions it. *But only rich men and fools follow the code, because it benefits them*, Semiramis thinks. *I was born in the dust, and I am certainly not a fool.*

'Give me your gold,' she repeats, 'and I'll carry you to the river.'

He is still for a moment, his breath shallow. She waits, knowing he has no other option. 'Take them,' he says eventually.

She hides the rings safely in her pouch. The man reaches out, wrings her hand as a wave of pain curls his body. 'Take me to the river now,' he says. 'Please.'

He is not as heavy as he looks, and she manages to put him into a sitting position. 'You'll need to hold tight,' she says. 'And you'll need to keep quiet – '

4

There is a sound like the wind before the man gasps in shock. Blood drips down Semiramis' fingers but she doesn't have time to wonder where it came from, because there is the sound again, and a flash of metal to her right. The second arrow sticks into the man's neck. His mouth is open, mute.

Semiramis stumbles back. *Run, run, run,* she silently screams, stepping away from him, her hands reaching for her small knife. Her back collapses into something. A hand grabs her, spins her around –

– and she finds herself face to face with a soldier. Four men stand behind him, grinning, their arrows nocked.

No one speaks. There is only the gurgling sound of the man behind her, choking on his own blood.

The soldier's face breaks into an evil smile. 'Tell me, little thief . . . which hand would you like to lose?'

Before any of them can shoot she launches herself down the slope. Thorns scratch her, rocks cut her, and she can barely see the landscape dance around her or the arrows flying, missing her. It feels like being punched over and over and she covers her face with her arms, tasting blood. A sharp pain in her hipbone and the rolling stops as she collapses against a tree. Behind her, the heavy tread of boots as the soldiers run after her.

Grabbing a branch, she stands, head spinning. Her feet slip on the rocks, her hair tangles in the bushes but she reaches the bottom of the cliff, where there are trees as old as gods and caves that hide bones and predators. Everything in her body is hurting, everything in her mind shouting. An arrow hits the giant tree on her right. The hill echoes with screams of outrage and she finds herself thinking, *If you scream I know exactly where you are,* which is what her father used to tell her when she was little.

She spots a cave, its dark mouth open and inviting. Surely the soldiers will think she is hiding in it, so instead she twists her body between the gnarled roots of a tree, taking a big mouthful of air before digging into the wetness of the earth. She forces her breath to still, her arms to stop shaking. She waits.

The soldiers' voices grow loud, their footsteps feel close. 'Go back and make sure the governor is dead,' shouts one, while another laughs, 'The thief is just a woman. She's worth nothing.'

'She can't have gone far,' says the one who wanted to cut off her hand.

The governor, she thinks. *The man I robbed was the governor of Eber-Nari.*

The soldiers walk around the tree and into the cave, and all the while Semiramis' thoughts are stuck on the huge curved knife soldiers use to cut hands, the edge so sharp you can't touch it without bleeding. She thinks of all those thieves dragged and chained and helpless as the knife is brought down on their wrists. Their severed hands lie in the dirt for days, until someone has the mercy to pick them up and throw them far away.

Her fists clench under the weight of her body and she can't feel her legs, but she won't move, not until there is utter silence, not until she knows she can leave whole.

She stays hidden as the men keep marching and the world turns to shadows.

*

Hours later there is finally silence. She lifts her head and spits blood and mud. The fresh air of the night is as welcome as cold water on a burn. She starts crawling out, head ringing. Everything looks blurred, contours and edges fading.

She limps to the river to wash her face, scrubbing the mud and blood from her tunic as hard as she can. The sound of the river is a slow hiss, and from here the valley looks menacing. But she isn't scared: she likes it when the land is all the same colour, a black as dense as if it has never been kissed by the sun. It makes her disappear.

There is a story her father used to tell her before bed. Nine wolves catch ten sheep. Since there is one too many, they do not know how to share out the portions. They brawl and bicker, until a fox comes along, takes all the sheep, and disappears before any of the wolves realize what she has done.

Semiramis smiles to herself as she wrings out her tunic. She hasn't been caught and she plans not to be caught for a long time.

2.

Semiramis, An Orphan Nobody

The village of Mari sleeps like a dead man. In front of the main gate, a soldier is standing with a torch in hand, the light enlarging his shadow on the wall. He is Ninurta, named after the god of war and always too willing to enforce the code whenever a villager breaks it.

Semiramis moves in the darkness, following the sound of the water, until she finds the place where the river Euphrates crosses the village. Her breath coils in the cooling air. Carefully, testing each hidden handhold, she climbs the vine-covered walls.

From above, Mari looks like a maze. The mud houses sit apart from one another, with narrow dirt roads snaking between them. In the small courtyards, cookfires have burned out, but the smells of meat and spices linger.

Semiramis jumps down, careful not to wake the guard dogs. Between the yards are the trees that look like prophetesses in long black robes, the kind who come to the village to interpret people's dreams. Her house is at the opposite end of the gate. It is one of the largest in the village – home of the chief shepherd of Mari. Three dwellings are cobbled together in the compound, with an oven and a grain keep in front. Through the window, she can see the embers of a dying fire, surrounded by bowls with the remains of supper. The dogs growl softly as she enters, but they settle down when she scratches them behind the ears. Measuring each step as if she were walking on shards, she reaches her mud-walled bedroom and lights a lamp. It sways like an eel, illuminating the small space with red rugs spread across the floor and a bed mat in a corner.

Semiramis pushes it aside to reveal a hole dug into the ground, where a handful of small possessions sparkle: a rock-crystal seal, carved animal figurines – a dog for the healing goddess Gula, a lion for the fierce Ishtar – obsidian amulets against demonesses, silver hair rings and agate eyestones taken from necklaces. The governor's rings tinkle as she places them in the middle of the hole. Her stolen prizes, her secrets, her way out of Mari. She touches them with the care that women in the village reserve for their newborn babies. She counts, making sure that nothing is missing, then carefully covers the hole with her bed mat again.

For months, she has been planning her escape, but now the time for plans is almost over. Her father has discovered that she has been having her monthly blood and, after making her pay for keeping her secret hidden, he has focused on finding a husband for her. Men have been coming to their mud house, shepherds and blacksmiths, small merchants and fishermen. Semiramis has pretended to smile obediently, all the while thinking about her precious possessions.

She does not want to marry a villager. She wants to go west to the merchant cities on the sea where life glimmers with possibilities, where palaces have walls so tall that they can feel the warmth of the sun, and ships from all over the world crowd the ports: Hittite, Greek, Egyptian, Libyan and Babylonian. Places made of gold and treachery, glory and blood, whose tales she has learned from the traders and sellers of songs that pass through the village, making her dream.

Her brother says those stories belong to a world she will never see. They are, after all, as distant and untouchable as the sun flying overhead. But Semiramis keeps her stories in her head, just as she keeps her stolen possessions under her bed mat.

No one will steal those dreams from her.

*

Light filters through the small window, pouring over Semiramis' face. For a moment she keeps still, listening to the quiet sounds of the yard rising and falling – clucking chickens, the grinding of the millstone, goats bleating. Then she stands quickly, brushing the dust off her arms and walking outside into the yard.

The mud houses are shrinking like figs under the sun. The dirt is red-hot beneath her feet, and the familiar smells of honey and almond dance in the air. Beyond the village gates, in the sun-bleached plain, women are balancing baskets on their heads and, beyond the fields, goats and sheep graze lazily on the hills.

Eber-Nari, the people in the east call this land, 'beyond the river'. Once, robbers lived in these hills, waiting for passers-by, like crows circling above a wounded man. They'd fall on their prey and leave them by the side of the narrow trails with nothing to cover them but their own skin. But these days, as long as the sun keeps floating, Assyrian soldiers walk the land, massacring each other, ambushing lone riders. They kill in the name of the king's eldest son, the man who split the empire into two raging factions five years ago – the prince Assur-danin. He waged war against his own father, claiming the throne before the king's death. His brother, Shamshi-Adad, has been fighting him ever since, weakening the empire to the point of despair and wetting the land with a thousand men's blood.

Eber-Nari might be far from the heart of the empire, its villages small and godforsaken, but without it the Assyrians wouldn't have access to the sea and the Phoenician cities that flourish on the coast. For the riches to flow from the west – jars filled with sweet wine, timber, carved ivories and sculpted amber – the Assyrians need Eber-Nari. And now the princes' armies ride in the province, forcing towns and villages under their control, both hoping to subdue the region before the other does.

'You look terrible. What did you do this time?'

Semiramis turns quickly. Her brother is leaning against a tree, watching her with a small smile. Amon, *the hidden one*. His mother named him after the Egyptian god of air, invisible and inscrutable. If it was a wish, it wasn't granted. Amon can be read as easily as a priest reads an omen.

'I am fine,' she says.

'You don't look it. Did you crawl through the mud to get back here? You stink.'

'Something like that,' she says. He laughs, and she shushes him, casting a quick look around, though their father is nowhere in sight.

'Am I in trouble?' she asks. 'I was gone for too long.'

He shrugs. 'You are always in trouble. But Father is with the sheep now, and he has other worries today.'

'What worries?'

He leans in. 'The villagers say that Assur-danin's soldiers have captured the governor. They killed him when he tried to run away.'

The breath stops in her chest, but she forces herself to feign surprise. 'What does this mean?'

'Our governor was one of the last men faithful to Shamshi-Adad. It means Shamshi-Adad is losing the war.'

'Losing a battle and losing the war isn't the same thing,' she points out.

Amon smiles. 'He lost most of the battles, sister. And, if what the villagers say is true, I expect that the soldiers will make a spectacle of the dead governor. Better not to leave the compound until it is over.' He ruffles her hair – she winces as he touches her head wound – then picks up a basket of grain and starts tossing it to the chickens.

He is a good man, kind and patient, unlike his father. Everyone in the village is charmed by him, because it is easy to like someone who doesn't have shadows within: it is like looking at the shimmering water of the coast, close to the land, where you can see every shell and starfish, and never swimming out into the deep dark sea.

Semiramis is grateful to him, because he loves her like a sister, even if they aren't tied by blood. He runs and plays and fights with her as if she were a boy, and offers her comfort when Simmas hits her.

She is grateful to him, but she also resents him, because every time she looks at him, she sees only a future she does her best to avoid: one in which she stays in Mari for ever, her days shapeless and unchanging, until the bright fire that burns inside her is quenched, and she stops dreaming of something more.

Some days she would rather die than face such a grey, ordinary life.

*

Amon has told her to stay in the compound, so she leaves as soon as she has finished her tasks.

The sun is high when she goes to draw water from the well. She takes the narrowest alleys to steer clear of the soldiers. A man is lining up bricks of clay to be sun-dried; two weavers are sharing some bread in front of their bright textiles. In the ivory workshop, each beautiful creation is on display – a cow and her suckling calf, a lotus flower, a bull. A group of women are sitting outside their houses, mending sandals. Semiramis walks by them as quickly as she can.

When she reaches the square, it is empty, palm and tamarisk trees casting cool shadows around the well. She fills the bucket to the brim, then hides in the nearest alley, waiting.

A sudden silence announces the soldiers' arrival. The villagers' voices die down, as if the world has lost every sound. Then five soldiers appear in the square. Ninurta is dragging the old governor's body behind him, pierced through his wrists with a leather whip. At his sides are two of the men who followed Semiramis down the cliffs.

'Impale him here,' Ninurta says, 'so that everyone can watch as he rots.'

They start cutting down one of the trees, their voices baying, echoing in the square. Semiramis remains hidden, barely breathing. She remembers the first time she witnessed an execution. She was ten and had to watch a woman accused of being unfaithful to her husband as her hands were tied before she was cast into the river. Semiramis hated the water, the way it silently killed the woman, showing everyone her pain. When the villagers had gone back to their houses and the square was empty once more, she asked Simmas why the code was so cruel.

'*I cut off their hands, I burned them with fire,*' Simmas recited, '*a pile of the living men and of heads against the city gate I set up, the men I impaled on stakes, the city I devastated.* The mighty King Ashurnasirpal had it carved on a monument in Kalhu when he made it our capital. It is a brutal world. Not everyone is made for it.'

'Do you think I am made for it?' she asked.

'I think that sometimes you forget you are a woman,' he replied, and she had wondered what he meant, for it seemed an answer to a different question.

Ninurta cuts the governor's chest, to show the others where to drive the wooden stake. Semiramis forces herself to look. The breath dies in her throat as the governor's body is crushed, the stake piercing it, like a giant spear.

When she was younger, she thought that the blood of kings and governors must be gold, for they are a different kind, closer to the gods and their constellations. But the drops that fall copiously from the governor's chest are red. No different from her own.

*

'When will the soldiers take the governor down?' Amon asks.

They are out in the yard, sitting around a fire, bowls of vine leaves and flatbreads all around them. At this hour of the evening, the soldiers are already guarding the gates, and all the villagers are eating inside the walls.

'It is an honour for Mari to witness such a spectacle,' Simmas says. 'Other villages will hear that the soldiers have left the governor here, and they will know that Assur-danin's soldiers value our village more than theirs.'

His eyes are pitch black and his thick beard covers a sun-darkened face. He always speaks with the blind certainty of a man who worships whatever his king tells him to. And in this western corner of empire, violence and ruthlessness are treated as if they are sacred.

'Will Assur-danin appoint a new governor, then?' Amon asks.

'Once he wins the war,' Simmas says, taking a mouthful of beer.

Semiramis looks at the crumbling mud walls that enclose their compound. She is seated as far from Simmas as possible, in case his mood changes for the worse. Lately, as the time for her marriage approaches and she spends more and more time wandering the hills, he seems always ready to find an excuse to humiliate her.

'Mari wasn't always like this,' Simmas says. 'It wasn't just a village passed between rival princes' hands. It was a splendid city once, with high, thick walls covered in frescoes and statues of water goddesses. Then its people rebelled against the mighty Babylon, and King Hammurabi razed it to the ground. Houses and temples were set ablaze, corpses piled in the streets and left to the crows. A handful of women and children were left alive, and the few walls and buildings that refused to collapse were allowed to stand. A merciful act on Hammurabi's part – to let the city survive as a village.'

It is a story he has told them many times, but Semiramis knows he likes to repeat it because it makes him feel important, as if he is part of something greater, and not just a speck of dust, like all the other villagers who live at the mercy of the empire.

Simmas turns to her. 'What lesson does this story teach us, Semiramis?'

That your life is in the hands of others, and that you must obey them or be crushed into the ground. 'That the fortunes of men keep changing,' she says.

He shakes his head. 'That kings reward those who deserve it.'

Sometimes she almost pities him. But the feeling is a flicker, and it goes away as quickly as it came. Simmas doesn't deserve her pity, just as he doesn't deserve her love. He has never done anything to earn it.

'Go to sleep, both of you,' Simmas mutters, pouring more beer for himself.

Amon yawns and stretches his arms, then goes into the house. Semiramis stands quickly, eager to leave Simmas' presence before his drunkenness turns into bitterness. She is almost at the door, when he calls to her: 'Semiramis.'

She stops.

'You can't keep roaming around looking like a wild animal,' he says. 'You know I want you married before the end of the season.'

I know. You keep repeating it. She waits for her brother to disappear into the house, then says, 'Amon is older. Shouldn't he marry first?'

Simmas throws a piece of food to the dogs. 'Your brother is a man. He can marry whenever he wants.'

*

She waits until she is the only one left awake before going back to the square.

Dates hang in moonlit clusters on the trees. The houses along the dirt road are silent. In front of some doors, Semiramis can glimpse chunks of flatbread, almonds, small jugs of beer: funerary offerings for the spirits of the dead. The house of dust has no food, no drink. If the dead aren't remembered, they return to earth to plague the living, finding scraps of food in the gutter, tormenting their loved ones for a sip of water. Semiramis can feel them sometimes, angry eyes gazing, skin bone-white. She does her best to ignore them.

The square is empty: no trace of soldiers or feral dogs. She takes a few careful steps. The governor's body is bent over a wooden stake by the well. His long, oiled hair has fallen over his face, and blood has poured from his crushed chest onto the post. The soldiers haven't even bothered to remove the arrows from his legs, she notices. They have nailed a placard right under his feet, the word 'TRAITOR' painted in black.

She stands in his blood for a long time, until she can smell nothing else: sweet like honey, sharp like iron. Then she tears off a piece of her tunic and goes to soak it in the well. Carefully, as if the governor could feel her touch, she starts cleaning the blood from his chest. Some has clotted, and she has to scrub, recoiling at the coldness of his skin.

High or low, we all share death, she thinks. It is a lesson that all Assyrians must learn, no matter how much they fear the house of dust. It makes her think of her favourite epic, which a seller of songs passing through Mari had once sung during a village feast. The man was old, his voice hoarse, but the story was beautiful.

It told of Gilgamesh, the king who was both god and mortal, and of how he couldn't prevent his brother's death. Helpless and distraught, he searched for the one man who was granted immortality by the gods: if he could learn his secrets, then he, too, might live for ever. But death's secrets weren't his to share, and Gilgamesh was forced to return home, having failed to gain the immortality he so longed for.

The rag in Semiramis' hand is dark and thick with blood. Cleaned and polished, the governor's skin is the colour of cedar-wood. Rich, as it should be. She hopes his spirit will find some peace, even without food or drink. With one of the small lamps by the funerary offerings, she burns the rag, until all that remains of it are ashes.

*

The next morning Amon joins her in the yard as she is cooking a lamb stew. She is still thinking of the governor – she even dreamed of him in the night, though in her dream he was alive, standing in the river, urging her to come closer.

'Do you know what day it is?' Amon asks. He is grinning happily.

'First day of the month of giving,' she replies, chopping the vegetables. Summer is ending, and the days are growing cooler without the sun slashing the sky like a whip.

'Yes,' Amon says. 'And you know what that means?' He moves closer to her ear. 'The boys are climbing tonight.'

She stops, hand in mid-air. 'What about the soldiers?'

'We will be careful.'

She looks at him, serious. 'I want to come too.'

He grins. 'And so you will. I convinced the boys already.' He dips a finger into the simmering sauce, licks it. 'Let us see if all those nights in the hills have truly turned you into a mountain goat.'

They gather at the foot of the cliff. There are ten of them, farmers, builders and blacksmiths, the best and fastest of the village. Semiramis stands at the end of the row, plaiting her hair so that it doesn't fall into her face. They have sunk a torch into the ground, wedged between two rocks. It illuminates half of the cliff, bathing its smooth face in pale gold. The upper part remains shrouded in darkness.

A boy, one of the climbers' brothers, stands watch by the opening between the two rockfaces. They all stand silent, waiting for his signal. Amon glances at Semiramis, but her eyes are set on a tall, lithe boy at the end of the row, who surveys the cliff with a haughty smile. His name is Baaz, and he is always the first to reach the top.

A long moment of silence, then the boy standing guard waves his hand.

They move in unison, like a pack of wolves, yet two figures quickly detach from the others. Baaz climbs easily, his muscles rippling as he tests each handhold. He is the strongest of the village, his hands and arms covered with scars from his work forging bronze blades and armour for the soldiers. Semiramis follows him, avoiding the weeds and bushes that grow from this part of the ravine, where birds like to hide and rest.

The shadows swallow them as they reach the higher part of the cliff. Baaz grows slower, Semiramis quicker – she moves better in the darkness. The rocks are sharp under her hands; her feet feel like wings. Balancing on a small outcrop, she stretches her body as tall as she can, reaching out for a root to pull herself over to the top of the ravine.

The air tastes different up high, sweeter. The black sky feels close enough to touch. Baaz hoists himself up straight after her, his arms scratched by rocks and thorns. They both stand, catching their breath, waiting for the others. The shadowed valley stretches below them. There is no light but that of the moon.

Slowly, the other boys appear, small cuts and bruises on their hands and faces. Everyone watches the last one to pull himself up: a small boy who looks like a mouse, grey and shivering. Baaz gives him a contemptuous smile, then, unexpectedly, turns to Amon. 'You said she was fast, but not faster than me,' he says, in his low, rasping voice.

The boys slowly edge away from Semiramis, as if she were plagued. Amon remains quiet. His face is blurred in the shadows, but Semiramis knows he must regret bringing her.

A boy with a lumpy face says, 'No one is faster than you, Baaz. She is a witch. It is her mother's blood.'

'Do not speak of my mother,' Semiramis spits out.

Baaz cocks his head with the satisfaction of a child who's caught a lizard and is ready to cut off its tail. 'Why?' he asks. 'We all know the rumours anyway. Your mother was a whore, a mad woman who preyed upon lawful men.'

Her face burns. The silence and the other boys' stares creep upon her skin with a stinging weight.

'Baaz,' Amon says, 'we need to go back.' He is standing at the edge of the cliff, looking down. They can hear a soft whistle coming from below: the boy on guard duty urging them to climb down. Baaz frowns, as if torn between the satisfaction of humiliating Semiramis and the threat of soldiers seeing them. Semiramis waits, hands shaking. If Baaz were alone, she would grab a stone and smash his face with it, but now, surrounded by all the other boys, she would only end up beaten twice: by Baaz, and then by Simmas when he sees her covered with bruises. The helplessness makes her choke.

Finally, Baaz turns. 'Crying won't bring her back,' he says. 'But do not despair. Maybe you will turn out just like her.'

She feels roiled and raw, as if he had slapped her. Some boys smirk; others look away. Semiramis watches them descend the rockface one by one, their shadows long and stark until they blow out the torch and the ravine is plunged into darkness once more. Then, slowly, fighting back the tears that stream over her face, she makes her way down the cliff and walks home, alone but for the moon god, who watches her from the heavens.

*

There was a time when her life might have been very different, if only fate had been kinder. But gods are cruel and slippery, and they deal out destinies however it amuses them most. And what can humans do? They cannot change their past. Semiramis has learned this the hard way.

Her mother killed herself when Semiramis was a baby. She was a beautiful woman and fell in love with a man who felt nothing for her.

That is all Semiramis knows about her – that she was beautiful. *Hair dark like a night river, skin the colour of the moon, eyes like black gemstones.* These are only stories, songs sung by the villagers: slippery words told in whispers, passed from old women to curious children. But Semiramis has nothing else, so she has no choice but to believe they are true.

When her mother fell pregnant, madness took hold of her: after Semiramis was born, she drowned herself in a lake. The elders of the village say that the water wanted to turn her into one of its creatures, but the gods would not let her give up her beauty. So they transformed her into something else: a woman with the tail of a fish. Others believe that Derceto's body is just a corpse lying on the seabed, putrid and bloated, another thing the water has swallowed.

Sometimes images appear in Semiramis' sleep – a woman with blue-green fish scales on her legs, urging her to join her in the water – but she can't tell if they are dreams or memories.

Alone on the rocks by the lake where her mother had dived, the baby clung to life with the stubbornness of a clam. Around her, on the plains that were beginning to bud, white-feathered doves were laying their eggs in nests of twigs and grass. They came to the lake shore in thousands in the months of spring, and when they heard a child's mournful cry, they mistook it for one of their own. They gathered beside the baby, keeping her warm with their soft wings, feeding her milk from their beaks.

When Simmas came upon the scene, he thought it was a sign sent by the gods. He took the baby, asking travellers and villagers if they knew her mother. No one would claim her, so Simmas took her home to Mari. His wife had died giving birth to his only son, and he thought a daughter might be useful in the house as she grew up. He kept her in the hope of arranging a good marriage, one that might give him land and sheep, maybe even wine and new fabrics.

He named her Semiramis, because a Greek traveller had once taught him the word. *Doves*, it means, in the language of Eber-Nari, and it is thought to bring luck because the birds are as sacred as goddesses. A strange name for a strange child.

And strange Semiramis was, no matter how Simmas tried to teach her the ways of the village. She liked danger and all things that were forbidden. She spoke to animals and begged travellers to tell stories of the great cities of the empire, where lions and leopards roamed in gardens with gem-trees of all colours. She was always looking for answers no one seemed able to give: where does fruit come from? Why do flowers blossom? How far is the vault of the heavens? She could name the constellations in the night sky, and how they traced the path of the sun and moon, knew which plants to use to create potions and ointments, could play the lyre better than musicians who passed through the village.

'Why do you want to learn everything?' Amon asked her once. She shrugged and said nothing, though the truth was that she enjoyed learning tricks and secrets because then she could use them to her advantage: she could show Amon how well she sang, diminish other children when they didn't know a proverb, heal herself when she was beaten. She was observant and curious in a way that no other villager was.

When she was a child, growing up in a house that wasn't her own, Semiramis would convince herself that she was special, that she was meant for greatness. She'd spend days fantasizing about her mother, who became a warrior, a queen, a goddess. In her dreams, Derceto died fighting, protecting her child, close to the man she loved. It didn't matter that the villagers whispered that Semiramis was different, or that Simmas told her she was worthless whenever she wouldn't obey him. Her mother was a goddess, travelling through the secret ways of water, drinking milk from the moon.

For years she has tried to give her life some sort of meaning, to convince herself that her destiny was charted when her mother left her alone on a rock. But then, on nights like this, when the village boys' words echo in her head, like an unwanted visitor, the truth hits her so hard that she thinks she might choke.

She is not special. She is just an orphan. She is nobody.

3.

Ninus, King of the World,
King of Assyria

Kalhu, capital of the Assyrian empire

Before the sun sets, his brother will die. And he will be the one to kill him.

Onnes brings him the news before the break of dawn. Ninus is in the throne room, tracing the shapes of the stone panels that line the walls, the tales of his grandfather's conquests. It is dark but he doesn't need the light – he knows the images by heart. The king campaigning in the east, the hills and mountains sculpted in patterns of lines and spirals, the horses carrying the chariot adorned with crests and tassels. The royal hunt, with the king shooting a bow as his horses jump over a wounded lion. There are arrows in the beast's neck, where the mane meets the jaw, and Ninus feels them under his palm. He traces his fingers around the lion's teeth, its mouth open, roaring in pain. And then the celebrations after the hunt, where his grandfather stands over a dead lion, two guards carrying maces on his left, four eunuchs on his right. Between two of them, a bearded officer, the crown prince. He is dressed as the king, but with only a diadem on his head – Ninus' father, Shalmaneser.

Ninus rests his forehead against the sculpted figure. In the relief, his father must have been his age now, if not younger. He wasn't king yet, and he had his own father by his side, trusted officers all around and an entire kingdom to worship him. What does Ninus have? A traitor brother, traitor officers, a kingdom weakened to the point of despair. And a dead father.

The sky is black, so black it feels like being under a deep sea. There are no stars, just the gold of the palace walls feebly glittering like a thousand lamps. On nights like these, the dead awaken to haunt the living, seeping through the cracks, speaking in hisses and whispers. Not even the *apkallu*, the protective spirits that guard the entrance to the king's quarters, can stop them. Ninus can feel the coldness against his arms, as if a thousand dead men were trying to grab him.

'Ashur has fallen, my king.'

He turns. A man lingers on the threshold of the throne room, dwarfed by the statues of the winged bulls. His face is handsome but tired, his eyes the colour of ageing copper.

Ninus steps out of the shadows to face him. 'And my brother?'

'Our men have captured Assur-danin.'

Ninus tilts his head, letting the words echo. 'Dead or alive?'

Onnes hesitates. He often does this before answering his king's questions. Ninus knows it is because he fears his impulsiveness and wishes to tame it as best he can.

'Alive.'

Ninus closes his eyes. *Good.*

'There is something else,' Onnes adds, and Ninus hears him emptying his voice of any feeling, as he always does before speaking of something horrible. 'The governor of Eber-Nari was found dead near the village of Mari. He was our last ally in the western provinces. He was killed by arrows and impaled. There was a wooden sign on the stake with the word "traitor".'

Ninus forces himself to laugh. The sound is strained. 'A final gift from Assur-danin . . . Well, now I can name you governor.'

Onnes doesn't speak. He merely looks at him with eyes that would be beautiful if they weren't cold.

'Eber-Nari is yours,' Ninus continues. 'Go there, make sure its people are loyal to us and the trade routes secured. Without the region, we have no access to the sea. I'll give you fifty men and horses.'

Onnes bows slightly. 'Yes, my king, Shamshi-Adad.' He uses Ninus' royal name, but Ninus isn't king yet and, besides, it is Onnes who speaks, his most trusted friend.

Ninus shakes his head. 'Don't call me that. Not here, when there is only you and me. Now let us go and speak with my brother.'

They ride, following the river. The land is burned and scarred. Five years, they have fought. When the war started, Ninus had barely seen twenty winters. Now he looks as if he has seen a hundred. The mean cawing of crows guides them, and soon they start seeing the bodies the birds have mutilated. Empty holes instead of eyes and noses, flies feasting around them.

Dawn starts breaking, creeping over each dead man. Ninus looks away, his mind full of shouts and shadows. He can see each battle as if it were still raging. Wounded men wriggling like worms. Tarred corpses, arrows flying in and out of sight. When darkness eats the soul, men don't look like men any more. Their screaming faces don't look like they belong to warriors. It is all mud and dirt, fire and pain, until one forgets what the world was like before.

His people believe that war is the way of life. That it keeps the earth clean, the minds alert. But *this* war wasn't meant to be. Brothers aren't meant to fight each other.

'You are one and the same,' their mother used to tell them. 'Two halves of the same heart. One cannot exist without the other.'

What happens when one half is sick, Mother? Ninus thinks. *When a tumour blackens it, corrupts it?*

The trenches around Ashur seem abandoned, shields and broken wheels stacked between fires that burn tiredly, bringing the smell of ash with them. They dismount in silence. In front of them, Ninus' army looks as endless as the sea, tents stretching out on all sides. Beyond it, the walls of Ashur, for so many years the empire's capital, before Ninus' grandfather built the mighty Kalhu.

Their boots sink into the deep ruts of the earth. Ninus almost stumbles. He quickly straightens, aware that many already think him young, weak, unfit. Around them, men and crows gather to watch the procession in silence. They reach a bigger tent, and the soldiers form a semicircle around their king, waiting.

An image floats in Ninus' mind, a memory. Red stains on small hands, slim arms and legs climbing a tree, childish laughter in the warm summer air as his brother threw cherries down on him. *Catch them, Ninus, catch them!*

'He is here, my king,' Onnes says.

Ninus lets the memory fade as he throws open the tent.

'How many times does a man die?' their father asked them once. This was before Ninus was Shamshi-Adad and Assur was Assur-danin. No royal names for them then, no expectations. Their world was simple, made of games and laughter, of bronze toys and boring processions.

'One, Father,' Assur said, because he always spoke before thinking. Shalmaneser shook his head. 'Ninus?'

Ninus thought about it. 'A man dies every time he fails, every time he is lost, every time he is shamed. There is more than one death.'

'You are clever,' Shalmaneser said. Ninus turned to his brother with a smile but found only anger on Assur's face.

That night, rather than whisper to him about the kings and gods of Assyria, as he often did, Assur turned his back to his brother and pretended to sleep. Ninus couldn't understand it. Assur was stronger and braver, the favourite among Father's generals, who petted him and let him play with their swords. Unlike Ninus, who sometimes read so much that his head hurt, Assur didn't care about epics or myths – but wasn't a true king meant to be strong rather than clever?

'Father told me he saw you fight today,' Ninus whispered, trying to find the right thing to say to make his brother feel better.

'Did he?' Assur asked, suddenly awake. His voice was hopeful and his eyes brimming with expectation.

'Yes. He said you reminded him of himself when he was younger.'

Assur smiled and looked at the ceiling dreamily, his jealousy forgotten. 'We will conquer the world, you and I.'

'With my tablets?' Ninus joked.

'With my armies *and* your tablets,' Assur said, and there was such fervency in his eyes that Ninus believed him.

Why do good memories always bring bad ones with them, the two inextricably linked, like the sun scorching the earth after a day of precious rain, or a nightmare sneaking into the mind after a peaceful dream?

The commemoration of the pact between Assyria and Babylon. A giant carved relief of two kings shaking hands was brought to Shalmaneser's new palace in Kalhu. A testimony to the power of Assyria and a promise of peace for the years to come. Ninus and Assur were cleaned and dressed and brought to their father. They had to hold a mace, heavy and precious. The symbol of the authority vested in the king as vice-regent of the supreme gods. It was a chance to prove their worth, more important than their training and the hours spent with their tutor learning celestial omens.

Ninus' hands were sweaty, but he gripped the mace with all his might. Assur didn't take the duty seriously enough. 'It is just a mace,' he whispered, with a smile.

'Not to Father,' Ninus replied, agitated. 'Not to the gods.'

Assur grinned, then pulled the mace towards him. It slipped from Ninus' fingers and fell, clanging onto the stone floor, like a gong.

Shalmaneser turned. His face was all disappointment. He was carrying a ceremonial sickle, the kind that gods use to fight monsters, or so he had told them.

Slowly, he said, 'Which one of you should I beat?'

Ninus looked down. He knew Assur was biting his tongue next to him.

'Assur,' Shalmaneser said. 'Did you drop the mace?'

'It was an accident,' Assur said stupidly.

'An accident,' Shalmaneser repeated. 'Ninus? Did you drop it?'

'We both did,' Ninus said. Then he stared straight ahead and added, 'But Assur pulled it first.'

Now the memory blurs, like the words carved on the clay tablets he loved to read, and all he can remember is the hand of Father on Assur's arm as he dragged him away.

Later, when the brothers were alone in their room, Assur made Ninus pay for it.

*

Inside the tent there is a hazy light. A young man sits in the middle, his wrists tied to a wooden post, his face covered in dirt.

'The traitor of Assyria graces me with his presence,' Assur says.

Ninus looks slowly over his brother. The skin around his wrists is close to breaking. 'You have tried to escape,' he says.

Assur smiles. 'What can I say? I was never suited to captivity.'

'Still, you are here.'

'I'm not as clever as you, remember? You'd have talked your way out of it by now.'

Ninus takes a stool and sits, hoping it will make his legs stop shaking.

'Ashur has fallen, but my army still stands,' Assur says. 'To disman-tle it, you'll have to kill me, and we both know you won't do that.'

'I won't?' Ninus says.

'You have occasionally enjoyed watching me suffer.' His face con-torts into a contemptuous smile. 'But that was different. It was Father hurting me, not you. You were just watching. You like to cause pain but don't want to be the one who inflicts it, because you are a coward.'

'A coward and a man who commits patricide. Surely Father hoped we'd turn out better.'

Assur looks away. There are deep shadows under his eyes. 'I used to think Shalmaneser would choose you as heir,' he says. 'You were nothing like our kings, but he liked you all the same. He liked that you read those stories and that you were fascinated by – what did he call it? – the *scribal art*.'

'You were the obvious choice,' Ninus says.

'And yet he didn't choose me, did he?'

'He would have, eventually. He appointed Dayyan-Assur because he trusted him. They had fought side by side for twenty years.'

'Dayyan-Assur was a minister, nothing more, and we were his sons. The army should have been ours.'

'You started a rebellion because Father didn't ask you to lead his army.'

'And you chose to defend him.'

'It was the right thing to do.'

They survey one another across the room. They haven't spoken to each other, *truly* spoken, since the day of the betrayal.

It was the end of summer, just like now, and the light was thick and golden. Father had called them to the Northwest Palace to announce that, from then on, his troops would be led by Dayyan-Assur. Dayyan was a good and virtuous man, which is why he is long dead now. Assur hadn't said anything, but Ninus had seen the shadows growing on his face, the anger twisting his features.

The tent door flaps open and Onnes walks in. He looks at Assur for the briefest of moments before turning to his king. 'Nineveh and two other cities have surrendered, Shamshi-Adad.'

'*Shamshi-Adad*,' Assur repeats. 'You never liked that name.'

Onnes ignores him, his expression betraying nothing. Ninus stands and places a hand on his brother's – his true brother's – shoulder.

'Accept the surrender. Do not slaughter anyone. Take the leaders and bring them to Kalhu. We will talk to them.'

Onnes nods and leaves. There are the sounds of boots marching and men shouting.

'You really believe you're decent, don't you?' Assur says.

Ninus turns back to him. 'Isn't that what we all tell ourselves?'

'Onnes surely doesn't. He has always been one of the bad roots of Assyria.'

'You used to respect him.'

'When we were children. He's grown too cold, inscrutable. How can you trust a man when you don't know what he's thinking?'

Ninus shrugs. He has asked himself the same question many times, but in the end, there is only one answer: he trusts Onnes. 'Trust isn't always a bad thing,' he says. 'Father trusted many men.'

'Father wasn't fit to rule.'

'Neither are you.'

Assur laughs. 'And you are? You used to turn away when men were being impaled on our walls. You gave water to servants chained outside the city.'

'Weakness and lack of cruelty aren't the same thing.'

'They might not be in that godless whorehouse you like so much, Babylon. Or in Israel, where every king prays for their god to be merciful. But this is Assyria. We don't wait for our enemies to strike before we strike back. We bend the world to our will, and what doesn't bend, we destroy.'

Ninus sees now why he has come. Deep down he has known it ever since Onnes came to tell him the news. He learned long ago that his family only understands the language of strength. And for those who can't speak it, there is no other option than to learn it.

Ninus draws his sword. Assur's eyes are wide, gleaming. Ninus kneels next to him, his face only a breath from his brother's. Just as when they slept in the same bed because they feared the spirits, or when they hid in a corner, scared of the dark. Arm against arm, knee against knee.

'I do not care what Father told you,' Assur says. 'You are, and have always been, weak.'

Ninus places the blade against Assur's neck. He can see a vein pulsing, a single drop of sweat rolling down. 'At least I am not dead.'

The knife cuts easily into his brother's skin. Assur drops to the side as blood pours out, thin at first, then thick and dark. Ninus closes his eyes.

How long does a palace stand before it falls? he wonders.
How long will brothers love before they fight?
Time after time the river has risen and flooded.
From the very beginning nothing has lasted.

4.

The New Governor

They have a new king, and a new governor.

Semiramis is preparing an ointment for the healing wound on her head when Amon bursts into the courtyard. 'Assur-danin's soldiers have gone,' he pants. 'All of them. Everyone is going to the square.'

She wipes her hands carelessly on her tunic and follows him, heart thumping. Villagers are gathering, voices rising in excitement. Semiramis slips into the crowd. She can see Simmas by the well, his dogs panting at his feet. Next to him, Baaz and two other boys are pushing children out of the way. All eyes are drawn to the man standing in the middle. He is young, with a dusty knee-length tunic: an envoy. Behind him the body of the impaled governor droops forward, skin decomposing. Though the envoy keeps glancing at it, the villagers seem barely to notice it.

'I bring news from our capital, the mighty Kalhu,' the envoy announces.

The square quietens at once.

'From the prince Assur-danin?' someone asks.

'No,' the envoy says. 'From our new king, Shamshi-Adad the Fifth.'

Murmurs ripple through the crowd.

'Shamshi-Adad the Fifth, King of the World, King of Assyria, has killed his brother,' the envoy says. 'Every city and village pledged to the traitor Assur-danin begs for the king's mercy.'

Semiramis watches the fear crease every villager's face – she knows they are thinking of the impaled governor, whose mutilated body suddenly feels like a demon, casting a shadow upon them all, and of those among them who swore their allegiance to Assur-danin as his soldiers galloped through the province.

'The new governor of Eber-Nari is making his way through the land between the two rivers,' the envoy continues. 'You shall be among the first to swear loyalty to your new king.'

The voices of the villagers rise and fall like a willow tree in the wind. Out of the corner of her eye, Semiramis sees Simmas' mouth curve into a proud smile. *He is already forgetting he was so sure Assur-danin would win*, Semiramis thinks.

'The governor will be in Mari in ten days' time,' the envoy says. 'He expects a welcome worthy of his stature. The great Shamshi-Adad has saved us all. The war is over. The time for glory has come.'

Semiramis almost laughs. It is strange to hear words of such greatness spoken in such a humble place. A figure shifts next to her. 'Everyone thought Shamshi-Adad was going to lose,' Amon says quietly, in her ear.

'What did I tell you about losing?' she whispers back. 'The king lost the battle, but he won the war.'

'And he has started his reign with his brother's blood on his hands,' Amon says. Around them, everyone is talking, faces dark with worry. The women give fresh water to the envoy before he mounts his horse and turns west, towards the villages close to the sea.

Semiramis can barely pay attention to any of it. All she can think of is what the envoy's words mean for her. *Assur-danin's soldiers are gone. The roads are safer. The cliffs will soon fill with merchants and travellers again.* And before the season ends, she will be on the road too, leaving Mari behind.

Excitement blossoms inside her, like a tree in spring. A change is coming, and while every other villager might be scared of it, to her it tastes like hope.

*

At night, after every man and woman has spoken of the news to the point of exhaustion, there is finally peace. Simmas' house is quiet, bodies breathing together as if part of one big placid creature. Semiramis slips into the main room, where Amon has fallen asleep with his back against the mud wall. Sensing her presence, he opens his eyes.

'Are you sneaking out again?' he asks, with a half-smile.

'Not tonight,' she says, sitting next to him. 'Tell me the riddle you used to love. The one about the governor.'

He sighs, stretches his long limbs. '*He gouged out the eye: the man lives. He cut the throat: the man dies.*'

'The answer?'

'You know the answer. You said it yourself.'

'Yes. A governor. But I don't understand it.'

'It describes his power. He is free to act as judge, to punish or sentence to death according to his whim.'

She looks at his profile in the shadows. 'Why did you like it so much?'

'I used to wonder what it would feel like to take lives and not pay the consequences.' He shrugs, then stands. 'I am going to sleep. You should do the same.' Then he disappears into the room he shares with Simmas.

The house smells of clay and cinnamon. Outside the window, the moon is fat and milky, and looks as if it could drip from the sky. *How does it feel to take a life?* Semiramis wonders, as she drags herself to her bedroom and curls up on the mat. In her mind, she sees an image of the old governor, the spill of blood from his pierced chest.

Power changes men, and not for the better or kings and soldiers wouldn't be so merciless. And on such power the world is built: gods and kings at the top, who are bound to no will but their own, then governors and courtiers, then soldiers and so on, until, at the bottom, common people such as herself. All commoners can do is pray and worship, gaining favours with loyalty and adulation. And, of course, subdue those even smaller and weaker than they are.

Whatever one's place in the great chain of terror, it is always the same: there are those who have power and those who don't. She has no intention of staying among the latter.

*

Over the next ten days the village comes to life as it prepares for the governor's arrival. Crumbling walls are repaired and freshly painted with bulls and lions. Torches are set in every alley, casting bright lights on the amulets hanging outside every door. Weavers spin new tunics, bright and thin, like butterfly wings. The men butcher the meat and bring it to the women who pick the tender bits to make soup. They prepare the *pita* – the fragrant smell of bread lingering outside each house – the *kadee* pastry, rich and buttery, and the pine pies. The older women wash tunics in the river, red, blue and yellow cloth floating, like strange and colourful sea creatures.

The previous governor's body is taken down, the wooden stake burned. There is no sign of him now except for a small patch of dark earth in the shape of a circle. Boys play on it, using small branches like swords, and around them girls gather the late olive harvest.

Semiramis kneels by the main gate, hands stained with green pigments. She has been helping other girls to paint the inner wall, plastering the bricks with chalk before painting flowers and animals on them. The girl beside her – another shepherd's daughter – is mixing different pigments. She passes Semiramis a soft, fine-grained powder for the leaves, then goes in search of burned bone for the darker colours. Semiramis applies the green powder with her fingers, tracing each leaf as if it were a water ripple. When she has finished, she studies her tree of life, adds a handful of white to brighten the middle of each leaf.

Behind her, children run after chickens, guiding them behind gates. The day is still bright. The women are speaking of husbands, and of a dancer from a nearby village who fell in love with one of Assurdanin's soldiers. 'He has left her and now she is alone and carries his child. Can you imagine such a fate?'

Semiramis walks away before they can turn their attention to her. There is something she wants to do before the new governor arrives with his soldiers.

She makes her way along the dirt roads, passing the flat brown houses and the courtyards where children are gathering flowers. Behind one of the walls, Amon is kissing a woman with hair as black as the midnight sky and bells sewn to the straps of her sandals. Suppressing a smile, Semiramis walks past them, between clattering carts and swaying donkeys.

At the end of the alley where the forge and the workshops are, she crouches behind a pile of empty reed baskets that stink of fish. She can hear the river rushing beyond the village wall and the singing of the women walking home with their clean clothes.

She doesn't have to wait too long. Baaz walks out of the door next to the forge, holding a dagger of freshly cast bronze. He looks around the alley, seems not to see her. When she is sure he's gone, she slips through the door where he came from.

The house is dim, the smell of rust overwhelming. The main room is decorated with seals of demons and lion-headed monsters. In a corner by a flickering lamp, a terracotta plaque catches her eye: it is finely engraved with a winged horse fighting a giant scorpion. Semiramis picks it up, hiding it under her tunic with some of the seals. Then she hurries outside again, walking around the forge to avoid the hound guarding the yard. The wall is easy to climb here, worn by centuries of draughts and storms. From the top, she looks at her figure mirrored in the river. It keeps changing as the water flows, like one of the shapeshifter gods.

She holds Baaz's possessions in front of her. For one fleeting moment, she wonders if she should keep them. But they aren't worth much, and neither is Baaz. Besides, he has to pay for insulting her. So she throws them all into the river.

*

Beyond the smallest mud houses, in a corner that is always quiet and shaded, are the remains of the old temples of Mari. Scattered between stones covered with vines, the statues of the gods look like relics from another world. Semiramis knows that the rich cities of Assyria have temples sacred to the highest gods that rule the heavens, but here in the village they worship the lesser deities: Aya, goddess of dawn; Lahar, who guards the sheep; Ashnan, goddess of grain. In front of their statues are terracotta bowls with food offerings so that the gods can always feast and bless those who revere them.

The sun slips behind the mountains, and darkness falls into the folds of the hills. Semiramis passes the statue of Nusku, god of fire and light, surrounded by small burning lamps, and she makes her way to the patch of grass that was once the heart of the temple. There, three larger statues are looking ahead blankly. A stone bull for Anu, king of the sky, stands in the middle. On his left, a feather-robed archer, Enlil, god of the wind and the air, and on his right a nude winged woman with bird's talons, the mighty Ishtar, goddess of love and war. Semiramis kneels by the sculpted lions at the goddess's feet.

31

Women always come to Ishtar before lying with a man. They touch the goddess's wings and ask for their husbands to go eagerly to their beds. Semiramis comes here whenever she has done something forbidden.

I stole Baaz's seals to punish him. Do you forgive me?

There is a legend about the goddess Ishtar and the ancient city of Eridu. Eridu was ruled by Ea, the most cunning and artful god, who was also the architect of the universe. When Ishtar travelled to meet him, he welcomed her into his rich palace, and she challenged him to a beer-drinking contest. As soon as Ea was too drunk to stand, she convinced him to spill his secrets. When she had learned the knowledge of the world and its mysteries, she stole it from Ea and gave it to her city, the ancient Uruk.

Semiramis looks up. The goddess's wings are painted crimson and there are two carnelian stones inlaid in her eyes. She doubts Ishtar will mind her stealing but, just in case, she says a quick prayer and kisses the goddess's feet.

*

She hears them before she sees them. Fifty men riding to the small village of Mari. She is perched on the wall, hidden behind an old tree whose branches are heavy with shiny olives. At her feet, unaware of her presence, the men of the village are standing in a little group. Simmas and Amon are at the front, with Baaz's family. Above them, the sky is of a bright blue, as if it knows Mari is about to be blessed with the presence of the king's new governor.

The valley starts echoing like a drum, and then, suddenly, soldiers are streaming across the plain, their sun-kissed armour spreading light all around them. As they ride closer, Semiramis can see their pointed helmets, rosette wristlets and short kilts. Their horses are fine, saddlecloths woven with bright geometric patterns. They come to a halt in front of the gate, swaying and shining like inhuman creatures.

A man dismounts. His head disappears behind the olive branches from Semiramis' view, and she has to move aside to follow him, careful not to fall down the wall.

'I come in the name of Shamshi-Adad the Fifth,' the man says, 'King of the Universe, King of Assyria, Son of Shalmaneser the Third,

Glorious King of the Lands, King of All Peoples, Grandson of Ashur-nasirpal the Second, King of the Four Corners of the World.'

His voice holds richness, like precious spices or molten gold.

Simmas takes a step forward. Semiramis can see him swelling with pride and reverence. 'I am Simmas, chief shepherd of this village. Mari welcomes you, Governor.'

The man looks young, maybe a little older than Amon, and his posture is remarkable. It exudes calmness, or coldness.

'We have travelled across the two rivers. We have passed village after village to give the news of our mighty king, and to see how war has affected trade. Here is your chance to pledge allegiance to Shamshi-Adad. The king is generous,' the word trips on his lips, Semiramis notices, as if it were foreign, 'and forgives even those who tolerated the traitor Assur-danin during the war.'

'Mari is yours,' Simmas says quickly, 'and loyal to the great Shamshi-Adad the Fifth. We'll hold a feast tomorrow night to welcome you properly.'

The governor nods, an almost imperceptible movement. 'We will make camp outside the walls,' he says. His eyes are steady, set on Simmas and no one else. Semiramis feels the urge to be seen. She shifts aside so that the olive branches don't hide her face and stares at the governor with all the intensity she can summon. He turns slightly, his eyes looking up and falling on her for a moment only. His expression doesn't change. Before she can pin his face to her mind, he turns his back on them and mounts his horse again, disappearing as quickly as he arrived.

*

She doesn't join the women who bring fresh cheese and figs to the men in the camp. She stays in the yard, healing a lame lamb. Amon sits on the ground, mending a stool, whistling.

'The governor seems strange,' he says, after a while.

'What do you mean?'

'I don't know.' He shrugs, unperturbed. 'There is something dead in his eyes.'

She is surprised by his unusual insight. 'Could you hear what his name is?' she asks casually. He lifts his head from the stool curiously. She keeps her face expressionless, though her heart is thumping.

33

'Onnes,' he says.

'Onnes,' she repeats. It sounds strange but soft in her mouth, like a precious secret.

*

Before dawn breaks, Semiramis slips out of the house. Everything is wrapped in a bluish light, the lit torches outside each house flickering. She goes past the alleys and the square, climbs over the wall and down the other side. The river is green and deep, flowing through the rust-coloured hills. The soldiers have made camp on the opposite bank. The tents are round and small, a winged lion with a human head on each. Horses are resting by a patch of trees, where drying tunics and waterskins are hanging from the branches. Even from beyond the river, Semiramis can hear someone snoring, and the gentle whistle of a boy as he fills the water troughs.

She walks on, finds the spot where the water is closest to the tents. On her side of the bank, she crouches in the shadow of a tamarisk tree, trails her hand in the current. She waits and listens, hidden under a low, thick branch.

After a while there is a movement from behind one of the bigger tents and the governor appears. He is naked to the waist, his trousers crumpled as if he has slept in them. He looks around, then walks to the riverbank. The water is cold in the mornings, but he walks into it with no hesitation. He stands in it waist-deep, looking at the village, then disappears under the surface. Semiramis follows his shape as he floats underwater. She wants to move closer, to see if the darker lines on his chest are scars, or simply tricks of the light, but he emerges, wet hair plastered to his face. He lifts his head and looks straight into her eyes.

'You are stealing my moment of peace,' he says.

She freezes. Drops of water slide down his neck between his collar bones. She was right: there are thin scars on his chest, reaching all the way down to his hips. He is handsome, in a careless, arresting way.

'I always bathe here in the morning,' she says.

His face is unnervingly blank. 'Bathe, then.'

She considers doing it – she would like to see his face as she wades in, but something holds her back. She rises like a bird uncoiling from its nest and goes to stand in the water. She is aware of her loose hair, her coarse tunic, the fading bruises on her arms.

'Are you afraid I will hurt you?' he asks. Despite the coldness of his expression, she likes the way he speaks: each word feels as if he has tasted it, held it on his tongue, like a spice.

'Should I be?'

'People usually are.'

'I don't like fear.'

He laughs, as if she is jesting. 'Nobody does. And yet we all feel it.'

'I try my best not to.'

He lifts his eyebrows, considering her. A sudden cold breeze tickles their skin. The branches of the tamarisk tree sway a little behind her, and a flower breaks loose and lands on the surface of the river, floating between them. She smiles, then dives into the water. She swims in his direction and comes up for air a few steps from him, hair falling around her shoulders in dark waves.

He is still standing there, gaze fixed on her. Behind them, the village is waking. The sun is rising behind the hills, and she feels its warm light falling on her cheeks.

He tilts his head. 'Your face . . .' he says, breaking the silence. 'Do people tell you you look like the goddess Ishtar?'

She blinks in the brightening light. His question feels more like a statement to her, as if he wanted to tell her she is striking but couldn't find the right words for it. *This is not a man who says what he thinks.*

'Do goddesses stand among mortals?' she asks.

He doesn't reply. She wrings out her hair, then walks out of the water, back to the riverbank opposite him. She allows herself to glance at him one more time before hurrying back to the village.

Our days are few in number, and whatever we achieve is a puff of wind.

Extract from *The Epic of Gilgamesh*

5.

Ninus, King of the World, King of Assyria

Ninus is reading. The words blur in his tired eyes, shadows leaping in and out of the tablets:

> For it is I, indeed, who have put my people into a pitiless hand,
> into a narrow strait with no way out.
> Who is the god that will spare my people from catastrophe?
> I fought and killed like a flood,
> a raging storm that made their blood flow.

Outside, evening is falling. The windows of the palace glow like shrines in the dusk. Through them he can see the temples, tall and menacing, and the ziggurats, the pyramidal stepped towers his grandfather built.

'The joyful palace of wisdom', the Northwest Palace is called, but it seems to Ninus that this place has been emptied of any joy and is filled instead with the spirits of dead men who crave his attention. His grandfather, who was cruel yet the best of the Assyrians, a man who could command a room with a single glance. His father, stabbed in his bed by his own son. His brother, whose recklessness dragged him down to the house of dust, where all who enter never see light again. Each reaches out and whispers to Ninus.

He puts down the tablets. How is he supposed to move forward, to be King of the Universe, with these spirits of clay dragging him backwards? Onnes might be able to help him, to anchor him to the world of the living, but he has gone to Eber-Nari. *On your orders.*

He doesn't want to sleep, for he already fears the moment he will wake, when the room will look like a battlefield, and the shadows cast on the walls will be distorted, stretched-out limbs and abused creatures.

His eyes close and the dead start to whisper. In his dream, the corpse of his brother becomes a beast that walks beside him, staring with vengeful red eyes.

*

He is woken by the sound of soft, careful steps. From the corner of his eye, he sees a woman draped in rich purple robes. The smells of sandalwood and ripe, sweet figs.

'The kingdom is crumbling, yet you read.'

He pulls himself up, head ringing. His mother stands in front of him. Her greying hair is loose down her back, and her skin shines as luminous as the moon. Nisat isn't tall, or beautiful, yet whenever she steps into a room, everyone else seems to fade, as if she leeches all colour from the world.

'Assur is dead.' Ninus hears the pain in his voice, the urgency.

'He is dead because you killed him.' The words are like a blade twisted in his heart. Seeing his pained expression, she sighs theatrically and waves her hand. 'You did well. Assur was a traitor and wouldn't have survived long anyway.'

'He was your son,' Ninus says sharply.

'He came out of my womb, yes, but he didn't have my blood. He was made of passions and stupidity, two things I certainly never taught him.'

Ninus stares at her, unblinking. 'You are cruel.'

'I am honest,' Nisat replies. 'Your father, the father Assur *murdered*, was clear. Strength and understanding are the two qualities that make a king. People usually believe that wisdom and knowledge can be learned, but people are fools. It is strength that can be learned. One either has understanding or one doesn't.'

'Not everyone can master strength. Some people can fight all they want but are still beaten.'

'Those people aren't meant to be rulers.'

'Maybe I'm not meant to be a ruler. Maybe I'm tired.'

She scoffs. 'Tired . . . You think you've seen horrible things because you've been at war? I've seen much worse than you and here I am, still standing.'

Nisat: the most powerful woman in the kingdom of Assyria. A queen made of will and purpose. Nothing can wear her down; nothing can beat her. Sometimes Ninus thinks there is no blood inside her, no veins or beating heart, only pure, unbridled ambition, driving her relentlessly forward.

'You have never been at war, Mother,' Ninus says.

'Women are at war every day of their lives because they're expendable,' she says. Her face is lined, skin starting to sag, but her eyes have the force of thunder. They are fixed on his, unflinching, until he looks away and sits on the nearest chair. She remains standing.

'You did the right thing,' she says, 'fighting for your father and your king, avenging him, killing a brother who was a traitor. How many other men can say this? None.'

He isn't so sure. After his coronation he had looked at his hands, guilt seeping into every corner of his body, and asked himself, *Are you a good man?*

As if reading his mind, his mother says, 'You'll make a good king. I made sure you were next in line to the throne. Assyria has bled for years and now it needs peace and wisdom.'

Ninus flinches. 'Father would have chosen Assur.'

She shakes her head. 'I convinced him otherwise. And your brother learned that soon enough.'

He feels as if a stone has dropped into his heart. 'Assur knew he wasn't Father's choice?'

Nisat ignores him. He can tell by her expression, by the frown on her face, that she is already moving on to the next plan, the next plot. *As if she hadn't just buried a son and made another king.*

'Now, here is what you will do,' she says. 'You will stop sleeping on the floor, like a beggar, and you will prepare for tomorrow. You will speak with all those men who betrayed their king and you will pardon them, except one. You can decide who that will be.' Her eyes cling to him, and he knows what she is about to say. 'You will impale him so that the others know how merciful you have been. If they complain or whisper behind your back, I'll remind them of what your father did to the men who were disloyal.'

41

His thoughts are too tangled, as always when she comes to speak to him. He needs to be alone. He rises slowly. She waits for him to speak, head slightly tilted, as if she were expecting him to complain, or contradict her. But he knows there would be no point in that.

'I will see you in the throne room at dawn, Mother,' he says.

There is the slightest annoyance on her face at the thought of being dismissed, but she covers it quickly. She reaches out and cups a hand around his cheek. 'You will face whatever awaits you, and you will win. You are my son, and a king.'

He closes his eyes, but before he can enjoy the rare moment of comfort, she draws away from him and leaves the room. He looks at the empty space where she was only a moment ago, as if willing her to come back. But, of course, she doesn't.

This is how Nisat has always been, offering love and guidance in moments as precious as Egyptian gold, then pushing him away, a boy alone in the greediest of worlds.

He believes this is where his weakness comes from. You can't give a man the feeling of being understood then snatch it away from him: he'll spend the rest of his life searching.

*

He goes to sleep in his old bedroom. He has been struggling to stay in the king's apartments, where his father died. But this is the room he grew up in and, despite Assur's shadow lingering in a corner, this is where he should be.

He casts a look at the other side of the room, where Onnes' pallet once lay. How many memories, how many nights he spent lying in the shadows, listening to his friend's even breaths.

They used to steal herbs from the women's palace together, opium poppy pods that they crushed into wine and savoured as they sat side by side on the pallet, feeling the room blur. Sometimes they could even hear the spirits whisper. 'Maybe the opium blurs the boundaries between our world and the house of dust,' Onnes would say, with a note of hope that Ninus didn't like. They moved their arms so that the shadows on the walls touched, their hands together, fingers like the petals of a long-stemmed flower.

Nisat found them once. They were lying in a corner of the court-yard, heads up to face the starry sky. They had been caught by a servant as they stole the jugs of poppy powder from a perfumed chamber, and had run as quickly as they could along windowless corridors and through clear courtyards, tripping each other, laughing, hiding in deserted rooms as if the world was after them.

'Ninus.' His mother came slowly into focus, the jewels wrapped around her body bright and blinding. When her eyes set on him, they were reproachful. She stared at him for a long time, then turned to Onnes.

'Do you know that your mother used to take opium? She would have my servants bring the pods to her, then lay down and chewed them until the ceiling looked like the sky, or so she said.'

Onnes stood up. His face in the moonlight was calm, but his breathing was slightly ragged, as if he had been running a long distance.

'Some people are dead long before we bury them,' Nisat said, then left.

Onnes lay down again. It was a while before Ninus found the strength to speak. His lips felt thick and heavy, and there was a familiar weight in his chest, the fear of saying the wrong thing. 'Maybe what she said isn't true,' he said tentatively.

'No, it is,' Onnes said calmly. 'I saw my mother eat the pods. She used to say it made the world peaceful.'

Ninus didn't reply. When he turned to his friend, a single tear was shining on Onnes' cheek. But his lips were curled into a blissful smile.

*

When dawn breaks, he goes to see his daughter.

Sosanê sleeps in Nisat's household, a large building nestled between the Northwest Palace and the city walls. Men aren't allowed inside, but Ninus is king and will do as he pleases. A grand feast must have taken place in the night, because slaves are hurrying away with empty dishes and the air is thick with drunken whispers. The smell of wine seeps into every corridor, and as he passes the wide bedrooms, he glimpses women with hair in thick, perfumed plaits, dark blue kohl smudged around their eyes.

In the last room at the end of the main corridor upstairs, a child is sleeping. Music, smells, whispers, everything floats into the room: his daughter could never sleep with the silence.

Sosanê lies on a bed swathed in crimson pillows, a pile of tablets next to her. Ninus can't help a smile: 'Descent of the Goddess Ishtar to the Netherworld' and 'The Ballad of Former Heroes', his daughter's favourites. The furniture of the room is rich, inlaid with carved ivories from Eber-Nari and Phoenicia. A stone harpy sits menacingly on a table, vultures at her feet, and a plaque shows a lioness mauling a young man.

Ninus sits by the bed. As if feeling his presence, Sosanê stirs. When she was born, she looked nothing like him, and he almost believed she wasn't his daughter. But the more she grows, the more like him she becomes: sorrowful blue eyes, hair dark like a storm, a tablet always in hand.

'I thought you would never come,' Sosanê says. What sad, sad words for an eight-year-old.

He takes her little hand. 'I am here now.'

'Can you stay?' She wipes her eyes, sleepy.

'Yes.' He lies next to her, under the watchful eye of the harpy. His daughter nestles into him, and he puts a hand on her head, as he feels fathers are supposed to do. He focuses on her breathing, slowing as she falls back to sleep. It helps him keep the nightmares away.

He is twenty-four years old. King of the Universe. Father to a lonely child.

6.

Village Feast

The feast started at dawn, and by dusk the air is slicked with the gold of the firepits set around the square. Men stand close to large vats of beer, drinking through long tubes. Women are seated on rugs, biting into flatbreads and ripe figs. Plates heavy with *mersu* cakes, freshly baked bread and tender meats are carried around by girls with hair tucked under light veils.

Semiramis is drinking date-palm wine, the sweet taste melting on her tongue. She has woven her hair carefully; her long, dark plaits reach down her back. The dress she is wearing, which belonged to Amon's mother, is too large for her, but the pale green fabric shines like river-stones in the setting sun.

Her eyes search for the governor. He is sitting on a carved chair close to the largest firepit, its flames leaping into the air, orange and bright. He is wearing a long, dark tunic and earrings with pendants in the shape of lions. Some of the villagers carry gifts to him and leave them at his feet: a freshly carved lyre, ivory statuettes, jars of scent, and amulets against the demoness Lamashtu, who strangles infants in their cribs. He watches them with no expression, and sometimes nods at something his soldiers say.

At the opposite side of the square, sitting in a dark corner, a woman is wrapped in a tunic the colour of silver smoke: a diviner from a village west of the river. She is holding a small lamp in her hands and waits patiently for the villagers to come to her and tell her their dreams.

Semiramis moves closer, then lingers. She knows of men who were told that their nightmares were warnings of imminent death, and the diviner's face, with flesh drooping off her bones, unsettles her. And what dreams should she tell her anyway? The one where her mother comes for her from the river, jewels of pearl and coral in her hair? The one where she rides away from Mari, in plains of grass so endless they look almost like the sea? Those aren't dreams, they are wishes.

A hand closes on her arm. 'We should dance, sister.'

She glances away from the diviner into her brother's eyes. 'You only want to dance to impress the spice-seller girl.'

He grins. 'As always, you are very perceptive.'

She shakes her head, laughing, and lets him guide her to the centre of the square. A boy takes out his lyre, caressing the strings. Two men start playing tambourines, and Amon takes Semiramis by the waist and makes her sway. She feels her hair brushing against her back, her arms. Everyone turns to look at them, and a soldier whispers something in the governor's ear. The music rises and falls like a pulse. Other villagers join them, women with hair as dark as winter clouds and boys grabbing the hems of their skirts as if they were dancers' arms. Amon pulls Semiramis, lifts her, lowers her; she laughs when he trips over her tunic and treads on one of the weavers' feet.

'Here she comes,' Semiramis says, as the spice-seller girl walks towards them, a shy smile on her face. Amon looks radiant, and Semiramis moves aside, letting them dance.

The feast keeps flowing, with meat and fish carried around, dressed with oil and herbs from the summer fields. Semiramis steps around the dancers, attempting a glance at the governor, but her back collides against someone. She turns quickly and finds herself face to face with Baaz. He is smiling, though there is no warmth in his expression.

'You stole my stone seals,' he spits.

The chatter is loud around them, and she is grateful for it. She looks back over her shoulder, towards the governor, but he is barely visible in the crowd. 'Why should I care about your stone seals?' she asks.

Baaz flushes. 'Be careful, Semiramis. You know what the code says about thieves. You are lucky you still have both hands.'

She snorts. 'What are you going to do? Speak to our new governor? The code isn't kind to those without witnesses. *If the owner of lost possessions does not bring a witness for his accusation, he is an evil-doer and shall be put to death.*'

This makes him angry, but then a thought occurs to him, and he tilts his head with an expression Semiramis doesn't like. 'I do not need witnesses to punish you,' he says, then leaves her alone in the middle of the feast. She watches him join the other boys around a beer vat, pushing one out of the way to drink. *Do as you wish*, she thinks. *I will be gone before your accusation can reach me.*

The evening is casting its blue shadows. The last few clouds drift away and, behind them, stars glow like fireflies. As the music slowly dies, the people begin to scatter. Amon is whispering in the spice-seller's ear, winding her hair around his fingers. Some of the governor's men are disappearing with the women, slipping away in the darkness beyond the firepits. Two shepherds are helping Simmas to his feet. Semiramis watched him gorge himself on spiced meat, beer-soaked cushions and overturned cups all around him. Now his eyes are unfocused, as always when he is drunk. *Good*, Semiramis thinks, as the shepherds carry him home. *He will be dead asleep before he touches his bed mat.*

She goes to fill her cup by the firepit in a corner. Across the square, the governor is standing, saying something to the soldier on his right. The soldier nods and sits down, helping himself to more beer. Semiramis watches the governor leave his cup behind. His gaze lifts and touches hers. Then he walks in her direction.

She keeps still by the firepit, feeling the flames warm her cheeks. He stops a few steps from her, as if she were a strange animal he must approach carefully.

'Here you are,' he says, in his rich, warm voice. 'The girl who looks like the goddess Ishtar.'

She doesn't like that he calls her a girl, not a woman, but smiles. 'You are kind. Most of the villagers say I am a demoness. They are scared I might bewitch them.'

She expects him to ask her why, but he simply shrugs. 'Common people are always unkind to those who are different. They insult them because they do not understand them.'

His answer surprises her. No man has ever taken her side. 'How do you know that I am different?'

'Anyone who looks like you is both blessed and cursed. Your mother must have been a beautiful woman.'

Must have been. She watches his face, trying to discern any thought written on it. 'So I am told.'

'You don't remember her?'

'She died shortly after I was born.'

'How?'

She stares at him as she speaks: 'She drowned herself.'

Something shifts in his expression, as if he were showing her a different face, hidden behind his mask of coldness. She is struck by the pain she sees underneath: dark and raw.

'My mother died too, when I was young,' he says, after a pause. 'I remember her from when I was a boy, but I haven't seen her for so long now that sometimes I think I made up those memories myself.'

His face is vivid in the flames, foreign and flawless. His eyes are like bronze discs. They probably change colour with the light, she considers.

'I am sorry,' she says. 'I have no memories of my own mother.'

'Your life must have been difficult.'

'Life is difficult for everyone,' she says, because the last thing she wants is his pity. 'We are not gods. *Our days are few in number –*'

'*– and whatever we achieve is a puff of wind.*' He smiles. The expression brightens his face, makes him look younger. 'You know the ancient poems.'

'Some. I wish I knew them all.'

'There is a place in the king's palace in Kalhu with myths from every corner of the world. Princes grow up there, reading the epics of creation and the stories of the first men.'

'It sounds like the gods' Heaven,' she says, careful to keep the longing out of her voice.

'Noblemen do not see it so. To them, reading is a duty.'

'Of course. If you spend your life feasting, you cannot understand it is a feast.'

He shakes his head. 'Feasts, palaces . . . those places can be cages too.' She does not know what he means, and is about to ask him, but he stands before she can speak. 'I haven't asked your name,' he says.

'Semiramis.'

'A foreign name. Greek?'

'Yes.'

He nods as if she has proved something he knew all along. 'A foreign name for a girl who feels like a foreigner.'

The need to read his thoughts is like a fire burning her inside, but he is slipping away from her. 'I must go back to the camp,' he says. 'My men will be too drunk to control themselves otherwise.' He hesitates. 'I will leave Mari in two days. I hope I will see you again before we go.'

She looks into his handsome face. There is something about him, like honey drops on the lips, that leaves one wanting more. He waits a moment, and when she says nothing, he turns and walks back to his men. She watches him cross the courtyard and disappear in the direction of the main gate. An unspeakable panic takes hold of her – the need to run after him, grip his arm and go with him to his tent, away from Simmas and the dust of her mud house. But he is gone before she can act, and then it is too late for her to do anything at all.

*

The fires are burning out in the pits, the last embers glowing tiredly. The diviner sits in a corner by the edge of the square, as motionless as an ancient oak. Semiramis walks to her. The night air touches her skin with its cold hands, as if trying to warn her. But she feels restless, pulled forward.

'Do you wish to tell me your dreams?'

She flinches at the sound of the diviner's voice: deep and cavernous as a man's. The woman's face bathes in a pool of lamplight, tens of amulets hanging from her wrinkly neck.

'I wish to know my future,' Semiramis says.

The diviner takes two jugs and a shallow bowl. First, she pours water into it, then oil. It coils over the surface, refusing to blend. A large, perfectly round circle forms in the middle, swallowing the smaller blobs as it grows. Semiramis looks around, but all the villagers are gone. *As if the diviner was waiting for me*, she thinks.

'Your future is shrouded in darkness,' the diviner says slowly. 'But this sign is a warning.'

'A warning,' Semiramis repeats.

The diviner looks up, and her eyes grow as white as milk. Her lips move and, when she speaks, her voice cracks.

'The woman arrayed in purple and gold,
with a cup in her hand full of lust and faults,
will be as great as Babylon,
the glowing city which reigns
over the kings of the earth.'

The words seem to echo in the following silence. Babylon. The greatest city on earth, greater even than the mighty capital of the Assyrian Empire. People say that its gates are made of glowing blue bricks and that there are gardens built on terraces that brush the clouds.

'What does this mean?' Semiramis asks. The diviner is skimming her fingers over the oil, tracing patterns she cannot see. 'Will a woman rule Babylon?' Semiramis insists.

The diviner does not answer. She is mumbling to herself, the words as slippery as smoke. Semiramis waits for a long time. Her thoughts stumble in her mind like children in the darkness. Finally, she stands. She leaves the diviner in the square, her eyes rolled back in her head, as if still seeing a future she cannot share.

7.

Ninus, King of the World, King of Assyria

'When will Onnes be back?' Nisat asks.

They are standing on the terrace of the Northwest Palace, looking at the shadows that enfold the river Tigris. Dusk is settling over the city, and a gentle breeze blows, carrying the scents of the terraced gardens.

'Ninus,' Nisat says. She rests a hand on his shoulder, and he feels her rings press into his skin. Ninus glances at her, bracing himself. She rarely asks about Onnes, and when she does, she doesn't mean well.

'He must be in Eber-Nari by now,' he says. 'He is bringing the province back under our control.'

Nisat nods, satisfied. 'Good. As soon as he returns, I will find you a wife, so you can have children.'

He struggles to hide his surprise. 'I already have a daughter.'

'Yes, and she is clever and beautiful. Maybe one day she will be queen.'

'Her mother was a scribe,' he says, despite himself.

Nisat tilts her head so that he is forced to look at her. 'I was the daughter of a cupbearer and there is no woman as powerful as me. Sosanê may be a bastard child, but she is your first-born daughter. Your blood, *our* blood, flows in her veins. As long as I am here, every member of our family will be respected, because if we are respected, we are feared, and if we are feared, we can rule.' She smoothes her dress, rich purple from the western city of Tyre. 'But whether you'll have more children or not, you need to marry. Rumours spread fast, and the last thing we need is people claiming you are unfit to rule.'

'What rumours?' he demands.

She pretends not to hear. 'And we'll find a wife for Onnes, too, unless he has already found one in Eber-Nari.'

'Onnes doesn't like women.'

'That is not what the slave girls in my palace say.'

Ninus shakes his head. Of course Onnes likes women – he has seen him disappear with girls into his quarters often enough – but what he meant to say is that he doesn't *love* them.

'You know nothing about Onnes,' he says curtly.

'I may know nothing about Onnes but I know everything about you.' Each word is a warning, spoken quietly, but clearly: 'Find a wife. Father new children. And put those rumours to rest once and for all.'

*

Onnes.

The first time they met, Ninus was alone in the gardens, going through a poem he read in his mind. Some words were soft as peaches, while others were jagged, as if they were wrong. Ninus wanted to change them but didn't know how.

A shadow moved behind a tree, a head of light brown hair. Ninus approached it. It was a child of about his age, his knees pressed against his chest, his eyes staring into the distance. He didn't turn as Ninus looked at him.

'Are you allowed to be here?' Ninus asked, because he didn't know what else to say.

The boy looked up. His eyes were sad, but his face was calm. 'I can go if you like.'

He didn't say it out of fear, but in a tone that told Ninus he wished to be alone. Ninus understood. He usually wanted to be alone too, though at that moment he felt unable to walk away. 'We can both stay,' he said. 'What is your name?'

'Onnes.' His voice was cool, but his face tightened a little as he spoke.

'I am Ninus.'

The boy studied him. Then a smile. 'I know who you are.'

That was the beginning.

Onnes wasn't shy. He faced life, no matter how difficult it might be, without hiding or fantasizing about other worlds. Ninus found it hopeful. He often felt as if he was slipping away from his body, mind wandering in the sky, in the recesses of the palace, in the stories he read. With Onnes, he floated away less and less.

'You're spending a lot of time with that boy,' Nisat told him once. 'Do you know who he is?'

'Yes,' Ninus said. Then, 'No.'

'His mother was one of the Assyrian women sent to the palace from the provinces. Her father gave her as part of a bounty in the hope of advancing his position in the army. She stayed in my household.' Ninus listened, bracing himself for some sort of blow. 'She hanged herself last winter.'

Ninus felt suddenly angry. 'Why are you telling me this?'

'Madness breeds madness,' Nisat said simply.

That spring they turned fourteen. Trees heavy with lush fruit, sun painting the sky, like honey, dripping down on the palace and into the courtyards. They had finished their fighting practice, and it was time for Onnes to go back. He didn't sleep in the Northwest Palace; only royalty did.

'Are you tired?' Ninus asked him. He had started to feel restless every evening when they were meant to part, his skin prickling as if stung.

Onnes looked at him for a long moment. 'No.'

'Come then,' Ninus said, and turned to walk past the bulls with human heads that guarded the state apartments. In the shadows, he could feel Onnes' steps behind him, his smell of lemon and spices.

Assur was in the bedroom, playing with a short copper sword. He frowned when he saw Onnes. 'So, you are the boy with the mad mother.'

Onnes' expression remained impassive, and Ninus felt a pang of jealousy. He was never able to hide his feelings well. Assur also seemed surprised: his taunting usually bore results. He stood and threw the sword at Onnes. The hilt hit him in the chest, but Onnes managed to catch it before it fell. 'Do you wish to fight?' he asked calmly.

Assur laughed. 'I like this one,' he said to Ninus. 'He can stay.'

Life was different after that, easier. Spring slipped into summer, and they fought and ran and slept without their tunics on. Their muscles felt constantly tired, arms and legs dangled as their bodies changed. Onnes' shoulders became broader, his jaw tighter, wider. Sometimes he caught Ninus looking at him, and they laughed. The way the sun fell on Onnes' skin. How the wind stirred his hair. Only his face remained constant, ever inscrutable. Ninus didn't care. He had come to learn there was a murkiness inside his friend, but wasn't there in everybody?

One night, Assur didn't come back to their bedroom. Ninus and Onnes had heard him whisper in a slave girl's ear at dinner and had left early, eager to be away from the chaos of the feast. In the room, there was silence. Ninus removed his carved gold bracelets and placed them on a table gently: an ibex, a heifer, a lynx. Onnes was by the water vessel, washing his hands.

Ninus couldn't help but ask: 'What do you think of Assur's girl?'

'I didn't notice her,' Onnes said, without turning. His back was broad, shoulder blades jutting out. Ninus went to sit on the couch. 'Why do you ask?' Onnes asked. He had turned to face him, and his hands were still wet.

Ninus shrugged. He rested his head back and looked at the ceiling. He felt a strange buzzing going through him but didn't know how to speak of it.

'I don't trust women,' Onnes said.

His voice had darkness in it, and Ninus felt the need to soothe it. 'Because of your mother?' he asked.

'I suppose so.' He crossed the room and sat on his pallet. He pulled off his tunic. Ninus averted his eyes from the muscles in the belly, the bones of the waist.

'It is different for you,' Onnes said, after a while. 'Your mother . . . I would trust her.'

Ninus snorted. 'She is hard to trust too.'

'Yes, because she is ambitious, but she is devoted to you and your family cause. I would trust a woman like her.'

Ninus closed his eyes, thinking, *I trust only you*. He knew it was foolish to say it, so he kept silent. Across the room, Onnes' breath was growing even. *And you?* Ninus wondered. *What are you thinking about? Do you trust me?*

He could hear a thousand voices and whispers coming from the palace, people's lives buzzing around them.

Outside, the incomprehensible world. Inside, the two of them, bound together, breathing together, going through life together.

Lonely souls rarely find each other, but when they do, they aren't meant to part.

8.

Semiramis, a Thief

In her small mud-walled room, Semiramis cannot sleep. The diviner's words are pressed into her mind as seals are pressed into clay, though what their meaning is, she cannot tell.

As great as Babylon, the glowing city, which reigns over the kings of the earth.

She had wanted to go west, but Babylon is east, towards the rising sun and the kingdoms that were born out of the gods' hands. Whatever the prophecy means, it must be tied to her in some way, or else the diviner would not have told *her*.

Some mortal lives drift aimlessly, like lost souls; others are tied to their destinies, as two lovers are tied to each other. Semiramis knows nothing about love, but she understands desire. It can bring nothing or it can give everything.

When the boys of the village look at her, all she feels is a sense of weight, anchoring her to the dust. But the governor's stare is different: it has power in it – the power of escape. And if she doesn't act upon it, their meeting will be like rain falling into the river – invisible, its impact no more than a few ripples. Her life will go on as before; she will stay in Mari for ever, growing old like every other woman, bearing children and nothing more.

She sits up. How thin the wall between different lives is, she thinks, full of cracks one might peep into. But how does one move from one side of the wall to the other? It must be done carefully, like water flowing, wetting the bricks but leaving no trace after it dries.

Yes, she thinks. *I must be careful.* She repeats the words like a prayer, until her thoughts stop stuttering around her head.

When she finally falls asleep, her mind is filled with promises. She doesn't notice that the rugs under her feet are not as smooth as they always are, and that, in the little hole dug beneath them, all her stolen possessions are missing.

*

She wakes with a jolt. The house is empty, the air thick and moist: it will rain soon. She washes her face and brushes her long hair quickly, until it is shiny, with waves that one aches to touch. A sense of purpose is tightening her body, and she feels the same excitement that runs through her whenever she is about to do something forbidden.

In the courtyard, nothing moves. Simmas' dogs are by the door. There is something eerie in the way they sit, watchful, ears flat against their heads. The sheep are bleating from behind the fence, eager to be out on the hills. *As they should be*, Semiramis thinks suddenly. *Why are they here?* She looks around, waiting for Amon to appear, but nothing seems to breathe. Then, a shadow walks out of the grain keep.

'Semiramis.'

She stops mid-step. It is as if a cloud has blotted out the sun. There are deep bags under her father's eyes, and a vein is throbbing on his neck. Her gaze drops to his fists, which are holding something small and glittering.

'The blacksmith's son told me you stole from him.' His voice cuts across the air. 'I didn't believe him at first, but then I went to your room.'

He opens his palms, where the dead governor's rings are shining with the silver jewels and amulets. Her life, in his hands. She moves back, involuntarily.

'You are a disgrace,' he says. 'Wilful and unbending, ever since I took you in. I hoped I would gain something from you, yet you keep finding ways to disrespect me. Which man wants a woman who steals for a wife?' He drops the jewels, tiny circlets of gold and silver and obsidian, onto the sun-cracked earth.

Her skin is stinging, as if it knows what is to come. Any other day she might have cried and pleaded, but not today. Her fate is close enough for her to reach, and she will not allow Simmas to be in her way.

'I did not steal those rings,' she says, keeping her voice low.

His face grows purple. 'What did you say?'

Behind him, the grain keep and the house. Behind her, the gate. She takes a small step back, then another, and another. 'I did not steal,' she repeats.

'Liar.'

She is halfway across the yard when he lunges. She breaks into a run, but his hands find her neck and she trips. He grabs her by the hair – she feels a sharp pain on her scalp, where her head wound was healing – and drags her away from the gate. She wriggles and punches, but he hauls her over his shoulder.

She has a flash of herself as a child, calling for her mother while she was dragged away from the square and the boys she was playing with. They had looked at her with wide eyes, their wooden sticks still in their hands, while she had fought back tears. 'Your mother is dead,' Simmas had told her. 'She can't hear you.'

'Put me down,' she says, then louder: 'PUT ME DOWN.'

She grabs the door of the grain keep, anchoring herself with all her might. He pulls her inside and she drops to the ground, hitting her head against the wall. The room sparks. A pot falls and shatters. She pulls herself up, panting. 'I want to leave.'

'You are staying here until you admit what you are.'

'Father. Let me explain.'

'You're not my daughter.'

The blow lands on her face. Her head turns sideways, blood trickles down, half blinding her. She grabs a pot and throws it at him. It smashes against his shoulder, and he looks from the shards to her face, like a madman.

Before she can grab another pot, a plate, a ladle, anything, he throws her to the ground, kicks her in the stomach, in the head, in the chest. She sees his foot going in and out of focus, as he commands, '"I am a thief." Say it.'

'No.'

His fist meets her ribs. '*Say it.*'

She turns onto her stomach and hides her arms under her body, so he doesn't break them. There is a gurgling, and she wonders if it's coming from her. Her eyes must be closed, for she can't see shapes, just sparkles of light against a deep red background.

At last he stops.

'Look at the mess you made,' he says.

She can't see the mess, can't see his face. She lifts her head, just enough to breathe, then vomits. The liquid spreads slowly, wetting the hair she had so carefully brushed.

She wishes she were a god. She wishes she weren't nobody.

You will pay for this, she thinks. *There will come a time when I am untouchable, and I will make sure you pay.*

She has only thought it – how could she have spoken when she can't even feel her face? – but maybe the words have come out of her mouth because, from the corners of her eyes, she sees his sandals move back towards her. He drops to his knees and his face comes into view. He is frustrated, as if he has failed to reach a rebellious child.

'Always so ahead of yourself,' he says. He punches her in the back.

She faints.

*

The next thing she knows is the rain, its sound flooding the keep. It hurts her skull, and she wonders if maybe she has lost a piece of bone, because she feels as if her brain has no protection against the world, no shell.

She lifts her head slowly, carefully. Her nose is bleeding, all down her face and over her hands. On her left, a sad little puddle of vomit. She rolls onto her back and keeps still for a moment, trying not to feel the pain that snakes under her skin. She can hear the brushing of the palm leaves outside, the faint echoes of songs. Lives unfolding without her.

I am alone. I have always been alone. If she closes her eyes she can see her mother, a pale figure in a land of shadows, beckoning to her. 'Come,' the figure says. She is the colour of a winter's morning, and Semiramis reaches out to touch her, but the woman retreats even further into the country of darkness. 'Come with me to the house of dust, Semiramis.'

She opens her eyes. *No. I am not like you.*

She crawls out of the grain keep, focusing on each breath – she has to open her mouth because her nose is clotted. The raindrops hit her face. Her palms sink into the mud, her legs buckle, but somehow she manages to stand, steadying herself against a palm tree, a gate, a wall. Out of the courtyard and into the narrow streets.

A few children are running around her, the last to take refuge from the rain. Their feet splash in puddles; they are so happy they don't even notice her. She could be a demon from the netherworld, a walking corpse. She could be Tiamat, the monstrous mother of all the gods.

Outside the village the river is dark, dancing under the raindrops. Semiramis feels her way into the water. It is calmer here, quieter. She steadies herself against a rock, her cheek against its smoothness. She stays still for a long time. She stays until she can't feel where her skin ends and the river begins. She could just let the water carry her away. She could never go back. The possibility makes her fearless.

We are not gods. Our days are few in number, and whatever we achieve is a puff of wind.

She can see herself at eight, at ten, at fourteen, crying angrily in the grain keep, hiding in the ravine, her wounds tearing at the skin. Every time she had imagined making Simmas pay, assembling her things and leaving. But she never did.

To humans, everything seems indelible, permanent. What would we do, she wonders, if we knew that our actions don't count, that everything keeps shifting and changing no matter our will? How would we act?

Night falls, and she knows what to do next.

*

The camp is darker than the village under the rain. The horses are snorting, pulling at the rings that tether them. Semiramis can see the soldiers' silhouettes against each tent – they are eating and drinking inside, the smell of stew mingling with the earthy scent of rain. Most of the torches have burned out, and the ones that remain cast feeble wavers of light.

The governor's tent is in the centre, larger than the others. There is one guard outside it. Semiramis walks slowly. Her aching skin stretches over her as if it belongs to someone else. When she is close enough to the tent, she grabs a torch and throws it into the air. The guard watches it fly. He takes a few steps away from the entrance, his eyes gleaming with fire. Semiramis sneaks behind his back, flapping the tent open and closed before he can notice.

60

Inside, there is a table with a dead sheep cut open, as if ready to be studied by a seer, and a pallet where two daggers are gleaming. Onnes is sitting with his back to her, a cup of beer in hand. 'I told you already, I don't want any company.'

'I need a place to hide,' she says. Her voice sounds different, as if something in her throat has been crushed.

He puts down the cup and turns. His eyes widen in shock at the sight of her. She likes it – for a moment he can't be elusive: even his face can betray something.

'You are bleeding,' he says.

She had wanted to be careful before but now, broken and bruised, she is past that. Her possessions are gone, her plan turned to cinders. She either takes her chances here, or she goes back to Simmas. And it will be a miracle if he lets her out of the house again. *I will die there. He will kill me.*

She takes a step forward while the governor stares at her dripping hair, the blood crusted on her face and arms.

'Let me.' He gestures for her to sit, and she does so, trying not to wince. The waves of pain cut into her skin like knives. He brings water to clean the wounds, and pomegranate juice. Dipping the cloth into the liquid, he offers it to her. Their fingers brush as she takes it. She presses it against her cheekbone and lips, wiping away the blood. When she has finished, he offers her his cup of beer, which smells strange and sweet.

'Opium powder,' he explains. 'It makes the pain go away.'

She drinks it in one long gulp. Her head is throbbing, and her throat burns when she swallows.

'Who hurt you?' he asks.

She looks at him. She doesn't know if it is best to lie or be truthful, so she settles for something in between: a lie that makes him understand she is lying because she can't be honest. 'I fell down a cliff.'

He nods, as if he understands. 'Boys who walk out of the training ground in Kalhu look like that. They never forget who hurts them because they always pay them back. Sometimes, they even kill, to make sure they aren't hurt again.'

'Have you ever done that?'

He doesn't answer.

'How does it feel, to kill a man?'

He looks thoughtful for a moment. 'It feels good.'

'How?'

'There is nothing like it. I have heard of people in the west who value order and control, some who believe in forgiveness and goodness, even. I cannot imagine how that feels – no Assyrian can. There is nothing like losing yourself when you kill someone else. Your thoughts, your pain, everything disappears.'

Unwillingly, she thinks about her mother. 'Like love.'

He nods. 'To lose your soul for the sake of another. Our king once said the same thing.'

'And what do you think?'

His gaze is far away, as if he were looking through time, at a memory only he can see. 'I think that to take one's darkness inside yourself can be dangerous. If you have to suffer, at least let it be because of your own shadows.'

He is silent. She sees him hesitate before he speaks again. 'I told you that my mother died, but I didn't tell you how.' Something flickers in his eyes. 'She thought the man she loved loved her too, but when she realized he didn't, she went crazy. She was shunned and hated at court. After a while, she could endure it no longer. She took a rope and hanged herself.'

It is as if a veil has been torn, and she can finally see behind it. *He is like me*, she thinks. *His mother killed herself. He knows what it means to be alone.* There is a humming in the air, and for a moment it feels like the whole world has gone: there is just their tent, the beating heart of the universe.

'Were you shunned at court afterwards?' she asks.

'I wasn't, thanks to our king. He treated me as family.'

'Is Shamshi-Adad a good king, then?'

He stares at her, as if considering whether her question is treacherous or insulting. 'It depends. There are kings who build the most magnificent temples, but impale people even after they submit to them.'

'Is he that kind?'

'He isn't.'

'He is good, then.'

'He is my friend.'

She frowns. 'Your king is your friend.'

'We have known each other since we were children,' he says simply.

How does that make you feel? Your friend is also your master. But she cannot speak such words, so she asks, 'And does your king choose a wife for you?'

He watches her curiously. 'I have no wife.'

Hope surges in her chest, like a swollen river. She turns away, fearing he might be able to see it in her eyes. The tent smells of rain – wet earth and something sweet. She is aware that their knees are touching, though she can't feel him, can't feel anything except the pain.

'If I stay here,' she says quietly, 'I will have to be married by the end of the season.'

He lifts his hand to her neck, and for a moment she thinks he will choke her. Instead, he touches her damp skin, traces her collarbones with a thumb. His eyes on her are unwavering.

'Keep pressing the cloth on your wounds. I will warn my men not to disturb me.'

He stands. Then, halfway across the tent, he stops. 'Why are you really here?' he asks.

She looks back at him. *Because I have nowhere else to be. Because, all my life, I have longed for something more.* She feels as if she is holding her fate in her hands and she could drop it at any moment. But other words are throbbing inside her, like seeds waiting to burst.

'I came here because I found some golden rings under my father's pallet,' she says. 'I think he stole them from the dead governor.'

9.

Semiramis, a Liar

When Semiramis wakes, she doesn't know where she is. She tries to stand, but the pain forces her onto the pallet. She tries again. Every movement is like a punch. She takes a few deep, excruciating breaths and looks around her. Then she remembers.

Onnes is gone. He has left a cup of beer at her side. As she stands, stumbling when she feels a sharp pain in her hips, she knocks the cup over. Beer spills onto the ground, filling the air with a sweet, sickly scent. Outside, a sound grows: villagers murmuring, and soldiers giving orders. She can't hear what they're saying, so she drags herself out of the tent.

Soldiers are packing their weapons, saddling the horses and wrapping provisions. She hurries past them, a sense of nameless terror driving her towards the village. The sun is creeping into the sky after the night's rain, and women are lingering in the roads, keeping children in their arms as they glance towards the main square.

When she reaches her mud house, it is empty. Inside, jars and pots are strewn across the floor, as if someone has hastily emptied them. In Simmas' room, rugs have been pushed aside, and the chest with his belongings emptied onto the mat. She runs back outside and towards the square.

A crowd has gathered around the shadows of the empty firepits. They are staring at a spot in the centre, where a man is standing on the red-hot dust, surrounded by Onnes' soldiers. Semiramis moves closer, pushing two women out of the way. She can hear Onnes' calm, controlled voice. She doesn't need to see to know that the man he is talking to is Simmas.

Onnes' words carry all across the square: 'These belonged to the dead governor of Eber-Nari. You stole them.'

The crowd bobs their heads to see the rings Onnes must be holding. Semiramis drags herself behind one of the trees, her body aching, like an open wound. She can see the village boys and Baaz standing by the well, horrified.

'Your daughter confessed you were hiding them in your house,' Onnes is saying. 'My soldiers found them under your bed mat. You know the law.'

'That is a lie,' Simmas says, the faintest trace of rage in his throat. There is only one thing worse than pain for him, and that is public punishment: he cannot stand the humiliation. 'She is a liar.'

Semiramis' hands start shaking. She clutches her fists until her palms are raw.

'Why would she lie?' Onnes asks. He speaks without feeling, or cruelty, even without interest. It is unsettling.

'Because she has bad blood inside her,' Simmas spits out. 'It comes from her mother, a murderess and a whore.'

He tries to say more, but there is a collective gasp and Semiramis catches a glimpse of the soldiers as they bring Simmas to his knees and push his head onto one of the firepits.

'Summon her!' Simmas screams, and his voice has changed: there is an edge of desperation to it now – it almost doesn't sound like him. 'Let her confess in front of me. I want to see her face as she lies.'

'There is no need.'

Everyone turns to her as she steps forward into the clearing. She can see herself in their shocked eyes: her swollen and purple throat, her bruised face, the blood crusts on her arms. Simmas lifts his head. His face is filled with hatred. All her life, she has looked at that face, soaked its contempt like a rag.

'Semiramis,' he says, 'didn't I teach you that you must not lie?'

'Yes,' she says. 'You taught me well.'

'Then tell the governor the truth.'

There are old breadcrumbs and soot on his wrists. She looks at him for a long moment, then shakes her head. He makes a strangled sound, as if he wanted to stand and hit her. She steps back, instinctively, but he cannot move. The soldiers yank his arms out in front of him.

'Which hand?' Onnes asks.

The women shield their children's eyes. The trees stir in the wind, as if waking from a bad dream. Amon's head appears among the villagers. He is staring at Semiramis from the opposite side of the square. She waits for him to make way among the crowd, but he stands frozen to his spot.

Onnes unsheathes his sword. It is broad and short, the hilt shaped like a crouching lion. 'You know the law,' he repeats, looking down at Simmas. 'Which hand?'

Simmas' breathing is ragged. Amon starts walking towards him, but slowly, as if he were moving underwater. When he reaches the centre of the square, Baaz grabs his arm, pulling him back.

'You don't have to do this,' Simmas says. His voice is low, a quiet pleading. 'I am your father.'

'Don't you remember?' she says. 'I am not your daughter.'

It is the last thing he hears before he screams. The sword comes down like lightning, too fast to see. Amon shakes Baaz away and runs to Simmas. Semiramis keeps still and watches as her father's hand flies, then falls into the dirt.

*

Lines of birds are stark against the pale skies. Red water drips onto the ground; it sounds like an eerie lullaby. Semiramis watches the women throw buckets of water around the firepit. The earth turns from crimson to brown, then pale and watery. Amon has disappeared. The world around her is heightened, a strange state in which every contour shimmers, past and future do not exist – only present.

She walks to her mud house, swaying slightly, bumping into the walls. The villagers move aside as she passes, as if she were a disease they were scared to catch. *Maybe Simmas was right. Maybe this is what I am.*

In the grain keep, everything is as it was – her vomit on the floor, stains of her blood on the walls. The memories of last night strike her and, before she knows it, she throws up again. It smells of the opium Onnes has given her.

'Semiramis.'

He is standing at the edge of the courtyard. There is a brown stain at his waist, close to the lion-shaped hilt of his sword. She wipes her mouth and walks to him.

'Your father is in the healer's house,' he says. 'He has lost a lot of blood, but he will live.' There is something different about his face, though she can't tell what.

'I can't stay here,' is all she says.

'My soldiers are readying the horses to go back,' he says. 'We ride to Kalhu before night falls.'

She wonders how many commoners he has punished, and what he thinks about, the moment they scream. If he thinks at all.

'I want you to come with me,' he says.

It is hard to tell if it is a request, or a demand. Either way, it does not matter. She knows the answer. She has known it ever since she first spoke to him, by the river.

'Yes. I will come.'

*

She finds Amon sitting at the top of the wall by the main gate, staring at the blackening sky. Simmas' cries have died down, and now the village is silent, as if in mourning. She climbs and sits at a safe distance from him. Every movement seems to rip at her wounds; her hands are still shaking.

Amon looks at her, then away again. 'You are leaving,' he says. His voice is hoarse.

'Yes.'

He snorts. 'You could have told me. About the rings.'

'You would have told Simmas.'

He presses his hands over his eyes. 'You *maimed* him. He is our father.'

'He is *your* father.'

'He raised you too!' he shouts. 'You can't change that, despite the things he did.'

She stares at him, throat tight. 'You know he hurt me,' she says quietly.

'So, you maim someone, because he beats you?'

67

'That is what the code says. An eye for an eye.'

'You are not a king, or a governor! It is not up to you to deal out punishment!'

Do you think hurting him gave me any satisfaction? I will carry my decision inside me, like a splinter, for the rest of my life. She wants to say the words, but she knows he wouldn't understand, so she keeps quiet. An owl screeches from somewhere in the village – they are a bad omen in their land, flying spirits of the dead who seek revenge.

'You should go,' he says. 'You are not welcome here any more.'

She looks at his profile and the way it blurs into the night. From her first memories, until this very moment, she has lived with him by her side. But she knows – has always known – that she will have to move forward without him.

She climbs down the wall, and when she looks up at him one last time, the tired shape of his face hangs in the darkness, like a star.

*

Can we grasp the instant when our fate turns? Or can we understand it only later, once the moment grows into a memory?

They have been riding for a whole day, and now they are making camp. In this slice of land – green and bronze mixing between the two rivers – she can still see the village, a small dot on the horizon. Onnes joins her at the edge of the camp. They didn't speak as they were riding, and now that the world has gone back to what it used to be – less vibrant, less sharpened – she feels the magnitude of her choices.

'What are we going to do when we reach Kalhu?' she asks.

'We are going to get married,' he says calmly.

Her head jerks up. 'I thought you didn't want to be married.'

'Neither did you.'

Behind them, a soldier shouts an order. Semiramis watches the men as they fix the tent poles and groom the horses.

Married. For years she has despised that fate, treated the word like a doom to avoid at all costs. But now she knows she has to go east, and that the governor has not entered her world by chance, or meaningless luck.

'You are brave,' Onnes says.

'You don't know that.'

'Oh, I know,' he says. 'I know it was you who stole the rings from the dead governor. The traitor Assur-danin's soldiers fight for me now. They said that a young woman was trying to help the governor when they found him, and that she stole all his gold, then disappeared.'

The words are a shock. He isn't looking at her, and she is afraid to breathe.

'Have you known all along?' she asks.

'No. Then you came to me the other night and told me it was your father who is a thief. My guess is that *he* beat you. Maybe it wasn't even the first time. So you planted the gold under his pallet and took your revenge.'

She takes a step towards him, so that they are facing each other. 'And if what you say is true? Would you bring me back to Mari?'

He glances at her. '*The hammer shatters glass but forges steel.* I've known a lot of men in my life who are glass. But you are different.'

The sun goes down – a tiny brushstroke of red in the sky. She reaches out and touches his chest. She can barely feel his heartbeat. It is hidden, like everything else about him. But she has seen a glimpse of him, and it was enough to make her understand: in the village square he had tested her, and she had passed the test.

'I will marry you,' she says.

Around them, the sun meets the land, colouring the sky with a thousand shades.

Thus my old life dies, she thinks. *Let a new one be born.*

BOOK II

823–821 BC

Man is the shadow of god, and slave the shadow of man.
Assyrian Proverb

IO.

Ribat, a Slave

Citadel of Kalhu, capital of the Assyrian Empire

He learned to read on the scar of his mother's back. If someone asked him what he wants to become, he would say: 'A scribe.' But no one will ever ask him. He is a slave and the son of slaves. An animal, a property, a unit. Assyrians value horses more than slaves. They have them brought to the empire from the north, feed them food that he has never tasted.

His mother always said that slaves are birds born with smaller wings. 'We lie under the trees, staring at the sky, twitching our little wings feebly, trying to learn what no one is willing to teach us.' Ribat often pictured these birds. They had a dull plumage, wounds that made them writhe in agony, bodies stretched out calling for help. Above them, birds with bright feathers – sunset orange and Egyptian blue – flying high in the luminous sky.

He is royal property, so he hasn't been branded. His mother had made sure of it. She had a brand, the mark of her previous owner's name burned with a red-hot iron into her skin. Ribat traced the letters of the scar as a child, even though it made his mother sad.

'What was his name?' he asked, and she said, 'Nabu-shum.' So he would try to read the scar, sign by sign. When he had worked it out, he wanted to learn more. He started reading the scars on other slaves' backs. He liked the sharp edges of each sign, tiny arrows lodged between the ribs. Two lines crossing: *star*. Five: *lord*. Six: *son*. He sat behind them as they rinsed and wrung sheets, mended and ironed tunics, sliced and fried vegetables. When they sent him away, he went back to his mother, and repeated what he had learned until she hushed him.

He knows there are hundreds, if not thousands, of clay tablets with more signs somewhere in the Northwest Palace, but he also knows he can't touch them. Punishment is an ever-present threat for a slave, an evil shadow lurking behind him, following his every step. There is a man who told his master, 'You are not my master,' and had an ear cut off. A woman who tried to run away was followed by the citadel guards before being whipped to death in front of her master's palace. A man who cut away his branding . . . Ribat doesn't know what happened to that one. All he knows is that none of them was careful.

He, on the other hand, is always careful. He has spent his life dodging dangers. He is good at it. He reduces his thoughts to the essentials: food, sleep, work. He prioritizes things that are important so that he doesn't steal a morsel of food unless he is starving; he doesn't look priests and courtiers in the eye even if they speak to him.

But even in such a life there is always a glimmer of hope. One can't live without hope.

*

The lower part of the citadel is a quagmire. His feet sink into the mud – the air is heavy with its odour. He tries to step around animal droppings, to follow the tracks of other passers-by. Above him he can see the pale and mighty shapes of the houses of the gods. Next to them, the walls of the Northwest Palace, so high they seem to touch the colourless sky. On his left, the palaces of the governors, beasts of white limestone crushing the small houses underneath. A line of people is waiting in front of a wine-house, children eating a roast goose, licking their greased fingers. He passes the sandal-maker's shop, the weaver's factory, the forge, the bakery.

At the market stalls, he stops. Cages with ducks, pigeons and turtle doves clatter. Delicious smells drift to him – broth, flatbreads stuffed with mutton and vegetable fillings, even roast grasshoppers. He closes his eyes as his mouth waters. A girl with bracelets in the shape of snakes offers him a platter of grilled fish. Spices waft from it and Ribat quickly walks away. On his right, stalls of incense from the east; on his left, jugs of wine from Eber-Nari. He finds a short merchant with a large golden necklace and shows him the royal seal. The man looks at the small clay tablet around Ribat's neck – his identity disc – then hands him a basket filled with folded cloths. Women's tunics, Ribat notices, not his master's usual. He takes the basket, careful not to crease the fabrics, then hurries out of the marketplace and into a narrow street. A drunk is lying down, his face in a puddle of spilled beer. Ribat steps over him and enters the house behind him. Everything is dark, and the air smells of healing herbs. Smoke comes out of small wooden vessels in spirals. On a table close to the door, the drawing of a sheep's colon on clay and the model of a goat liver.

Ribat clears his throat, and a man with no front teeth appears from behind a curtain. The healer, he calls himself, though Ribat has noticed he doesn't dress like one – his tunic is plain, brown stains on the sleeves.

'My master needs more opium,' Ribat says.

The man laughs. It is an unpleasant sound, a hissing. 'You need to repel evil from that palace.'

Ribat ignores him, waiting in silence. The healer hands him a small jug crafted in the shape of a poppy pod. Then, he shows him pressed flowers of blue water-lily. 'Your master should try this,' he says. 'They come from Egypt. Steep them in wine for weeks and they will make your master happy.'

'He doesn't want happiness. He just wants the numbness.'

The healer puts away the flowers. 'Has your master called an *asu*?'

Ribat shakes his head. 'Nothing a physician could do.'

The healer raises his eyebrows. 'A man who can't sleep is being punished by the gods. A man who is scared of his own dreams is paying the consequences of a crime.'

Ribat hides the small jug in the pocket of his tunic and leaves the house. Outside, a little boy is looking at the drunk, giggling. As evening falls, the smell of mud mixes with the scent of flowers that the breeze carries from the gardens. Ribat walks back to the palace, thinking about the healer's words.

*

In the dark corridors of the palace, the flickering light of oil lamps illuminates glimpses of the bas-reliefs. The head of a lion. The wing of a protective spirit. A purple flower.

Ribat steps into the courtyard, where a group of women is hauling water by the well. Blue and yellow glazed bricks glitter above the columns, the ornamental designs in the shape of bulls. In a corner by the wall, there is a post with a chain attached to it, the bronze rusty and stained with old blood. Ribat avoids it carefully and joins the women, who are deep in a hushed conversation.

'Master is coming back,' one says, when she sees Ribat. She has short black hair and plump lips like a pomegranate split in half. Her name is Ana, 'grace' in the western land she comes from. Ribat thinks it fits her well.

'Good,' Ribat says.

'He is marrying a villager from Eber-Nari,' Ana adds.

'A villager?' Ribat repeats.

'Yes, a shepherd's daughter.'

A woman by the name of Zamena scowls. 'A commoner . . . How could this happen?'

Ana smiles as she balances the water on her shoulder. 'Let us hope she is good.'

A good woman would never marry our master, Ribat thinks. 'We should clean the old blood from the stone before they arrive,' he says, looking at the post.

'I will do it,' Ana says. Ribat nods, grateful. Then he leaves to put away the tunics. They are smooth to the touch, golden like the sun and crimson like a slave's blood.

✻

In Master's room, he grinds the poppy pods into a powder and pours it into a cup. When he has closed the lid, he leaves the clothes on a stool. He does each thing slowly and carefully, taking time. The bedroom makes him feel calm, shielded. He can collect his thoughts here.

He knows everything about the palace, every corner, every room, every courtyard. He knows where the other slaves steal small bites of food, where they go when they want to hide, how they pass pieces of information to other palaces.

Outside, the streets grow dark, and the citadel prepares to rest. The buildings take on the colour of the sky. The earth of the gardens is rain-drenched, their trees and flowers bright even as shadows grow longer.

He doesn't just know about the citadel, he also knows about its people. What they do when no one else is supposed to see them. He can glance around and listen, because no one ever notices him. Each thing he sees is carefully stored in his mind, like tablets in a library.

The king always paces, in the palace, in the gardens. His head is so full of thoughts that even the air around him is dense, as if he brought with him little clouds of mist. He seems lighter, happier, only when he comes to see Ribat's master.

The king's mother is more feared than the king. They say that whenever a man dies in the citadel, she is the one who gave the order. Slaves don't mention her name when they speak: there are those who work for her, and those who avoid her as if she were a poisoned blade.

The commander of the army, the *turtanu*, touches himself in his palace. Ribat saw him once, when he was sent to bring him a message. He tiptoed to the reception room, tablet in hand – how he liked to hold it, to feel each letter carved into it! – and rested his ear on the door. The *turtanu* was moaning loudly, in a way that was so intimate, so private, that Ribat felt compelled to listen. When he peeped inside, he saw that the *turtanu* was standing naked in the middle of the room, facing a bas-relief of a warrior that looked eerily like himself.

His mother once said that the more powerful men are, the stranger their tastes. Ribat thought 'perversions' was a better word for it but he didn't tell her. She was clever and brave. Now she is in the house of dust, lost with kings and governors. She left Ribat behind in this unjust world, teaching him one last lesson: for a slave, the only way out is up.

The light is dimming, and the room smells of opium. Ribat smooths the tunics one last time, then hurries to join the preparations for his master's return.

II.

A City Built by the Gods

Semiramis enters the citadel of Kalhu through a massive gateway flanked by colossal human-headed bulls. Above her, the sun reaches its peak, bathing the city in gold. She looks up at the glazed buildings catching the light and thinks this must be a city built by the gods. The palaces are made of brilliantly coloured brick and tiles, their surfaces gleaming green and blue and yellow. Behind them, higher than the walls, she sees what look like mountains covered with lush green trees.

'Those are the gardens,' Onnes explains. 'They are planted on the terraces of the ziggurats.' He uses the word for the buildings they have often seen as they travelled from Mari, temple towers that reach towards the sky. The ziggurats are barely visible under the flowering plants. She glimpses orchards with almonds, olives and date palms, canal water gushing from above like a gateway to the heavens.

People stream past them as they ride in the lowest part of the city – women with tunics the colour of sand, merchants with bulls and camels, men dragging prisoners on a leash. They speak in strange languages, their voices blending, like a prayer. Beyond the citadel, on the river, a hundred boats with carved figureheads of horses carry logs of timber.

She rides in the crowded streets wearing a leather vest that Onnes has given her. Her legs are sore, her hair filled with sand, long plaits hanging with the old governor's golden rings. *Do not look back*, she thinks, as they pass a gleaming black obelisk and take a wider road that leads to a magnificent palace basking in the sun. *Only forward.*

By the gate, they dismount. Onnes gestures for his men to stay behind, then walks between two giant lions made of bronze, gold leaf shimmering on their manes. Semiramis follows him through three large courtyards where dignitaries and priests in bright blue robes are speaking in hushed tones. There is an eerie quiet, like that of a temple. The men turn to them as they pass, skin like ivory and eyelids painted dark. They look as cold as statues, and Semiramis wonders if there is blood inside them, or simply stone.

In the fourth courtyard, Onnes stops and waits by a wall covered with reliefs of tribute bearers. Semiramis stares at the figure of a man with two monkeys on a leash. It looks so real and vivid that she expects it to jump out of the wall. She reaches to touch it, then catches herself, resisting the urge to trace the animals' contours with her fingers. Everything around her is so vast that she feels small and meaningless. If a god reached down from the sky, he could pluck her out of the courtyard.

A courtier in brilliant green robes appears, eyes staring at Onnes' feet. 'The king will see you now.'

'Come,' Onnes says, closing his hand around Semiramis' arm.

At the door of the throne room, two winged bulls stand sentry. A bird watches them, perched on the bull's head, its feathers like rainbow shades. *Everything is watching here, everyone is alert*, Semiramis thinks. Then she steps into the shadows.

She is in a long corridor, incense burning from a brazier at the centre. Beyond it, the king is seated on a throne dais, his lean figure framed by a large stone panel where a tree of life is carved. Its branches stretch to the ceiling, like dancers' arms. A few men stand near the throne, their faces dimly lit by tall torches.

'You are in the presence of Shamshi-Adad the Fifth, King of the World, King of Assyria,' the courtier announces from the shadows. His voice echoes: a faint humming against the walls.

Onnes bows deeply and Semiramis copies his movements. She can feel everyone's eyes on her, and the stillness of the room, thrumming with power.

Then, a laugh. 'Come, Onnes, there is no need for such formalities.'

The voice is low and musical, each word rolling out with perfection. Onnes and Semiramis stand and walk closer to the dais. As they pass the brazier the air is cleared of incense, and she can see the king more clearly.

Shamshi-Adad has the aura of a man who isn't aware of his own beauty. His skin is luminous, the colour of freshly pressed olives, and his richly embroidered tunic is the same dark blue as his eyes. At his waist, he carries a sword with a hilt shaped like a roaring lion, similar to Onnes'. He touches it absentmindedly, and his gaze passes over Semiramis as if she were a ghost.

Next to him an older woman is richly dressed. A crown of golden flowers and intricate leaves frames her forehead. The woman's lips curl before the king can speak. 'I see you outsmarted me, Onnes.' Her voice lacks the musicality of the king's and reminds Semiramis of a blade sharpened so carefully that it would make one bleed with the slightest touch.

Onnes bows. 'How so, my queen?'

'We had a wife ready for you, yet you come here with another woman.'

Semiramis bites her tongue. She is aware of her chapped hands, of the smell of horse that still lingers on their bodies.

'I'd rather choose my own wife, my queen,' Onnes says calmly.

'Of course. But now we have an unmarried princess in the citadel. What should I do with her? Send her back to the kingdom of Urartu?' She speaks as if she is used to being the only woman in the room. The men glance at her with respect, though with no liking, Semiramis notices.

'The princess of Urartu can stay,' says a large, beardless man. His dark hair is oiled and plaited, and his voice is high-pitched, like a child's. 'We need her now more than ever.'

'So she will stay,' the king says.

'*You* intend to marry her?' the queen asks.

Semiramis expects the king to punish her for addressing him so, but he merely shakes his head. 'Urartu is an enemy. The princess is here as a hostage, not as breeding stock.'

The beardless man clears his throat. 'My king, Urartu is proving more powerful than we thought. If King Sarduri sent his daughter here, it is because he wants to make peace.'

'You can't make peace with savages,' says a tall man with greying hair. His face is lined and might once have been handsome, if not for the promise of violence it carries.

'With due respect, my *turtanu*,' the beardless man says sweetly, 'you can't despise all the peoples who don't have Assyrian blood. The

80

empire isn't what it once was. If you hate anyone who isn't born between the two rivers, you'll find yourself surrounded by enemies.'

Onnes shifts next to her. Semiramis follows his gaze and sees that the king is looking at her husband as one looks at the sun. It is unsettling.

'Ilu is from noble lineage,' the king says. 'He can't understand your interest in foreigners, Sasi.' His eyes are still on Onnes, even as he is speaking to the beardless man, who nods reverentially. 'But Onnes has travelled for many days. We'll let him rest and discuss these matters tomorrow.'

'Thank you, my king,' Onnes says.

All the others bow, except the woman, who stares at Semiramis as if she were a worm. She is glad to follow Onnes when he leaves the room and its whispers behind. As she walks next to him, it occurs to her that the king hasn't looked at her, not once. As if he was pretending she didn't exist.

*

Onnes' palace is on the opposite side of the citadel, nestled between other identical buildings – the homes of the governors. When two guards open the heavy wooden doors, Semiramis' eyes need a moment to adjust.

The place has the beauty of the dreams she used to conjure as a child. A courtyard paved with terracotta tiles leads to suites of rooms where she can glimpse paintings of blooming flowers and running animals. The lower parts of the walls are decorated with panels of alabaster, carved in low reliefs of bulls. Between a well and a wooden post, a line of servants is standing. They look grey and silent, like small spirits from the house of dust. *Not so different from the villagers*, Semiramis thinks unwillingly. *Not so different from me.* She wonders if they can feel it too, if they can see that she is more like them than the governor she married.

A girl with ink-black hair springs forward and guides her to the upper floor, where rooms are reached from a wooden balcony that extends all the way round the courtyard below. Golden torches light windowless corridors that lead to a more private side of the palace, with views across the hills and fields. The brilliant wall paintings are of protective spirits, lion-headed men and sphinxes.

The slave accompanies her to a sealed room: her vapour bath. As soon as Semiramis enters, she pours water on heated stones, then leaves. The air grows moist, to clean away the sand that has lodged in her hair, and on every inch of her skin. Semiramis removes her tunic and sits, resting her head against the wall.

The silence wraps her like a woollen blanket. She has never heard such stillness, she realizes suddenly. Even when she was alone in the village, there was always some sound in the distance, a goat bleating, a child crying. But this quiet feels different, like the still heart of the world.

Outside, the light pours into the halls and chambers. When she was younger, she wanted to be closer to the sun, thinking its radiance might make her shine. 'Or you might catch fire,' Amon would object. He had always feared the great forces of the universe, while she would run straight to them. The thought of her brother, small and far away in their village made of dust, makes her feel a brush of coolness, as if a shadow is pressing its hands to her.

She pushes it away and stands, wet hair dripping down her back. She remembers the young women from her village praying to Ishtar before lying with a man. Semiramis does not pray. She looks at the sky and makes promises. She promises she will be bold and fearless. As luminous as a star and as raging as a lion.

*

In Onnes' bedroom, two torches pour long stripes of gold across the walls. The smell of incense lingers in the air, so rich Semiramis can almost taste it. Onnes sits on a couch opposite her, a cup of beer in hand.

'Do you like the palace?' he asks. He is clean and perfumed, strands of light brown hair falling around his face.

'Yes,' she says, taking a grape from a platter set between them.

'And what did you think of our visit to the Northwest Palace?'

'The man with no beard in the throne room,' she says, 'who was he?'

He swallows some beer. 'Sasi. He's a eunuch, one of the closest to the king.'

Eunuch. She has heard there are men at court who have been mutilated to diminish the risk of them inheriting too much power. Men who can't have children can't threaten the throne.

'Is he a governor?'

'He is a spymaster. He holds the role that was once Shamshi-Adad's when he was still prince.'

'A spymaster,' she repeats.

'Yes. It is tradition that the king's son has a network of spies and sends reports to his father to help him make foreign-policy decisions. But since Shamshi-Adad has no son yet, that role is now Sasi's.'

'Why not yours?'

Onnes frowns. 'Sasi was the perfect choice. He offered himself and the king couldn't refuse him.' His tone suggests that speaking of the eunuch displeases him, so she doesn't enquire any further.

'Is it true that the king's mother wanted you to marry another woman?' she asks. The crimson gown she is wearing is smooth against her hips, unlike anything she has ever worn. She can feel Onnes' eyes tracing the curves of her body.

'I imagine so, yes.'

'Did you know before you left the citadel?'

'No.'

'She doesn't like you, does she?'

'She never did, which is a pity because I find her formidable.' There is a hint of respect in his voice, and she thinks about the king's mother, standing in the throne room and teasing her son. Her face was like a well, so dark and deep it was impossible to glimpse the bottom. And so were the faces of the men around her – everyone keeping their secrets buried under sweetened words. She suddenly understands why Onnes decided to marry her, why he wasn't upset, but rather pleased when he found out that she had lied to him. In this world of fiddlers, he needed an ally. *I will be that and much more.*

Blood beats in her, faintly humming. Onnes is staring at her, as if waiting for one wrong move. 'You are unconquerable,' he says, after a while, and that makes her smile.

'You have your walls, and I have mine.'

They are close, two people who have avoided intimacy all their lives. A man made of coldness, and a girl who slips into the shadows, like a thief.

He puts down his cup and covers the distance between them. His breath is warm and rich with spices against her lips. Outside, the birds whistle and the priests start chanting. Onnes pulls her into his arms. A choking feeling takes hold of her – the same she felt when they spoke in the village square. It is the need to pull his skin off his body, peeling layers away to discover something no one else knows. But she can tell he likes to be the one who guides her, who touches her as if she were his. In this, at least, he isn't unreadable.

In this golden room in the capital of the Assyrian Empire, they are naked, lowering their defences, looking for pleasure in each other.

*

Semiramis has grown up hearing tales of kings and governors – how they live in cities made of gold, dress their perfect bodies in silver and lapis lazuli, sleep with lions and serpents in their wide, silky beds. Though those were all stories, there was a kernel of truth in them.

Every corner of Onnes' palace is filled with richness. Glowing lyres inlaid with carnelian. Collars and necklaces made of sheet gold. Wine-filled goblets on smooth ivory tables. Onnes himself sometimes seems to have jumped out of a myth. They lie together in his bed, wrapped in lion skins, bathed in the glow of the torches. As they travelled from Mari to the capital, he had mostly kept quiet, and Semiramis had wondered if it was because he regretted his decision. But here, in the comfort of his home, as the moon god travels across the sky, he pours opium powder into his wine and tells her of his life, one story after another, as if he were unwinding a twisted thread.

He tells her about the eunuch Sasi, who once, after a feast in the Northwest Palace, came to Onnes' room and asked him if he would join him in his bed. The eunuch is from the Phoenician cities by the sea and was deported, with many others, during one of Shalmaneser's campaigns. Semiramis thinks about the man's features, small and delicate, and about the subtle accent hidden in his voice, like a secret waiting to be discovered.

Onnes tells her of his own mother, a general's daughter from the eastern provinces. He recounts the days spent with her in the women's palace, where all they did was play hide and seek until she was too tired and fell asleep, her breath smelling of opium poppy. His face darkens when he speaks of her, as if a wound inside him is bleeding, staining everything. In those moments, it is strange to think of him as the man who fought in the rebellion, who destroyed the city of Ashur and captured the king's brother.

'Did you know Assur?' Semiramis asks. She always feels dizzy lying next to him, as if she has drunk the world's best wine.

'I knew him well. We grew up together. He thought the world owed him everything.'

'Maybe it did. He was a prince after all.'

Onnes' eyes are lit, the fire caught in his face. 'His mistake was to think himself untouchable. But anyone can be killed.'

She nods, because she likes the way he speaks, with no regard for anyone's title or station. It allows her to feel equal to him.

In all his tales, he never mentions the king, and she finds it strange, for she noticed how they looked at each other in the throne room. But she does not question him. She simply looks at him and listens. She listens to make sense of this world, to give it a shape so she can inhabit it.

*

Their wedding feast is held in the Northwest Palace, on a wide terrace that overlooks the river. Semiramis is wearing a dress the colour of pale sunrise with an elaborate embroidery of a lioness on a background of lotus buds. Onnes' tunic is simpler, made of cotton and of a deep purple.

The terrace has been transformed into a lush garden. Flowers and vines climb around painted columns, fill the air with their scent. Men and women recline on crimson couches, hair plaited with beads of rare amber, arms covered with bracelets. Between them, three-legged tables are laid with roasted ducks and pigeons. Attendants wind through them, their arms heavy with wine jars and trays of honeyed almonds.

Semiramis looks around. The eunuch Sasi is eyeing her curiously from a corner. At the opposite side of the terrace, a woman is standing by herself, looking at the river. Her hair is like a field of golden wheat, and her tunic is embroidered with a winged goddess that doesn't look like any Assyrian deity Semiramis knows.

Onnes' hand closes around her wrist. 'I want you to meet the king.'

He takes a cup of beer from a passing tray, then makes his way to the couch where the king is reclining, listening to two men with thick beards dressed in horizontal rows of curls. Semiramis follows, blood beating in her chest so loudly that she fears they might hear it.

The king's face lights up when he sees Onnes, then darkens when he notices Semiramis beside him. With a wave of his hand, he orders the men to leave. Once again, she is struck by his beauty, refined like the most magnificent statues. But then, she considers, artists shape their stone after him.

'Ninus,' Onnes says, with a small smile.

Ninus. She likes his real name, for it fits him better than his royal one. Ninus seems surprised to hear Onnes use it in front of her: the knowledge of a king's name gives power over its owner, which is why kings, queens and princes keep their real names from becoming known to the masses – only the people closest to them may know and use them.

'Onnes,' Ninus says. 'I thought you would never get married.' There is the slightest trace of emotion in his voice, like a lyre chord strung and echoing quietly.

'You *hoped* I would not get married,' Onnes replies. 'Now you will have to marry too.'

It sounds like an old joke between them, though both are serious.

'Is the thought of marriage such a burden to you, my king?' Semiramis asks.

Ninus turns to her. His face is startling. While Onnes' eyes are flat, Ninus' are filled with a thousand emotions, all racing quickly, like a mountain stream. 'Marriage is a duty all men must endure,' he says.

She smiles. 'I am not sure the goddess Ishtar would agree.'

'What do you know of gods?'

She is struck by the contempt in his words, as if she was committing a heinous crime in speaking to him. She thinks about the prophecy she heard in the village square, about the diviner's white, unfocused eyes. *The woman arrayed in purple and gold will be as great as Babylon.*

'Gods' wills are unknowable,' she says. 'Yet we crave their knowledge.'

'It's curious, isn't it?' he asks. 'Mortals crave what they can't have. It's a never-ending need, like eating food that never fills you.'

Is he speaking about her? *They*, he said, as if he weren't mortal. But, then, he is king, she considers, and kings are closer to gods than to men. Before he can dismiss her, she bows to him and walks away. Courtiers and noblemen whisper and skitter out of her path. She stops in the middle of the terrace and stands alone surrounded by strangers.

Slowly, she becomes aware of a shadow staring at her from behind a column: a man with no beard and lush black hair. Semiramis joins him under the colonnade. When she is close enough, she sees that the eunuch wears an earring on each lobe, in the Assyrian style, and his hair ends in a row of simple, shiny plaits.

'A *joyous* wedding,' he says, in his high-pitched voice. 'The goddess Ishtar must be looking down from the heavens.' His tone unsettles her, shrouding words in meanings she cannot decipher. She is aware of the men and women around them, casting glances in her direction. The spymaster laughs softly. Semiramis has the uncomfortable sensation that he is reading her mind, a suspicion she confirms when he says, 'They stare because they have never seen a common woman in their midst. A fascinating sight.'

She remembers what Onnes told her about the eunuch, in the long hours they spent chatting before the dawn. 'I thought you were common too, my lord,' she says.

He cocks his head, interest (or surprise? she wonders) brightening his eyes. 'Common *and* a eunuch. A double slight. But I have long grown used to their stares.'

'No one seems to be staring at you now.'

'You are the more exotic animal here,' he says. 'And a novelty. Maybe it will wear off, maybe it won't.' He winks and bows to her, walking away as if the paving under his feet were made of water.

He does not want others to see him talk to me. The thought makes her feel angry, as well as lost. There is no one she can talk to, and nowhere she can go. Around her, wine and beer keep flowing like rivers in winter, and nobles are laughing and touching each other's jewels. The night is growing dark, but the terrace remains lit. The torches are crackling, and the men's faces look luminous, almost divine, as they shout their toasts.

May the gods make us powerful.
May the goddesses make us splendid.
May the king trample his enemies.

Onnes is still speaking to Ninus. There is tightness in the king's face – it is clear he wants to be anywhere but here. Semiramis watches as Onnes leans towards his ear to whisper something. His lips almost touch it. Ninus shakes his head, then turns to look at Semiramis, his eyes the same colour as the evening sky. She looks back at him and, as she does so, a strange, dream-like feeling surges through her, like the longing for a memory that was never really hers. For a moment the terrace becomes a sweet, indistinct blur, where nothing exists but the king and her husband, sitting together on a high couch that seems impossible for her to reach, as toasts keep echoing feebly like lost creatures in a cave.

May love make us undying.
May we live, for ever, in memory.
May we defeat death.

12.

Semiramis, a Governor's Wife

She stands in the pillared portico of the palace, watching attendants come and go in the temple below. The portico is cool, with cedarwood columns and bas-reliefs of deer and gazelle running in open countryside. It separates her quarters from Onnes' and, from up here, she can see the temple of Nabu, the god of wisdom, and the priests that pray, swaying like spikes of grain in the wind. On her right, reaching up to the sun, are the hanging gardens and, beyond the walls, a great sand arena surrounded by hills, orchards and fields.

In Mari, the diviner had spoken to her of Babylon, the greatest city that reigns over the kingdoms of the earth. But surely, she reasons, no city can equal Kalhu in greatness, with its terraced temples and palaces, huge and shining against the sky.

'Do you need anything, Mistress?' a quiet voice asks.

She turns. A slave is standing by the columns, looking at the floor. He is small, limbs thin, like those of an insect. There is a clay tablet around his neck, which she wishes she could read.

'What is your name?' she asks.

'Ribat, Mistress.'

She wonders if he is supposed to speak to her, or if he dares to do so because he knows she is common-born. *I should send him away.* But she is too curious, and too lonely in this strange new place.

'How long have you been in this palace?' she asks.

'My whole life. I served the previous governor, before Master arrived.'

His face is unremarkable, features arranged in a strange way, as if the gods were bored when they created him and didn't pay too much attention to his looks. But his eyes are striking: alert and full of sorrow. He must be her age, though he looks much younger.

'And where did Onnes live, before he took this palace?' she asks.

'With the king, in the Northwest Palace.'

'You have been to the Northwest Palace?'

'Many times. I go whenever Master sends me.'

'And in the lower part of the citadel?'

'Every day.'

She stares at him. 'You must know every corner of this city, then.'

He nods. 'Slaves are the eyes and ears of the mighty Kalhu.' He falls quiet, though she can almost hear the rest of his thought, the part he is not saying out loud: *You are going to need one, if you want to stay afloat.* Then it occurs to her that he came with the pretence of asking her if she needed anything, when actually he was the one who needed something. It makes her smile, though she does her best to keep her face expressionless. She is sure that, even if Ribat is staring resolutely at the ground, he can *see* her.

'And what do slaves want, in return for information?' she asks.

If her question surprises him, he takes care not to show it. 'Nothing, Mistress.'

'Everyone wants something.' *I know that well. I had dreams, even when I had nothing.*

A flame burns in his eyes, like a candle suddenly lit in the darkness, but he remains quiet. She does not ask him more: she does not need to. There is one thing that slaves want, above all else: freedom.

She walks up to him. He is standing so still that she is surprised to hear him breathe. Placing a hand around his wrist, she says, 'You will be my eyes and ears, then.'

He startles and shifts back instinctively, then moves forward again, as if he needed more of her touch. But she has already left the portico.

*

The best way to make allies is to start with the household. She can rise as high as she likes, but if a servant wants to slit her throat while she sleeps, nothing will stop him. So Semiramis learns all the slaves' names. Ana lines her eyes with colourful pigments, plaits her hair, oils her body. Zamena cooks the meat just as Onnes likes it, tender and spicy. Ribat organizes Onnes' tablets – from the way he traces the signs on the clay, Semiramis suspects he can read them. She learns to recognize their shadows as they leap across the floor, the sound of their whispers. She smiles at them as they enter a room, asks them if they grew up in Kalhu or if their families were deported by the king's father. They come from every corner of the empire, from the jewel-like cities of Egypt to the glittering shores south of Babylon and the wild mountains beyond the kingdom of Elam. At first, they think her mad, but slowly they smile back, ease up a little in her presence.

Ribat is the one Semiramis likes most. He is as serious as a man and as slippery as a shadow. He always lingers outside doors before coming in. His face, raw with some unnamed grief, breaks into a flickering smile whenever she talks to him. When she asks him how he came to be owned, he tells her his mother was a slave.

'Was she born a slave?' Semiramis asks him, but he is already speaking of something else, his mind constantly focused on the next task, the next snippet of information to share. He speaks warily about others, and almost never about himself. He is cautious, and rightly so: Semiramis knows that cautious is how you survive.

He always appears when she needs him, as if the simple thought of him is enough to bring him to her. She asks him all the questions she is too ashamed to ask Onnes.

What Babylon looks like – he has never been there but describes how each gate glows blue and green in the light and how sculpted lions guard the streets, like creatures fallen from the sky.

What the common people say about the king's mother – 'She once executed a dignitary in the throne room after he claimed she should submit to her husband,' Ribat says, as if that explained everything.

'And what did King Shalmaneser do?' Semiramis asks.

'He liked that. He chose her because she was fierce.'

When she asks him about Onnes, Ribat tells her nothing she does not know already, except that her husband often welcomes a priest in the palace and asks him to divine future happiness and despair from a lamb liver.

'He always enquires after his health, his future, his dreams,' Ribat explains.

'Why?'

He shrugs, does not answer. But she sees that a thought is forming in his mind, one she wants to grasp. So she asks, 'What is the thing Onnes hates most?'

She sees him frowning, thinking. 'Weakness,' he says eventually.

*

'Can you read those tablets you always carry, Ribat?' she asks him one day. They are in the reception room, Ribat arranging the narrow-necked jars, Semiramis eating plums. When he hesitates, she adds, 'Do not lie to me.'

A small smile passes over his face. 'Yes, I can read, Mistress.'

'Can you teach me?'

A long silence. Then: 'It would be my honour to teach you.'

They settle in the portico every afternoon. They read proverbs and prayers, charms and curses – against snakes, flies, scorpions. Ribat is superstitious: he sees bad luck as a constant shadow, hovering behind every corner, every closed door. When a wild cat sneaks into the main courtyard of the palace, he quickly seizes it and throws it outside, 'Before it can howl,' he explains. 'That would be an evil sign.' When a line of red ants crosses the floor of the kitchen, he finds a tablet filled with rituals against evil portents – 'So we can loosen the grip of these forces,' he says wisely.

In the evening, he leaves tablets with proverbs on Semiramis' bed, which she reads in the flickering light of the lamps, fingers pressing into each sign as she tries to decipher it. Her bedroom overlooks the portico, with its smell of cedar-wood, and has waves painted on the walls with a brilliant copper blue. It gives the impression of being underwater, which makes Semiramis think of her mother.

Sometimes, she can hear Ribat hovering by the door, wondering what words she is practising without him.

'You can come in,' she tells him one time.

His head appears at the door. She is sitting on the floor with a tablet on her lap: a numerical hierarchy of the gods. Ribat has explained that numbers are sacred in the empire and they are assigned to each of the gods, according to the place and order to which they belong.

'Come,' she repeats.

He takes a step inside. He glances at the tablet and says, 'The god Anu has the perfect number: sixty.'

She puts aside the tablet. She has read enough about Anu. 'You haven't told me who taught you to read.'

His eyes darken. 'My mother.' She had thought his mother was alive but now, seeing his face, she understands that she must be dead.

'And how did she learn?'

'She didn't. She . . . I learned from reading the scar on her back.'

There is a hint of challenge in his eyes, as if he is daring her to pity him. He reminds her of herself.

'You are very clever,' she says.

He blushes violently. 'Thank you.'

Around them, the waves seem to move in the light of the lamps. Semiramis feels a strange and sudden sadness. 'Go,' she tells Ribat. 'I will sleep now.'

*

'Have you ever fought a woman?' she asks Onnes one evening. He has come back from the training ground and is undressing for his bath. Muscles ripple under his skin, showing the scars on his chest. He pauses to consider the question. It is something he always does, no matter how strange, or surprising, the question is.

'No,' he says.

'You should fight me.'

He looks at her placidly. Any other man would have laughed, she knows it well. But Onnes merely says, 'You do not know how.'

'Then train me.'

It is winter, a month since she arrived in Kalhu, and she has barely left the palace. She longs to roam the city, and the training ground is one of the places that interest her. She can hear the soldiers' shouts sometimes, coming from the palace beyond the gardens.

Onnes does not reply. He makes his way to the bath, and she follows. In the room, the vapour is thick, blurring their features. Onnes sits on the stone carved in the shape of a bench and rests his head against the wall. 'You can come with me tomorrow.'

She says nothing, hiding her smile.

*

93

They go the next evening, when the training ground is empty. The building sits between the Northwest Palace and the hanging gardens, overlooking the royal road with its obelisk. It has brick walls the colour of sand and, as they walk inside, dust dances with the soft breeze. In the wide courtyard, spears and shields rest against the walls. Semiramis brushes her fingers against the metal – iron, unlike the bronze weapons she used to see in Mari. Onnes disappears into a corridor, and when he comes back, he is holding two long spears. He tosses her one and she catches it awkwardly before it falls. She knows how to use a dagger – has done so countless times in Mari while hunting – but has never held a spear before.

'Find your balance,' Onnes says calmly. 'Whichever leg is forward, the same hand should be forward too. Defend your front by moving the forward arm across the body to block me. Keep your knees bent.'

'I do not know the movements to block you.'

'You will learn as I attack you.'

Instinctively she brings her hands to the scars on her arms. They are itching, and when she feels their thin edges under her fingers, she sees her father's face, the way his black eyes gleamed when he was angry.

'Attack me, then.'

Onnes swings his spear. The movement is lazy, as if he were toying with her. She catches the blow on her own spear, holding on to the shaft with all her strength. If he is surprised that she blocked him, he does not show it. He stabs at her again. She catches it once more, gracelessly, but he is so strong that the blow sends her weapon flying from her hands. She steps back, hurrying to pick up another from those lined against the walls. Onnes barely gives her time to compose herself. He swings his spear at her casually, without effort. She dodges, feeling a drop of blood trickling down her arm where the iron head grazed her skin. Fear fills her chest, quickly turning into rage. Rather than retreat, she flies at him, knocking him against the table where daggers are laid. The weapons fall and clatter. He grabs her arm and throws her against the wall. Her spear slips from her hand, and she stumbles but doesn't fall. They look at each other. He could hurt her at any moment, but she does not care. There is a new thought inside her, a hope: *This is what it means to be able to defend myself. Not to be helpless.*

She is ready to attack again, when a voice cuts the air like an arrow. 'Fighting with women now. Should I worry?'

A man walks out of the corridor and comes into the light. His black hair is streaked with silver, and his cunning face is lined with age. Semiramis recognizes him from the throne room: Ilu, the commander of the king's army. She wipes the blood from her arm, but Ilu is not looking at her. He is staring at Onnes with a vicious smile.

Onnes puts down his spear. 'I didn't think you could worry about me.'

'How are you going to learn to beat me,' Ilu asks, 'if you train with your wife?'

'I can beat you,' Onnes says coolly, picking up a short sword.

Ilu laughs. 'Never have. Never will.' His teeth flash, like a wolf's. Then he unsheathes his sword. 'Come,' he says. 'Let us show your wife how dirty your blood really is.'

Onnes says nothing. Ilu walks to him, sword raised. He pokes it at Onnes' chest – still, Onnes doesn't move – and stops before the blade can pierce the skin. He opens his mouth to speak again –

– but Onnes' sword slashes forward like an angry snake. It meets Ilu's with a hissing sound, and the two step back and forth so quickly it is hard to follow. It is Onnes who attacks, and Ilu moves aside with the speed of a man half his age. The swords rise and fall, flashing in the air like lightning. Ilu dances backwards, parrying Onnes' blows as if he had four arms, instead of two. His blade slices the air as he dodges Onnes', his body moving like sunlight across the water. There is the clank of iron against iron, and for a moment it seems that Onnes' blade will find Ilu's skin. But then Ilu grins, his sword slips past Onnes' and lands at his neck, where it stops. Onnes grows still. A vein is pulsing frantically against Ilu's blade.

'You might be stronger than all my men,' Ilu says, 'but you are still a bastard.' Then he leaves the yard without a scratch.

The sky grows red; the sun god must be angry. Semiramis watches her husband, ears still ringing with the clanging of swords. Onnes' eyes are bloodshot. There is something different about him, anger twisting his features. When he finally speaks, his voice is raspy. 'He used to taunt me when I was a child. He couldn't bear that I was close to Ninus. He'd rather his own sons were friends with him, but they are brutes, and Ninus liked only me.'

He breathes deeply, caught in a memory he does not share. She walks to him and cups a hand around his cheek. He tenses, taut as a bowstring.

'You are the king's favourite, not him,' she says quietly. 'That is all that matters.'

He does not look at her. But she knows she has said the right thing, because his body loosens a little under her touch.

'You were good,' he says. 'We can come here again tomorrow.'

*

Thus her days pass, flowing forward like a river. Winter passes into spring. The month of beginning slips into the month of blossoming. Gardens become rainbows of fruit, and priests pray to Ea, crafty god of water, magic and mischief. Semiramis spends her days with Ribat and her evenings with Onnes.

When he gives her a polished bronze mirror and she looks at her image, she scarcely recognizes herself. Her robes are purple, with a gold sash. Her dark hair is shining, reflecting the light of the torches. *The village girl is gone*, she thinks. *This is the governor's wife.*

And yet, if she looks closer, she can see the tiny scars on her arms and shoulders, the memories of her humiliation. If she were a goddess, she would make them fade with a touch of her hand. But she isn't.

Her glowing future unfolds, but she never forgets her past. It is written on her skin, and to cut it away would mean losing a part of herself. A part that, no matter how much she denies it, will always be there.

13.

Blood Mixed with Dirt

She is upstairs, looking at inventories from Eber-Nari, when voices float from the main entrance. A few moments later, Ribat appears.

'You have a visitor, Mistress,' he says.

'Who is it?'

'The spymaster, Sasi.'

She startles. No one has visited her in the palace until now and she cannot think what the eunuch would want with her. *Only one way to find out.* 'Bring him to the courtyard,' she orders.

She wears sheer blue linen embroidered with lapis lazuli and open-ended bracelets around her arms. When she walks downstairs, the eunuch is standing in the shadows. He bows to her from a distance, then walks in her direction before she can invite him to come forward. He moves slowly and strangely, like a fish gliding through murky water. His face looks different in the light of the day: his skin is pale, almost translucent – a man who despises the outdoor spaces but thrives in the shadows of dimly lit rooms.

'It seems the rumours about you haven't died down after all,' he says with the hint of a smile. Behind his lips, his teeth are so bright they catch the light of the sun. 'Semiramis, the governor's wife. Every-one in the citadel is still talking about you.' Her name in his mouth sounds different, less foreign. Onnes has told her that Sasi speaks many languages, Greek included.

She takes the jug Ribat offers her and pours beer into two cups. 'Are they saying anything of interest?'

'Just that you have bewitched Onnes with your beauty.'

'Not interesting, then,' she says, handing Sasi a cup. She wonders if she is supposed to lead him to a different room to entertain him, but she would rather be whipped than admit her lack of knowledge of the palace to the spymaster, so they remain standing, a few feet from each other.

'You don't think beauty a topic worthy of conversation?' he asks, curious.

'It bores me that people think beauty is the only reason why a man would marry a woman.'

He laughs. It is a childish, unnerving sound. 'You find it boring. I find it amusing.' He his cup to his lips – she notices he barely drinks – then looks at the glazed bricks above the columns. The bulls seem to be swimming in an ocean of blue and golden waves. He is staring at them in such an enraptured way that she expects him to comment on them, when he asks, 'Has Onnes spoken about me?'

She is taken aback by the question. 'He has.'

'And?'

'He says that a man who knows everyone's secrets is as powerful as a king,' she replies. 'He can unravel lives as he wishes.'

Sasi's smile grows wider. 'I am flattered,' he says, though she didn't mean to be flattering. 'I like your husband. A clever man, despite his inability to understand others' feelings.'

'I think he understands. He just isn't interested in them.'

'Maybe you're right. You would know better. After all, you've been married for, what, two seasons?'

She is torn between the impulse to laugh and the need to slap him. 'Is there any better way to know a man than to share his bed?'

He chuckles. 'I wouldn't know. I have never shared anyone's bed.'

'Yet you know everything about anyone.'

He shrugs modestly. 'My spies have spread as far as the sea to the west and all over the mountains to the east. They whisper secrets that are worth as much as the precious stones on your dress, if not more . . . secrets about every man and woman in Kalhu, including your husband.'

Talking to him is like learning the intricate steps of a dance he has performed countless times and she can't follow. 'And what is the most precious secret you have learned about my husband?' she asks.

It seems he was waiting for the question. A sweet, malicious smile spreads on his face. 'Onnes is a loyal man, despite his status. He could easily have claimed the throne, yet he didn't.'

She raises her eyebrows, and he reads the confusion on her face. It lights something in his eyes. 'You do not know?' he asks. 'Shalmaneser was Onnes' father. Your husband is not just a governor and the king's confidant, he is his half-brother.'

Her throat closes. Sasi's words echo in her head, like a bell that refuses to be silent. They bring something with them, a soft undertone, a memory: Onnes' face as he spoke to her at the village feast. 'I wasn't shunned, thanks to our king,' he'd said. 'He treated me as family.' *Because he is family.* Then she remembers Ilu's taunting in the training ground. *You are still a bastard.* What he meant was: *the king's bastard.*

Sasi is watching her, eager for a reaction. *This is why he has come. To see if I am just a dull girl from the provinces, or a woman worth remembering when he gathers his spies.* But she does not want to fit anywhere in his tapestry of secrets.

'You are telling me my husband is the king's brother,' she says, voice dripping with sarcasm. 'And I married Onnes only because I thought he was handsome.'

The laugh that emerges from Sasi's mouth is loud and crystalline. It echoes in the courtyard, as if a hundred children were laughing with him. 'I think you will fit well here, Semiramis,' he says. 'But remember to be careful. Palaces are slippery places where powerful men stab each other in the back.'

She wonders if he is truly warning her, and if he is, why he would do such a thing. 'You haven't been stabbed yet.'

He lifts a dark, fine brow. 'I understand the way the game is played.'

'And what game is that?'

'Power.'

For the first time since he came here, she feels she is gaining something from the conversation, not only losing it. She smiles at him, as guilelessly as she can. 'Power isn't a game that is played in palaces only,' she says. 'Do not fear, Spymaster. I know how to play too.'

*

She leaves the palace as soon as Sasi has gone. She takes the wide street lined with the other governors' houses, then follows the royal road. Guards are standing stiffly by its side, their eyes fixed straight ahead. To the left, the hanging gardens tower over her: endless sets of stone and brick terraces bursting with plants.

She climbs the first flight of stairs, white limestone smoothed to perfection, until she is high enough to have a view of the road below, and the narrow streets and houses beyond it. There are more stairs that lead up – she counts as many terraces as six – flowers of different colours blossoming on them. A flock of orange birds takes flight from the palms, circling the ziggurat. She can hear voices to her left and makes her way past columns so covered with vines that the stones are barely visible. The terrace widens, forming a clearing of lush green where a herd of gazelles is grazing. Beyond it, on a portico guarded by bronze sphinxes on stone pillars, a group of women is lounging, playing lyres. Some are holding cats and ferrets on leashes, and one has a lark perched on her shoulder.

Semiramis climbs more stairs, reaching an orchard rich with fruit trees – shiny olives, ripe golden pears, sweet figs. Streams of water flow between rows of plants. It makes her think of the garden of the gods in *Gilgamesh*: *There were trees that grew rubies, trees with lapis-lazuli flowers, trees that dangled gigantic coral clusters, like dates. Everywhere, sparkling on all the branches, were enormous jewels: emeralds, sapphires, haematite, diamonds, carnelians, pearls.*

Semiramis keeps moving. The spymaster's words follow her. Onnes is Ninus' brother. His father was the king, Shalmaneser. *But why didn't he tell me? Why keep it a secret?* The palm trees sway slightly, leaves brushing against each other like shy lovers. *There must be more to it.*

She stands in the breeze, trying to steady the rushing of her thoughts. It takes her a while to realize that there is a woman with long pale hair between the rows of fig trees, looking at the fields beyond the walls.

Semiramis approaches her. The woman turns. From up close, Semiramis can see that her skin is bright like sunlit gold, and her face isn't painted like everyone else's in the capital.

'You must be the princess my husband was meant to marry,' Semiramis says.

'Taria,' the woman says. 'And you are Semiramis.'

They bow to each other, Semiramis gracefully, like a reed, Taria more stiffly, as if the movement was foreign to her.

'I keep hearing the most outrageous things about you,' Taria says. 'I thought you were a witch, or a demon, perhaps. But then I saw you at the wedding feast.' She sounds disappointed. 'Assyrians often forget that common people aren't so different from them.'

Oh, trust me, we are different. 'The only thing common people and noblemen share is death. In the house of dust, we are all equals.'

Taria tilts her head. It is a hawk-like movement, as if she were considering what to do with the woman in front of her. 'You are wise or a fool. I often find it hard to tell the difference.'

'Wise men live. Fools die,' Semiramis says. It makes Taria smile – a bright, bold expression that lights her face as if it were water under the sun.

'You are a guest in the queen's palace?' Semiramis asks.

Taria's smile turns into a sneer. 'I prefer the word *hostage*, for it better depicts my situation.'

It is Semiramis' turn to smile. 'Are you allowed to be in the gardens, or have you escaped?'

'Are you going to call the guards? You should not be here either. Women are usually accompanied in Kalhu, yet I see no guards or slaves behind you.'

'I do not like to speak with an audience.'

Taria nods. They start walking past the fruit and trees, towards the edge of the terrace. Beyond the walls, the fields are dry and thirsty. There is no green in them in the summer. All the water flows into the capital, its gardens lush and fruitful even in the hottest months.

'Tell me about your land,' Semiramis says. 'Is it true that your palaces are so high on the mountains that you hear the gods whisper?'

'Assyrians call it Urartu, but for my people it is Biaina,' Taria says. '*Place of fire.* We lived in villages around fire temples once, before we were attacked and started hiding in the mountains. Now we build our fortresses on rocky heights and carve funeral chambers out of the mountain walls, where the ashes of our ancestors rest. I like to come here because it reminds me of my home. It makes me think of our mountains and the forests around them.' Her expression is sad, eyes filled with longing.

'I hear that these gardens were built by a king for his concubine,' Semiramis says. It is something that Ribat has told her. 'She longed for the mountains of her home so the king ordered his builders to create the highest gardens ever seen.'

'I am not surprised. Assyrians love to live close to the heavens.'

'And your people don't?'

Taria shrugs. 'We live in fortresses frescoed with scenes of everyday life. We are humble. Here in Kalhu, all nobles care about is glory. You have bas-reliefs to showcase your deeds and conquests, to mirror your power, but we do not care about greatness.'

'You must miss it very much,' Semiramis says, because the longing in Taria's voice is like a flame, burning her words as she speaks. Semiramis cannot imagine such a thing: if she thinks of Mari – and she tries not to – all she sees is her father punching her, her brother's face under the moon, disdainful, disgusted. She removes the images one by one, like splinters.

'I miss a world that doesn't exist any more,' Taria says. 'When the Assyrians campaigned in our land, they plundered every town. They impaled men and women and set fire to the villages. The flames reached higher than the mountains. The bodies piled up in the lakes until the air smelt of death.'

'That is the Assyrian way, yes,' Semiramis says.

'Your husband's way too, I imagine.'

Semiramis stills. There is an edge to Taria's voice that she can't quite understand.

'I went to the training ground once,' Taria says. 'Your husband was there, and the king. They weren't fighting, just watching younger boys challenging each other. One made a comment about the king. Something about him being weak, about your husband being stronger, I think. The king pretended not to hear, but your husband took the spear from the boy's hand and broke it in two. Then he beat him until the boy fell to the ground and stopped moving. When he left, the others called a physician, but the boy was dead. His face wasn't a face any more. I saw it.'

Semiramis keeps quiet.

They have reached the end of the orchard. From here, they hear a voice, a glimpse of richness. To their left, framed by branches of bright yellow flowers, is a columned pavilion with feasting couches set in a circle. Taria and Semiramis stop a few steps away from it, watching the two figures that are standing between the columns.

Onnes is speaking to the king, his voice carrying in the women's direction. Ninus is staring into the distance as he listens. He and

Onnes are the same height, Semiramis notices, but the similarities end there. They do not look like brothers. Yet there is something between them, in the way they move and speak, so close to each other.

Then, the movement so quick that Semiramis thinks she has imagined it, Onnes touches Ninus' neck. Ninus closes his eyes and makes a sound like a sigh. Something tugs at Semiramis' chest. Onnes and Ninus are standing as they did during her wedding feast, as if they were two halves of the same person, as if neither was whole without the other.

Without speaking, she turns away from the portico and hurries through the orchards, then down the endless stairs, away from the whispering branches and the blooming flowers. She is aware of Taria's eyes following her, but she never looks back, not until she is safely out of the gardens and back on the royal road.

*

She waits for Onnes in his bedroom. He arrives as evening creeps in, bathing the city in a deep blue light. His hair is damp and his face tired. He brushes his lips against her cheek before sitting on a stool and looking at the tablets Ribat has left for him on the bed.

She watches him read one, then forces her eyes to the bas-reliefs on the wall, away from the calm precision of his movements, the coldness of his eyes. She wants to tell him of what she has seen in the gardens, of what Taria has told her, but she doesn't know how to speak of it.

So instead she says, 'The spymaster, Sasi, came to see me today.'

He does not look impressed. 'I knew he would. I will order the guards to keep him away from the palace.'

'I handled him.'

He raises an eyebrow. 'What did you think of him?'

'He is perceptive, though I suspect also quite ruthless.'

'There are worse people in the capital.'

Like who? Like you, who beat a boy to death in the training ground? But this isn't something for which Onnes owes her an explanation. She turns her gaze to his. Sasi's words keep hissing in her mind, like a trapped animal.

'Sasi was eager to speak about you,' she says.

There is something calm and patient in Onnes' expression. 'Was he?'

A long silence. She waits before speaking, hoping he tells her before she has to ask. But he doesn't. She takes a deep breath. 'When you told me your mother fell in love with a man who didn't love her back . . . was he King Shalmaneser?'

He lays aside the tablets. His face is starkly lit by the lamps, eyes glowing like amber. 'I am not surprised that Sasi told you this. He isn't a man who understands loyalty.'

'So it is true.'

A grim smile pulls up his mouth. 'You know what they say when a king has children with women of a lower status? That the blood of the children is mixed with dirt.'

'It doesn't matter what they say,' she says. 'Your father was king. You have a claim to the throne.'

He shakes his head, a tense movement. 'Don't speak like that.'

'Does Ninus know who you are?' she insists.

'How could he not? He is his mother's son and, besides, no secret stays buried in this place. But we don't speak of it. Blood doesn't only bind. Sometimes it poisons.'

She can see his hand on the king's neck, the way Ninus edged closer to him, as if Onnes were a fire in winter. 'I don't believe he could be poisoned against you. He seems to worship you.'

He pours some wine into his cup, takes a large swallow. 'He does, doesn't he?'

'Does his affection mean so little to you?'

'It means everything to me. But sometimes it would be best if it weren't there.'

She knows what he wants to say. 'Devotion can make people do dangerous things.'

He turns to her. 'Yes,' he says quietly. Then, 'Come here.'

Something twists and coils within her. *If you keep your enemies confused, it is easier to attack*, he had once told her on the training ground. At the time she'd thought he was right, but what if he always behaves as if he is in a fight? Even when the two of them are alone in his bedroom?

Outside, a gentle breeze brushes against the palace walls. She goes to him, tilting her head back. Onnes' palm against her chest rises and falls with each breath. He touches her as if she were a riddle he needs to solve, as if her pleasure was a prize he must win.

As for his pleasure, she has learned that he fears it, for he doesn't want others to see him so raw. So she does everything in her power to make him so.

14.

Ninus, King of the World, King of Assyria

'I have heard the most curious rumour, my king.'

The eunuch is standing in the throne room, facing the inner court-yard that leads to the king's private suites. The day is ending, and the throne room feels like a cage. The governors are all gone, except Sasi. He and Ninus are facing each other, Ninus in the fading light, Sasi in the shadows.

Ninus waits, knowing that Sasi will speak again after a suspenseful pause.

'A rumour that Onnes,' Sasi continues, clearly savouring every word, 'is training his wife, teaching her how to fight.'

Of all the things Ninus expected him to say, this was the last. But Sasi knows how to play people's strings, as if they were all harps in his hands, their chords waiting to be struck at the eunuch's pleasure.

'I was hoping you'd have some rumours on Babylon to share,' Ninus says flatly, 'but if you are so interested in the gossip of the capital, perhaps I will find myself another spymaster.'

Sasi bows so low that his plaits tinkle, heavy with silver rings. 'Of course,' he says quickly. 'I have rumours on Babylon too. The prince Marduk has settled in one of our old governor's palaces, the one clos-est to the gardens.'

Marduk, the prince of Babylon, second son of the king. When Ninus was losing the war against his own brother and was desperate for an alliance, he met with the king of Babylon under the blue and golden gate of Ishtar. The terms were clear: the Glowing City would come to his aid if Ninus swore loyalty to them, a thing his brother would never have done, or his father. *Weak. Coward.* But there are different ways to fight a war, and only one thing matters: to win. So Ninus swore and Babylon came to his aid. The pledge to their mad alliance? A spoiled prince with a reputation for fathering bastards and killing men out of boredom.

'I hear Marduk is happy there,' Sasi continues. 'With enough riches and women to satisfy him. Though, I will confess, I am quite worried. Every report on the prince tells me he is . . . erratic.'

Erratic, ruthless, vile. 'Should I send him back then and openly declare war on Babylon?' Ninus asks in tones that drip sarcasm.

Sasi bows again. 'Forgive me, my king, I am not well versed in military tactics. The only weapons I trade in are secrets.' His voice is as smooth as the most precious fabrics, but Ninus has long learned how to resist its charm.

'We won the war against my brother thanks to Babylon's support,' he says. 'So we have no other choice.'

'Some might say that the conditions of the treaty you signed were humiliating,' Sasi says.

'Yes. And if Babylon attacks now, have we the men to push them back?'

'As I said, I am sadly ignorant on—'

'We don't,' Ninus answers. 'Now go. I thank you for your counsel.'

Sasi doesn't move. Ninus can feel him organizing his thoughts, folding them, trying to find the most considerate way of sharing them. 'After the war, your mother suggested you impale one of the dignitaries who betrayed you . . .' he says eventually. 'But you didn't.'

Ninus thinks about his mother's face as he stood in the throne room, weighing the lives of his enemies in his hands. In the end, he could not bring himself to crush them.

'I am king now, Sasi,' he says. 'You will answer to me, not my mother.'

*

He goes to the training ground at sunrise, anger filling his body like poison.

A rumour that Onnes is training his wife, teaching her how to fight. This is how a king is betrayed, he thinks. By a woman with sand in her hair and dirt on her knees. A commoner who stinks of sheep. During his brother's wedding feast, Ninus had looked at Onnes' *wife* – just the word makes him want to smash something – and wondered how such a common woman could have trapped him. He had seen Onnes sleep with many women – from servants to scribes, dancers and even priestesses – but he had never thought he would marry one. How could he be so stupid? How could Ninus be so blind? *Maybe I do not know him after all.*

The palace lies pale and flattened in the light. Shalmaneser built it years ago, straight after his first campaign against Urartu. After years of training in its wide courtyards, from dawn till dusk, this is almost like a second home to Ninus, one filled with violence and dark memories.

The burning sun still hangs low in the sky. At the centre of the courtyard, Onnes is already practising. Ninus watches the sunrise touch his shoulder blades, his arms tensing as he shoots his bow.

'You are up early,' Onnes says, without turning.

Ninus grabs a dagger, feigning carelessness. 'So are you.'

'I couldn't sleep. Semiramis kept me awake.'

Something inside Ninus twists. He throws his dagger. It swirls in the air, breaks the arrow Onnes is holding in two. He turns to him, eyebrows raised. His patient expression – as if Ninus were overreacting – enrages Ninus. He picks up a sword and swings it in Onnes' direction. Onnes bends, moves swiftly aside, picking up a spear from the ground.

'Do you remember what Shalmaneser used to say about women?' Ninus asks. He follows Onnes' movements, his blade slashing the air, missing Onnes' head by a breath. Shalmaneser taught them to read the expression of their opponents to anticipate their moves, but Onnes' face is always as calm as windless water.

'I've never heard him speak about women,' Onnes replies.

'Of course you haven't,' Ninus says savagely. 'He would speak only with me and Assur of such things.' He steps back as Onnes tries to reach out and disarm him. 'He would say that women are meant to be distractions.'

'Your mother wasn't a distraction to him,' Onnes points out. 'He always listened to her because he valued her opinion.' He grabs Ninus' wrist, bends it, but Ninus doesn't let go of his weapon. He throws himself to the ground, bringing Onnes with him. Red dust flies around them. Onnes usually overpowers him, but today he is distracted and Ninus is angry. He rolls Onnes onto his back and pins his hands to the ground, kneeling over him.

'*A woman's love and a man's duty,*' Ninus recites. '*There comes a point in our lives when every one of us must choose. And there is only one right choice to make.* That is what Shalmaneser said.'

Onnes pushes him aside. Ninus swings his sword, and the blade grazes Onnes' shoulder: a thin red line, like the cuneiform sign for 'star'. Onnes looks at the blood as it drips slowly down his arm.

The sun is rising. Voices gather from the corners of the palace, warning them that men are coming to train. Ninus stands, brushing dust from his tunic. In a corner of the courtyard, basins of clear water are used to clean away sweat and blood. He puts down his sword and washes his face. Onnes joins him to clean his cut. Ninus follows his slow, controlled movements as he wets a piece of clean tunic, dabs at the wound.

'Here,' he says. 'Let me.'

Onnes hands him the cloth. Ninus can feel the warmth rising from his skin. His pulse flutters in his throat; his father's words echo in his mind. *Love and duty. Every one of us must choose.* But Ninus disagreed with his father on most matters.

He looks at Onnes as he wraps the clean cloth around his shoulder. He is still, so still.

The poets say that men are made for glory, but gods want glory for themselves. So, to make men vulnerable, they gave them the gift of love.

*

Large sheets of sunlight illuminate the walls of the council room. They are covered with battle scenes that depict Ninus' grandfather's attack against the Elamites, the bull-like people who live in the shadow of the Zagros mountains. Under the reliefs of dying soldiers, Sasi and the *turtanu* Ilu are sitting on cushioned chairs. The *bârû*, the royal diviner, claims the place at the end of the table, as far from the eunuch as he can. His nervous hands play with the hem of a heavy bag, filled with models of sheep livers. Ninus sits on a carved ivory chair, between his mother and Onnes.

'Let us begin,' he says. 'Ilu, what news from our borders?'

The *turtanu* leans back comfortably, as if his chair were a throne. 'Quiet on the east and west. But we need to secure the northern borders quickly. Your father started his campaigns with the territories in the north because he knew that if we leave the northern border open to incursions, the empire remains threatened.'

His voice exudes calm and confidence. Shalmaneser once told Ninus that the first thing he noticed about Ilu, when he came to be educated at court as a child, was his arrogance. He carried the noble lineage of the Bit-Adini tribe in his blood and took pleasure in diminishing other boys of his age. Shalmaneser liked him for it, and they became friends. As soon as Shalmaneser was king, he named Ilu governor of the Bit-Adini territories, the land east of Eber-Nari, between the rivers Balikh and Euphrates.

'Should I follow my father's steps?' Ninus asks.

'We have two enemies, growing stronger every day,' Ilu says. 'Babylon and Urartu.'

'Babylon is an ally, not an enemy,' Sasi intervenes, his voice as sweet as cream.

'Babylon will never be an ally, no matter how many treaties we sign,' Ilu retorts.

'Shalmaneser launched five campaigns against Urartu,' the *bârû* says. 'How are they still standing?'

'Their capital is impregnable,' Onnes says. 'It is a rock fortress on a lake called Van. The mountains between our kingdom and the lake . . . The army can't march there in winter, and even in summer they are hard to cross.'

'We need the flow of resources from the north,' Ninus says.

'Urartu won't attack us,' Onnes points out. 'Not now that their princess is in Kalhu.'

'Good,' Ninus says. 'They can't attack us, and we can't attack them. A temporary truce. As for the resources, we'll conduct raids through the eastern mountains to secure at least part of our borders. That way, we can keep wood and horses coming in from our tributary states, the ones my father won with all that effort.'

Ilu smiles. There is an undertone of malignity in it. 'May I suggest we eliminate the tribespeople of the Medes? Their city straddles the Great Khorasan Road, and it has become quite a burden to my troops.'

'*My* troops,' Ninus corrects him.

'Of course,' Ilu says, though there is nothing respectful or reverential in his tone.

Ninus casts a glance in his mother's direction. She is quiet, dangerously so.

Sasi notices too, attentive as ever. 'And how is the princess of Urartu, my queen?' he asks. 'Is the women's palace to her liking?'

Ninus glimpses a glimmer of rage in Nisat's eyes: there is nothing his mother hates more than to speak of 'womanly things' in the council.

'We must speak of the war,' she says firmly.

'The war has ended,' the *bârû* says, with a frown.

She continues as if he hasn't spoken: 'I have a list of the men who fought for you, Ninus, governors and commanders and noblemen's sons, each with his own request.'

'If the requests are reasonable, they shall be granted,' Ninus says.

'They are. As for all the traitors,' *the ones you refused to kill*, he can almost hear her think, 'they should be stripped of their lands and properties, so that their titles can be granted to the men who were loyal to you.'

'Traitors must be punished as a warning to others,' Ilu says. 'Break their arms, skin them, whatever you think best. They will not betray you again.'

Ninus' ears are ringing. He wonders if his mother and Ilu, who have always been close, have spoken of this behind his back. 'I have decided to keep those men alive,' he says. Ilu's eyes fasten on his, sharp as blades. Ninus knows that expression: it is a threat, the warning that comes before violence. He answers with a warning of his own: 'But I can think of a thousand punishments for those who wish to disobey me. Luckily my grandfather has filled this palace with detailed depictions of torture.'

The *bârû* shifts uneasily in his chair. Sasi's face is in the shadows. Nisat's head is tilted, a chilling look in her eyes.

'Leave the list of requests with me,' Ninus says. 'You are dismissed.' They all stand to leave. 'Not you, Onnes,' Ninus adds, in spite of himself.

Sasi and Ilu disappear into the archway that leads to the courtyards. The *bârû* gathers his bag under his arm and quickly tiptoes away. Nisat's lips curl with disapproval but she follows them. As the room empties, the air seems to clear. Ninus stands, controlling the beating of his heart. Onnes remains seated, waiting. He has cut his hair, Ninus notices, so that light brown strands don't hang over his eyes any more. *Maybe his wife did it.* He pushes the thought away. He is behaving like a child.

'What do you think?' he asks.

'I think the council has changed,' Onnes says.

'The game is the same, and so are the players.'

'Yes, but they were easier to command when your father was here.'

'Because they knew what happened when they disrespected him. They feared him so they rarely spoke the truth. But a king needs truths, much more than he needs lies.'

'Shalmaneser used that fear to build the vastest empire the world has ever seen.'

The words tug at Ninus' memory, make him think of Assur. He would say things like this as a child: *We will be the fiercest warriors of our generation, we will rule the greatest empire, and our names will be whispered among the gods.*

'Yes, my father ruled with fear,' Ninus says. 'And how did it end for him? Murdered by his son.'

A shadow stains Onnes' eyes. For a moment his face becomes like the sea in winter, dark and restless. Then he stands and walks to Ninus. Their shadows merge on the walls. He pulls his king close to him, a brotherly embrace. His words are whispers in Ninus' ear.

'As you once told me, you'll never be like your father.'

*

Memories exist outside time and place. They are windows onto other worlds, faraway lands where everything glitters like sunlit gold, but the air tastes like rust.

They were fifteen and celebrating one of his father's campaigns against the Hittites, the iron workers and chariot-riders from the west. Shalmaneser was resting on a raised couch, listening to his counsellors as they praised him. Nisat was on her wooden throne, female attendants oiling her plaits and fanning her with fly-whisks. Ninus and Onnes sat next to each other, silent.

Amid the conifers and palms, the hands of drummers and harpists danced like dragonflies. The men laughed and drank. They all pointed at the branch of a palm, where a severed head was hanging, dried blood at the neck. The Hittites' leader. Ninus couldn't stop looking at it. A slice of brutality in a place of such lushness.

'Here is a king who rules supreme among mankind!' Ilu shouted from his couch, making all the men cheer. 'The protector of the people, the raging flood that destroys all cities! As powerful and fierce as the war god Ninurta!'

Shalmaneser sat without smiling among the shouting men. Black curly hair grew thick on his head and beard, covered his chest. Earrings inlaid with gems made his strong jaws sparkle.

Ilu stood, shiny goblet in hand. His eyes were gleaming with power, as they always did whenever he and Shalmaneser came back from a successful campaign. 'A king can do whatever he wants!' he shouted. 'He can take the son from his father and crush him! He can take the girl from her mother and use her! No one will oppose him!'

Ninus shivered. He thought of Gilgamesh, the arrogant hero Assyrians love to read about in the epics, who tramples his citizens like a wild bull. From somewhere on his right, Assur laughed, mocking the dead leader. He had followed his father onto the field, his first taste of war, and had come back with blood on his hands and a smile on his face. As a king's son should.

Ninus turned to Onnes, but his friend was a statue, his face a mask of disgust. He didn't eat, didn't drink, didn't acknowledge the bleeding head. He just looked at Shalmaneser, eyes filled with pure hatred. It was frightening.

The feast went on, but Onnes walked away. Ninus followed. He moved from the garden to a small courtyard where they used to take poetry lessons. Onnes was standing under the painted bas-reliefs, figures falling and dying all around him: archers shooting from mighty walls, soldiers escaping into the river, the dead and wounded together in the dark blue waves.

'My father can be cruel,' Ninus said. The severed head was still vivid in his mind, the whites of the dead eyes, the helpless mouth. 'I am sorry if he upset you.'

'He didn't upset me.'

Ninus smiled. 'No one ever does.'

Onnes didn't contradict him. They were close, their faces all shadows. The sky above them was filled with a thousand stars, as if every god and goddess held a torch. Ninus reached out. He wanted to touch

Onnes' cheek, but he hesitated and his hand lingered in mid-air. Shouts and laughter came from the banquet, and both of them jumped. Ninus dropped his hand.

'You are not like your father,' Onnes said. His voice was strange, angry but hesitant.

'No.'

'But do you think you will ever become like him?'

Ninus didn't understand the question, yet he could tell Onnes needed some sort of reassurance. 'I won't.'

Onnes breathed out, as if he had been holding too much inside him. He, who had always looked like a god to Ninus, cold and inaccessible, now seemed just a scared boy. The sight filled Ninus with longing. Onnes' eyes were on him, bronze and green blending like the texture of old swords. Ninus shifted forward, slowly. His lips found Onnes'. He tasted him – sweat from the heat and spices from his body. Then he stepped back, waiting. Onnes was gazing at him. His lips parted, as if he would speak, but then his face was distant again. Ninus would have given the world to be able to tear it open and look inside.

*

When evening falls, they dine together in Ninus' apartments. The moon is up, and slaves bring platter after platter of food – vegetable soup, *mersu* cakes, duck pies, cheeses covered with sweet plums. Onnes eats everything silently and methodically, sipping blood-red wine from a silver cup. Ninus looks at him, picking at his own food without enough appetite to eat it.

'It has been a while since you and I ate together like this,' Ninus says.

Onnes finishes his meal, as if he hadn't spoken. When his bowl is empty, he fills his and Ninus' cups with wine. 'What do you think of Semiramis?' he asks.

Ninus stares at him, bewildered. *I don't want to talk about her*, he thinks. 'She seems quite ordinary,' he says. Then, in spite of himself, he adds, 'Quite common.'

Onnes drinks some wine. 'She is fierce, because she has nothing to lose.'

Ninus knows that everyone has something to lose but keeps quiet. Onnes is unfolding a bundle tied to his belt. Inside, Ninus glimpses a tiny bright jug. Onnes empties its contents into his palm, revealing flowers of blue and violet shades.

'These are called the Sacred Lily of the Nile in Egypt,' he says. 'My slave bought them from the healer. They have been steeped in wine for weeks.'

As always, Ninus wonders how Onnes can change the subject so quickly, without his thoughts bleeding behind him, as if they'd been suddenly severed. 'What do they do?' he asks.

'Euphoria,' Onnes says. 'They make you happy.' He takes a flower and puts it between his lips.

Three slaves enter to clear the platters. Ninus waves them away. Herbs and drugs have always had a dangerous effect on him, ever since Onnes made him try poppy pods when they were younger. When he eats them, his feelings are like tides, swelling and pulling everything into the waves. But he has never been able to deny his friend.

He takes the petals: they are sharp, the pistils orange like the brightest sunsets. He puts them into his mouth and chews. Onnes watches him quietly. From the courtyards he hears footsteps and whispers, soft sounds echoing with an uneven rhythm.

They keep drinking, wine turning dark as blackberries. The stars are white, clouds rushing past them. The effect of the Sacred Lily is spreading through Ninus' body. Everything is quiet and glowing. The bas-reliefs on the wall are peacefully staring at him, their eyes warm and forgiving. *Maybe nothing has truly changed between us*, he thinks suddenly. *Maybe all will be as it was.*

He stands, flecks of light moving in his eyes, and knocks the jug onto the stone floor. Onnes laughs as the wine wets his hands. Ninus opens his mouth to complain, then bursts out laughing too. They are leaning against each other, trying to gather the shards, failing, laughing harder.

When the excitement dies down, they sit with their backs against the wall, speaking of things as if they were children: lion hunts and men from their training, Ilu's ambition and Sasi's network of spies. They speak as if they weren't king and governor, as if the shape of the world didn't depend on them.

'Why did you marry?' Ninus asks him.

Onnes gives him a look as if to say, *You know why.* 'You'll have to marry too.'

'Yes. But why her?'

'I think she understands me.'

I understand you.

The torches are on, and the light bathes them in warmth. The walls are swinging a little, and Ninus grabs Onnes' arm to keep still. Onnes' light brown hair is gleaming, like honey. The earring on his right lobe sways slightly. Ninus reaches out to touch the lion pendant. It is cold under his fingers. Onnes' gaze is steady. Like a piece of metal, never bending, never breaking. Ninus forces himself to be still. He takes a deep breath. Then, without thinking, he leans forward. Onnes tastes different from how he remembers: like the Sacred Lily, like sweet wine. When was the last time they kissed like this? Before the war, before Ninus was king. He can feel the pounding of his heart against Onnes' chest. It is like lightning setting the sky on fire. His hand slides around Onnes' neck. Onnes opens his lips, draws closer, then back.

They look at each other. Too much to say, too little time.

Onnes stands. 'I must go,' he says. His voice seems to come from afar. 'Semiramis will be waiting for me.' With sudden striking composure, he takes the jug, then walks out of the room. Ninus stands too, steadying himself against the walls. He watches Onnes until he reaches the end of the corridor and disappears.

15.

Semiramis, an Intruder

The temple of the god Nabu, the divine scribe of destinies, lies peacefully under the cold sun. Two men are carrying dead sheep on their shoulders, dribbles of blood staining their white tunics. A group of lamenters is kneeling in the main courtyard, chanting to soothe the gods.

Semiramis walks past the first courtyard, careful not to disturb the lamenters, then slips into a small corridor where incense curls up in the darkness. She blinks as she passes from the corridor to the white light of another yard. Trees are planted in regular rows here and even the columns are sculpted in a way that imitates the trunks of date palms. On one side there are the twin shrines of the god Nabu and his consort Tašmetu, goddess of wisdom, silently gazing at the scholars at work in another bright, spacious room that opens onto the courtyard.

Under the shade of the shrines, is the king's mother. She is seated at a table laid with cakes and pomegranates, a cohort of slaves behind her. Ribat has told Semiramis Nisat's story countless times already. The queen was married to Ninus' grandfather, the cruel Ashurnasirpal. Then, when her husband's firstborn son was old enough to marry, Nisat seduced him even though she was his stepmother. It is rumoured that, in her quest to keep the throne, she eliminated all competition. She was older than Prince Shalmaneser by nine years, but the moment Ashurnasirpal died, Nisat was by his side, ready to console him.

People say he could have married hundreds of other women, more chaste, of nobler birth, but Nisat gave Shalmaneser something no other could give him: a powerful ally.

Under the light of the courtyard, Nisat's face appears more lined, her eyes more dazzling. It is impossible to tell her age – she could have seen forty or sixty winters. Her lips curl slightly when she sees Semiramis approaching. 'I knew you would come,' she says.

Semiramis stops a few feet from her, bows gracefully. 'You did, my queen?'

'You have come all the way from the dust of Eber-Nari to our glowing capital. Surely you didn't plan to spend all of your days in Onnes' palace, hidden from everyone.'

'No, my queen.' Semiramis would sit, but she suspects Nisat should invite her to do so.

'Have you already learned who counts in this citadel? You decided to come to me, because I am a woman and the closest to the king.'

Semiramis can't help but smile. 'Do people always come to you because you are a woman?'

'Yes. Women are more pliable, in their imagination.'

'You don't seem pliable, my queen.'

Nisat laughs. The sound scratches the courtyard, as if it could leave marks on the stone. 'The hierarchy of the palace is strict. The closer you are to the king, the more power you have. The more kings you are related to, the higher your status. I was married to two kings, and I am mother to one.'

'And before you married the king, what was your claim to status?'

The queen raises her eyebrows, then gestures to the slaves. 'Bring more wine.' She pats the stool on her left. 'Sit. Your name is Semiramis, is it not? A Greek name.'

'Yes,' Semiramis says, sitting carefully.

'And you're an orphan,' Nisat says. 'A shepherd's stepdaughter.' When Semiramis keeps quiet, Nisat continues: 'People talk here. Spies, soldiers, defectors, guards, slaves. There is nothing you can say or do without me knowing.'

Semiramis accepts the cup a slave offers her. 'I am Onnes' wife now, my queen.'

'Tell me,' Nisat says, 'did you charm him with your beauty? You certainly have a striking face.'

'Beauty alone is no use. Certainly not to Onnes.'

'Of course not. He likes you. He isn't a man who likes many people. Don't tell me you didn't work to win his affections because I wouldn't believe it. Look at you. You are already here, trying to win over the queen.'

She feels as if Nisat is baring her mind, unspooling her thoughts one by one. It is a strange, scary sensation: no one has ever managed to guess what she is thinking.

'A woman does what she can with her gifts,' Semiramis says. 'I imagine you would have done the same.'

Nisat snorts. 'You dare think you and I are alike.'

'I do not think I am like anyone else, my queen.'

'Everyone in this world thinks they are different, but most of the time they are all the same.'

'You certainly aren't.'

'I am *queen*,' Nisat says.

'Are queens born? Or are they made?'

Nisat sits back. Semiramis wonders if she has gone too far. *The verdict of the queen is as final as that of the gods*, the people whisper in the streets of Kalhu, and Nisat's verdicts are rarely merciful. Semiramis is ready to bow and take her leave before the queen can cut out her tongue when Nisat grabs her wrist. She is looking at Semiramis with a force that threatens to split her skull in two.

'You speak bluntly, Semiramis. So will I. You think queens are made? That is true. It is the woman who makes the queen, not the title, not her husband, not her son. But *you* will never be queen. You are ambitious and reckless enough, but my son has never loved a woman in his life. Do you know why?' Something flickers behind her eyes, and she lowers her voice to a hiss. 'Because he is in love with your husband.'

Her words cut the air like poisoned lashes. It is the way she has spoken that makes Semiramis stumble. As if Nisat were using a blade that hurts her to wound Semiramis too. *There must be more to it*, she had thought when Onnes hadn't told her about his father, and there it is. The truth, coming through layers of lies.

Semiramis stands. She has the distinct feeling that, if she does not leave the temple, she will crawl out of her skin.

'I will leave you to your prayers, my queen,' she says.

The sky is darkening, and the temple attendants light the torches. Nisat's blue eyes glower. 'You have come here with hopes, Semiramis, I am sure of it,' she says. 'But hopes are not so different from dreams: both are as far from real life as the house of dust is from the world of the living.'

*

The walk to the Northwest Palace isn't long, but by the time Semiramis arrives at the gate of the first courtyard, raindrops are already falling. Two guards look at her warily, but do not stop her. It is quiet, except for the shuffling of feet and the passing of shadows. The small rooms that open onto the Great Northern Courtyard – archives, storage, reception suites – reveal themselves in glimpses. The palace itself feels like a big, shy creature, showing its secrets in flashes of torchlight that lead to hidden rooms and corners. Semiramis plunges deeper into it. In the throne room, two courtiers dressed in pale yellow linen stop her.

'I am looking for my husband,' she says. 'Onnes.'

The courtiers exchange a glance and let her through. The throne room leads to a long, narrow corridor with several doors. Semiramis can feel the quiet of each chamber, bursting with hidden life. She is not far from the terrace where her wedding feast took place. She goes in the opposite direction, into small rooms that are connected to each other like parts of a labyrinth. Her heart is racing in her chest, as if she were doing something forbidden. *I probably am.* But she can't go home, can't stay still, waiting for Onnes to come to her.

My son is in love with your husband. She wants to believe it is a lie, but lies should be welcoming, coated in illusion. Nisat's words have no warmth, no softness. They are just blades. *Better to know the truth than to be fed lies.*

And if it is true that Ninus loves him, what does Onnes feel? Unwillingly, the lines of *The Epic of Gilgamesh* come to mind: *Each loves the other as his own soul.*

Two servants cross the small, dimly lit room, carrying trays of dates and figs. She follows them into a courtyard grey with rain where two eunuchs are speaking, their bald heads as smooth as ivory. Their eyes hunt her as she enters another chamber. Onnes and Ninus are in a corner, whispering. They do not notice her as she stands by the entrance, dwarfed by the eagle-headed spirits.

'Representatives of the government are everywhere,' Onnes is saying. 'You have an army of secret agents, ensuring that you are treated as the absolute authority.'

Ninus shakes his head. He seems upset. 'Yes, but I also live in a court surrounded by men with ambitions of their own.'

'Half of your governors are eunuchs. They are no threat.'

'Ilu has two sons –'

'Ilu is the only one left who fought for your father.'

'– and a daughter. I expect he'll soon try to convince me to marry her.' Ninus breathes out, passing a hand through his hair.

Semiramis steps forward. 'Onnes.'

Her husband turns. There is a seed of surprise in his eyes, which he covers quickly. 'Semiramis,' he says. 'It is wet outside. Come, join us.' His voice is calm, polished.

She walks to them and bows to the king. When she lifts her head, he is looking at her, puzzled. His lips part slightly. It is almost as if he is seeing her for the first time. Up close, he reminds her of his mother, though faintly, as if she had tried to make him in her image but he slipped away before she could finish.

Then he looks away from her, abruptly. 'We will continue tomorrow,' he tells Onnes. 'Join me in the throne room when you are ready.' His posture changes as he leaves the room: his back straightens, his face poised and serious. It strikes her that there is a different, more human version of him that exists behind closed doors, in the hidden corners of the palace.

'He hates me,' Semiramis says when he is gone from sight. *Of course he does. I have come to take the one he loves.*

'He dislikes most people, for that matter,' Onnes replies.

She stares at him. She imagines him and Ninus together as children running between the palm trees of the hanging gardens, as young men fighting side by side, as adults dealing with an empire.

My son is in love with your husband.

She waits until Onnes' eyes are back on hers, then presses her mouth to his. She breathes into him, then steps back and rests her head against the bright blue wall. She is aware that she is an intruder in this palace, that courtiers and slaves are passing just beyond the door. But she wants to leave a part of herself here, to give her own secret to this quiet place.

Onnes watches her, his eyes reading her face, like a priest studying the sky. Then he cups his hands around her neck and kisses her collarbones, pushes her dress down to her waist. She wraps her arms around his head, feels her heart beat wildly against his skin.

Let him have a different memory of this place. Let him forget his king.

*

The next day the clouds are gone, and the sky is pale and light. Semiramis leaves her guards behind as she walks into the training ground, looking for Onnes. It is late: the soldiers are all gone and the courtyards seem deserted. There are no sounds, except the faint echo of voices coming from further down the palace. Semiramis follows it. As she walks closer, it is clear none of the voices belongs to her husband. She is thinking she should leave when she hears the king say, 'You cannot touch me any more.'

She stops by the opening of the corridor. In the small courtyard in front of her, Ninus and the general Ilu are facing each other. Ninus seems distressed. His eyes are gleaming, and his fists are clenched. The scene is strange: from the way they are standing, it seems Ilu is *scolding* him.

'Your father and brother are gone,' Ilu says. 'The empire is on your shoulders now. You must be strong enough to bear it.'

'Don't speak of my brother,' Ninus says quietly.

'I will speak of Assur and so will you! Look at me!' Ilu raises his voice. Ninus looks at him. 'People see you as a god now. Your *duty* is to take lives as if they were nothing.'

'I don't want to be a—' Ninus starts. Then Ilu smacks his head against the wall. Semiramis starts, as if she was hit. Ninus' nose is bleeding and Ilu reaches out to wipe it.

'Don't.' Ninus turns his head away from him, towards the corridor. To Semiramis' horror, his eyes meet hers. She takes a step back, but he is already moving in her direction, face filled with unbridled fury.

'Who is it?' Ilu's voice asks.

Ninus stops. Semiramis is still, heart hammering its way out of her chest. They look at each other. *He will kill me. He will skin me alive.* Something passes over Ninus' face.

'No one,' he says. 'Nothing.'

Get out, his eyes seem to tell her. She runs out of the training ground.

*

The royal road that connects the governors' homes with the North-west Palace shimmers like snakeskin under the afternoon sun. Semiramis walks, two guards behind her, and stops under the Black Obelisk that rises in the sky, like a tower of doom. The monument is decorated with relief scenes that depict foreign kings bringing tribute to the Assyrian ruler. From the king's appearance – long, curly hair and beard, a ceremonial sickle in hand – he might be Ninus' father, but it is hard to tell. At the top and bottom of the reliefs there is a long inscription recording the king's military campaigns. She tilts her head to try to read the ones at the top. *I received the tribute of the people of the land of Omri: silver, gold, golden tumblers, golden buckets, a staff for a king and spears.*

The guards behind her mutter, 'My king.' She turns quickly and is surprised to see Ninus joining her in the stark shadow of the obelisk. He is alone – his own men left behind. His expression is guarded, controlled. She can't help but notice the bruise on the bridge of his nose, swollen and purple.

'Leave us,' he orders her guards. They obey and the two of them remain alone, shrouded in the cool shade. She bows slightly and waits for him to speak. When he does, he isn't looking at her. 'Some people dare go to the wrong place at the wrong time, and of course they are punished for it.'

Her pulse starts throbbing in her neck. 'My king.'

He blinks and turns his attention to the Black Obelisk. 'My father had this built to commemorate his deeds. It was commissioned by his commander-in-chief, a man named Dayyan-Assur.'

She is taken aback by the swift movement of his mind. One moment he is in deep dark waters, the next he is floating on the surface. She does her best to follow. 'What happened to him?' she asks.

'He died. He was the first man my brother murdered during the war.'

She brings her hand to the obelisk. It is black limestone, fresh to the touch. Under her fingers, subdued kings, prostrating before Shalmaneser. 'Who are these people?'

'Some are from the house of Omri, others from a small kingdom in the mountains in the east. Those,' he points at the second register from the top, 'are Israelites. People from the west, further west than Eber-Nari. They worship a single god and believe in the power of mercy.'

She traces the engraved shapes. 'It is beautiful, though brutal.'

He follows her arm with his eyes. 'My father believed brutality made things beautiful.'

'My own father didn't understand beauty, only brutality.'

He looks at her, his expression suddenly more open – it seems that some of his hatred towards her has ebbed. She thinks about all the rumours she heard in Kalhu, how he was beaten by boys older and stronger than him, until Onnes became his friend and started beating them for him. Then she thinks of how Ilu hit him in the training ground.

He must be thinking the same thing, because he says, 'What you saw yesterday . . .'

'I didn't see anything.'

He nods. Then he laughs, though there is no humour or happiness in it. 'Everyone thinks kings are gods. They don't know anything.'

She tries to read his face, but there are too many thoughts chasing one another, and she can't grab any of them. 'Even gods have burdens,' she says.

He opens his mouth to reply, but his guards are walking to them. 'The ambassadors are waiting for you, my king.'

Ninus' expression changes quickly: once more, he is guarded. She bows to him, and he walks away from her, back into the sunshine that bakes the royal road. His unsaid words linger in the shadow of his father's accomplishments.

I imagined that you would look like a god.
But you look like me, you are not any different.

From *The Epic of Gilgamesh*

16.

Ninus, King of the World, King of Assyria

He summons the council early, before he meets dignitaries in the throne room. The chamber is cool, painted in a soft pink light. He takes his carved chair and waits as everybody else – his mother, Onnes, Ilu, Sasi and the *bârû* – are seated.

'What news from the east?' he asks.

The question is directed at the whole table, but it is Ilu who answers. 'The king of the Medes has been executed.' His lean, muscular body is wrapped in a dark tunic embroidered with gold. Ninus can feel the bruise on his nose throbbing. For a moment, he imagines sinking his dagger into Ilu's hand. *But I need him, just as my father needed him.* Besides, what would Ilu do if he stabbed him? *He would pull out the dagger and pour himself a cup of wine.*

'My soldiers kept his head, as a gift to the king,' Ilu continues. 'We can hang it by the city walls.'

'The tribespeople won't like it,' Onnes comments. 'They will plan a revolt.'

Ilu smiles lazily. 'Let them. Then we'll deport them.'

'Burn the head,' Ninus orders, ignoring the flicker of annoyance in Ilu's eyes. 'It would attract vultures. What about the Aramean tribes?'

'We pushed them south of the river,' Ilu says. 'They lost more than half of their men. I doubt they'll try to invade again.'

'My father decapitated their leader in his last campaign,' Ninus points out. 'Won't they look for revenge?'

'These people are different, my king,' Sasi intervenes. 'Vengeance isn't their way. They are not warlike, just looking for land.'

'Then we will give it to them, as long as they submit to us,' Ninus says. 'What else?'

Nisat clears her throat. Something in her lit, focused expression fills Ninus with foreboding. 'What do you know of the kingdom of Bactria?' she asks him.

Ninus frowns. He has heard about the religious land, home of the 'mother of all cities' Balkh, where sun gods are worshipped and the hills are so green they look like carpets of emeralds. 'Not much,' he says. 'There aren't many records of it.'

'No, there aren't,' Nisat says, though, for some reason, it does not feel as if she is agreeing with him.

The *bârû* intervenes. 'Their capital is a city that far surpasses others in greatness. A city blessed by gods.'

'That is unfortunate,' Nisat says. '*Kalhu* is the most splendid city in the world, built by Ninus' grandfather with the blood of Assyria's enemies.'

They want me to go to war again, he realizes. From the way Sasi looks down and Ilu carefully avoids Nisat's eyes, Ninus understands that the three of them have discussed this already. 'Why should I concern myself with a place so far away?' he asks.

Nisat is quick to reply. 'Neither your father nor your grandfather travelled so far. If you conquer Balkh, you have access to all the main trade routes. Spices, gold, horses, everything flows along that road.'

'Balkh hasn't threatened us,' he points out.

'My king, their richness is a threat—' Sasi starts, but Ninus interrupts him.

'If we campaign so far east, how long will it take?'

'A year, maybe two,' Ilu says. 'Balkh is nestled between a fertile plain and the mountain range. An attack would be difficult but not impossible.'

Sasi clears his throat. 'A campaign such as this might help us get the riches we need after five years of war against your brother.' His hands, smooth and soft, peep out from the long sleeves of his tunic. He has never been on a campaign, never been to war. Ninus looks at him with deep contempt.

'You almost speak as if I *wanted* the war against my brother, Spymaster,' he says. 'Maybe I should have let him take the throne.

He would be here now, ignoring all your suggestions and clever plans.'

'My king knows I would never—' Sasi begins.

'I want more reports on Balkh,' Ninus says firmly. 'Their cities, their weapons, their king. If I lead my men into battle, I want to be sure we can win.'

Nisat is looking at him with a small smile. Ninus does not have to ask her what it means. He is learning the game. He is behaving like a king.

*

He leaves the throne room after the last suppliants have gone and walks through a single doorway in the southern wall that leads to an anteroom first, then to a large central courtyard. To the right are the banqueting suites and the terrace where Onnes' wedding feast took place. Ninus used to love the splendid view of the river and countryside, but now the place has a bittersweet feel.

He has told them to come before the moon is up. He changes, removes his crown and dagger, then goes to wait for them in a large room with tapestries on the walls. They arrive a little later. Onnes' arms are bare, except for a pair of cuffs whose round agate jewels are the colour of his eyes. The dress Semiramis is wearing is white and gold, leaving her shoulders naked.

'I am glad you could join me,' Ninus says, sinking back into a pile of crimson pillows. 'Ilu wanted me to dine in his palace with his sons.' He gestures them to the opposite couch.

'I could have come with you,' Onnes says, sitting.

'They hate you, you know that,' Ninus says.

Semiramis takes the place next to Onnes. Now that she is here, Ninus wonders if inviting them both to dine with him was a mistake. But he cannot deny her presence any longer. He must find a way to live with it, and to understand where Onnes' loyalties lie.

There are no torches, and lamps cast a golden, hazy light. Between the couches there is a rich bowl filled with pure, unmixed wine. The tables around it are laid with plates of spiced lamb and honeyed cheese.

Ninus points at the wine bowl, whose gold is decorated with battle scenes. 'This is the wine that my grandfather imported from Persia to celebrate Kalhu as the new capital,' he tells Semiramis.

Her face is mirrored in the bowl, contours blurred and crimson. 'I have heard about that feast. People say it lasted days.'

'It did,' Ninus says, 'with citizens from across the empire and leaders from neighbouring kingdoms. None had ever tasted wine: it was a delicacy, available in small quantities and used for religious ceremonies. And suddenly Ashurnasirpal was serving ten thousand skins of it. The sun kept rising and setting, but they never stopped drinking. When they finally left, they had learned that my grandfather had the power and the riches to feast like a god. Wine was the drink of the greatest rulers, the conquerors, the human gods who walked the earth.'

Semiramis smiles. There is a wistful quality to her expression, as if she yearned for a past that does not belong to her. 'Do you have memories of it?' she asks.

'I wasn't born,' Ninus says. 'But my father's feasts were often just as grand. He invited foreign dignitaries so they would bend the knee before the King of Kings, then sent them back to their cities, drunk and happy.'

Semiramis takes the bowl and drinks. When she bends, her face comes into the lamplight, and her hair falls forward. It makes Ninus think of a dark, dripping stream.

'Any news on the high officials we need to replace?' Onnes asks. Ninus had expected him to be colder, more formal in front of Semiramis, but he is speaking with the ease he always reserves for Ninus only, as if he were allowing Semiramis to be witness to it. Even more, to be a part of it. *But you do not know how he behaves when he is alone with her.*

'I have decided to appoint more eunuchs.'

'Is it wise, to set aside the noble families?'

Ninus watches Onnes' throat moving as he swallows. 'Assyria isn't what it once was. My father and my grandfather expanded the borders and surrounded themselves with nobles from the provinces, but a bigger empire demands a different approach to ruling. Posts need to be awarded on merit, no more through family ties.'

'Is this why you have Sasi and other eunuchs as state officials?' Semiramis asks.

'Eunuchs can't betray their king,' Onnes explains. 'They give up their family connections in order to serve him, often taking new names in the process. They can have no legacy, so they can hold no power.'

Ninus thinks a man doesn't need a legacy to be ambitious. Semiramis catches his eye, and for a moment he feels as if she has heard his thought. He looks away. 'I am tired of politics,' he says. 'If I'd wanted to talk politics, I would have invited Sasi.'

Onnes lays a hand on Semiramis' leg. 'Let us play the game Assur liked so much when we drank this wine together.'

Ninus' heart clenches at the mention of Assur, but he has no intention of showing weakness in front of Semiramis. He forces a smile. 'He liked it, yet he was horrible at it.'

'What is the game?' Semiramis asks.

'We ask each other questions in turn,' Onnes says. 'If you lie, you must drink.'

'And if you tell the truth?'

Onnes shrugs. 'Then we know something about you.'

And that is always a loss, Ninus thinks.

She narrows her eyes. 'And if I don't want to answer?'

'Then you drink.'

She turns her head to Onnes. Her loose hair is thick and black, and Ninus can't help but think how different she is from the other women of the palace, always wearing tight coils and plaits. She seems to consider something. Then her face breaks into a smile.

'I will start,' she says, eyes still fixed on Onnes. 'What do you fear?'

Ninus flinches. All these years, he has never asked such a question of Onnes for fear of . . . what? That he would grow uncomfortable and leave him. But Onnes' expression doesn't change. Staring straight ahead, he says, 'Madness.'

Semiramis bites the inside of her lip. 'I think that is the truth.'

Ninus suddenly feels angry with her. *She can't know him as I do.* 'Your turn,' he says, trying to keep his voice even. 'What do *you* fear?'

Her dark eyes meet his. She takes the bowl and drinks, as he expected her to do, but then she sets it down and, as if emboldened by the wine, says, 'Helplessness.'

They stare at her. Ninus remembers the way she looked at him after Ilu hit him, anger and sadness blooming on her face. It was as if she understood.

'Now you ask Ninus a question,' Onnes tells Semiramis. She nods, turns to him. The look on her face is as if she is daring him. It makes his chest burn with a feeling he cannot name. He decides it must be outrage.

'What is your most precious secret, my king?' she asks.

He almost spills the wine bowl. He glances at Onnes, who is impassive. For a single mad moment, Ninus imagines cupping his hands around his face and kissing him in front of Semiramis, just to see what she would do. He takes the bowl and drinks.

'If you do not answer, may I ask another question?' she taunts.

'You can ask a thousand questions. It does not mean I will answer them.'

She hesitates. 'What do you hate most?'

In this moment, you, he almost says, but there is another answer, one he can easily share. 'Cruelty. The need to crush those who are smaller and weaker. Assyrians believe we must rule over everyone else. That the world is made of opposites: darkness and light, chaos and order, death and life. And for them, one thing must always destroy the other. Kings need to subdue their people; strength must win over weakness. But opposites coexist inside us: we have equal light and darkness. We are not simple beings.'

There is a moment of silence, then Onnes says, 'You read too many poems.'

Semiramis laughs. Onnes is smiling and Ninus can't help but smile too.

'And you don't read enough,' Ninus says. He stretches on the couch, making himself more comfortable. His foot almost touches the hem of Semiramis' dress.

Onnes seems not to notice. 'You spent your childhood quoting lines from *Gilgamesh*,' he says, grinning.

'And you spent yours smashing people's faces in the training ground.'

They laugh again. The lamps flicker, tickling the tapestries. In the courtyard, the light has faded. Onnes stands, walks outside, under the stars. From their couches, they see him take the opium pods out of a pouch around his waist and chew them. The shadow of a servant passes, quick and breathless. The last courtiers make their way out of the royal suites, towards the large courtyards that lead out of the palace.

'Are we still playing?' Semiramis asks.

Ninus tears his eyes away from Onnes and looks at her. Her eyes are lit with a quality that is hard to describe. It is neither arrogance nor curiosity, but rather fervency, as if she could burn through him. He nods. *Why not?*

Her question comes quickly. 'Have you ever slept with a man?'

He leans back, trying to hide his surprise. 'I have slept with men, and I have slept with women.'

'Have you ever slept with Onnes?'

He is aware that his leg is touching her dress, yet she doesn't move. 'No.'

'How do I know that that is the truth?'

'You don't. But you can ask him.'

She touches the rings on her fingers as if she is unaccustomed to them. 'He never speaks of you when he is with me.'

'He doesn't speak of anything with anyone.'

She shakes her head. 'That isn't true. He tells me many things. Memories of his childhood, the way Ilu treated him, what his mother was like.'

Something breaks in Ninus' heart. 'He never talks to me about his mother.'

Onnes walks inside. Ninus sits up, and his leg moves away from Semiramis' dress. The room blurs for a moment, as if he were looking at it from underwater, all sounds and colours faded. Onnes passes him the bowl. The wine tastes sweeter with each sip. Some of the lamps have burned out and, deeper into the palace, the sound of lyre notes echo, bright and sweet.

Onnes sits and cups a hand around the nape of Semiramis' neck. He pulls her to him, brushes his lips against her cheek. Then he rests his head back, looks at the ceiling. 'Ilu wants to organize a hunt soon. Have you heard?'

'I can hardly wait,' Ninus says. His voice seems to come from afar. The wine is making him float away, down and down into a world made of water. 'Have you ever seen a lion hunt?' he asks Semiramis.

She shakes her head. He can feel the movements of her mind, her thoughts hidden beyond his reach. To his surprise, he realizes he wants to uncover them. *She hides her pain well, like Onnes. She gives you crumbs, and makes you ache for something she will never yield.*

Desire is a strange thing. What makes us want one person over another? Is it the memory of the past, the excitement of the present or the promise of the future? Ninus does not know. All he sees is that whatever mystery is in Onnes, he can see a glimpse of it in Semiramis too.

17.

Lion Hunt

The lion-hunt arena is outside the city walls, encircled by a canal that feeds on the river Tigris. Two rows of soldiers armed with spears form a barricade around it. Others are inside, standing at the edge with barking hounds on leashes.

Semiramis watches from the top of the hill that overlooks the arena. Governors and officials are sitting on a high platform to her right, while to her left are the women of the queen's palace. Below them, closer to the canal, is what seems like the whole population of Kalhu. Water-sellers walk through the crowd, while women keep their children close, away from the bottom of the hill.

Semiramis squints, trying to find Onnes' head in the arena. It is a vast space, sand brushed and cleaned to perfection. Ninus is counting his arrows on the royal chariot, wearing a fine hat and a gilded dress. Ten of his men are behind him, armed with swords and spears.

'A sport for kings,' a high voice behind Semiramis says.

She turns. Sasi is smiling at her, small eyes glittering with excitement.

'Except my husband isn't a king,' she says.

'I sometimes suspect Onnes wants to die young. But, then, aren't the best Assyrians arrogant *and* reckless?'

She smiles back at him. 'Onnes isn't arrogant.'

He bows, feigning seriousness. 'Of course not.'

A roar echoes in the arena. The spectators start shouting, pushing one another to see better. Ten wooden cages are dragged through the large gate. Small boys jump on top of them, ready to release the animals.

'Lions are sacred to Ishtar,' Semiramis says. 'Why do we kill them?'

'Lions embody the chaos of this world,' Sasi says. 'Assyrian kings must bring order to it. Besides, doesn't Gilgamesh humiliate Ishtar when she tries to seduce him? Sometimes even goddesses must learn their place.' He covers his pale hands with the sleeves of his tunic. Semiramis wonders why he isn't wearing something lighter in this heat but, then, she has never seen Sasi's arms, not even on the hottest days. 'The mighty King Ashurnasirpal, our king's grandfather, killed hundreds of lions with hunting spears. He would capture them in forests and hills, and breed their cubs in large numbers.'

'And his son? The king's father?'

Sasi's mouth curves into an odd, joyless smile. 'Shalmaneser would let his prisoners into the arena and make them kneel, foreheads to the ground, while the lions ran at them. He wanted to show the world everyone was at his mercy.' He looks at Ninus' figure in the arena. 'Our king isn't like that. He is a decent man. Sometimes too decent for his own good.'

Onnes appears next to the king's chariot. He checks his bow and quiver, then mounts a black stallion. At the opposite side of the arena, the cages are opened. The lions slide out slowly, elegantly. The spectators quieten, holding their breath. The horses take a few slow steps, coming out into the open. The lions raise their heads in unison, staring. One moves forward. He looks at the men defiantly, daring them to come for him. A rain of arrows sinks into his mane. He roars and thrashes, then falls. Flowers of crimson form at his neck. He dies, resting his head on his paws.

A moment of silence, the heat around them so thick the crowd can almost hear it buzzing. The lions growl. The king spurs the horses. The chariot takes speed as the men disperse around him. The crowd screams and stamps, and so the hunt begins.

It is a mesmerizing, terrifying sight. Semiramis has seen men hunting on the plains and hills of Eber-Nari, in the pitch-black caves of the ravines. She has hunted several times, but this is something else entirely. It is glorious and brutal, grace and violence blending together like the deeds of gods.

Ninus looses arrow after arrow from his chariot. He tracks the lions' movements, looks for the weakest junctures – he fights to kill, not to wound. A man of grace and mercy.

Onnes doesn't let the beasts come too close to him. He aims his spears with a look that could be pleasure, or anger, or both. He always keeps an eye on Ninus, and when a lion ventures too close to the chariot, he shoots him dead with a dagger through the neck.

Two young men with axes fight together, circling a lion before they throw their weapons. From the way in which Ilu watches them from the high platform on Semiramis' right, she knows they are his sons.

Another soldier catches her attention. He is wearing a bright blue mantle over his armour and his sword gleams like the most precious of jewels. He moves alone across the arena, fearless, and approaches the wounded lions, stabbing them again and again, blood spattering his face. When a beast tries to bite him from behind, he swings his sword and the blade cuts across its face, blinding it. The roar of pain threatens to tear the arena in two.

'Who is that man?' Semiramis asks Sasi.

'The prince Marduk, from Babylon.'

She watches as the prince sinks his sword in the lion's neck. 'He seems to be enjoying this.'

The eunuch leans in. 'There are two things to know about Marduk: he is a second son *and* he has slept with every woman in Kalhu.'

'*Every* woman in the capital?' she repeats.

'He beds with boys as well. He has quite the reputation.'

In the arena, Onnes retrieves his arrows from the dead beasts. Ninus places a hand over a dying lion's mane, as if to feel the life ebbing away. For a moment, his eyes glisten, but it might have been the light. The last wounded lioness drags her body closer to the barricade. The people pull back, screaming. Semiramis follows her with her eyes, heart racing. *If she lives, I will take her with me.*

But no lion survives the arena. There is the sound of savage laughter, then the prince Marduk slaughters the beast before it can escape.

*

It is dark by the cages. The smell of blood and meat is heightened, and Semiramis feels sick, as if she is gorging on raw meat. She walks with Ribat at her side, looking into the slices of darkness to see the animals hidden in them. They are in the low building next to the arena, where sunlight filters through small windows, striping the ground and blinding all those who walk in it. The lion tamers are dragging the dead beasts inside, blood trailing behind them in crimson carpets. They will clean the animals before carrying them to the king during the feast.

The lions in the cages hiss and snarl. When Semiramis walks past them, their gleaming eyes fasten on her. Some share a cage in pairs, circling each other, shoulder muscles rippling under their fur. Others lie alone, heads resting on their paws.

'Their mates have been killed,' Ribat whispers, and Semiramis can hear the pity in his voice. He is trembling, slipping in the shadows as if he could disappear.

They pass several empty cages, the iron bars old and rusty, and stop in front of a smaller one, away from all the windows. The fire from a single torch falls upon an animal slightly smaller than the lions, its golden fur spotted with dark markings. It lies in the middle of the cage, yellow eyes radiating light.

'A leopard,' Ribat says, in a fascinated whisper. 'Far rarer, equally dangerous.'

Semiramis moves closer to the cage. The animal is watching them, as if trying to understand what to make of them.

'There used to be more of them, but Ashurnasirpal hunted them all,' Ribat says.

The leopard stands, moving from light to shadow. She comes to a halt in front of the iron bars, eyes made of sunlight fixed on Semiramis. In the shadows, her fur looks paler, like cream, the dark spots changing from her torso to her limbs, each one different from the next, as if painted by a distracted god.

Semiramis thinks of the statue of Ishtar that she used to visit in her village. The goddess's feet were resting on the lions' manes, and Semiramis used to touch them and speak to them as if they were real. It is said that when the goddess goes to war, she rides a chariot drawn by lions, just as the weather god Adad always walks beside raging bulls.

What do you say? she asks the leopard. *I am no goddess, but I was a prisoner too, once.* The animal turns away her head but moves her body closer. Her rich, spotted fur is close enough to be touched. Semiramis reaches out, finds the soft place where shoulder meets spine. The leopard's head snaps back, growling. Her mouth closes a breath from Semiramis' hand. A dare. Behind her Ribat murmurs a panicked 'Mistress,' but she does not move. She does not breathe.

Do not be afraid of me, she thinks. *I am not afraid of you.* The leopard's heart beats under her hand. From up close, she looks like a forbidden deity, as if one of the bas-reliefs of the palace sprang out of the walls, alive and hungry.

A moment, dropping like a leaf from a tree.

Then the leopard moves her head again, laying it by Semiramis' palm. Semiramis smiles, turns to Ribat. 'Go and speak to the tamers. We are taking her to the palace.'

*

The gardens smell of blood and spices. A flock of birds flies over them, their black shapes stark across the sunset. Four soldiers are carrying a dead lion towards Ninus, followed by drum and cymbal players. When they reach him, he rises from his couch and pours a libation over the lion's head.

'I, Shamshi-Adad the Fifth, King of the universe, King of Assyria, King of the land of Ashur and Adad, make this offering to the goddess Ishtar, lady of battle.'

The wine trickles over the lion's mane. Ninus looks down, and Semiramis thinks he will touch the lion's head, but then he lies back on his couch, as eager courtiers and attendants crowd around him.

Incense burns thickly from the carved altars. Naked dancers leap over the dead beast, their arms like long, frail wings. They follow the rhythm as musicians march around, striking drums and cymbals with their hands. Semiramis sits with Onnes by a table near the king's couch. She is looking at the dead lion, so small at the king's feet, like a helpless cat.

Assyrians gain their fame by destroying anything that brings chaos to the universe, she thinks. *And from the spilled blood of their enemies, they build their own shining world.*

Sasi appears and takes the empty space on Semiramis' couch. 'If you do not mind, I will sit here,' he says, though he is already seated. He has changed for the feast, and his earrings – ivories in the Phoenician style – swing slightly against his perfectly groomed plaits.

Onnes snorts. On his arms are thin, fresh cuts from the hunt. 'Tell us, Spymaster,' he says, voice dripping with spite, 'what secrets have you gathered this lovely night?'

Sasi sighs, an exaggerated gesture, and turns to Semiramis. 'Your husband has always struggled to trust me. I fear it is because I once asked him to join me in bed. Though can you blame me? He is handsome.'

Semiramis laughs, but Onnes doesn't smile. 'I don't trust you because you have hundreds of spies spread across the empire, and your position in the capital depends on others' willingness to sell you their lives.'

'Well, yes, there is that,' Sasi concedes. 'But each of us has his job.'

'You are certainly good at yours,' Onnes says, before standing and walking away, towards a group of diviners. Opposite them, Nisat rests on a throne, stroking the hair of a small, dark-haired child. The child's locks are warm and lustrous, with precious beads plaited into them, and her face is as grave and serious as a woman's.

'That is the king's daughter,' Sasi says, following Semiramis' eyes. 'A clever girl.'

She looks like him, Semiramis thinks. The searching gaze, black hair against a thoughtful face. The girl listens to Nisat in silence, and when the dancers sway around them in a circle, she pulls back against her grandmother, as if afraid to be touched by strangers.

'Look,' Sasi says urgently, leaning close to Semiramis' ear. 'The Babylonian prince is coming here.'

She barely has time to fix her dress as Marduk walks over, a blue cloak fluttering from his shoulders. He is dark-haired, fair-skinned – fairer than any Assyrian – and wears rings and bracelets fit for a king. The eunuch bows and, with a humble voice that Semiramis has only heard him use with the king's mother, says, 'You fought well today, my prince.'

Marduk smiles at him, unfazed. He is standing, towering over them, as if that is where he belongs. Semiramis can't help but think he is the opposite of Ninus, who never looks at ease anywhere.

'So this is the commoner Onnes has married,' Marduk says.

'Not a commoner any more,' she corrects him. 'Would you care for beer, my lord?'

He sits next to Sasi, smoothing the golden fringes of his cloak. A slave comes forward, ready to give Marduk a cup, but the prince waves him away. His eyes are fixed on Semiramis. Up close, they have a preying quality, like a wolf's. 'Now that I see you, I'd care for many things,' he says. 'With that face, you could be a whore I would actually pay for.'

She tries not to flinch. His tone reminds her of the boys of her village, who used to taunt her because they knew they could. Sasi is smiling when she turns to him: he is watching them as one watches an immensely entertaining play. *Let him be entertained, then.*

'You don't usually pay your whores, my lord?' she asks Marduk. 'Or do you just assume they come to you willingly?'

He opens his arms wide. 'Can you blame them? Everyone wants to fuck a prince.'

'Or maybe they are just clever enough to know princes won't take no for an answer.'

There is a slight twitch in the clenching of his jaw, as if he isn't used to being questioned. He stares at her, assessing whether or not he likes it. 'In the poems, goddesses are lustful, treacherous and hungry for love,' he says. 'Kings must learn to subdue them, and every other woman in their path. The hero Gilgamesh is the first to take the lawful wives of all his citizens. Virgins wait for him in their new husbands' beds, because this is the order the gods have decreed.'

'Is that how you seduce women?' she asks. 'Reciting poems?'

His smile is slow and dawning. 'You tell me. Is it working?'

She forces a laugh. 'I am not easily seduced.'

'Then your husband is lucky. I haven't met a single woman in Kalhu who wishes to remain in her husband's bed.'

'I didn't say I want to remain in his bed,' she says. 'I just don't want to join you in yours.'

Unexpectedly, he reaches out and his hand brushes her hair. She keeps still, surprised by his boldness. Marduk exchanges a look with Sasi.

'Isn't she entrancing?' the eunuch asks. His voice is carefully amused, but his smile doesn't reach his eyes: Semiramis can tell he dislikes the prince. *But it is more than that. He is afraid of him.*

'Like a demon,' Marduk says.

She stands, and Marduk's hand drops. Her skin twitches where he touched her. 'Perhaps you should be more careful, then,' she says. 'Demons are even more dangerous than gods, because they are the most subtle.'

She does not wait to see Marduk's reaction. She walks away before he can speak, leaving him alone with Sasi.

*

The dark-haired child is sitting on the ground at the edge of the pavilion, drawing figures on the red sand. Semiramis approaches her quietly, trying to discern the shapes.

'Hello,' she says.

The child turns. 'Hello.' She casts a quick look behind Semiramis' shoulder. 'If my grandmother sees you here, she might have you whipped.'

Semiramis almost smiles. 'Does Nisat think me so dangerous?'

'Yes,' the child says simply, going back to her sand drawings. They look like a flock of water birds – long, thin necks and sharp, dark beaks.

A shadow appears next to them. 'Go back to the banquet, Sosanê,' Ninus orders. He is staring at Semiramis. His dark hair curls behind his ears, and his fingers, without the rings he usually wears, are long and elegant. Like a musician's, not a warrior's.

Semiramis bows to him, as the child scampers away. She expects Ninus to leave too, but he remains standing in front of her, face framed by the leaves and fruit.

'That is a beautiful name,' she says. 'Sosanê.'

'Her mother picked it,' he says. 'She was a scribe.'

He doesn't elaborate, so she asks, 'And your royal name? Did you decide on that?'

Adad, the storm and rain god. The bull that holds thunderbolts in his hands. He is everywhere in Kalhu – on monuments and cylinder seals, on the bas-reliefs of the palace, on the lips of priests and diviners as they inspect the liver of sacrificial animals.

'My father did,' Ninus says. 'He thought Adad was the epitome of all a prince should be, bringing rain and relief during droughts, but also storms and destruction in moments of anger.' His voice is raw with discomfort. Something has changed between them since she saw him with Ilu on the training ground, though she cannot tell what. All she knows is that the wall that was between them is gone, and that now she could reach out and touch him, if she wanted to.

'If you could have chosen differently, which name would you have picked?' she asks.

'I don't know. I've never felt much of a god.'

The words, so simple and honest, fill her with surprise. Assyrian kings believe their power is divine, bestowed upon them by the mightiest deities. But here Ninus stands, looking all too human. He turns as if to leave, then thinks back on it.

'I saw you speaking with the prince Marduk,' he says.

'I was.'

'What did he want from you?' He seems curious, rather than suspicious. It is easy to speak openly with him. In this, he is the opposite of Onnes, who seems never to care for anyone but himself.

'He wanted to tell me I look like a whore he would be willing to pay for.'

There is a flash in his eyes, like water when it is touched by the moonlight.

'Do not worry, my king,' she says. 'Taunting doesn't offend me.'

'You are lucky.'

What he means by that, she cannot say. 'To be taunted?' she says, with a smile. 'I wouldn't say so.'

He waves a hand, and for a moment, he resembles his mother. 'People always enjoy preying on the misery of others. It makes them feel powerful.'

'Oh, but I am not miserable, my king. Only different.'

He doesn't reply but simply stares at her as he did in the Northwest Palace, when the three of them were drinking wine together. He has the bluest eyes, a colour so pure it should only belong to the gods. They make her think of deep pools one can dive into, filled with treasures at the bottom. She excuses herself and walks back to the feast.

18.

Ribat, a Slave

The dry season has come, with its heavy days and taste of sand. Slaves move in the shadows of the burning buildings, like lizards. They spit on their hands and wipe them on their faces so their eyes don't hurt. Ribat likes the season: everyone is so disturbed by the heat that all they concern themselves with is how to survive it. This allows him to do things without being noticed.

In the early hours of the afternoon, the city is as still as the desert. Houses shine under a sizzling sun. Ribat moves from one patch of shade to the next. There is dust everywhere, coating buildings and people as if dressing them before swallowing them. Kalhu is always hungry. For slaves, for riches, for blood. It fools and tricks with its magnificence but, under its glorious disguise, it stinks and sweats and lashes. And Assyrians endure its cruelty: anything, in the name of greatness.

The gods bestow different gifts on different people, Ribat considers. To his mother, they gave light, even if she was born in the darkness. To Ana, the pretty slave who sleeps next to him in the servants' room, they gave a generous heart. Whether that is truly a gift or not, Ribat isn't sure, but Ana treats it as such. To him, the talent of survival. He can move swiftly; he can blend with the walls; he can stand so still that he seems to vanish. And so he has lived, surviving – for a slave in this world, often the most difficult feat – with a forbidden dream kept inside him, like a water supply in a drought: to become a scribe.

But lately he has been longing for more. He has been longing for justice, for love and, even though he can barely form the thought in his mind, for freedom. He wants to go back in time and understand what happened to his mother. He wants to touch and be touched, to listen and to be heard. He wants things he is not supposed to want. Maybe that is proof that he is just like everybody else: slaves, mortals and gods – they all long for things they cannot have.

He threads his way between the green and blue brick houses, towards the city walls at the opposite side of the square. At their foot a line of five slaves is tied to wooden posts under the merciless sunlight. Ribat looks around. There are no guards, no soldiers. Black birds are flying overhead. The slaves are punished under the eyes of the sun god Shamash, who sees everything that happens in every corner of the world, from sunrise to sunset. Ribat wonders if the god can see him now. But don't proverbs say that slaves are the shadows of men?

He grasps the waterskin that hangs from his waist and takes a careful step towards the other slaves. He should walk away from this place; he should be bringing Onnes' accounts to the Northwest Palace. But he is thinking of his mother today and the thought of her always makes him do something he later regrets. *What kind of person do you think you will become if you turn away from those who are like you?* he can almost hear her ask.

'One who wants to stay alive,' he mutters. But there is no one to listen to him. Only the heat, swallowing his words.

An invisible force drags him to the figures under the wall. He moves closer and closer, then pours a trickle of water into each mouth. One is a man as thin and straight as a spear. Then there are two boys, whose lips are cracked and swollen. A grey-haired woman whispers a blessing when she drinks, while the girl next to her looks at Ribat as if he were a mirage. He is putting the waterskin back, when he becomes aware of a presence at the edge of the road. Slowly, he risks a glance in the figure's direction. His heart almost stops.

The spymaster is standing by a blue-painted column, his oil-black hair gleaming. To his horror, Ribat realizes that the eunuch is staring right at him. He quickly looks at the ground, willing himself to disappear. Usually, it works. But when he looks up again, the eunuch is much closer. The corners of his mouth are turned up in what should be a smile. To Ribat, it looks like a sneer.

'Tell me,' the spymaster says, 'what is the punishment for a slave who gives water to those who are condemned in the name of Shamash?'

Ribat stares resolutely at the ground. His heart is beating savagely in his ears. 'A whipping, my lord.'

'You are lying,' the eunuch says. Ribat can hear a tinge of amusement in his voice. 'It is the gouging of the eye.'

Ribat remains silent. There is heaviness in the air, weight.

'Have you ever been whipped?' the eunuch asks.

'Every slave has been whipped, my lord.'

'I imagine you less than others.'

He feels that every word is a test, and a wrong answer might plunge him into a world of darkness. 'Would you like to see the scars, my lord?'

Sasi's voice changes slightly, the sweetness drained from it. 'I avoid the sight of scars and wounds, when I can. Sadly, I do not have the stomach for it.' Ribat is sure the eunuch has the stomach for anything but keeps quiet. Behind him, one of the slaves starts moaning softly. Ribat realizes he is asking for more water.

The eunuch ignores him. 'Is it true that your mistress has a leopard in the palace?' he asks.

Ribat buries his surprise quickly. He didn't think the eunuch knew who he was. 'It is. She bites anyone who comes too close and eats from my mistress's hands alone.' He risks a glance at the eunuch. He wants to scare Sasi, but the spymaster looks only mildly interested, as if he and Ribat were discussing dinner.

'I keep hearing whispers about them,' he says. 'Some people even say that they sleep in bed together.' Ribat doesn't contradict him. Sasi chuckles, amused by the thought. 'But of course,' he continues, 'no matter the stories the people spin about masters and mistresses, kings and queens, they remain what they have always been: mortal.'

Ribat stares at him. 'Semiramis isn't like the other masters.'

This makes the eunuch smile. 'You almost sound as if you are in love with her.'

Ribat looks down, so Sasi does not see the flush on his cheeks. 'She is my mistress. I am loyal to her.'

'In my experience slaves are loyal to their masters until they aren't. Give them a chance to avenge themselves on those who owned them, and they won't think twice.' Ribat lifts his head, stunned. He has never heard anyone speak so. Seeing his expression, Sasi smiles. 'You will forgive me if I speak freely to you. I was also sold, once. I know what it means when your life is in someone else's hands.'

Ribat knows this already, but he is surprised to hear him say it so easily. This is why he has become so powerful, he considers, because he uses his wounds as ways into other people's lives.

'Look,' Sasi says. 'Soldiers are coming.'

Ribat turns quickly. A line of men is marching in their direction. Ribat hides the waterskin under his tunic.

'I would disappear, if I were you,' the eunuch says. 'You do not want to be caught helping other slaves. I imagine you are not so prone to forget what the punishment for such a sin might be, when a guard asks you.'

Ribat does not need to be told twice. He slides back into the alley he came from, controlling his breath, easing his fears, convincing himself that he is nobody, that he is nothing.

In such a way, slaves become invisible to the world.

*

Back in the palace, he finds Semiramis in the portico, a pile of tablets in front of her. The leopard is sitting by her side. She shows her teeth when she sees Ribat but does not move.

'You took longer than usual,' Semiramis says, when Ribat joins her. It is cooler in the portico. The sky is stretched over them, a bright arch, and the paving is warm under their feet.

'The spymaster found me,' he says, careful not to mention *where* he found him. 'He wanted to know if it is true that you have a leopard roaming around the palace.'

This makes her laugh. The animal lifts her large spotted head, as if she knows they are speaking of her.

'And?'

'I told him the truth. That should keep him away for a while.'

'I do not mind him,' she says, going back to her tablets. 'I find him amusing.'

Ribat thinks that the eunuch is as amusing as a poisonous snake but keeps quiet. He settles more comfortably by Semiramis' side – as close as the leopard allows – and waits for her to ask him questions as she reads.

They have learned the simplest symbols – *star, sun, night* – and are now reading the more complex ones – *man, king, son, power*. Semiramis says they look like arrows, but Ribat believes they are more like slim bodies, stretching their limbs, bending down, showing their angular shapes. She is reading a tablet on demonic beings: how they look, what kind of diseases they bring, the rituals that can defeat them.

'Why don't they bear names?' she asks. There is no fear in her eyes, just a constant, burning curiosity. Ribat wants to remind her that there is a demon with multiple heads and claws whose plagues sweep across the land, and that there are red-eyed devils who can travel from the underworld to catch wrongdoers and punish them.

'Because you don't want to call them, or bring disease, misfortune and death upon yourself,' he explains.

'Gods can bring as much disaster, yet we have names for them.'

He is always astonished by her thinking. 'Yes, but spirits are more subtle.' He tries to impress her, because he likes the way she smiles when he says something right. 'They creep through cracks and enter the house to steal and murder. They wait in desolate alleys and pin down their victims.'

She studies him. It seems she is wondering whether he truly believes it. Then she laughs. The sound spills out of her as a fountain. Her face is like the sun in the clear blue light, and he presses it into his mind as shapes and words are pressed into clay. At night, when darkness envelops him, the memory will help him drift to sleep.

*

Attached to the Nabu temple, at the feet of the governors' palaces, there is an ancillary building: the training school for scribes. Ribat looks at them through the windows as he walks past. Five boys occupy each bench and, next to them, little water-troughs are filled with pure clay to be kneaded into cakes. A priest paces between the benches, speaking in a low, musical voice. On the wall opposite him, two inscriptions:

The scribe of proved skill will shine like the sun.
Memory is what is required of a scribe, first and foremost.

Ribat thinks he has a good memory, and that he would wish to shine like the sun.

'Would you like that?' Semiramis asks. 'To study, like a scribe?'

He turns. Her face goes from light to shadow as they move past the statues of the gods. There must be longing still painted in his eyes. He wipes it away quickly. 'Yes. I would like it very much.'

'And leave me?'

'Of course not.'

She half smiles, then reaches out and caresses his head. It is done so quickly that Ribat hasn't time to capture the feeling. He has stopped walking, but she is already moving on, as if nothing happened. Ribat hurries to follow her.

Around them, a group of slaves watches them, frowning as the two of them speak and laugh together. For a moment Ribat feels sorry for them, because they do not know what it feels like to be in the real world, to be flesh and blood, not just shadows sliding over walls and floors, closer to the land of spirits than the land of men.

*

Down in the servants' room, he cleans one of her dresses by the lamplight. It is quiet. Ana is sitting on the floor, plaiting her hair. Zamena walks into the room and sits next to Ribat. She has grown older – his mother's age, if she were still alive.

For a while, she watches Ribat in silence as he scrubs the tunic. Then she says, 'What do you talk about, all day long?'

'Who?' he asks, though he knows very well to whom she has referred.

'You and Semiramis.'

'Proverbs, mostly,' he replies truthfully.

Zamena sighs. 'You want a proverb? *Our worthiness is the result of chance.* Your mother used to say that.'

He stands to leave, folds the dress carefully. He does not want to think about his mother.

'You like her too much,' Zamena says. 'Nobles are not like us. Never forget it.'

'She is different.'

'Why? Because she was born common? She isn't common now.'

But that isn't why Ribat thinks Semiramis is different. He sees something in her that is inside him as well. He doesn't know what it is, doesn't know if it is a good thing, but knows that it is there: a spark that refuses to be put out and extinguished into nothingness.

*

It is not yet dawn. He is wandering the palace, trying to avoid the heat of the servants' room. Close to the storerooms it is cooler, so he paces the corridor there, each step as silent as a feather. A strange sound is coming from one of the rooms, and a sweet smell that pulls him closer to the door. He peeps inside.

He is surprised to see Semiramis, framed by the blooming flowers painted on the walls. She is standing by the jars of palm oil, holding a bowl with honey and long hanging beans that look green in the feeble light. Acacia fruit? Ribat wonders. Semiramis adds ground dates in the bowl and starts grinding. When she is done, she pushes her night tunic up to her waist. Her belly is flat and smooth and, between her legs, thin dark hairs. She dips a piece of cotton in the paste then inserts it between her thighs. She doesn't make a sound as she moves her hand up, then fixes her tunic down.

When she is done, she turns and looks Ribat straight in the eye. He winces; he should have expected that she knew he was here. She always does.

'Is the bedroom too warm, Mistress?' he asks tentatively.

She stares at him in silence for a long time. It is a strange look, one she always reserves for others. As if considering what to do with him. Ribat feels hurt.

'Come in,' she says finally. 'And be careful with that paste. It's not for eating.'

He moves carefully in the shadows, a safe distance from her. 'What is it for?'

She ignores his question. 'You have been taught to obey your masters.'

He nods. He wonders where this is leading.

'If someone asked you who your master is, what would you say?'

He thinks he understands now. 'Slaves don't receive many kindnesses. We never forget the people who have been good to us.'

She smiles. 'Good.'

He doesn't like her tone, as if he were a child who is being taught a lesson. Unwillingly, Zamena's words pop into his mind: *She isn't common now.*

She starts collecting the ground dates and acacia fruit. 'I read something yesterday,' she says, as she hides the mixing bowl under a cloth, behind a line of long-necked jars. 'I thought you would like it.'

'A proverb?'

'Something a diviner once said.' Ribat wonders where she could have found a diviner's manual. '*Sky and Earth both produce portents*,' she recites. '*Though appearing separately, they are not separate: Sky and Earth are related.*' She looks at him. 'What does it make you think about?'

In his head, he tries answers that would please her. But then, a thought: 'It makes me think about us.'

She nods. 'I thought the same. We come from the dust; the kings of Assyria come from the sky. But are Sky and Earth really so different? When evening comes, and the land blends with the sky, do they appear separate? They don't.'

He stares at her, speechless. She walks out of the storeroom, as if she hasn't just spoken words as dangerous as poisoned arrows, as treacherous as a slave hitting his master. Ribat follows her.

*

Later, he casually asks Zamena about unripe acacia fruit and honey. She raises her eyebrows and explains to him that some slaves use the paste to prevent pregnancies. He doesn't comment, but for a while, whenever the women whisper and wonder why Semiramis doesn't become pregnant, Ribat keeps his head down and thinks of how she had pushed the paste inside her. No fear or hesitation. As if she had done it many times already.

*

'Onnes doesn't call for me any more,' Ana tells him one day. They are in the reception room, clearing the soup-smeared bowls. Night is falling and the palace is warm from the day's heat. Ribat dries a large bowl with a clean cloth, keeping silent. He thinks about the day Ana was brought to the capital – as part of the booty taken during the war with the king's brother. Ribat was there with Onnes when the prisoners were hauled into the market square. They stood for a long time under the summer sun, while Assyrian men nudged and pinched them.

Some of the prisoners cried, which distressed Ribat because he knew that the more they cried, the less likely a good master was to pick them. Ana didn't shed a tear. Onnes chose her because of it: he doesn't tolerate people who show their suffering.

'Why do you think he doesn't want me?' she asks again.

He wonders if she deluded herself that Onnes actually cared for her. Onnes doesn't care for anyone, except the king. And now Semiramis.

'Because he has a wife,' he says.

He hears her steps coming to him. She rests her forehead on his back. 'Semiramis has something different about her,' she says. 'She doesn't behave as other women do.'

Ribat puts down the cleaned bowl and turns. Ana's face is pretty, eyes soft and hesitant. There is a single lamp next to them. Ribat closes her fingers around it, and the room is plunged into the shadows. When it is dark, the palace sleeps, and the night belongs to the slaves. A momentary change in the order of things. The seeds of freedom, bursting from the earth before they are buried again.

Ana kisses him. Ribat's mouth opens of its own accord. She guides his hand under her dress so he can feel the warm, fragile skin. He closes his eyes and sees the contours of Semiramis' naked body, Onnes' hands on her flesh. He thinks that Onnes was inside Ana just like he was inside Semiramis. He shouldn't be thinking about this, but the thought excites him, and he finds the space between Ana's thighs. She lets herself be held, her body as small as a bird's.

Afterwards, when he stands breathless and alone in the blurry room, he almost convinces himself that it was Ana's body he thought of when he was touching her. But that isn't the truth.

*

In the servants' quarter, everything is dark. The shapes of the other slaves are shadows around him. It is hard to tell if it is day or night. Ribat often thinks the house of dust might look like this. It makes him think of another dark room.

A bloody dagger.

A father's dare.

A king's last words.

Sometimes, when the memory resurfaces, he considers sharing it with Semiramis. But as much as he loves her, he can't predict what she would do with such a precious piece of information. So he keeps it to himself.

19.

The Wings of War

Semiramis cannot sleep. She sits on the floor by the bas-reliefs of waves and fish, and imagines that her mother is among them, floating in the moonlit water. Back in Eber-Nari, the people said that water had healing powers, that its creatures could speak to the rain and mend a broken heart. Semiramis never believed it. It was love that broke her mother's heart in the first place.

Do you love Onnes? It is a question she has asked herself many times. Across the room, her leopard stares at her with yellow eyes. The corner that opens onto the portico is her favourite place to curl up and sleep. Semiramis keeps her in her apartments, except when she takes her to the gardens, walking her on a leash. She likes to see how women and courtiers move aside as they pass: it makes her feel feared, untouchable.

She stands and walks to the portico. The leopard stalks behind her. Semiramis can feel her breath on her ankles, the soft sound of her paws on the floor. The city is dreaming in the breeze. Semiramis crosses the portico and slips into Onnes' apartments. He is resting in his bed, the chamber still warm from the day's heat. His shoulders are the colour of dark honey in the shadows. She removes her earrings and slowly unplaits her hair, then sits by his side. He stirs and wraps his arm around her leg.

'Did you take the opium?' she asks. He shakes his head. The bags are dark under his eyes, his arms tired as he clutches her. She pours the opium powder into the cup by the side of the bed and gives it to him. He drinks as if he were dying of thirst. The leopard paces the room, her eyes glowing faintly, then jumps onto the bed and settles upon their feet.

Onnes lies down again. She watches his shoulders rise and fall with each laboured breath. She thinks he has fallen asleep, until he whispers: 'Ninus wants to campaign again.'

The crack in his voice stills her. 'When?'

'Soon.' His words are so quiet she isn't sure she has heard him correctly. 'I don't want to go back there.'

'Where?' she asks.

But his dreamless sleep is coming over him now. His breaths grow even, and he leaves her alone with her leopard in the shadowy room.

*

At dawn, she slips away. The moon is thin, fading as the sky grows brighter. The rooms are empty except for the statues of the *apkallu*, staring at her with their cold bird eyes. She wears a necklace of gold beads and hanging pomegranates and a blue dress with fringed sleeves. When she walks out of the palace a single guard accompanies her. They take the royal road and enter the courtyard of the North-west Palace, which is deserted except for a figure standing by the bas-reliefs of tributaries: Sasi. He seems lost in thought. Still, when Semiramis approaches him, his face doesn't show the faintest hint of surprise.

'When are they leaving?' she asks.

He raises an eyebrow. 'Why don't you ask your husband?'

'He is sleeping.'

'And you can't?'

'I am not tired.'

He smiles. 'You never seem to be.'

'I could say the same of you.'

He sighs and moves in the direction of the throne room. She follows.

'Summer has ended,' he says, as the guards move aside to let them pass. 'The men haven't campaigned since the end of the war with Assur. But the city has recovered now, and the soldiers are restless.'

The throne room is silent, two slaves poking the brazier at the centre. The shy light of dawn spills through the door, like buttercream.

'Where are they campaigning?' she asks.

'There is a city in the east, by the name of Balkh. It is one of the richest the world has ever seen, and the king has set his eyes on it.'

'Did he set his eyes on it, or did you?'

He chuckles. 'Nisat and Ilu did. But they are older and more experienced and know what is best for the empire.' It sounds like an act he has learned to play, one he has performed countless times.

'Balkh,' she repeats. She has never heard the name. It can mean only one thing: 'It is far.'

'Yes. They will be gone for a year, or more.'

'When are they leaving?' She repeats the question he has not yet answered.

'There is a sandstorm coming. They will leave Kalhu when the storm is over.'

'Storms don't last more than a few days.'

'You'd better be ready to say goodbye, then.'

The brazier is burning orange and bright. The slaves light a few torches, then leave the room. Sasi watches them go. 'If you will excuse me, I don't want the king to find me here. He would think I am *conspiring* against him.' The word seems to amuse him deeply. 'And you should go back to your husband.'

*

As Sasi promised, the sandstorm comes. Sand gathers in the air like a swarm and starts slapping against roofs and walls. Semiramis follows its dance from Onnes' apartments. The air is so dry that her throat is parched. The leopard is restless: her tail lashes and her face is alert, scanning the shadows for an invisible enemy.

Onnes is sitting on a couch, examining a tablet with a list of resources from Eber-Nari: fabrics, olive oil, ivories and cedar-wood. When he speaks, he doesn't look up. 'When the storm is over, the army will leave.'

'I know,' she says. 'Sasi told me.'

Onnes snorts. 'What does he know of war?'

'He knows something of its consequences,' she says. 'It was a war that brought him here, after all.'

He ignores her. He despises Sasi, with his secret power and information, so different from Onnes, all coldness and bleakness and carefully built walls of stone.

'I don't know if I'll come back alive this time,' he says after a while. 'These campaigns beyond the known borders of the empire . . . they are essential, but dangerous.'

Semiramis watches him. Her leopard hisses uneasily. 'You are stronger than all of your men,' she says. 'If someone can survive this, it is you.'

He looks up from the tablet. His stare has an intensity she has never seen. 'When I am out there fighting,' he says, 'I have moments when I want to cut everyone to pieces. I want to drag them all to the house of dust, and I don't even mind if I go down with them.'

His guard is slipping. It is always hurtful for him when the defences come down. When he is like this, there is an ache in her chest. She knows that she cannot mend him, for she has never managed to mend herself. But isn't it always easier when the pain is someone else's?

She walks away from the window and goes to kneel by his side. She cups a hand around his cheek, feels the coldness of his skin. 'Sometimes when I feel the need to hurt I think about my mother,' she says. 'Everything she did or people say she did . . . I think it's in my blood, something rotten that I can't uproot, no matter how hard I try. And it disgusts me.'

Outside the window, the sand covers everything – temples, palaces, the city walls. The wind thrashes and the sky is closed, a vault golden like the desert.

Onnes closes his eyes. 'Before I met you,' he says quietly, 'I thought no one could ever understand me.'

*

On the third day, the sand settles, and the world looks burned. Slaves sweep the dust from floors and walls, slowly revealing the images under it. The head of a bull appears before the rest of its body; flower petals float on the walls without their stems.

Down by the citadel the streets are busy, but the royal road is quiet. Semiramis follows it, past the obelisk and the Northwest Palace, until she reaches the two temples that sit at the foot of the western wall. She enters the house of Ishtar, dodging prophetesses in white and red robes. A sweet smell drifts from the censers. Groups of supplicants are clustered around the courtyards, and Semiramis slides past them, through a narrow door that opens onto a small portico, where each column is covered with prayers: they are hymns to the goddess, 'she who transforms men into women'.

She finds Ninus as he is talking to two priests dressed in female clothing. Onnes has told her he likes the chaos of the temple as a respite from the silence of the Northwest Palace. Sensing Semiramis' presence, Ninus turns. With a quick wave of his hand, he sends the priests away. They bow and disappear, soft-shoed and reverent. The portico grows quiet. Semiramis and Ninus look at each other.

'You have sand in your hair, my king,' she says, resisting the strange impulse to brush it away.

He smiles. 'It is a miracle I don't have sand on every inch of my body, after the storm.' He seems calm, less restless than usual, as if the prospect of the imminent campaign is soothing him. 'What do you need?'

'You are leaving soon. I have come to ask you to look after Onnes.' Ninus raises his eyebrows. 'He can be . . . reckless,' she adds, in spite of herself, aware that she is echoing what Sasi once called her husband.

Ninus makes a fond expression, as though Onnes' flaws were the most precious jewel. 'He has always been like that. There is nothing I can do about it. Believe me, I have tried.'

'He is even more reckless when it comes to protecting you.'

She can tell that he is annoyed by the boldness of her statement, his displeasure showing on his face like ripples in the water. 'Do you know how he broke his nose?' he asks. She shakes her head. 'Ilu's sons were taunting me during a feast. Everyone was there, my father included. They didn't care: Assur was the prince everyone wanted to impress, not me. Ilu's sons called me weak. They said I might be able to read but couldn't even hold a spear properly. Onnes stood from his couch and banged his head into Bel's, then did the same to Sargon. It was a mad thing to do in front of my father, but that is how Onnes is: mad, because he isn't afraid to be hurt. Ilu dragged him away and threw him into one of the storage rooms by the Great Northern Courtyard. Later, Bel and Sargon beat him up so badly that, when I finally found him, there was blood everywhere, on the floor, on the walls.'

Her chest is hurting. Her skin feels worn and bruised. She is in another storage room, one halfway across the empire, in the small village of Mari. She steadies herself against a column. 'I don't want Onnes to die for you,' she says.

'I am his king. He should be ready to die for me.'

'I know.'

'I don't want him to die for me either,' he admits. 'But I don't have the power you think I have. *When the gods created mankind, they also created death, and they held back eternal life for themselves alone. Humans are born, they live, then they die –*'

'*– this is the order the gods have decreed*,' she finishes.

Ninus is looking at her with soft, inquisitive eyes. It is unsettling how he carries his feelings in his hands, so openly that others could snatch them away if they wanted to.

'Please, my king,' she says. 'Remember to protect him.'

He doesn't nod, but he doesn't need to: she knows he will do anything for Onnes. When she was a child it was her greatest wish to have someone who loved her so much that he would protect her from any danger. But life wasn't kind to her, so she became that person for herself.

Ninus keeps looking at her, and she feels a strange pull towards him. It would be so easy to indulge it. To take one step closer to him and then . . . And then what? She doesn't know. She bows to him and leaves.

*

Their last night together: Onnes orders the slaves to leave the courtyard as they are eating. In a corner, close to the well, his armour has been polished, his weapons displayed on a table, gleaming and sharpened: an iron and silver forged sword, a bronze pointed helmet, a double sheath decorated with lions holding a dagger and whetstone, spear heads glowing like mountain peaks under the moonlight.

Zamena has prepared a sweet vegetable soup, which is still untouched in their bowls. As the slaves' soft steps fade, Onnes sets aside his cup and stands by Semiramis' couch. He touches her neck, cups his palms around her shoulders. She starts undressing him, but he stops her, kneeling by the couch, and opening her legs, until he is pleasuring her, and she has to cover her mouth with her hand to be quiet, or be heard by everyone in the citadel.

When he stops, he lies back next to her, hair unkempt and lips glowing. The soup is cooling, its smell growing fainter. She looks at his profile in the dark. The ridge of his nose is slightly crooked, where Ilu's sons must have broken it. She had never noticed it before.

'Let me come with you,' she says. 'Do not leave me behind.'

I have built a life here. What will happen to me, if you leave? Maybe Ninus might have heard her thoughts, but Onnes can barely acknowledge his own.

'No,' he says. 'This is our war to win.'

Above them, the moon shines like a precious pearl. Her thoughts keep growing in the dark, but she does not share them. Next to her, Onnes drifts to sleep. He is still, like a corpse; it is only when she is beside him that he can sleep so.

There are no sounds, except their quiet breathing.

She watches his face, memorizes each line, each bit of skin, until she feels he is safely tucked into her mind. When she finally falls asleep, the gods are already parting the sky with their fingertips, revealing the light of dawn behind the veil of darkness.

*

The army leaves under a sky the colour of dusty gold. Hundreds of soldiers are gathered by the city gates, surrounded by cavalry and scythe-bearing chariots. The people of Kalhu cheer, whispering promises of riches and glory. Semiramis stands at the foot of the gateway, right under one of the giant human-headed bulls. She rests her hand against the stone, thinking about Onnes' face as he said goodbye to her. He didn't reassure her that he was coming back, didn't ask if she was afraid. And she didn't complain, knowing he had married her exactly because she knows how to float, no matter how deep and dangerous the waters.

The drums begin to beat and the men at the head of the army mount their chariots. She looks at Onnes as he soothes his restless horse. He doesn't look back. The soldiers are beating on their shields with their spears, their bodies moving in unison under the sun like a creature with a thousand heads.

'Shamshi-Adad the Fifth, King of the World, King of the Universe!' the soldiers shout.

Ninus makes his way to the chariot that is waiting for him at the head of the army. He looks different in his armour, older. His face gleams, as if he were god-born. He steps onto the chariot and turns, scanning the crowd as they cheer. His eyes find Semiramis, with a strange, haunting expression. It strikes her that this might be the last time she sees him. She bows to him slightly just as he turns and takes the reins of the chariot, leading his army away from the citadel, onto the endless road that will take them to Balkh.

BOOK III

821–818 BC

Since you must do this, I must go with you.
Let us leave. Let our hearts be fearless.
From The Epic of Gilgamesh

20.

Ninus, King of the World, King of Assyria

Balkh, capital of Bactria

Ninus bends over the water, looking at his shadow as it gently floats away from him. It makes him think of the ancient poems: *I looked into the water. My destiny was drifting past.*

Next to him, Onnes washes his face. Water drips down his neck, traces paths towards the scars on his chest. He pushes his hair out of his eyes, then lowers himself into the stream. Ninus does the same. As the water washes away the smell of war, he feels a sense of calm: he is here with his brother, the only person he trusts, and nothing else matters. As always, the feeling is accompanied by fear of the moment when it will go away.

'Will you burn my body, when I die?' Onnes asks, breaking the silence.

'When you die,' Ninus says, 'I will be dead as well. We will be together in death just as we are in life.'

Beyond the trees, the walls of Balkh loom, like a giant creature of sand. Beneath them lie hundreds of dead Assyrian soldiers. Their camp is spread out in the forest, or what remains of it. It reeks of pain and hopelessness, and soon they will have to go back to it.

Ninus sits up. Onnes is staring at him with a dead look, the same he has whenever he is exhausted. He finished his opium weeks ago, and Ninus knows he hasn't been sleeping. He puts a hand on Onnes' back, feeling the slow, tired heartbeat. 'We have grown up longing to rule the world,' he says, 'and now we are turning it to dust.'

Onnes shakes his head. His hair is darker in the evening light, wet strands falling into his face. 'You must not think so,' he says. 'You fight because that is what you were trained to do. You conquer, because you are a king.'

As little comfort as the words should bring, they calm Ninus. He lets his head tilt so that it touches Onnes' shoulder. Onnes' body is always cold, even on the hottest nights. Ninus can feel the warmth of his own skin on him, like a fever. Above them, the passage of the clouds is quiet and soothing. It seems impossible to feel such harmony with the world in this vicious place of death. And yet they have found this corner of peace.

A cloud moves past, revealing a handful of stars. In the morning the wind will come, and they will drift away, like withered leaves.

*

It has been worse than they thought. They crossed the Zagros mountains into a land so arid that all they could see were dried lakes and abandoned ziggurats. They passed through the kingdom of the Medes, where rocks the colour of the moon were covered with the tribes' signs.

Then, out of the Assyrian Empire and into the wilderness. Access to Bactria was a bloodbath: the Bactrians let them into their country, hiding in walled cities built on top of rocky hills. Then they met Ninus' army in narrow passes where Ninus couldn't attack in full force, as his men were stuck in crevices that felt like the walls of the underworld.

Those days still ring like nightmares in Ninus' head. Screaming soldiers trying to climb the rockface, like cockroaches. Bodies of men and horses twisted unnaturally on the ground – he had had to walk over them to get to the end of the pass, to climb a mountain of his own dead men. The Bactrian king had pushed them back into a plain that, by the end of the day, was painted crimson. It was as if the soil were crying red tears.

For the counterattack, Ninus had split his forces into three groups, led by Ilu, Onnes and himself. They surrounded every city, cut the ropes used to collect water, so that the people were forced to retreat further and further into their homeland. They pulled back from one stronghold to another, until all that was left to take was Balkh. But 'the mother of all cities' refuses to surrender. Inside, the Bactrians have food and water enough to last years. Its walls are too high even for the Assyrians' siege-engines. Their war equipment is too deadly. An endless attack that Ninus can either abandon or continue to the death.

A faint sound rises from Balkh, like a song. Foreign people, praying to their gods. Ninus imagines skinny children running about the moonlit streets until their mothers catch them, men lingering outside the bakeries, hungry for warm bread, the sounds of the armoury, the hisses of burning metal being quenched in water.

An ordinary city, filled with ordinary people, all of whom wish Ninus and his army dead.

*

He dines in Ilu's tent. Cold meat and a jug of beer, passed between the two of them. Ilu's helmet and armbands gleam faintly in the light. His armour is rich, with sparkling inlaid gems: he always goes into battle wishing to be singled out.

They are tired and don't speak. At last, when the meal is over, Ilu turns to him. 'You are fighting well. Your father would be proud of you.'

Ninus looks at him. When he was still prince, years before his father was murdered, he had walked into his mother's apartments to find her sitting on a stool. Ilu was standing behind her, his hands smoothing her long, wavy hair. It was an intimate gesture, one of a lover, and Ninus had thought of his father, betrayed by his second in command.

'How do you know?' he asks Ilu now.

Ilu's expression, for once, seems honest. 'Because I am proud of you.'

*

The night is black and rich with stars, campfires smoking thinly, rising in the dark like spirits. Onnes is standing by the edge, looking at the city they can't seem to conquer. Ninus walks to him.

'How long shall we keep going?' Onnes asks. He has bound his hair back with a piece of brown leather. His jaw is clenched, the muscle pulling at the skin as if to pierce it.

'How long *can* we keep going?' Ninus says.

Onnes keeps silent. When they were stuck in the narrow passes, he and Ninus had fought together, two bodies as one. There were moments when Onnes raised his arm and Ninus felt like it was his, when a blade cut Ninus' cheek and he heard Onnes scream. Shalmaneser believed that violence is the strongest way to intimacy, stronger even than lovemaking. *When you fight side by side with someone,* he used to say, *it is as if you carry each other's souls.*

Ninus takes a deep breath. 'Ilu won't accept a retreat,' he says. 'He'd rather die on the battlefield.'

'Of course he would.' Onnes rubs his tired eyes. His face is all stark edges in the shadows.

'*War cleans the soul,*' Ninus says. 'Do you remember when my tutors kept saying it?'

'My soul is far from clean,' Onnes says.

Ninus reaches out and touches his wrist. His pulse is faint, as if his heart was barely alive. Onnes looks down at the place where their bodies are joined. Then his arm rips away, as fast as a snake. He grabs the dagger from Ninus' belt and throws it. Ninus follows it with his eyes. The blade flies and sinks into a young boy's neck. He has no helmet, no scale-armour . . . just a headband tied at the back: a Bactrian.

'Ambush,' Ninus says quietly, and before he can run back to his tent for his sword, more lightly armed archers appear among the trees. 'AMBUSH!' Ninus cries, drawing his dagger from the body of the Bactrian boy. He is wriggling on the ground, eyes like moons in the darkness.

Then, it is chaos.

The Bactrians are everywhere, the arrows ripping the air, setting the tents on fire. Assyrians swarm around their king, shouting, spears in hand. A hand seizes Ninus' shoulder, and he is thrown against a tree. He bends down, dodges the blade that swings to slice his throat. He cuts the man's knees and sees him fall without even glimpsing at his face. He can hear Ilu's voice – 'They are coming from the trees! Cut them down! *Cut them down!*'

Ninus runs back into the fight, head buzzing, the taste of iron in his mouth. He isn't even wearing his armour and feels eerily aware of his nakedness, his flesh so thin under his tunic. Arrows keep flying down on them. He lifts a dead body from the ground and uses it as a shield, advancing in the midst of the burning tents. A spear flashes out, sinks into the soft place just above his hip. He bends over, stumbles, presses his hands to the wound to drown the pain. Blood spurts weakly. He sees an arrow flying down on him and thinks, *This is it*, when someone's blade catches it.

'Come!' Onnes says. 'Follow me!' He grabs Ninus' hand and drags him up. Black smoke envelops them, a snake strangling its prey. There is a bearded head, separate from the body. They step over it. Faces appear in flashes, gasping, pools of sweat and spit.

Onnes stops by the stream beyond the camp, helps Ninus down. 'Wash the wound,' he says, but he is already doing it himself, cupping his hands into the water and pouring it down onto Ninus' flank. He lifts the tunic, and there is the open flesh, the veins and tendons visible underneath, pulsing slightly. Onnes presses his hand around Ninus' hip. Blood runs through his fingers and onto the ground.

'Stay here,' Onnes says, and then he is gone, back into the chaos.

Ninus tries to stand. He can't see anything. A figure runs out of the smoke towards him, and Ninus reaches for his dagger before the man collapses in front of him. There are arrows in his back like grotesque wings. He is an Assyrian, one of Ilu's. And not a man, but a boy, without a full beard yet. Ninus grabs his hand and squeezes it.

'Hold tight,' he says. 'Don't be afraid.'

The boy lifts his head. His eyes are wild with fear. Ninus waits for him to stop breathing. His own body is shaking, strength pouring out of him as he bleeds.

Overhead, the moon is gone. The gods must be grinning down at them. He leaves the boy by the stream, his hands thrust into the smoky air like claws. Then he stands and staggers back towards the battle.

21.

The Royal Council

Kalhu, capital of the Assyrian Empire

The Northwest Palace is silent, priests quietly staring at Semiramis as she walks past them. The scent of spring is all over the capital, buildings and statues striped by the late-afternoon light. In the Great Northern Courtyard, she stops. Rather than enter the throne room, where she can glimpse the king's mother dealing with suppliants, she turns left, under an archway that opens onto a long, narrow room, where tall torches burn thickly.

The walls are covered with battle scenes, Assyrian men waving the severed heads of their enemies, defeated people being pushed into a river. Seats and couches are set around a table, where four men are sitting. She recognizes Ilu's younger son between Sasi and the prince Marduk, and opposite them a priest, eyes coated with kohl. Semiramis has seen him before, in the temple of Nabu: he is the *bârû*, the seer who charts men's destinies. They all fall silent when they see Semiramis.

'I've come to take the place of my husband,' she announces.

They stare at her. The *bârû* draws a sharp, shocked breath.

'Your husband isn't dead yet,' Marduk says, with a half-smile. His gaze slides over her body, assessing her as if she were a slave.

'What a *pleasure* to see you here, Semiramis,' Sasi intervenes. 'Did Onnes tell you to join us before he left?'

'Yes,' she lies.

'Fascinating,' Sasi says, his black eyes glittering. 'Sit, sit. The *bârû* was just telling us of his divinations.'

She takes the empty place on Sasi's right, ignoring the priest's outraged expression. Marduk's eyes never leave her. Ilu's son sits smirking, winding a lock of black hair around his finger. 'Do governors' wives sit in the king's council now?' he asks. 'Counselling on trades and war tactics?'

Semiramis turns to him. 'Before Nisat joined this council, queens didn't sit with kings and governors. Yet now would you deny her a seat in this room?'

'But you are no queen, are you?' Ilu's son taunts.

Sasi chuckles. 'She is right. We mustn't always fight change, Sargon, sometimes it benefits us.'

'Of course you speak like that, Eunuch,' Marduk says. 'You are a foreigner. If King Shalmaneser hadn't thought you were useful, you'd be in a pleasure house down in the citadel.'

Sasi's smile doesn't curl. 'No one here is a true Assyrian, my prince, except Sargon.' He bows to Ilu's son, then looks back at Marduk. 'You are from Babylon, Semiramis from the province of Eber-Nari, I am Phoenician, and the *bârû*, I believe, comes from a village on the south border of the empire.' He nods to the priest, who blushes violently. 'Why pretend we are different from what we actually are?'

No one answers. Sasi's smile widens. 'Well, then,' he says, 'shall we begin?'

Semiramis sits back in her chair, feeling the precious carvings under her fingers.

Sargon shrugs. 'The sooner we start, the faster I can be away from here,' he says.

What a fool he is, Semiramis thinks. *He doesn't understand that a seat in this council is a gift*. She straightens her back, raises her chin. She is poised, as if before a fight.

They start with the war. Another city of the Bactrian kingdom has fallen. The Assyrian army has cut the rope the fortress needed to collect water from outside the walls, then used siege-engines to pluck the city. A war tactic often employed by Ashurnasirpal, as Ilu's son points out. 'That will make for a most interesting bas-relief,' Sasi comments gleefully. Semiramis can't help but think of Onnes' face as he spat out, *What does Sasi know of war?*

But the city of Balkh still stands. They have not received news in weeks, and Sasi suspects his spies have been held in the camp for need of more Assyrian men.

'Find some others, then,' Sargon says lazily.

Sasi turns to the *bârû*. 'What do your readings suggest?'

The priest sits up, a severe expression on his face. 'My latest reading of a lamb's colon has been unfortunate,' he announces. 'The coils resembled the face of Humbaba, the guardian of the Cedar Forest.' He looks at them gravely. 'It is an omen that a usurper will soon rule this land.'

Sasi opens his eyes wide, in what Semiramis doubts is genuine shock, but Marduk laughs. 'Nonsense,' he says. 'We have no time to listen to his disastrous premonitions.'

When it is his turn, he shares the news from Babylon: his father is keeping the peace with Assyria, while his brother is trying to expand the territories to the south.

'As long as he respects the Assyrian border . . .' Sasi says.

Marduk laughs. 'My brother is no diplomat. You have grown too used to your king.'

Sasi raises a brow but, rather than retorting, he calls to the courtiers waiting outside the room. They slip into the room, one after another, reporting on the men who come and go from the city, the goods they bring, the crimes they have committed.

A priest recounts the movements of celestial bodies.

An apprentice physician brings a new medical catalogue: he wrote it as he observed the activities of the high priests of the goddess Gula. 'It is an attempt to classify medical knowledge,' he says. 'It has sections on skin diseases and battle wounds, infertility and illnesses of the mind.'

Sargon claims there is no such thing as an illness of the mind, but Semiramis notices that Sasi keeps the catalogue for himself as he dismisses the apprentice.

Once the meeting is over, everyone leaves, except Marduk. He stands by the door, and when Semiramis tries to walk past him, he brushes his hand against her neck. 'I am glad you have joined us,' he says. 'At least now there is a pretty face I can feast my eyes upon.'

His smile reminds Semiramis of the one Simmas gave her before she ordered Onnes to cut off his hand. She bows mildly as she imagines smashing Marduk's face against the stone wall.

'I am glad I can be of use, my prince,' she says.

The next morning, when Semiramis walks into the council room, Nisat is standing by the king's chair. Two slaves linger in the shadows, trays in hand, but the men of the council are nowhere to be seen.

'I sent the others away.' Nisat stares at her, unblinking. 'Sit.'

Semiramis claims the nearest chair. Although the sun god is pouring his heat across the city, the room is chilly. It is as if Nisat draws all the warmth from around her.

'Onnes must be proud of you,' the queen starts, 'sitting here, usurping his place.' Her eyes linger on Semiramis' bracelets. She has covered the thin faded scars on her arms with a powder Ribat has given her, but still, no matter how richly she is dressed, she always feels like a beggar in front of the queen.

'I am sure he will be,' she replies, 'when he comes back from the war.'

'*If* he comes back,' Nisat corrects her. She pours some wine for herself. Then, after the smallest hesitation, she pours some for Semiramis too. 'When Shalmaneser went campaigning he always promised me to Ilu. The second in command. I didn't like that. You can't take a step lower once you are at the top. You must fight to keep your place.'

Semiramis thinks about Ilu punching Ninus' face in the shadows of the training ground, about his blade glinting against Onnes' neck. 'I don't think Ilu would make a good husband, my queen,' she says.

'Oh, he's been loyal enough to me.' What she means by that, Semiramis can't say. 'Who do you think you'll marry if Onnes doesn't come back from the war?' Nisat asks. 'Surely you won't go back to your village.'

'I'd rather not,' she says flatly.

'Then what? You will stay here, a woman unmarried in the capital?'

'I'll seduce someone with my beauty,' Semiramis says. When Nisat doesn't smile, she adds, 'Some of us are born into the right families. Others resort to whatever means we have.'

'You are very resourceful.'

'I have to be.'

'I often find that the less people have been given in life, the more eager they are to prove themselves.'

'Does that come from personal experience?'

Nisat laughs. On her lips, the faintest shade of purple. 'My father was a cupbearer. He gave me to King Ashurnasirpal in marriage when I was ten.'

Semiramis flinches. She knew of Nisat's first marriage but had no idea the queen was only ten. A child. 'Your father must have been an ambitious man.'

'No more than others. Everyone in this court would sell their children to gain favour with the king. When the time came for Ashurnasirpal to marry, my father pointed out that I was young but I was the cleverest child in all of Kalhu, and the most obedient.'

Semiramis tries to picture her. Small and pale, with the biggest blue eyes and words that could cut you if you came too close.

'Was he right?'

She smiles, though there is no warmth in the expression. 'My father was always right. I owed my obedience to my husband, and no one else. I tolerated his cruelty, told him every secret I could gather, and welcomed his children as if they were my own. Soon, I became his closest adviser.'

'And when he died, you married his son.'

Nisat drains her wine, then says, 'You said yourself that we resort to whatever means we have. Besides, it was not a betrayal. Shalmaneser needed someone to teach him how to rule, and I was there for him. I made him king.'

They look at each other. The words hang between them. If anyone else spoke them, it would be treason. But who can accuse Nisat of such a thing, without having to pay the consequences? *She can't have been beautiful as a girl*, Semiramis muses, *but there is something in her face, cunning and wisdom, that makes one want to be close to her.* Danger, tempting you like a charming lover.

A courtier appears from the throne room. 'There are envoys from Babylon waiting, my queen.'

Nisat stands, adjusting her headdress. 'Duty awaits,' she says, keeping her eyes on Semiramis. 'Or maybe you want to sit on the throne in my stead, since you are so eager to take part in the empire's business.'

Semiramis smiles, as charmingly as she can. 'You said it in the temple of Nabu, don't you remember? I will never be queen.'

*

That evening, Ribat brings her lamb and *pita* and a plate of dates soaked in honey. She isn't hungry, but she forces herself to eat. The day is vanishing like a shadow at night. The animals on the walls of the portico are blurred, yet she has long learned their shapes: wild horses running between palm trees, goats with horns as long and sharp as bronze swords, deer running straight into hunters' nets. Ribat is crouched, reading some inventories.

'Did you know that Nisat was ten when she married Ashurnasir-pal?' Semiramis asks.

Ribat looks up. 'Her father was a cupbearer,' he says, with the smallest shrug. 'People say he had great influence on the king.'

She drinks from her cup of sweetened wine. She feels restless, looking for something, though she isn't sure what. A story that casts the queen in her true light, perhaps, or a glimpse into her feelings. She stands, leaning against the low brick parapet to look down at the Nabu temple.

The queen's greatest pose is that she never feels untouchable while acting as if she is, with her knowledge and power, allies and ruthlessness. Every thought of hers, a dagger in the dark. Semiramis wonders if she has always been so, even as a little girl. But maybe Nisat was never a little girl.

'She had a brother once,' Ribat says. 'He died as a child, a few years before she married.'

The darkness of the night is coming, plunging into the room like an unwanted visitor.

'I had a brother too,' Semiramis says quietly. She had never mentioned him before.

Ribat puts the inventories aside. 'Is he dead?'

She remembers Amon laughing, eating in the courtyard, his knees covered with dust and his fingers sticky with dates. Sometimes, when she went out at night, he waited for her, making sure she came home safely.

'No,' she says. 'But I am dead to him.'

*

Council meetings bleed into each other. The days pass, and Semiramis spends her mornings with Sasi's spies and Nisat's diviners, listening to the endless disputes of the day. In the evening, she trains alone in

Shalmaneser's palace, testing different swords, throwing spears against wooden targets.

Time passes, and the news from Balkh becomes scarcer still. The *bârû* starts sharing the most disastrous prophecies. Nisat firmly claims that no news is better than bad news. 'At least we know that my son isn't losing.'

'That isn't the same as winning,' Semiramis comments, but Nisat silences her with a look so sharp it could have cut out her tongue.

At night, she falls asleep thinking of Onnes, though Ninus always creeps into her dreams too. They fight in rivers of blood, holding on to each other desperately. Semiramis' hand tries to grasp them, but the crimson waves carry them beyond her reach. Then Ninus turns and sees her. *Help us*, he says. *We are drowning.*

She wakes with a jolt, heart hammering. The room is grey, the colour of ghosts, of a dawn without sunlight. Her nightdress is drenched with sweat.

Help us.

'What do you want me to do?' she asks, hating the fear in her voice.

But, of course, they are too far away to answer her. Her husband and her king. If one of them dies, she knows he will drag the other down with him.

*

A long line of people is forming in front of the Ishtar temple, children holding their mothers' hands and thieves trying to cut the line, sliding seamlessly between the hungry citizens. Semiramis stands behind baskets of fresh-picked dates, fragrant bread and honey cakes. On her left, Ribat and Ana are busy drawing jugs of beer, which they distribute to the people when it's their turn in line.

It's the month of Ishtar and, for the goddess's festival, Semiramis has decided to make donations to the temple. She has seen hundreds of commoners gather around the houses of the gods, hoping to be fed, as attendants wave them away, sending them back into the streets.

'Governors make donations to the temple in exchange for prophecies,' Ribat explained to her, but that is only one of the reasons that brought her to the temple. Those people with hollow cheeks and empty bellies remind her of herself: in her village, when there were shortages of food, everyone would hope for the governor's support. Some lived through those shortages thanks to his donations, just as others died, when the food didn't come.

The sun warms the courtyards, flooding the temple with gold. The line of people seems endless: men with foreheads creased like a turtle's skin, olive-skinned girls with painted eyes and mouths, boys as skinny as dogs. When it's their turn, they grab their flatbreads and cakes, mumbling for Ishtar to bless Semiramis, the governor's wife. A thin man touches her hand, whispering words she cannot catch, before disappearing into the crowd.

'He said it is good fortune to touch a woman blessed by the gods,' Ribat explains. 'He called you . . .' he hesitates over a word, lowering his voice '. . . *sēgallu*. Woman of the Palace.'

'Woman of the Palace?'

'Yes.' Ribat nods. 'It is a great honour, a title that belongs to the king's mother too.'

'And what do you call a woman who rules in her own right? A queen?'

Ribat thinks about it. 'A ruler is a *šarru*,' he says, weighing the words carefully. 'So a female ruler must be called a *šarratu*. But that is only for goddesses or queens of foreign lands. No woman has ever sat on the Assyrian throne.'

It is true. No woman has. And yet what did the diviner in Mari tell her? That a woman will rule over Babylon, that she will be greater than the kings of the earth. Those words had felt like a promise, and Semiramis still carries them inside her, like a light.

When the line starts thinning, she makes her way to the inner part of the temple. Corridors and rooms are empty, except for a couple of attendants who are sitting in the shade, jugs of beer in hand. At the entrance to a dark chamber that radiates heat and incense, she stops. The *bârû* is inside, praying. His tunic is embroidered with crescent moons and eight-pointed stars: the moon god Sin and the Queen of Heaven side by side. Semiramis waits, until he senses her presence.

'I know why you have come,' he says. Though his head is hidden by a cloud of incense, his voice is as clear and sharp as a knife slicing flesh.

Semiramis takes a step forward. Her eyes slowly adjust to the shadows. The walls of the chamber are carved with images of the goddess and her lions. On a table, there is a collection of clay tablets, the guides for reading omens and the gods' prophecies.

Well, then, she thinks, *will you give me what I want?*

'You have made offerings to the temple,' the *bârû* says. 'And now you expect a prophecy in return.'

'Yes.'

'There is nothing for you here, for you are a woman. You already know your fate.'

She feels a pang of anger, followed by hopelessness. It is an ancient feeling: that no matter what power she might achieve, it will never be enough. 'I sit with the king's councillors in the Northwest Palace,' she says sharply. 'My husband is the governor of Eber-Nari, and the closest adviser to the king.'

'But you are a woman still.'

'Are all women's destinies doomed to be the same?'

'You know they are.'

You are wrong, she thinks. She turns her back to him and leaves the room. In the main courtyard, supplicants are still whispering their reverent thanks to the governor's wife. Semiramis lingers, listening to their chant.

My name is on their lips, not the bârû's. *He believes I am worth nothing because he cannot see beyond what he has always seen. He will not see a change until he is forced to do so.*

What had Ribat called a queen? A *šarratu*, a woman who rules in her own right. A leader. A conqueror. A ruler.

*

She invites Sasi to dine in her palace. They sit in the courtyard on couches with embroidered pillows, while Ribat serves them a spicy fish soup. The leopard is unsettling the eunuch, as much as Sasi tries to hide it.

'I remember how this palace was before it became Onnes',' he says, looking around as he edges away from the leopard on his couch. 'It belonged to a man called Dayyan-Assur, one of the closest generals of King Shalmaneser.'

'Yes,' Semiramis says. 'Onnes told me about him.'

'Dayyan was killed under the city gate by Ninus' brother,' Sasi says ruefully. 'A pity. Assur used to look up to Dayyan when he was a child.'

'Children can't remain innocent for ever,' she says.

'Especially in this world.'

The air is cool, and the ornamental bulls are majestic in the light of the torches. Onnes has been gone for more than two months. Outside, the green shoots are sprouting with the first autumn rains. In the month of giving, Anu, the most compassionate of all the gods, watches humans from the high heavens but doesn't interfere. It is a blessed month, before the crueller gods take over.

'You believe other places are different?' she asks.

'I believe they are. *City of blood, full of lies, full of plunder.* That is what Israelites in the west call this place. I kept hearing it when we were deported, and I used to imagine a city of pain and darkness. Who would have thought I'd find myself so at ease in such a place?'

'Nothing good comes with ease,' she says. 'You built a life here.'

He smiles mischievously. 'You think too highly of me. Fate plays its part, too.'

She sips some beer. 'Do you really believe that?'

'Yes. Fate always leads us where we are meant to be.' He is quiet for a moment, enjoying a dramatic pause. 'I wonder what you are bound to become.'

Her leopard stands. Semiramis lays a hand on her back, feels the slide of muscle over bone.

Sasi sighs and continues, 'In the Ishtar temple there are thousands of clay tablets with prophecies written on them. Every year the gods speak, and the scribes write down men's destinies.'

'I asked the *bârû* to foretell my future, but he believes there is nothing to say to a woman,' she says, more stiffly than she wants to.

'He once said the same to the king's mother,' Sasi says.

'And?'

'And she proved him wrong. Now the *bârû* obeys her in everything and recites to her the oracles that reveal the fate of every Assyrian king.'

'What does she do with such knowledge?'

'She shares it,' he says, with a slight smile. 'With me.'

She wonders why he is telling her this, and whether a trick is coming. She keeps her face carefully expressionless. 'Any prophecy of interest?'

'Oh, yes. Here is my favourite.' He glances around, making sure no one is listening to them, then recites:

'The raging flood,
the king destined for joy and grief
shall make Assyria bleed
with his brother's blood.
He shall die young and forgotten,
at the hands of his own madness,
To the gain of his wife.'

The torches light his face, and his smooth skin glistens. He is surveying her, waiting for a reaction. She blinks, takes in each word. *The king destined for joy and grief.* Isn't that what Gilgamesh was called before he went mad?

'Which king does the prophecy refer to?' she asks.

'Priests don't tell.'

'And you think this speaks of Ninus?'

'Who else?' he says. '*Shall make Assyria bleed with his brother's blood.*'

'Other kings have killed their brothers,' she says cautiously. 'And Ninus has no wife.'

Sasi's mouth twists into a wry smile. 'We can easily speak of the past and present, but who can tell the future?'

For a moment she wishes he would stop speaking in riddles and share what he truly thinks, but then it occurs to her that maybe his real thoughts are hidden from himself, too, buried in a place he has forgotten how to access. She picks a bite of fish and feeds it to the leopard.

'Sometimes the past can be equally unreadable,' she says. '*Lots are drawn by the gods' will. From former days only empty air remains.*'

'"The Ballad of Former Heroes".' He nods sagely. 'A song sung as men drink in front of the fire, seeking warmth in the great heroes of the past. If they vanished too, despite shining so brightly in their lifetime, then who are we to complain?'

'Not everyone vanishes,' she says, because she doesn't like his tone. It is as if he is saying: no matter what you achieve, you count the same as the others. 'The names of some survive the passing of time.'

He seems to read her mind. As always, her discomfort only makes him bolder. 'Indeed they do. But is memory a force strong enough to let them live again?'

22.

The Princess of Urartu and the Whore of Kalhu

She walks to the women's palace accompanied by her leopard and two guards. The walls are painted green, with bas-reliefs of Ishtar and her sister Ereshkigal, queen of the underworld. At the entrance, the guards open the heavy doors for her.

In a large, sun-dazzled courtyard, women are reclining on feasting couches. Their hair is oiled and lustrous, their fingers heavy with rings. They are a strange mixture – young aristocrats without a male protector, villagers sent to the citadel for diplomatic marriages, foreign hostages, palace administrators, scribes and musicians. They all grow silent when they see Semiramis, one almost falling from her couch at the sight of the leopard. The animal studies them placidly, then pulls at the leash to take a bite of meat from the table. The women around it edge back, terrified.

'Come,' Semiramis says softly. 'Do not scare them.'

She finds her way upstairs, to a large, bare room that overlooks one of the smaller courtyards. A bronze bull head and a statuette of a winged woman are placed on the only ivory table, and the Assyrian bas-reliefs have been covered with tapestries that represent fires, thunder and storms. Semiramis wonders how the king's mother feels to have the statue of a foreign goddess in her palace.

'She is called Tushpuea,' Taria says, emerging from a corner of the room, following Semiramis' stare. 'She is the goddess my people pray to most.' She stands straight, eyes steely, her simple tunic the colour of a dark bruise. Her fingers caress the goddess's wings, which are long with pointed tips, like a falcon's.

'She seems more benevolent than Ishtar,' Semiramis says.

Taria laughs. 'Everyone is more benevolent than Ishtar. Your gods are cruel.'

'Some more so than others.' The leopard stretches her long limbs, amber eyes glowing.

'Is she going to attack me?' Taria asks calmly.

Semiramis admires her steadiness. 'Not as long as I am here.'

'Why did you bring her?'

Semiramis shrugs. 'She becomes tired of the palace. She needs more space – she is a wild animal.'

'Assyrians kill everything that is wild.'

Semiramis smiles and lets the leopard free, removing the leash. The animal goes into a corner, rubs herself against the tapestries, slowly, seductively. Semiramis watches her. 'They are afraid of the chaos wild things bring. But I do not mind wildness.'

Taria nods, then sits on a soft-pillowed couch and gestures for Semiramis to take the other.

'So,' she starts, 'is your husband still alive?'

'I expect you know as much as I do about the war. You live in this palace with Nisat after all.'

Taria shakes her head. 'The queen does not like to share council talk with other women.'

'No, I expect not,' Semiramis concedes. 'That is why I have come. I wanted to ask you something.' Taria inclines her head, listening. 'I have been joining the royal council –'

'Yes, I have heard.'

'– and I think you should come with me.'

Taria raises a pale brow. 'I am a foreigner.'

'You are a princess. The prince Marduk sits in the council. Why shouldn't you?'

Taria looks at her. Slowly, she says, 'You know why. I am a hostage, not an ally. Besides, I have no wish to. They *despise* me. Just like they despise you.'

Semiramis shakes away the words. She has been thinking about an alliance, and Taria seemed to her the most sensible to make. There is fire in her, self-righteousness, which sets her apart from the other women of the palace.

'I am not looking for acceptance,' Semiramis says.

'What do you want, then?'

The answer to the question is easy. 'Everything.'

Taria's face makes her smile. It is as if the sun has forgotten how to burn. Semiramis stands and meets her leopard halfway across the room. 'I will come back tomorrow.'

'And if my answer is the same?' Taria asks.

'Then we will do something else,' Semiramis says. 'Have you ever seen the shows of *The Epic of Creation*? *Gilgamesh* is my favourite.'

'I do not know the story.'

Semiramis smiles. 'I will tell you.'

*

When she goes back to the women's palace the next day, Taria is waiting for her in the reception room. As soon as she sees Semiramis, she comes forward and holds out her hand to the leopard. To Semiramis' surprise, there is a piece of raw meat in it. Slowly, the leopard meets her. Semiramis watches as they remain still, assessing each other, before the leopard devours the meat in a single bite.

Taria looks up, her face as bright as summer. 'Let us go to the gardens,' she says.

They spend the day together. They walk up the steps of the ziggurat, cool their feet in the fresh water of the canals, pick the fruit from the plants over their heads. The terraces are rainbows of colours, yellow and pale green leaves that the jewellers copy when they make pendants for the richest necklaces. The leopard catches a bird and brings it to them, teeth bloody and tail lashing. From the top terraces, they can watch the round-boats woven from bundles of reeds as they are loaded and unloaded on the city quay, hear the shouts of the sailors. The sun throws sheets of bright light over the river, making it shine.

When the sun god starts his descent towards the earth, they go to the large portico surrounded by bronze sphinxes, where other women are seated, waiting for dancers and acrobats to perform the shows of *Gilgamesh* and *Adapa*. Taria and Semiramis take a couch between bushes of tamarisk flowers, keeping the leopard close. Around them, the women's clothes are as rich and bright as the plants: violet and sunset orange, green and sky blue.

The performers start with the myth of Adapa, the Sumerian man who was blessed by the god Enki with immeasurable intelligence. Summoned by the king of the gods, Anu, Adapa is warned by Enki not to eat or drink anything offered to him. When Anu realizes how clever Adapa is, he decides to offer him the food of immortality, which Adapa dutifully refuses. The performers sob as Adapa realizes what he has lost, and, when Semiramis looks around, she sees that tears fill the audience's eyes too.

'Adapa's refusal is the reason behind humankind's mortality,' she explains to a bewildered Taria. 'It shows that mortals do not deserve eternal life, because when it was offered to them, they refused it.'

The sun fades and the breeze grows stronger as the performers change for *The Epic of Gilgamesh*. Two beardless men play cymbals and kettle drums. Dressed as birds and scorpions, the actors move between the couches while the women accompany the music with claps and cries. When they quieten, one of the dancers starts the story:

'Surpassing all kings,
Powerful and splendid beyond all others,
Gilgamesh suffered and accomplished all . . .'

Gilgamesh, the king with divine blood in his veins, who had everything the world has to offer, except a friend he could call a brother. When he dreams of a stone falling from the sky and turning to warm flesh in his arms, his mother tells him that the boulder stands for another hero, a man named Enkidu.

'He will be your double, your second self,
A man who is loyal, the companion of your heart.'

The audience cheers. Gilgamesh and Enkidu are inseparable, fight the forces of the world together, defy the gods. Until Enkidu dies, and Gilgamesh grows mad.

'For six days, I would not let him be buried,
I thought, "If my grief is violent enough,
Perhaps he will come back to life."'

Above them, date palms and poplars shield them from the sky with their dark green leaves. The audience is wailing.

'They are all about immortality,' Taria says in a whisper. She is not crying, though her voice is rough. 'I did not think Assyrians were so terrified of death.'

Semiramis says nothing. She watches the dancers in silence, as they unveil the stories of those born of greatness, glory and tragedy bursting from their fingertips. It is only later, when they are walking back to their palaces, that a momentary sadness spreads over her at the thought of how happy and careless Gilgamesh and Enkidu were, before death took everything they held dear.

*

One morning she leaves the council meeting only to realize that she has left the inventories of Eber-Nari on the table. She crosses the Great Northern Courtyard, hoping that Sasi hasn't stolen them, and that Nisat is already gone. It is a pale day, the light carried by the god Shamash white and blinding. She hurries under the archway that opens onto the council room, then stops before going in. Voices float feebly to her. She takes a step forward, looks inside.

To her surprise, the prince Marduk is still there. The torches have been put out and the room is darker than usual. It takes her eyes a moment to adjust. Then Marduk groans, and Semiramis sees a woman in front of him, her back against the wall. Pale hair flashes like lightning in the shadows. Then Taria's head shifts and her eyes find Semiramis.

She hesitates for a moment too long. Taria draws a sharp breath and steps away from Marduk. Her long dress has been pushed down around her shoulders, revealing a necklace with the pendant of the winged goddess shining on her chest. She quickly covers herself, her cheeks flushed with shame. *Her gods are more prudish than ours*, Semiramis thinks.

Marduk turns. The look that passes over his face makes her freeze. It is hatred – mad and simmering. It goes away quickly, replaced by a laugh.

'Do you wish to join us?' he asks, reaching for his blue tunic. The lions embroidered on it are angry, showing their sharp teeth. Somehow it sounds more like a threat than an invitation.

'I will leave you,' Semiramis says. She quickly retraces her steps, back in the glaring light.

She is halfway across the courtyard when she hears Taria's voice. 'Wait.'

She does not wait. Taria catches up with her, blocking her way. Semiramis stops, looks at her. Her lashes are almost white in the light, her face red as if she has been slapped. For some reason, Semiramis feels betrayed, though Taria owes her nothing.

'Where are you going?' the princess asks. She is searching Semiramis' face for a reaction.

'To my palace.'

'You disapprove.'

'You can do as you wish. It doesn't concern me.' *If your wish is to be used then discarded, I won't stop you.*

Taria tilts her head. 'You are a good liar. But I don't believe you.'

'He looks down on you, you know that,' Semiramis concedes. 'Babylonians do not see Urartians as equals.'

Taria's eyes burn suddenly. 'And do you think your husband sees *you* as an equal? A common woman from the province he *owns*?'

Before I met you, I thought no one could ever understand me, Onnes had told her. Semiramis looks away. 'No. I don't think he does.'

Taria opens her mouth, closes it. Semiramis' words echo in the still air. Semiramis waits for their sound to fade, then says, 'I won't speak of this to anyone. I hope you will remember it.'

'Why? Because we are friends?' There is cruelty in her tone, though it is not directed at Semiramis. Rather it feels like a blade Taria is using upon herself.

'Because I know there are always consequences to pay for witnessing someone's secret in this place. And I have no intention of paying them.'

She turns and crosses the rest of the courtyard. This time, Taria does not follow her.

*

The next day, Taria does not come to her, so she goes to the training ground. Everything is neat and shining in the wide courtyards, blades resting against the walls. She grabs a spear, plays with it until it feels like part of her arm. Sometimes training by herself feels like a dance, trying different moves, imagining soldiers of dust coming at her as she slips through their lethal fingers. When she used to fight with Onnes, everything was different: the shapes around them felt stunted, familiar, yet deceptive. She was always on edge around him, waiting for him to do something unexpected. She smiles to herself as she throws the spear, thinking about the times he corrected her posture, his hand on her shoulder guiding her as if they were part of the same body, then quickly attacking her when her guard was slipping.

The spear flies and clatters to the ground. It is the sound that distracts her. Out of the corner of her eye, she glimpses a shadow moving towards her a moment too late. Before she can turn, a hand grabs the back of her neck, pushes her forward. She twists away, trying to break free, but the grip is like a claw. She is pulled up, turned around.

The prince Marduk's face looks back at her. 'I thought you might need someone to practise with, since your husband is away.'

He lets her go and she stumbles. 'I'd rather train alone,' she says, straightening. He is blocking the way out of the courtyard, so she moves closer to the walls to retrieve her spear.

He laughs. It is the same laugh he had when he cut down the lions in the arena. She grips the spear tightly and moves towards him.

He shakes his head. 'That is not the kind of practice I had in mind,' he says, amused. As fast as sunlight on water, he grabs her wrist and bends it, forcing her to drop the spear. She tries to shake him away, but he closes the distance between them. He looks like the cruellest of gods, his skin pale and unscarred. She can feel its heat, anticipates the burn. *Do not let him see your fear. Do not give him the satisfaction.*

'What?' He smirks. 'Didn't you come looking for me yesterday?'

She slaps him. The sound is like a whip. When he looks back at her, there is bright resentment in his eyes, as if she had just ruined a particularly entertaining feast. She moves aside but he seizes her dress and pushes her against the walls. Her head hits the stone. The courtyard goes out of focus.

'If you touch me, I will make you pay for it,' she gasps.

'I hope you will. I need some fun, and this place is killing me with boredom.' His face is closer, until his lips are on her neck. She closes her eyes and prepares to leave her body, to float in the place she used to go when her father hurt her.

'Mistress.' A voice echoes on the walls, quiet yet firm.

Marduk turns. Semiramis swallows, the world suddenly bright again. Ribat is standing in the courtyard, face red. Rather than stare at his feet, as he always does in public, he is looking straight at them.

'The spymaster is waiting for you outside your palace,' he says.

She knows he is speaking to her, but she seems unable to form words to reply. Her chest is hurting, as if her heart was trying to tear it apart.

'The eunuch can wait,' Marduk says.

'He is expecting you, Mistress,' Ribat insists. 'He was most displeased to see you were not there to welcome him.'

She jolts back to life. She pushes Marduk away, running towards Ribat. She reaches the corridor that leads outside and steps into its darkness. Marduk's laugh follows her, rotting in the air. Ribat's feet hurry on the polished stones. He says nothing as they walk from the training ground to her palace.

Semiramis fixes her plaits before stepping into the courtyard, steadying herself for the eunuch. But, when she walks into the light, the place is empty.

'Has Sasi already left?' she asks Ana, who is gathering the empty jars. Her mind is still struggling, her breath panicked. She hides it as best she can.

Ana frowns. 'He was never here, Mistress.'

Across the yard, Ribat blushes. Semiramis draws a sharp breath. Everything in her mind aligns, thoughts bright and sharp as if suddenly under the light.

'Leave us,' she tells Ana.

The girl casts a glance at Ribat but does as she is told. Her steps echo feebly, then fade. Semiramis turns to Ribat. He is standing at the entrance to the corridor, a strange expression on his face. It takes Semiramis a moment to realize it is anger.

'You saved me,' Semiramis says.

Ribat lifts his head. 'He would have hurt you.'

She moves closer to him. 'I have been hurt before. Do not think I cannot survive it.'

Ribat shakes his head. 'He would have hurt your reputation. You would have lost respect and power.'

She stares at him. She had not thought of this. She had expected Marduk to rape her, hit her, but had not considered what might happen afterwards. Ribat is right: Marduk could have stripped her of everything in a moment, if he'd wanted to.

Then another thought occurs. *Ribat intervened because if I lose everything, he does too. I am his way to a different life, just like Onnes is for me.* An endless rope, tied from person to person, that can be snapped in a moment.

The sky is darkening; the first stars come out, warm and bright like lamps. She walks to him and touches his wrist. His heartbeat flutters, like the wings of a nervous bird.

'How did you find me?' she asks.

'I always find you,' he says simply.

Their shadows slide over the floor, over the painted walls. It is just them under the stars, and the sounds of the city preparing for the night. Kalhu is never quiet. Doves sing, merchants yell, priests chant.

They remain side by side, in silence, while the city keeps whispering and the stars look at them from above.

*

She is woken by a panicked whisper.

'Mistress,' Ribat says. 'Mistress.'

She sits up. The covers fall from her, and the breeze presses against her bare skin. 'What is it?' She hears a deep, menacing growl from downstairs. 'Where is the leopard?'

'You must come,' Ribat says. 'Outside.'

She does not bother to cover herself. She runs downstairs, following Ribat, to the main courtyard, where her slaves are all standing, trying to tame the leopard. The stones of the paving are spotted with blood, and it takes her a moment to realize that the animal is bleeding from a cut in her flank. She snarls and spits, her jaws snapping as the slaves come too close. Semiramis crosses the courtyard, pushing Ana aside. The leopard stops. There is pain in her eyes and, when she steps forward, she limps. Semiramis kneels. She knows that if she goes any further, the leopard will be angry. So she lets her come to her. Her slaves and guards watch as the animal growls angrily then collapses, letting Semiramis touch her flank. She cries then, almost biting Semiramis' arm off as she assesses the wound. It isn't too deep, or too grave.

'Who did this?' she asks. Two slaves back away from her and she realizes that her voice is shaking with rage.

'There is more,' Ribat says.

They go outside, where the sky is shading to dawn. Pale yellow torches light the street between the governors' houses and their palace walls. By the side of the heavy wooden doors, the bricks are stained crimson. Writing, made with blood. Semiramis reads each sign slowly, tripping over the words. *Here dwells the Whore of Kalhu.*

'It is pig's blood,' Ribat says. 'He came in the night. I saw him and I could not see your guards so –'

'I asked them to watch my apartments,' she says, regretting her mistake. But she could not sleep without them outside her room.

'– so I sent the leopard hoping she would scare him, but he wounded her. I am sorry.'

She watches the writing grow starker as the sky pales. 'The prince Marduk,' she says. Ribat nods. She feels a sick anger as her throat aches where Marduk touched her.

'I will clean it,' Ribat says.

'No,' she says. 'Not until nightfall.'

'But the nobles might see,' he complains. 'Soon, the attendants of the temple will wake.'

'Yes, they will.'

All her life, people have taunted her. She has been called an orphan, a whore, a thief, a liar. So many times, she prayed that they would leave her alone. But she knows that her wish could never be granted. She is a woman who allows herself to dream. The world will always try to crush her. *Let them try*, she thinks, walking back into her palace. *Let them come.*

*

She summons Taria to her chambers in the evening, when the cool air fills the palace with its scent. The blood is still on the walls – Semiramis has ordered the slaves not to clean it until night comes. She welcomes the princess in the portico, bids her to sit on a cushioned couch. Taria looks pale, tired eyes surveying Semiramis warily.

'I assume you have seen the new decorations on my palace walls?' Semiramis asks. From her room comes the angry hiss of her leopard, though the animal does not join them. She is resting, her wound dressed and bandaged.

Taria's hands fidget in her lap. 'It was hard to miss. Aren't you going to order your slaves to clean it?'

'I wanted you to see it first.' She pours beer into two small cups, offers one to Taria. 'You were right. They despise me, just as they despise you.'

Taria brings her lips to the cup. She drinks, taking her time, then asks, 'Who is responsible?'

'I think you know who he is.'

Silence. A look passes over her face. 'I do not know what you are talking about.'

Semiramis leans forward, smooths the sleeves of her dress. 'The prince Marduk came to find me in the training ground the other day. He made me an offer, of sorts. My silence in exchange for his attention. I told him I had no interest in his attention, but of course he did not believe me. Men like him truly think that the world exists just to please them. Can you guess what he did next?'

Taria looks away from her, as if Semiramis had slapped her. 'I do not want to play this game.'

'It is no game. He tried to take me with force until I was called back to the palace.' Taria's fists are clenched. Her eyes are stubbornly fixed on the window. 'The next morning, the writing appeared.'

'You cannot be sure it was him,' Taria says. Her words are stones. It seems as if she is clinging to them as one clings to the edge of a cliff.

'My slave saw him.'

Taria turns to her, eyes flashing. 'And you believe him?'

She is hopeless, Semiramis thinks. It makes her sad, because she was starting to like Taria, more than she cares to admit. But now she sees that a friendship with another woman can be a weakness in the capital: men use it as a vulnerable point, pitting women against each other as if they were lions in the arena.

She rises. 'I want you to tell Marduk that if he calls me a whore again, or if he spreads lies about me, I will send my leopard into his room so she can devour him while he sleeps.'

Taria's eyes hold Semiramis'. 'Do you think this will scare him?'

'I don't. But it is the language of cruelty and threats, the only one he understands.'

'There are other languages he can speak.'

'No. There are other languages *you* can speak. But you are not like him.'

Outside, the slaves are cleaning the blood from the stone, red water dripping into a basin. Semiramis watches Taria walk away, along the royal road that takes her to Nisat's palace. Part of her wants to slap the princess, another part to run after her.

Her brother used to say that she always wanted to bend the world to her will. He was right. But some people cannot be bent.

And so she can either break them, or let them go.

23.

Semiramis, a Fighter

News arrives in the capital from the city of Balkh in the month of flooding.

Semiramis is sitting in the main courtyard when Ribat bursts inside, his hands red and chapped. It is cold, but the torches give them touches of warmth, licking the naked parts of their bodies: faces, hands, ankles. Her leopard lies at her feet, lashing her tail lazily. She is almost healed, the cut a fading scar.

'What is it?' Semiramis asks.

'There is news, Mistress,' Ribat says, breathless. 'From the city of Balkh.'

Her head snaps up. They haven't heard from Balkh in more than a year. 'Tell me everything.'

'Ilu's son has come back with messengers. He is about to speak in the marketplace.'

She stands quickly, wrapping a fringed cloak around her shoulders. 'Let's go.'

The marketplace is as crowded as Semiramis has ever seen it, every corner clogged with labourers and merchants, weavers and carpenters. Groups of slaves crowd around noblewomen; priests and priestesses stand in the sunset, their white tunics making them look like flocks of doves.

At the centre of the crowd there is a lean man with thick black hair and small eyes: Ilu's first-born son. His brother Sargon stands a step behind him. City guards force the people to give them space, pushing men and women back towards the stalls. Semiramis takes a place next to the priestesses, flanked by two of her guards. It takes a while before the chatter dies down – everyone is speculating, rumours racing from one mouth to the next.

When the square is finally silent, Ilu's son speaks: 'My name is Bel. I am our *turtanu*'s son. My father fights with our king under the gates of Balkh.' His voice rings in the air like a bronze bell.

'Does our king live?' someone from the crowd shouts.

'Our king lives,' Bel says, 'and our army has crushed the reign of Bactria.' Cheers and shouts. 'But the city of Balkh still stands. It is an ancient city, legendary in size and strength, and its walls won't be breached. The king of these foreigners has gathered an army to the number of four hundred thousand. He tried to destroy us with cunning in the open field, but when we answered with strength, he cowered and hid behind his walls. Our army still stands,' he pauses, as if considering his words, 'but to pluck Balkh we need new recruits.'

New men? The crowd erupts in questions and complaints. Kalhu is already weak – its food provisions scarcer, its defences vacillating. To send the remaining soldiers across the rivers, to a land so far away . . . If Urartu or Babylon attacked them, they wouldn't have the men to defend the city. The guards struggle to keep the crowd in place.

'We won't need more than fifty,' Bel shouts.

Semiramis is startled. Bel has travelled all the way back to the capital just to ask fifty men to join him? Then he speaks again: 'Climbers. Men as light as dancers and as silent as hunters. Our king promises wealth and reputation to those who wish to fight for him. I will personally take the names of those who will bring glory to Assyria, and I will lead them to Balkh. We'll leave at dawn in two days' time.'

They are all silent now. The cold sun fades and sinks between the temples. The marketplace slowly empties, as Bel disappears in the direction of the Northwest Palace, his brother and guards following him. The stalls are cleared, baskets filled with the few leftovers of the day – blemished fruit and palm hearts, handfuls of pistachios. Some children linger. They cast careful glances around, waiting for the best moment to steal something, then disappear in the narrow streets before anyone can punish them.

*

When she steps into the council room, Sasi and Bel are already there. Bel frowns when he sees her. Up close, he looks older than Semiramis remembers from the palace feasts. There are deep lines of worry on his forehead, and a bad scar that coils around his wrist. He stares at her, torn between confusion and annoyance.

'I expect you remember Onnes' wife?' Sasi asks, inviting him to bow to Semiramis.

Bel doesn't. 'I do.'

'Semiramis has been joining me in the council,' Sasi explains, 'helping me with some matters.'

'Does my husband live?' Semiramis asks.

'He does.'

'But he is in grave danger,' she prompts him.

'War is danger, yet we live and die for it.'

'You wouldn't be here if the war was going well. You are losing.'

Bel and Sasi exchange a glance. Bel hesitates before answering. 'That isn't what I said to the people.'

'But it is what you implied.'

His eyes fill with shadows. 'It is a massacre,' he admits. 'If we don't find a way to breach the city, our army will be destroyed.'

Her blood runs cold. She turns to Sasi, but the eunuch's expression is unreadable.

'The men who come with you should know the truth,' she tells Bel.

He doesn't answer her, though she knows what he is thinking: if he tells them, they will not come.

'Does the truth matter?' Sasi asks sweetly. 'The army needs climbers, and what is more glorious than fighting for our king? Whoever joins them will grow ageless. Songs will be sung about them, the people who fought against the mightiest city of the east.'

Bel shakes his head. How empty those words must sound to him, after he has seen his soldiers die on the battlefield.

'And if Balkh won't surrender?' Semiramis asks.

Neither can answer her.

*

She doesn't walk back to her palace until night falls. The citadel turns grey, shadows lengthening as the last few men move through it. A guard, scolding a child. Two noblemen, cloaks fluttering in the cold wind.

Sasi spoke of greatness and glory, but is that what war truly is? Are

196

campaigns as glorious as the bas-reliefs that cover every palace wall? Soldiers richly dressed, shooting arrows from their chariots, riding over lions and enemies alike, causing fear and wreckage wherever they go? Surely not. Surely war is blood and mud, cheating and back-stabbing, deeds that no poet would write about. *A massacre*, Bel had called it. And Onnes and Ninus are there, in the midst of it all.

A weight is pressing on her chest. A change will come soon, and she must act upon it, carve her own path before the gods weave her destiny for her. A line of 'The Ballad of Former Heroes' comes to mind, one that made her heart clench when Ribat first read it to her.

The whole of a life is but the twinkling of an eye.

It made her think of her mother, rotted at the bottom of a lake, and of all the times she felt death was near, so near she could feel all the light dim and the shadows darkening like spirits' fingers. Those words unsettled her, because there is no greater grief than living with no purpose than to go back to the dust. Why, then, do some men rise above others, like fires so great that the gods are forced to look down and take notice of them?

All women's destinies are doomed to be the same, the *bârû* had told her.

No, she thinks. *They aren't. Let the gods learn that.*

*

She finds Bel in the blacksmith's workshop of the artisans' quarter. He is giving orders to the bronze workers while he examines the long daggers that are arranged on the tables. He steps aside when he sees her, the frown deep on his face.

'I will come to Balkh,' she says, before he can speak. 'I will be one of your climbers.'

Bel raises his eyebrows. 'I have my climbers already.'

'Bring one more with you. I grew up in Eber-Nari, lived my whole life in the hills, climbing walls and slopes. I was the best and fastest in my village.'

'This isn't a game. This is war.'

'Is this what you told the men who came to you to fight?'

'They were men. Women can't fight.'

'You know I can. You've seen me train with Onnes in Shalman-eser's palace.'

'I have,' he says. 'And I have seen him kick you to the ground.'

'I always stood up again. He believed I was a good fighter because I wasn't afraid. Wouldn't you want someone like me beside you? Someone who isn't afraid?'

He turns to the furnaces. Behind him, the blacksmiths are casting them curious glances.

'I know you believe women are weak,' she says. 'You believe that I couldn't bear such a long journey and then a war. The only way I can prove to you that I can is if I come. And if for some reason I slow you down – though I assure you I won't – you can send me back. Once we get to the camp, it'll be my husband who decides if I can climb or not.'

He looks back at her, the firelight orange on his face. 'You are mad.'

'If you leave me behind, I will follow you,' she insists, 'all the way to Balkh. And then what will you tell the king?'

'I might execute you.'

She almost smiles. There is something about him that reminds her of the boy Baaz from her village: the arrogance, the empty threats. 'We both know you won't do that. My husband would make you pay. And, besides, execute me for what? There are no laws that say I can't come.'

'The code doesn't mention women at war.'

'Neither does it forbid it.'

He looks around. There is simplicity about him. Maybe his father might see it as dullness, he who is used to sitting with kings and bending their thoughts to his advantage. But to Semiramis it looks like hope.

'You may come,' he says. 'But if you slow us down, you will travel back. You will keep your word. And when we arrive at the camp you will tell your husband exactly what you told me. I won't be punished for bringing you.'

'You have my word.'

'We leave tomorrow. Meet me at the front gate with your own weapons.' And before she can say that she has no weapons of her own, he stalks away.

The cold morning sun filters through the door. Deeper inside the workshop it is all soot and sparks of fire. The daggers gleam on the tables, the handles inlaid with roaring lions. They seem to call to her, whispering promises of death. She thinks about her dream, about the ghost of Ninus begging her. *Help us.* He had blood on his hands, and when she had tried to wipe it away, it stained her too, arms, chest, everything.

The swords hiss as the workers quench them in water. Semiramis stays still. It doesn't take her long to become aware of a large shadow by the door, staring at her with small bright eyes. She turns to face him.

Sasi's face is impossible to read under a veil of mildness. He is wrapped in a purple tunic with sleeves longer than his arms. Only the tips of his fingers appear, pale and smooth as a baby's. 'I expected Bel would fight harder to oppose you,' he says, joining her inside the workshop. 'But I was wrong. A governor's wife, travelling with the *turtanu*'s son to go into battle.' He is amused by his own words and chuckles. 'I don't think I've ever heard a more curious tale.'

Semiramis forces a smile, though she knows that Sasi can tell when an expression isn't sincere. 'Isn't this place too far from the safety of the Northwest Palace for you?'

He slides closer to her. 'On the contrary, these alleys . . . this is where I feel most at ease. I grew up in a Phoenician city, Tyre. Do you know of it?'

'Yes.' It is one of the cities she had wanted to go to before Onnes came to her village, before her life changed for ever.

'The alleys are all narrow there,' Sasi says. 'Sticky as if covered with spilled honey. The houses are piled on one another like a bee-hive. You have to push people out of the way when you walk. It gives you a sense of chaos but also of protection. Assyrians don't like chaos, of course. I find the Northwest Palace – and all palaces for that mat-ter – too spacious. They leave people alone with their thoughts.'

She knows what he is talking about. Onnes' palace had felt the same the first time she had stepped into it. As always with Sasi, she wonders why he is here, and what she can do to be rid of him.

'You have come to convince me to stay in Kalhu.' She offers the words as bait.

He brings a hand to his heart, as if she had hurt him. 'You under-estimate me. I am merely concerned for your well-being.'

'Of course you are. Have you ever fought in a war yourself?'

'My talents lie elsewhere, I'm afraid. Besides, have you ever seen a eunuch fight? A priestess once told me I was fated to become a king's shadow.'

'She was right.'

He smiles in his childish, unnerving way. 'I wish you good fortune in Balkh, Semiramis. I will be praying for your return. You have been of good use for the king's council.'

'I will come back,' she says. She realizes, a moment too late, that she is telling herself so, as well as him.

'Oh, I am sure you will. You and I, we are alone in this world. Losing isn't an option for us.' He winks at her, then walks out of the workshop with his slow, crawling steps.

She rests her back against the wall, looking at the figures of the workers as they cast iron swords, dark against the glow of the fires. *Losing isn't an option for us.* After endless games and conversations, she finally understands why Sasi has taken an interest in her. *He thinks he and I are the same.* She almost smiles. *Let him think that. Anything to make him a friend, rather than an enemy.*

She makes sure that no one else is stalking her, then approaches a young man with a close-cropped beard and asks him to show her the newly forged daggers.

*

Back in the palace, Ribat is alone in the reception room, pretending to polish already-gleaming silver. Her leopard appears as soon as Semiramis enters. She seems angry, snapping her jaws when Semiramis tries to scratch her head. She lets her be and reaches for a cup of beer. There is a new dagger at her waist, inlaid with an image of the goddess Ishtar. Ribat glances at it, then goes back to the polished bowls.

'Bel has found his climbers,' he says. 'Or so the slaves whisper.'

She looks at his face, sees the tightening of muscles under the skin. The faint voices of Ana and Zamena cooking dinner in the courtyard drift to them. Usually at this time of the day she comes back from the training ground for her bath, where Ribat unplaits and brushes her hair as they discuss the council together, unpacking each bit of information. But not today.

'I have been thinking about Gilgamesh,' she says.

'Gilgamesh?' Ribat asks, puzzled.

'He was wrong,' she says. 'Immortality doesn't mean *living* for ever. It means surviving even after your heart stops beating and your body is burned. It means living in myth, in stories.'

He bites his lip. 'I am not sure death always leads to myth, Mistress. For most men, it leads only to ruin.'

'I *have* to go,' she says. The words ring in the room. 'There is no other choice.'

'You could stay,' he says. The leopard moves closer to him, as if taking his side. The courtyard turns to gold as the torches are lit and incense fills the air.

'When I was a child, I used to hate the water,' she says. 'People from my village said that my mother drowned herself in a lake, so every time I went swimming I thought the bottom was filled with dead bodies. I imagined their clothes clinging to their skin like fish scales, mouths and lungs filled with water. But I didn't like the fear. Fear paralysed me, held me down and took my breath away. So I forced myself to swim. It wasn't easy at first but, in time, it gave me strength. Every time something scared me, I made myself face it, until all the fear was gone.'

Ribat's face is dark in the firelight. He looks at his feet for a long time, then says, 'I understand.'

She reaches out and touches his hand. 'I know you do.'

*

They leave at dawn, the sun colouring the sky with brushstrokes of pale pink. Under it, the land looks blue, otherworldly. They mount the horses at the main gate, the city sleeping all around them. Semiramis is wearing one of Onnes' tunics, a long-sleeved garment that protects her skin from the heat of the deserts and the cold of the mountains. Her hair is plaited in thick braids wrapped tightly around her head and, over it, a turban tied at the nape of her neck. She feels the light weight of her spear against her back, and her dagger on her waist. Around her, the other climbers are humming with anticipation, faces blurred in the bluish light.

Bel rides first, his rich cloak stirring in the wind. They will take the road network towards the Zagros mountains, he explains. They will travel quickly and lightly, no more than a few supplies. They will live off food provided by the stalls and posting stations along the route, and what they will capture in enemy territory. The army has left boats made from inflated animal skins to cross the rivers, so they will follow the water course when they can to shorten the route.

Semiramis' body sways on the horse. She turns to look at the city one last time, temples and palaces like clouds against a lightening sky, then sets her eyes on the mountains in the distance, the whispers of gold and glory from the men around her like a prayer that guides her to Balkh.

When the gods assemble, they decide your fate,
they establish both life and death for you,
but the time of death they do not reveal.

From *The Epic of Gilgamesh*

24.

The Gate of the Netherworld

She enters the country of Bactria welcomed by corpses and pained whispers. The land seems deserted, yet the whispers keep following them, eerie, malignant. Semiramis looks at the trees, dark and sad against the silver sun, as they ride past empty cities made of shadows. Low clouds stream above them, and a treacherous wind makes the bare branches shiver.

It didn't take them long to understand they were in enemy territory. The Assyrian army has left nothing but ruins behind them. Cities have been burned and all that remains are villages nestled between rocks and streams. Bel has instructed them to hide their Assyrian clothes in case Bactrian soldiers are still hiding in the rock formations. They dutifully obeyed, though Semiramis can smell their fear at night, when they camp around the fire pretending to sleep, the whispers growing louder as the land grows darker.

They have travelled through the months of spring. The colours are different in the east from those of the capital, land stretching endlessly around them in stripes of black and green. Now summer has come, bringing no warmth with it. The mountains around them carry cold wind, and when it rains, everything becomes a dark blue-grey.

'We should find the camp soon,' Bel says one day.

They have entered a long, narrow pass filled with decomposed bodies. They fought here, Bel tells them, and lost many men. Most of their war chariots were destroyed. Semiramis can see broken wheels spread out among what should be dead men but have long lost any human shape. The sun makes the smell unbearable during the day, and in the evening, they must light fires to keep hungry animals away. The nights are black, with only a small slice of star-filled sky above their heads. It makes Semiramis feel as though she is in a gaping mouth, one that has swallowed men, rocks and fire.

When they finally ride out of the pass, they can see the tents of Ninus' army and, beyond, the mighty city of Balkh.

*

The smell around the camp is something Semiramis has never breathed. She lingers for a moment, looking at the wasteland around her.

'Don't let the stench scare you,' Bel says. 'Death lives with us here. You will grow used to it.'

But it is worse than that. It is the smell of bodies trapped *between* life and death, trying desperately to stay in the world of the living while they are dragged away from it. The air buzzes with a strange sound – a whisper? a breath? – as if they are violating something sacred.

'I am taking the climbers to my father,' Bel tells Semiramis. 'You should find your husband.'

She nods. She makes her way through the camp, past stinking latrines and lines of laundry, where tunics dance in the breeze, like birds of shadow. A group of soldiers is examining a dead sheep's liver. Clouds of flies move thickly around every tent. She walks to a man who is sharpening iron swords with a sandstone. There is a stain of old crusted blood on his cheek, but he seems not to notice.

'I have come to see my husband,' Semiramis says. 'The governor of Eber-Nari.'

The soldier's head snaps up. He stares at her as if she were a ghost.

'Do you not know where he is?' she asks, impatient.

His hands shake slightly as he puts down the sharpened sword. 'Onnes is with the king.'

'Take me to him, then,' she demands.

He leads her to a large tent in the middle of a clearing, then flaps open the entrance. It is spacious, with a couch and bed on one side, a table on the other. It looks much cleaner than the rest of the camp, though the smell lingers here too. Ninus is standing by the table, looking at a map drawn on a clay tablet. He is alone.

She clears her throat, and he turns, a scared sudden movement. Their eyes meet. For a long moment, he stares at her, speechless. 'Semiramis?'

His hair has grown longer: it is dark against his cheeks. He is wearing a short-sleeved tunic underneath a long-fringed shawl. She notices a small stain on his waist – blood had soaked through the bandages.

'My king,' she says. 'I was told Onnes was here.' She is aware of the lightness of her voice, as if she hadn't just crossed half of the empire to join them. She is about to explain herself when Onnes enters the tent behind her.

His eyes are bloodshot, and his cheeks hollowed. There are fresh cuts all over his arms, and an old gash on his neck is yellowish and infected. He walks past Semiramis without seeing her and joins Ninus at the table.

'Onnes,' she says. Quiet, tentative: the voice almost sounds as if it doesn't belong to her. He does not hear her.

'Brother,' Ninus says.

Onnes startles, as if brought back to life, and follows Ninus' eyes. This time, he stares right at her. There is a long and uncomfortable silence. Both Semiramis and Ninus wait for him to speak.

'You shouldn't be here,' he says. His voice is rough, a strangled sound.

She takes a step towards him. 'I've come to join Bel's climbers.'

He stares at her. Cold, unnerving. 'You shouldn't be here,' he repeats. 'You must go back to Kalhu.'

'Are you mad?' she asks. 'I can't go back.'

He looks at her blankly and then, to her horror, he screams: 'YOU MUST BE MAD TO COME HERE!' He turns his back to her and slams his hand onto the table. Semiramis looks at Ninus, but he seems as shocked as she is. Onnes' arms are shaking as he grabs the edge of the table, his knuckles as white as bone. Ninus reaches out and rests his hand between Onnes' shoulder blades. When Onnes doesn't push him away, Semiramis feels a pang in her chest.

'She can't go back now,' Ninus says. 'It's too dangerous.'

'Is she your wife or mine?' Onnes asks, between gritted teeth.

Ninus lets his arm drop. Semiramis' heart seems to be beating too slowly, as if crushed by a giant stone.

'I won't leave,' she says. 'I will climb and fight.'

Onnes turns to her. His rage seems to have gone – all his feelings seem to have gone – and now his eyes are emptied, as if someone had stolen his soul. 'You want to stay here and fight? Do as you wish. But you will die. We will all die in this place.'

He walks out of the tent. Semiramis and Ninus remain, looking at each other, speechless.

*

She sits at the edge of the camp, on a fallen tree that marks the boundary between the forest and the expanse of yellow grass that must once have been rich arable land.

Beyond it, Balkh stands proudly on a rocky outcrop. It is the biggest city she has ever seen, even bigger than Kalhu. Its walls are smooth and gleaming, as if kissed by the Bactrians' sun god; they are too high for siege-towers, the gates too thick for breaching. The city's front walls stand proudly over a not-so-steep slope, heavily protected by archers. Climbing through that route would be impossible, Semiramis notes. She can see that the army has already tried: bodies are spread all over the slope, dark smudges among the light green shrubs. The side walls, on the other hand, are nestled in a tall, steep ravine. It looks like a stairway to the heavens, the walls so high they almost reach the sky. There are archer posts in the form of stars to track attackers if they attempt to climb through that way, though it seems that not all are manned. *Of course they aren't. They know that no one is mad enough to climb that way.*

She watches the city for a long time, thinking. The branches of bare trees entwine above her, like dying lovers. Strange figures are carved into the trunks: horned animals, wide-eyed owls, and hands in prayer.

When she finally walks back to the camp, the low, creepy murmuring that has accompanied them ever since they entered Bactria follows her, like an angry spirit.

*

She eats with Onnes in his tent. The evening is quiet, soldiers sharpening their swords and spears. Onnes is sitting on his bed mat, a cup of wine in hand. His eyes are vacant, and his hair has darkened to copper. Almost two years they have been apart, and now her heart craves him, the taste of his skin. But he seems too far away for her to reach.

'Are you still angry with me?' she asks.

'I am not angry.'

'What are you feeling, then?'

He closes his eyes. 'Tired.' She looks around and, for the first time, realizes there is no trace of the sweet smell that usually accompanies him wherever he goes: his supply of poppy pods must have run dry. Slowly, she goes to sit on the mat behind him, and pulls him back, gently, so that he can rest against her chest. He doesn't fight her, simply lets himself be moved.

'Can't you sleep?' she asks.

'No. I have tried.'

'What happens?' She brushes a strand of hair out of his eyes.

He lets out a shuddering breath. 'I dream of the days in the passes, when the Bactrian army wouldn't let us out.'

'Those days are gone,' she says. 'It is the Bactrians who are trapped now.'

'When I am awake, I can hear the spirits talk. They never stop.'

'I can hear them too.'

His eyes are glassy and wide. 'This campaign . . . it isn't like any other.' He turns his head on her shoulder and looks at her. Up close, the wound on his neck is purple and swollen.

'Are you scared?' he asks her.

'No,' she says, knowing it is the answer he wants to hear.

'That is why you are different from the others.' He leans forward and presses his lips to hers. His hands find her skin as if it were the only thing that might save him. They don't even undress. He breathes against her collarbone while he is inside her. It is different from how it was in Kalhu: before, he wanted to be present; now he just wants to lose himself. She grabs a fistful of his hair and lets him disappear. She wonders where his mind is going, if it is a place she will ever be able to reach.

When they are done, she grabs a wet cloth and dabs at his wound. He lies down on her chest again. She cleans the cut carefully, then dresses it with a mix of daisy and tamarisk she has brought from the capital. He doesn't wince at the pain and lets her work in silence.

'Did you mean it when you said you wanted me to go back to Kalhu?' she asks, after a while. The lamp has burned out and the tent is made of shadows.

'Yes,' he says. Then: 'No. I don't want you to go.'

'I won't.'

He stirs slightly in her arms. Then, to her relief, he falls asleep.

*

In the king's tent, the generals stand in a semicircle. Ilu and Bel are standing side by side and, behind them, a couple of Bel's climbers. Ninus is sitting in a wooden chair that has been fashioned into a throne. His mouth is slightly contorted as though he is in pain but trying to hide it. Onnes takes the place next to him. Semiramis lingers, unsure where to stand, then moves beside Bel. Everyone's eyes follow her.

'For what reason is your wife in the camp, Onnes?' Ilu asks, breaking the silence. 'To advise on military tactics?' Among all the generals, he is the only one who doesn't look wounded. Having seen him fight, Semiramis isn't surprised.

'I came with Bel as one of the climbers,' she says calmly.

A few men laugh. Onnes remains silent.

'Is this true?' Ilu asks Bel.

'It is, Father,' Bel says uncomfortably. Semiramis can tell he is regretting his choice, now that he has to account for it in front of his father's men.

'Women belong in the shadows of the house,' a general comments, with a lazy smile, 'or in a man's bed, not in a camp.'

'Balkh won't surrender,' Ninus intervenes sharply. 'We have lost hundreds of men. The last two ambushes weakened us further. We need all the help we can get.'

'What we need are climbers,' Ilu says. Semiramis can see a seed of annoyance on his face and knows that Ninus sees it too.

'Semiramis can climb,' Onnes says.

Ilu turns to him. 'She came here without your approval, didn't she? You must learn to control your wife, Onnes.'

The king's voice cuts across the room. 'Just because *your* wife would never do anything apart from drink and gossip, Ilu, it doesn't mean you can judge Onnes'. If Semiramis wishes to climb, let her,' he adds, and his tone is definite. 'We have an attack to discuss.'

Ilu nods, just the slightest movement. Semiramis suspects he will make Ninus pay for this later, but now it doesn't matter. She is allowed to stay. She tries to catch Ninus' eye, but he isn't looking at her. Bel seems to relax. Onnes stares blankly ahead of him, his face all stark edges and shadows.

'Seizing Balkh becomes more difficult with each passing day,' Ninus says. 'We have slaughtered many, but we are now at a disadvantage: an army of hundreds inside the walls can easily hold off thousands of attackers. Our main assault strategy is, and has always been, to attack with a large number of men, hoping to spread the defences thin and take advantage of a weak point. This usually ends with too many casualties.'

'*This* strategy has brought us victory after victory for years,' one of the generals points out.

'It has,' Ninus replies. 'But how many men need to die on the field so that we can go home with tales of glory and conquest?'

Semiramis notices the unease spread across the men. Assyrian soldiers, let alone kings, see casualties as a necessity. Her people might fear death more than anything else, but cities must be conquered, lands must be ravaged. There is no escape from the battlefield. Still, Ninus ignores it all.

'Our approach needs to change,' he says. 'The few Bactrians who remained behind might not have recognized our climbers as Assyrians, but we can't risk losing the advantage. We must attack as soon as possible.'

'We have been scouting the latrine tunnel that should lead directly into the lower part of the citadel,' Ilu intervenes. 'It looks abandoned and, surprisingly, accessible, considering the numbers of people in Balkh. Our men have been cleaning the entrance without drawing attention. That way should be clear.' He hesitates, then smiles, without warmth. 'Onnes will take his men through the tunnel.'

Semiramis glances at her husband, but he says nothing, looking somewhere above Ilu's head. His fist clenches, almost imperceptibly.

'Then the climbers,' Ilu continues. 'You will make your way up the slope, as fast as you can. The first part of the climb isn't hard. Archers won't be able to see you properly at night, so you'll use that advantage.

Then, climbing the walls will be harder, but more difficult for the archers to shoot you.'

He looks at Bel, who nods. They seem not to realize that his plan is madness.

'If we climb that way, we'll die,' Semiramis says.

Everyone turns to her.

'The slope is covered with the bodies of men who have already tried it,' she says. 'If they didn't succeed, neither will we.'

'If you are scared, you shouldn't climb it,' one of the generals says.

'No one should climb that slope,' she says. 'We should make our way up the ravine on the left of the city, the one that leads to the acropolis. We can climb at night. Then we make it into the city and burn the acropolis. A diversion, so the army can crash the main gate while the Bactrians are distracted.'

'There are archer posts on the ravine,' Ninus points out. 'They shoot attackers if they attempt to climb. And the way is too long. You'll never make it to the acropolis by dawn.'

Semiramis shakes her head. 'All we need to reach before dawn breaks are the archer posts and kill those men so that they can't give the alarm. No more than two or three of the posts are manned. Without those archers, it is impossible for the Bactrians to shoot us as we climb to the acropolis.'

There is a moment of silence. Every general is thinking. To her surprise, it is Ilu who turns to his son. 'You think you can do it?'

'It would be hard,' Bel says, 'but not impossible. And we will have fewer casualties as we go up, as well as a chance of arriving unnoticed in a part of the city that is surely unprotected. All the soldiers are on the walls and at the gates now.'

Semiramis nods. 'They will be expecting us under the walls. No one would think we'd go straight to the acropolis.'

It has grown darker outside, and the torches cast large shadows against the tent canvas. Ninus is staring at Semiramis. His shoulders are rigid, his hand clenched to the side. Before he speaks, she knows what he will say. She knows because he has no other choice.

'Let us scout tomorrow, then.' He speaks slowly. 'If the walls can be climbed, you'll go that way. But no more than a day of scouting, or we'll give the Bactrians a chance to attack us again.' He brings his hand to his waist. 'You are dismissed,' he orders. Then, to her surprise, he adds, 'Not you, Semiramis.'

She stays, watching the men as they file out, except Onnes. The three of them remain, unsure of where to stand. Light rain starts pattering against the canvas.

'My king,' she says. 'Thank you.'

Ninus nods, pushes the hair off his face. 'I am giving you a chance. Do not waste it.'

She bows to him, listens to the dance of the rain above their heads. *I have never wasted a chance in my entire life. What would happen to me if I did? Where do orphans and commoners fall when they take a false step?*

*

They spend the next day scouting. The clouds have gone, and the sky is a flat grey. Semiramis and Bel stand with the other climbers at the foot of the ravine, testing the indentations in the rock: it is pale and smooth to the touch, but there seem to be enough handholds to climb it.

'We will need to pick two climbers each,' Semiramis says. 'Or the guards will notice us.'

'The others can go with the rest of the army,' Bel agrees. He chooses one of his father's men and a climber who comes from the mountains of the north, close to the border of Urartu. Semiramis picks Mannu and Luqa, the youngest and lightest of the group.

They will cover their faces with dried mud and wear tunics that camouflage them. Inside the acropolis, they'll slaughter the guards and set the citadel on fire. Onnes' men will go through the abandoned tunnel and join them inside. They will open the gates for Ninus and the rest of the army.

They stand in the shadow of the ravine, contemplating the plan. A few steps from them, Ilu watches them. When Semiramis notices him, he smiles, like a wolf.

'This is the gate of the netherworld, Semiramis,' he says. 'Let us see if you can enter the land of the dead and come back unharmed.'

*

Behind the camp, a stream flows peacefully: it is the only place that the stench doesn't reach. The water isn't deep, so Semiramis squats by the bank, feeling smooth, cold rocks under her soles. Across the fields Balkh casts a huge shadow, darkness bleeding into the forest.

A low crescent moon is rising. Its point pierces Semiramis' mirrored face. Her people believe that, when the moon is shaped like this, it is the boat in which the god Sin sails through the heavens. In Bactria they worship the sun, but in Assyria, the moon is far more powerful. The early-morning light might warm the earth and chase away the evil spirits, but as the day wears on and the sun travels on its course, it becomes a murderer, causing sunstroke and bringing droughts and suffering.

Semiramis rests her forehead on the wet ground. *When the sun rises, Balkh will have their god and his protection. But the night belongs to us.*

There is a feeling inside her, old and familiar. It is the awareness that what awaits her can either bring her closer to the heavens or plunge her into the house of dust, and the loneliness that comes with knowing that most men would never risk so much, when the outcome is so uncertain. But she isn't like most men.

She waits for the moon to reach its peak and prays for her fate.

*

In the king's tent, Onnes and Ninus stand side by side, two untouched cups of beer in their hands.

'Do you think we'll come out of there alive?' Ninus asks.

Onnes smiles tightly. 'I can assure you, *you* will.' His neck seems clean: the cut isn't swollen now. Ninus presses his hand to the wound on his waist, a mess of skin and stained cloth. It refuses to heal.

'Perhaps you shouldn't fight tomorrow,' Onnes says.

'And where is your wife?' Ninus asks, with a small laugh.

Onnes stares unseeingly at the canvas. 'If she lives, and I don't . . .' he starts.

'Don't,' Ninus says. He grabs his arm and tugs him close. Onnes smells of a childhood that lately Ninus can't seem to remember. 'Please don't.'

25.

The Climb

Semiramis

Semiramis looks down at the lights of the camp. From above, they seem as small as fireflies. The world spins, lights blending with the stars. She closes her eyes, knowing it is the only way to stop the spinning.

She is suspended in the darkness, bruised hands tight around rocky handholds, arms aching. Her breath is warm, her face cold. She repeats the plan in her mind. *Reach the posts. Kill the guards before the city wakes. Slide into the acropolis.*

They have climbed far, but not as fast as they thought they would. There is no light on this part of the ravine, so they must move blindly, feeling their way up without knowing what they'll find hidden between the rocks. Luqa, the boy Semiramis picked as her climber, touched a snake at some point, giving off a soft cry. Bel would have killed him, Semiramis suspected, if he wasn't worried about the body making too much noise as it hit the ground.

Soon it will be dawn. There is a moment in the night when the mountains are darker than the sky, and the stars are like ships following Sin through the twinkling heavens. The moon has grown paler now, the stars scarcer and, beyond the city, a brushstroke of dusky amber. If they don't reach the posts before the sky grows light, they will be seen.

Reach the posts. Kill the guards before the city wakes. Slide into the acropolis. The other climbers are moving, blurred figures between earth and sky. Semiramis rests her head against the rock, for a moment only. Then she hurries upwards, as fast as a lizard.

*

Onnes

Onnes takes his hand out of the putrid water, ignoring the reek that permeates the tunnel.

They have covered their faces with thick pieces of cloth, but the smell sneaks into every corner. Two of his men vomited as they passed the second fork. It would have been disgusting if the slime in which they are walking wasn't already made of shit and muck, urine and putrefying things. Not even rats come down here. Only creatures that crawl and thrive in the darkness can be found. And fifty Assyrian men. The flames lick the vaulted ceiling, and small shadows creep away from them, annoyed by the light. Two torches have gone out: one man slipped into the water, bringing it down with him, and the other burned out with the humidity. They hold their remaining lights as high as they can.

'If someone is left behind, we keep moving,' Onnes says. His voice is like a hiss in the tunnel. He knows his men are afraid – he can feel it – but there is no space for fear in such a place. The tunnel is growing warmer, and there is a faint humming somewhere above them. They must be in the underbelly of the city.

'Put out the torches,' Onnes orders. The men plunge the lights into the water, and their faces become one with the darkness. Onnes waits for his eyes to adjust.

There is a glow in the distance, at the end of the tunnel. As they move forward it grows larger, like the wide eye of a giant staring at them. They squat in the muck. Contours are visible now, shapes gaining substance and colour. Fruit peel floats next to animal excrement. Onnes dodges it. A breeze comes to them, and they remove the cloths from their faces, inhaling. When they had entered the tunnel, the night was made of shadows, but now a golden light is dawning.

Onnes walks out of the water. He looks around, then nods to his men, who make their way out carefully. Brown matter and filth cling to them, weighing them down. Their hands rest on the handles of their swords, ready. But in the clearing in front of them there is no one, the emptiness of the back alleys of a city that has yet to wake.

A little girl appears. She is scampering, moving her mouth as if chewing, though she clearly has no food. She kneels by the pond of dirty water where food leftovers are piled, then notices them. What they must look like to her, Onnes muses, animals, monsters, dawn creatures?

He takes a few steps forward. 'Which way is the main gate?' he asks her, in the Bactrian language. His accent is thick, but he has learned the words from a prisoner. Behind him, they are all waiting. The girl points a finger at the wide road to her left, then sets her eyes on the rest of the group. There is something fearless in her face that reminds Onnes of Semiramis the first time he saw her.

Before the girl can speak, he slashes her throat. Blood spurts from her neck and spatters his face. She sinks into the pile of mud, and Onnes' men hurry past and over her, as if she is part of the city's waste.

*

Semiramis

Her arms are throbbing. The post is a few feet above her. She does not look down: if she does, she is sure that she will fall. They have formed two vertical lines, one under each of the star-shaped shadows. The boy Mannu is the first of her line, then Semiramis, then Luqa. On the left, Bel leads the way to the post closer to the acropolis, two men behind him.

The mud on their faces has dried; their tunics are stuck to their backs. They can hear the guards yawning, muttering – there are two, one for each post. As she moves up the steep rock wall, Semiramis sees her shadow, the contours suddenly clearer. Around her, the shadows of the other climbers grow starker too. It takes her a moment to realize the guards aren't speaking any more. She stops climbing. Her body clings to the wall, her fingers shaking as they grip the cracks in the rock.

There is a whisper, then an arrow flies to her right: a flash of metal against the rising sun. It pierces the head of the man under Bel. He gives his death-gasp, eyes white, and his hands let go of the holds. Semiramis' heart thrashes against the rock. She shuts her eyes, waiting for the crack of his body as he hits the ground. When it comes, it sounds far away, as if from another world. They are closer to the sky now.

For a moment, no one seems to breathe. Bel makes a gesture as if to say, *Do not move*. The climbers stay still. The guards are alert now; the Bactrian above Bel is looking down, and soon he will turn and see her.

Her arms reach up, fingers finding the hollows in the stone. Knees and wrists bruise as the edges cut her. She's next to Mannu, who is shaking his head. 'They will see us,' he mouths.

'Up with me,' she mouths back, 'or die.' Her body slides into the shadow of the post. Her head scrapes the wood above her. It is shaped like a star. She just needs to grab one of the points and push her body up.

She clenches her fist once, twice, then grips the edge of the post. Her shoulders burn as she hoists herself up. There is no time to stand, as the guard turns, looks down at her in shock. She grabs her dagger and cuts his tendons. He stumbles back, his legs collapsing. His body forms an arc, and he is about to fall down the post – *He can't*, Semiramis thinks wildly, *he will scream* – so she grabs his ankle and pulls him towards her. His back hits the stone, his hand reaching for his sword. But she is quicker – she crawls by his side and cuts his throat.

A group of bats flies above her head, disturbed. She catches her breath as his blood trickles between her fingers. A hand emerges, then a head: Mannu pushes himself onto the post.

She looks beyond him, at the guard on the next post. He is nocking an arrow, eyes fixed on them –

– the arrow sinks into Mannu's hand. He grunts, legs dangling, and before Semiramis can grab his arm, he falls down the post into the paling sky. He doesn't make a sound as he flies – Bel has forbidden it. *If you fall, do not scream*, he had ordered them.

Semiramis stands, legs shaking. She looks for cover as the guard nocks another arrow –

– but Bel has made it onto the post. He sticks his dagger into the guard's foot, and his arrow flies into the horizon, away from Semiramis.

There is a struggle, Bel and the guard thrashing on their post like snakes. Then a cry that rings in the air like a heron's call before Bel silences it, sinking his blade into the guard's chest.

Luqa emerges at Semiramis' side, his little body tense as a bowstring. 'They must have heard us,' he says.

'We don't know yet,' she says. Her body is still shaking, though her voice is firm. On the other post, Bel and his man are standing, taking the guards' weapons.

'We must hurry,' Bel says. 'Before someone raises the alarm.'

They look up. The acropolis still looks silent, massive palaces and temples resting. Above them, a path is cut roughly into the rock that leads to the highest part of the city. Each step gleams as the sunrise caresses it. Semiramis and Bel exchange a glance, then start to make their way up, panting, running.

*

Onnes

The Bactrian army is coming towards them, like a swarm. They spring up from everywhere: out of windows, down from rooftops, from behind doors and columns.

The climbers are late, but they don't matter: the plan doesn't matter. He will open the gate for Ninus' army, even if it's the last thing he does. A new shower of arrows rains down on them and men fall to the ground to his left and right. As he plunges forward, he looks around and sees he is alone: all his soldiers, the ones who were running with him at least, are down. He turns: the rest are standing out of arrows' reach, lingering.

'Follow me or I will come back and kill you myself!' Onnes shouts. Then an arrow knocks into his arm, and he throws himself into the shadows of the nearest building. He breaks the shaft, grunting, just in time, before Bactrian soldiers come at him. His head pounds as he cuts them down, left arm slowed and stinging.

He stands in the wetness of their blood. His weapons stick out of the bodies all around him. One of the wounded soldiers stands up and tries to stab him. Onnes dodges him, then closes his hands around the man's neck.

'Die,' he says. '*Die.*' The man's eyes bulge, his arms shake, and then he is still and silent.

Onnes takes up a spear, then walks back out of the building, towards the high gate, where the Bactrian guards wait for him, like angry watchdogs.

*

Semiramis

They gather twigs and pieces of wood as silently as they can, then place them around the temples and palaces of the acropolis. Bel takes his waterskin, which he filled with oil before climbing, and pours the liquid over the wood, careful not to waste a drop. There are no guards here. They must be further down, stationed at the gate. Semiramis squints, trying to see the city's lowest part, where black holes lead into the tunnels that grow like roots under Balkh. She is distracted by movements close to the gate: dark shapes, gathering.

'The main gate,' she says. 'They are already fighting under it.'

Bel follows her gaze, then flattens himself against the wall of a sand-coloured building, dragging Semiramis behind him. 'There are soldiers coming.'

Luqa and the other climber crouch. They can all hear the clatter of armour now, and the thud of feet coming in their direction. Bel tosses his empty waterskin to the side and unsheathes his dagger. 'We kill these men,' he whispers, 'then start the fire.'

Semiramis feels the coldness of the dagger handle in her palm. From the large paved street that connects the acropolis to the lower part of the city, she can see the Bactrian guards coming in their direction. She tries to count them – one, two, three, ten. Too many. And they are only four.

The guards stop when they see the wood gathered around. One looks up, understanding dawning on his face. He shouts something in his tongue, before his knees waver. He falls, Bel's dagger deep in his throat.

'Now!' Bel shouts.

The climbers run against the Bactrians in unison, from shadow to light. Semiramis lifts her arm, flashing her dagger against a guard. The

Bactrian parries it so forcefully that he knocks the weapon out of her hand. He punches her, hard, and she falls to her knees. She manages to drag him down with her. As he raises his sword, her fingers close around a stone. She brings it down on his head. He lowers his grip, dazed, and she rolls away from under him, picking up her dagger.

'Start the fire!' she shouts.

Bel picks up a torch, running towards the biggest pile of wood. Semiramis looks as he cuts down the Bactrians. She sees his ankle twist as a blade grazes his leg, and the torch rolls away from him, onto the stone paving, away from the wood. She sees a Bactrian wrench a spear from the broken body of Luqa and thrust it into Bel's face.

No. Someone takes her by the throat with one hand, a sword gleaming in the other. She kicks him in the groin, and they fall together. All his weight is on her left arm – the bones may break. She stabs him in the face, once, twice, three times. Blood spills out, painting his cheeks. She crawls away, the dagger in her hand the only thing that matters. Around her, men travel to the house of dust, slowly, painfully. Their arms reach out to her, and she dodges them.

I'm not made for death and death is not made for me.

She pushes herself up. Guards follow her as she runs, but she knows they won't catch her. They have armour burdening them, and she has spent her life running, light as the wind.

She picks the dying torch from the ground and throws it over the twigs of oil and wood, setting the acropolis on fire.

*

Ninus

They come down on the Bactrians like wolves. Men gleaming in purple and gold, with spears glimmering like stars on the sea. From Ninus' chariot, the world feels made of wind. They crash through the gate like a storm bursting from the belly of the sky. In front of it are lying Onnes' men, and the bodies of the Bactrians they slaughtered before pulling the heavy doors open.

Inside the city, it is chaos. Soldiers in shining armour sway towards him. Common people run away from the acropolis into the arms of the Assyrians. The horses gallop after them, hoofs plunging into their welling blood as if into a river.

Ninus throws his spear into the leg of a Bactrian man. It slices through flesh and muscle. He bends to retrieve it as his chariot passes by. The wheels spatter filth everywhere. There is a battle cry from somewhere on his right: Ilu, tearing apart the armour of a Bactrian with his bare hands. Ninus steers his horses to the left, to avoid a woman dragging her children to safety, and crashes against a building. The chariot shatters, and Ninus jumps down, rolling away from the chaos of broken wheels and horses.

'Get out of there!' a familiar voice shouts. He turns and, a moment later, a woman's face appears: Semiramis, filth-spattered and breathless. She grabs his shoulders and pushes him to safety as a wave of fire burns the spot where he was before. He doesn't see where the fire comes from. The cut on his waist has opened, and he is bleeding profusely.

'Stay with me!' she says, taking his hand. 'Don't let go!'

Every breath makes his lungs sting. They move away from the main street, over men and women who lie moaning on the ground. Semiramis stops behind a giant round column, and he sees that she has strapped a wet cloth over her mouth. Behind them, what might have been a rich garden, the ground now spattered with weeds and Assyrian corpses. He tries to stand up, but she is removing his armour, looking at his wound. She holds its edges together, then grabs his hands and puts them over it, murmuring, 'Keep pressing,' as she covers it with a piece of cloth she tears from her own tunic. Her hands are bleeding, and it takes him a moment to understand it is her blood, not just his. He takes her fingers and looks at her palms – deep cuts cover her wrists and arms. They look up and their eyes meet: hers dark and fierce, his blue and storm-like.

A shout slices the air, followed by running steps. Semiramis looks around in panic, but he squeezes her hand and says, 'Do you trust me?'

She frowns and he can see that there is no trust in her, not for him anyway, but he doesn't care. He drags himself closer to the bodies in the garden, pulling her behind him. The shouts grow louder and Ninus forces her to lie down. Then, before she can complain, he covers her body with the corpse of an Assyrian. He lies down beside her and does the same. All he can see from under the bodies is her face, wide eyes staring at him. He reaches out and grabs her wrist. Her pulse beats against his fingers. *Alive, she is alive*, is all he thinks, before he takes a deep breath and closes his eyes.

The steps echo as the Bactrian soldiers march past the columns into the garden. He keeps still, feeling the soldiers' feet move around them, checking every corner. They spear the bodies, to make sure they are dead, and Ninus feels the iron tip graze his chest as the corpse that covers him is pierced. Then, they are gone, their voices blending with the chaos of the city.

Semiramis sits up with a jolt, gasping for air. She pushes the corpse away from her, touching her chest and arms, checking that she is whole.

He takes her shoulders. She is shaking, but he finds that touching her is the only way to sanity. 'They've gone,' he says. 'You are not wounded.'

She looks up at him. Her eyes are flaming torches, burning suns. *You saved my life*, they seem to say.

So did you, he thinks.

Then she is gone as quickly as she came.

*

Semiramis

She runs down the acropolis, looking for her husband. The world around her is worse than her deepest nightmares. Blood and urine spilling from dying men, the wounded wriggling before someone finishes them off. The screams blend with the crackle of fire, like an obscene song. The flames are orange waves, crashing down the path from the acropolis. There are trees in every corner of Balkh, and the fire carves its path through them, lighting them one by one, from the trunks to the branches, to the flowers that burn red and white before they wither.

Semiramis keeps moving, down slippery steps, past screaming women and wounded soldiers. A boy steals water from a guard, trying to heal a burn. A man kneels in front of a bundle, sobbing. Two girls are trying to pull their mother up, but she can't stand.

'Go,' the woman shouts, pushing them away. 'Run!'

Semiramis grabs their arms, dragging them down the steps. The girls look up at her, cheeks covered with soot and tears. 'You must get out of here,' Semiramis says. They stumble after her, missing a few steps, their heads turned back to their wounded mother. 'Your mother can't be saved!' Semiramis shouts. 'You have to keep moving!'

Men swarm towards them, stabbing their spears into the wounded. Semiramis races past them, dragging the girls with her. She sees the Assyrian chariot flying towards them a moment too late. She throws herself onto the ground, hands covering her head. One of the girls goes down with her, the other runs back up, her arms outstretched like a bird. The soldier cuts her head before his chariot disappears in a cloud of black dust.

Semiramis doesn't look any longer. She pulls herself up and runs, under archways that threaten to crack, past thick columns that used to hold roofs but now carry nothing but the sky. The houses around her are shadows, their colours bled away by thick clouds of smoke. She can see the gate to her right and, fighting in the streets under it, Onnes' men. They are pushing Bactrian guards into a square.

She sways, the hot air choking her, and holds on to a wall. It is carved with what seem like hands in prayer, hundreds of them. The carvings are bright, almost glowing, and for a moment she thinks Balkh's sun god is sending her a message. Then she realizes that the building is on fire.

She stumbles back to the steps that lead to the gate. She slips and her body folds as she lands on her ankle. The fall takes her breath away. Her arms thrash as she searches for handholds. She can't seem to pull herself back up.

She lifts her head. Onnes is standing at the foot of a burning building, covered with muck. He is looking at her, lips moving, but he is too far away for her to hear. She starts crawling down to reach him. Her leg is useless, a dead weight. The Bactrians are running past her, taking refuge in a temple to her right.

When she looks up again, she sees that Onnes is shouting, running to her.

A torch flies above her, spins in the sky like a glowing bird. It lands at the feet of two giant trees on her right. The temple catches fire. The Bactrians run back into the open, their bodies dancing and burning and melting. They are running away from the house of their sun god, like tongues of flame, bringing death with them.

Semiramis tries to stand. The sand scalds, the air tastes like burned flesh. A swarm of arrows dives from the sky, stabbing the screaming men. Pain bursts in her chest. She falls down, human torches running around her, their screams piercing her skull.

She wants to cry but suddenly there is a piece of wet cloth over her mouth. She wants to surrender but someone is speaking to her, urging her to stay awake, dragging her towards the gates, away from the burning city.

26.

The Secret to Immortality

She wakes slowly, darkness fading as she fights back to life. A sharp pain is piercing her chest. Ninus is standing by her mat, covered with soot and blood.

'My king,' she croaks.

There is the taste of ash on her tongue. She tries to sit up, but the pain is too intense, so she settles for moving her head. The tent's light is dim, the air dark and musky. She feels as if she is looking at the world from behind a curtain. Everything is muffled, sounds and colours sucked out of the earth.

'I saw you fall,' Ninus says. 'I thought you were dead.' His wet hair is stuck to his forehead, and his face is raw.

'I am not easy to kill.'

He almost smiles, though his eyes are haunted. She remembers flashes from the battle: his wound as she tried to stop the bleeding, the strength of his grip on her wrist. For a long moment, when they were both hiding under corpses of their own men, his hand on her skin was the only thing that had kept her from suffocating.

'The wound isn't deep,' Ninus says, 'but you have lost a lot of blood.'

'What was it?' Her voice is so faint she can barely hear it. Her chest is wrapped in a clean cloth, her wound packed with herbs.

'An arrow. It pierced your skin between your ribs. The healer pulled it out, so it won't fester.'

She wonders if he was by her side as the healer worked on the arrow shaft, what he saw of her body as she lay there, unconscious and vulnerable.

'Where is Onnes?' she asks.

'Gathering the prisoners.' A shadow passes over his face. 'Do not leave this tent. What happens now is not something you deserve to see.'

He turns to leave, then stops. His shoulders are rigid, and she cannot see his face as he speaks: 'You were brave. I owe you my life.'

He flaps the tent door open before she can answer. Outside, she glimpses a blur of shadows and fire. The spirits are screaming, or maybe it is the prisoners. She rests her hand on her throbbing chest and closes her eyes, focusing on each painful breath, on how it anchors her to the world of the living.

*

When she stumbles out of the physician's tent, she finds herself in Hell.

In front of her, between the camp and what remains of the city, Assyrians are rounding up prisoners, shouting orders, building pyres. Statues of gods are carried away from the temples. They are piled at the foot of the walls and, when the Assyrians melt them, the gold streams down their faces as if the gods themselves were crying. Enemies' heads are counted, while men go through the booty, recording details on a scroll – jars, jewels, harps, gems, tunics, weapons. Somewhere beyond the walls, the army searches every house where the wounded are hiding. They drag them out, one by one, and butcher them. Cowards do not make good prisoners.

A cloud of smoke hovers over the city. The war god Ninurta's ancient name was Imdugud, 'rain cloud'. In the earliest stories, he was a giant black bird, floating over the earth, roaring his thunder cry from a lion's head. He must be flying over them now, choking the sun.

The Assyrians wash their dead with water and wine, lay them on logs of dark wood. Then they burn them. It is the biggest fire Semiramis has ever seen, flames lapping at the sky like the tongues of a thousand hounds. The dead burn quickly. She imagines their shadows, crowding into the house of dust.

When the pyres grow smaller, bodies and wood black and charred, the generals turn to the Bactrian prisoners. They are standing in a corner, men, women, children. Most will be deported, forced to move to the opposite end of the empire, in a land so far from home they won't know how to find their way back.

Semiramis waits at the edge of the Assyrian army, eyes stinging, wound pulsing. She can see the Bactrian women holding each other. A mother covers her daughter's eyes. *Yes*, Semiramis thinks. *What you will see now, you won't be able to unsee.*

Ilu steps forward. As his son's body was burned, he had stared into the fire, eyes empty if not for the flames dancing in them. But Semiramis had seen how he tightened his grip around the blade of his sword, blood slowly dripping from his palm onto the earth, like tears.

'Show subservience to your captors,' he shouts. 'Show your submission to the king!' There is something monstrous about him, and as Semiramis looks around, she can see it on the other generals' faces too, as if a disease is spreading among them.

They force the prisoners to strip naked. The women watch as husbands and sons, fathers and soldiers remove their armour. When they have finished, it lies in front of them like a shed skin.

Ilu selects the leaders: a hundred men with defiance in their eyes. To the west, everyone knows who the Assyrians are, what they are capable of. But here, in this land so far east where the sun god used to protect its people, they do not know what awaits them. They do not know that the treatment of enemies depends on their readiness to submit.

The men are brought forward to a clearing where thick, large stakes are waiting for them. They sway a little as they see the stakes, moving like unrooted trees in the dusty light. One by one, Onnes' men take them. They shove the points of the stakes into their ribs. The cry that leaves them is agony, a tear in the sky.

Semiramis wants to look away, but where can she turn to? There are heads lying in heaps, burned bodies, pleading prisoners. There is no escape from this nightmare, no peace from the putrid smell. It has soaked her body, slithered under her skin, and now she is part of it, a thread woven in this tapestry of violence.

The women are wailing. The cries might be curses or prayers. Semiramis doesn't know: she can't understand them. The stakes are erected. The prisoners' heads sag forward, the bodies' weight pushing the wood deeper and deeper inside. With their blood, the land is dyed, like a carpet of red wool.

How long will this go on? Semiramis wonders. *How long does it take for a man to die?*

But it doesn't matter how long it takes. Assyrian men are no longer men. They gather at the feet of the stakes and cut off the hands and feet of the impaled men. A woman with hair the colour of bronze runs forward, throwing herself at the foot of a stake, before Ilu's men take her. For a moment, Semiramis wonders why the world has gone black, then realizes she has closed her eyes.

She opens them again, slants of grey light cutting her pupils. The woman is gone, and this is all she sees: Onnes, cutting a man's hand with studied precision, his gilded knife against the skin of a man who is alive but very much dead. When it is done, he throws it onto a pile of other human pieces, like a discarded cloth.

Behind him, far from the carnage and the prisoners, Ninus brings his hand to his stomach and vomits, then walks away.

*

She finds Onnes alone by the river, cleaning his sword. It is hard to tell if it is day or night – the light is all the same. He is still covered with blood. It sticks to his face and arms, dried and darkened to rust. He looks like an angry god fallen to earth to exact his vengeance.

Without turning he says, 'You should be resting.'

'I cannot,' she says. She can barely stand: she is so tired that her body feels numb. But rest, peace, those things are now inconceivable. 'Did you carry me out of the city?'

'Yes,' he says. 'As mad as your plan was, it worked.'

He turns to her. His eyes are strange, wild. She wants to cry, because she had crossed a city for him, and now he is in front of her, alive. But this man isn't him. He is someone else.

And yet he had warned her before leaving for Balkh, hadn't he? *When I am out there, I want to cut everyone to pieces.*

'What you did was brutal,' she spits out.

She glimpses the pain on his face before he turns away again, but she doesn't care if he is hurting, not when all she can see is the way in which he cut off an impaled man's hand.

'You stayed and watched,' he says.

'You didn't need to impale them! You didn't need to mutilate them!'

His sword shines, and he turns his attention to his daggers. 'Our war is not only fighting in the field and plucking cities. It is also threats and tortures, omens and spectacles. It is all part of it. Why do you think the walls of our capital are covered with bas-reliefs of dying enemies?'

She thinks of the first time she saw him, how his voice had sounded like something she could hold in her hands – colourful spices, a ripe lemon, a piece of warm gold. It still sounds like that, yet now there is something else: menace, corrupting everything.

'Do you do it because you have to or because you want to?'

'Is there a difference?'

'No, maybe for you there isn't.'

He kneels, dips the blades in the water. The dirt flows away. 'When I was a child, Ashurnasirpal won a war against Elam. The Elamites had resisted as long as they could, even when all their allies were submitting. Do you know what Ashurnasirpal did to them when the war was won?' She keeps still, and he sheathes his daggers. 'He flayed them and draped their skins over the walls of Kalhu. For days we lived with clouds of flies at our gates, and stray dogs barking, trying to reach the pieces of skin that dried under the sun.'

She imagines Nisat, a cupbearer's child, forced to marry a king who made carpets of his enemies' skins.

He puts a hand to her neck, and she feels the coldness of his palm. 'What you saw today was nothing. Today we have been merciful.'

*

The smell soaks the land, and so do the cries, echoes that grow fainter but seem never to die. Everything was the colour of sun here, rocks, walls, temples, plains, *before we came and destroyed it*. Semiramis suspects that in a thousand years, when people travel to this place, they will find it grey and dead, spirits still wailing with sorrow and outrage. The sun god certainly won't be shining his light on these ruins.

A thought is untangling inside her, slowly and painfully, like a snake that has been still for too long: *I did this. Their blood is on my hands.*

I owe you my life, Ninus said. One life saved, and how many taken? How many burned when she set fire to the acropolis?

But if she hadn't come up with her plan, the Assyrians would be burning now, not the Bactrians. For one army to triumph, another must fall. So what is the answer? Can one rise without hurting others?

She has entered a world of men who forget they are mortals and treat those beneath them as if they are nothing but beetles scurrying at their feet. *But I will never be truly like them. Because no matter how much power I hold, I will never forget what it means to have nothing. To be nothing.*

And if I am not like them, what am I?

The sky offers no answer. She presses a hand to her wound and keeps walking, wandering around the camp, looking for a redemption that she knows will never come.

*

The Bactrian women are grouped at the edge of the Assyrian camp. A girl cries as one of Onnes' soldiers grabs her arm, drags her away. Semiramis walks past them. There is the bronze-haired woman who had run towards the soldiers, an older woman with scraped knees, a girl with dark eyes and skin covered with ash . . . It takes Semiramis a moment to recognize her: the girl she had tried to save in the city, with her mother and sister. Her black eyes burn into Semiramis' back as she walks away from the women and into the king's tent.

Ninus is standing, bare-chested. A healer is studying his wound, prodding it with a metal instrument. She bows, wincing at the stab of pain in her chest, then says, 'I have a request to make, my king.'

Ninus lifts his head. 'Speak.'

She straightens, slowly and painfully. 'I wish to keep some of the Bactrian prisoners for myself,' she says. 'Women and children.' She hesitates, thinking of the girl who was dragged away: outside the tent, her cry has faded to an eerie silence. 'I do not want your soldiers to harm them.'

Ninus raises his eyebrows. 'My men won't be pleased. They expect to keep those women for themselves.'

'Shouldn't your subjects revere you? How can they do so, if you don't give them something to live for?'

Ninus pushes the healer away and reaches for a clean tunic. As he pulls it over his head, he grimaces. 'Something to live for,' he repeats bitterly. 'Do you imagine every man lives for something, even the lowest slave in the province?'

'I think they do.'

He bites his lip, considering her words. 'A true king should trample his enemies, not embrace them,' he says. She knows it is his father

231

who is speaking, and his mother, and every other person who taught him to be ruthless, rather than kind.

'Didn't we trample them when we burned down their city, killed their soldiers and impaled their leaders?'

He looks at her for a long time and she thinks that maybe he is lost, like Onnes, that the war has dragged him into the house of dust and he cannot see the way back. But then he asks, 'How many women do you want?'

Hope bursts inside her. Her hand flies to her chest, as if to calm the throbbing of her heart. 'As many as possible. I won't keep them all. I will arrange for some to be deported to another region of the empire, Eber-Nari perhaps.'

He nods. 'I will order my men to guard those prisoners without touching them. Once we reach Kalhu, you will distribute them as you see fit.'

'Thank you,' she says.

His eyes are shifting enquiringly over her face. 'I told you not to come out of your tent. I told you not to look.'

How can she explain? This is the path she has chosen, and if she wants to keep going, she must not be afraid. 'If you have to bear it,' she says, 'I will bear it too, my king.'

*

Joints of glistening meat are being cooked on an open fire. The generals sit around it, passing beer jugs from hand to hand. There are a hundred other small fires by the camp, soldiers gathered around them. Someone is playing one of the captives' lyres. The sand moves and drifts with the breeze. The landscape shifts, like a veil pulled across a face.

Semiramis looks into the fire until her eyes are burning. Onnes is sitting beside her and, in front of her, Ninus' figure is sharp against the darkening sky.

'Tonight we drink to our king,' Ilu says. His voice is hoarse, and Semiramis wonders if he has been crying. She doesn't think him capable of it.

'The ruler of the world!' Ilu shouts. 'There isn't a corner of this earth that he hasn't conquered, people he hasn't forced into submission!' There are no shouts or cheers. The men listen, faces solemn in the firelight.

'We drink to our generals, who plucked "the mother of all cities"!' Ilu hesitates, then his eyes land on Semiramis. 'And we drink to Onnes' wife, the woman who took the acropolis with my son!'

The men raise their cups. Ninus stares at her. 'To Semiramis,' he says.

She stands. There is an eerie quiet, except for the notes of the lyre, which pulse in the air, like raindrops. 'There is a story I love, from *The Epic of Gilgamesh*,' she says. 'I wish to recite it tonight, in honour of the men we lost.'

The soldiers sit back. From the edges of the campfires, the women gather to listen too. She wonders if they can understand her.

'Gilgamesh,' she begins, 'the great king, both god and mortal, and his friend Enkidu, who is like a brother to him, offend the goddess Ishtar. She is furious, distraught, and unleashes the Bull of Heaven, the mythical beast of destruction, on earth. The land grows dry, and the Bull's breaths crack it open, trapping hundreds of men in holes deep in the ground. Enkidu almost falls with them.

'It is Gilgamesh who saves him, and together, they slaughter the fiery Bull. They rip out its heart and one of its thighs, and fling them into Ishtar's face, humiliating the goddess. Together, they think themselves invincible. *Who is the handsomest of men?* they ask, and the people shout, *Gilgamesh! Who is the bravest of men?* they ask, and the people cheer, *Enkidu!*'

When she and Taria had seen the play in Kalhu, Taria had said, 'No man can think himself invincible. The gods will come and take what he holds dearest.' And she was right.

'That night, Enkidu has a terrifying dream. He dreams that he is in the house of dust, where all who enter never return to sweet earth again. He wakes and falls sick, lying in his bed in agony, and every day he grows worse. "Are you leaving me behind, my friend?" he asks Gilgamesh. "Are you abandoning me?"'

Two people grown up together, bound to each other by friendship, love and obsession. It is impossible not to think of her husband and her king as she tells the story. Onnes stares unseeingly at the fire. Ninus' eyes are on her, as if on a tablet.

'When he hears his friend's death rattle, Gilgamesh cries.

"Beloved, don't leave me.
Dearest of men, don't die,

233

don't let them take you from me.
My beloved is dead, he is dead,
My brother is dead, I will mourn him.
As long as I breathe, I will sob for him."

'Then he veils Enkidu's face like a bride's.

'Gilgamesh weeps and weeps, fear of death driving him forward. Refusing to accept his brother's fate, he decides to find the one man the gods made immortal. So he travels over seas and mountains, wastelands and deserts, a journey no mortal has ever done. He finds the garden of the gods, and then, beyond the Waters of Death, he finds him: the man whom the gods made immortal.'

She wants to cry. It is a strange story: of a king so strong and ruthless who becomes weak when he loses the one he loves.

'The ageless man is stunned to see that Gilgamesh has found him. But when Gilgamesh asks him how he became immortal, this is what the man tells him:

"Yes, the gods took Enkidu's life
But man's life is short, at any moment,
it can be snapped like a reed.
Though no one has seen Death's face or heard
Death's voice, suddenly, savagely,
Death destroys us, all of us, old or young.
And yet we build houses, make contracts,
brothers divide the inheritance, conflicts occur,
as though this human life lasted for ever."'

Ninus' face floats in the darkness, like a secret the fire wants to reveal. The men are silent, mourning their dead. Semiramis can feel a single tear stream down her cheek. When she sits, Onnes wipes it from her face.

A girl, one of the Bactrian prisoners, starts singing – the sound is full of sorrow. The land is coloured like a dream, where everything exists in a blur: a strange, unreal place, where the living fade and the dead take shape.

*

'The way you told Gilgamesh's story, it was beautiful.'

She looks up. Ninus is standing outside her tent. The stars are veiled above his head: the gods have left, hiding away from the wreckage of this place.

'Gilgamesh crossed the oceans for his friend,' she says. 'He challenged the gods who climb the sky, and for what? Nothing brought him back.'

He sits down beside her. They are close, their shoulders almost touching. 'Things that are lost aren't meant to be found again. We must let them go.'

She puts her arms around her knees. They keep silent for a while, until she fears he might leave. Then it occurs to her that, with Onnes asleep, he might not have anywhere to go either.

'Sometimes, when I sleep,' she says, 'I am afraid I will never wake up. That I won't be able to find my way back to the land of the living.'

His eyes are dark in the shadows, like the deepest waters. 'Death and nightmares aren't the same thing.'

'In my dream, a flood bursts through, overwhelming everything and everyone. As the water rises higher and higher, the people die, and the gods fly to the highest heavens. I see that the gates are closing, that the people cower at their feet, like dogs, and I try to find a way through.'

He stares at her, wakeful, intent. His attentiveness is unsettling, as was his disinterest the first time she saw him. She looks back at him, thinking she has never shared this with anyone else. 'That's it,' she says. 'That is the dream.'

His eyes are shining. For a long moment he is silent, and she feels foolish for telling him. But then he says, 'You have just burned the acropolis of Balkh. I believe you could find your way even into the halls of the gods.'

She suddenly needs to touch his face, to clean his wound, just as she had done in the city. There is a loud roaring inside her, begging her to move closer. *He is your king. Your husband's brother.* He turns his head away from her, and she wonders if he is thinking the same, if he, too, is filled with this strange longing.

They stay like this, sitting next to each other, until the camp starts whispering and a grey light dawns.

BOOK IV

817–815 BC

Do not fall in love. A woman is a pitfall, a hole, a ditch, a woman is a sharp iron dagger that slashes a man's throat.
From 'The Dialogue of Pessimism'

27.

Ribat, a Slave

Kalhu, capital of the Assyrian Empire

The afternoon sun blazes off the yellow bricks of the palaces. In the governors' houses, nobles are feasting on terraces, and the smell of sweet lamb drifts all the way down to the square. Ribat and Ana stop and inhale greedily, then catch themselves.

'Come on,' Ribat says, taking her hand and guiding her past the taverns and wine-houses. In front of the *asipu*'s shop, Ana hesitates. 'The healer scares me,' she whispers.

Ribat almost smiles. 'He scares everyone,' he says. 'But if the army truly is coming back, we need a fresh supply of opium poppy.'

Inside, it is dark. They wait as the healer prepares the jugs. Ana observes the models of colons and livers on the tables, keeping close to the door. Ribat glances at her. In the past months they have spent long hours together. They roamed the citadel and stole food, and did other things Ribat isn't proud of. They had no choice. The famine left them with most of the city's resources sent to the army across the mountains. The food that remained went to the nobles and governors, and since there is no governor in Onnes' palace, nothing came to them. First, they ate the eggs and greens stored in the kitchen, then the peas and lentils, until those were gone too, Ana started fainting, and two other slaves stopped having their monthly blood.

'I do not like this,' Ana said once, after they had taken a cask of smoked meat from an old man's house.

'Who lives longer? The man who gives or the man who takes?' Ribat retorted, and Ana had looked disappointed, as if he had betrayed her somehow. It hurt him, even if he did not show it. She has a good heart, despite a world that does its best to snatch it from her.

When they step outside the healer's shop, light is falling into the alleys. The streets are growing crowded: common people and nobles are lingering to listen to a priest dressed in the fashion of the goddess Ishtar.

'The army has crossed the Zagros mountains,' the priest is shouting. 'They will be back in days!'

Ribat and Ana exchange a glance, then slip out of the crowd. Prisoners are carrying bags of rubble to the main gate, where massive bull statues are being cut. From beyond the city walls come roars and shouts: new lions have been captured for the arena. Ribat gives a small prayer to Ishtar, hoping that Semiramis is alive. If she isn't, then . . . He can't bear to think of it.

'You and Semiramis are close,' Ana says suddenly, distracting him from his thoughts. 'Do you think she will ever free you?'

The question surprises him. It is the first time anyone has asked him. Slaves keep their hopes well hidden in their hearts, nursing them in the dark hours of the night when no one is watching. He thinks about the few slaves he has known who were freed: children deposited as security for a short time, men who saved money while dealing with their masters' commerce, concubines who were freed after the death of their master. He isn't in any of these categories.

'We do not hope for what we cannot have,' Ribat says.

Ana's eyes are soft as she glances at him. 'But you hope. I see it.'

Strange, he reasons, how dull he had thought she was the first time he had seen her, when she is anything but. Maybe he was scared. He knows that if slaves are too clever, they are likely to be less careful.

*

He sits on the floor of the portico, the leopard by his side. Ever since the start of the famine, she has taken to disappearing for long days, when Ribat looks at the window anxiously, fearing that the guards will tell him she has killed someone in the citadel or eaten one of the children who play in the narrow alleys by the walls. But when she comes back, she brings rabbits and birds – doves, ducks and geese – from the gardens. Once, Ribat was so hungry that he tried to move closer as she was eating. She leaped up, teeth bloody, and grappled him by the neck. She is growing wilder, more restless.

Somewhere down in the citadel, a child cries, and his mother hushes him. Ribat looks down, as if he could track the sound. He was never loud as a child: he didn't cry, didn't wail, as if he already knew he couldn't afford to. At night, he would lie still on his mat, looking at the feet of the other slaves as they tiptoed between the lamps. When his mother appeared and lay down next to him, he would glimpse the dimples of her smile.

'You haven't brought me anything,' he said sometimes, disappointed, seeing her hands were empty.

'I have brought you secrets,' she whispered, and cupped her hands around the air as if they were filled with something precious. He imagined the secret unfurling, like a bird stretching its wings before it takes flight.

'What secrets?' he asked eagerly.

'I think the young prince may be in love with Onnes,' she told him one night.

Then, on another: 'The spymaster pays commoners for their secrets. He meets them in an alleyway by the city walls.'

And on another: 'When the king was away, the queen kissed the *turtanu* Ilu. I saw them.'

Ribat reached for the scar on her back and touched its wrinkled edges – a habit to soothe himself. 'The *turtanu* is scary,' he said, because even though he liked the secret, he wanted her to be careful.

She smoothed his hair back from his forehead. 'He is a small man.'

'He seems rather big,' Ribat replied, thinking of the *turtanu*'s figure, large and muscular.

'He is big in size, but small in character,' she said. Then, with a mischievous smile, she added: 'You know what the proverbs say: *Whenever there is excess, an axe remedies it.*'

That was the last thing she ever said to him. The next morning, she was dragged away from Onnes' palace and poisoned with other slaves in the Northwest Palace.

*

Zamena is in the storeroom, hanging jars of lentils from the ceiling to keep them out of reach of mice. The pale light coming from the courtyard illuminates her face: grey eyes and a sad mouth. Ribat joins her, casting a quick glance around to make sure they are alone.

'You never told me why my mother died,' Ribat says.

She raises a brow. 'What makes you think I know anything about it?'

'You were her friend. You know.'

'I loved your mother,' she says. 'And I warned her. But she was a curious woman.' She speaks the word as if it were an unforgivable fault.

'Warned her about what?' Ribat says.

'She was the one Onnes always sent to the other palaces, and this made her feel important. I would always tell her: "They think we exist for them. They don't understand that we have an existence of our own."' Her eyes dart nervously around his face. 'But she used to pry into things, then come back here and want to tell me all about it, even if I didn't want to hear.'

'Why did she die?' Ribat repeats. He is surprised to hear the menace in his voice.

Zamena lowers hers to a whisper. 'She had seen something she shouldn't have seen in the queen's palace. That is all I know.'

Her voice throbs with fear. Ribat pities her: fear is good, because it allows one to survive, but it can also be a cage. He has lived in it all his life.

'Have you ever had children of your own?' he suddenly asks.

She shakes her head. 'I was so jealous of your mother when she had you. But then I learned that, for us slaves, small joys always bring big misfortunes.' She casts him a sad look, then slips away from the storeroom before he can reply. Her shadow moves past the torches and disappears. The silence grows heavy with things left unsaid. Ribat knows spirits can feast on such things, so he lights a lamp to drive them away. He cups his fingers around the flame and thinks that, for his mother, he was much more than a 'small joy'.

*

After days of blazing sun trapping the city with its heat, the army comes back and brings the breeze with it. They ride through the gate, welcomed by the giant human-headed bulls and a cheering crowd. Ribat watches from behind the bronze statue of a lion. His eyes search for Semiramis. She rides a black stallion, gold rings in her braids, sun on her face. To Ribat's surprise, she is flanked by Onnes and the *turtanu* Ilu, the three riding behind the king.

They welcome her and Onnes in the palace with a feast of lamb and figs, pomegranates and sweet wine. Onnes does not touch the food and disappears upstairs, asking Ana for the opium. Semiramis eats as Zamena lights sweet incense to perfume the courtyard. When she is done, she walks upstairs, and Ribat follows her.

In her apartments, she strips off her dusty tunic, revealing a blood-stained cloth wrapped around her chest. Ribat removes it carefully: the cloth threatens to peel off the skin. He works in silence, casting a glance at her face every once in a while. She seems paler, as if she has spent too long in the darkness and brought something out of it with her.

'You were right,' she says suddenly, breaking the silence like a spell. 'I shouldn't have gone.'

Why? he wants to say, but there is something in her expression that tells him it is better not to ask. He washes the wound and binds it with a strip of clean linen. She doesn't wince, as if it weren't her skin that Ribat is touching. When he is done, he lingers, unsure whether to stay or leave.

'I am glad you are back,' he says.

She doesn't reply. He leaves her alone in the darkness of the room, staring blankly in front of her, as if she were still in Balkh.

*

He waits until the hour is late, and the sky has grown black. Then he sets out towards the queen's palace. Now that Semiramis is back, there might not be any other chances, so he must take this one while he can. The streets are empty and the ground still warm from the day's heat. He walks past the guards who are yawning in front of the main door and takes a narrow side alley that leads to the storeroom. Through the windows, he can see it is empty. He pushes the door until it gives way, and he finds himself inside. The steps that lead to the main courtyard are steep, the passageway narrow. At last it opens onto a courtyard with bright columns and flowered wall reliefs. Two women are sitting on the couches, playing the game of Ur. Their eyes are on the dice, and Ribat moves in the shadows, slipping behind the columns. His feet are silent on the stone. He takes a corridor where torches are burning. It leads him up another flight of stairs, where doors open onto richly decorated rooms. This place has a strange quiet, every room brimming with secrets. He just needs to find the one he is looking for.

In the first chamber, two lyre players are practising a song for the goddess Ishtar. In the next, there is a strange yellow bird in a cage. It glares at him, and Ribat hurries past it. Two other rooms are empty, winged statues presiding over discarded dresses and empty cups. Voices drift from the last door that opens onto the corridor. Ribat approaches it, keeping his eyes on the stairs.

'You don't look wounded,' a woman is saying. 'A little tired, perhaps.' Ribat recognizes the voice. It is unmistakable: each word a clean, deep cut.

'Still handsome enough for you?' a man asks lazily.

A small silence; Ribat does not breathe. Then the woman speaks again. 'I am sorry about your son.'

'I didn't come here to speak about him.'

Ribat shifts a little closer to the door, so that the man comes into view. The *turtanu*. He is sitting on a stool, shirt open at his chest, eyes following the king's mother as she paces the room. Gold glimmers at her throat, and her dress spreads like a pool of crimson around her feet.

'Ninus seems different,' Nisat says.

'You know how he is,' Ilu says dismissively. 'He can't stand death and torture. But he is growing used to them.'

'I worry Semiramis is trying to charm him. They rode into the city together.'

The *turtanu* barks a laugh. 'You see dangers everywhere. Semiramis burned down the acropolis: she had the right to take the place behind him. But even if she tried to charm him,' he points out, 'she would still lack Ninus' favourite feature. A cock.'

The queen turns to him sharply. 'Ninus doesn't like men. He would have found endless boys to bed otherwise. He falls in love with *people*. He was in love with me, once. Though that was a different kind of love, of course.'

'I can't blame him. You are hard to resist.'

The queen looks at him, half amused, half affronted. The room is darker than the rest of the palace, with small lamps failing to fight the impending darkness. 'I told you the last time,' she says, 'you can't come in here.'

'I have been away for months. Winning a war *you* wanted. I expected a better welcome.'

'The guards might complain.'

'The guards complain, I cut off their useless heads,' he says, with a dark smile. 'Now I am tired of talking. Come here.'

'You might talk to your wife like that, but I am your queen.'

He stands. The cuffs are tight around his wrists, and his shoulders are thick with muscles. 'I am sorry, my queen.'

She regards him with the faintest trace of distaste but doesn't push him away. Then he kneels in front of her, opening her dress. The queen closes her eyes and brings her jewelled hands around his face.

Ribat looks at them, hidden in the lengthening shadows of the corridor.

This is it, he thinks. This is the secret my mother died for.

28.

Ninus, King of the World, King of Assyria

Ninus wakes up, gasping.

He was dreaming about her. A goddess lay in his bed, covered his nakedness with a blanket of raven hair. It was as soft and shimmering as the purest fabric. Ishtar, he thought, for the goddess used to visit his dreams when he was a boy. But then she lifted her head, and Ninus' heart stopped. Semiramis. His body moved of its own accord, begging for her skin. But as soon as he touched her, she slipped away.

He walks to the window to calm himself. The sky arches like a woman's back; the stars are a thousand glittering eyes. The madness of his dream lingers. She should have knelt before him. Instead, she stared at him, as if daring him to touch her. If he closes his eyes, he can see her naked shoulder, feel the warmth of her skin.

He can't sleep. He will go insane.

*

In the large, inner courtyard of the Northwest Palace, his mother and daughter recline on luxurious couches. A table has been laid with platters of cheese, dates and pomegranates.

Ninus kisses his daughter's forehead and takes the place by her side. Sosanê has grown while he was away, but her face remains the same: pointed and serious, with sad eyes like a night sky ready to spill its tears. Nisat's eyes on him are like a hawk's beak, snatching details of his face as if she could gorge on him.

'I am proud of you,' she says, raising her cup to him. 'You have done what no Assyrian king before you did. You have taken the holy city of Balkh.'

Her tone is celebratory; Ninus hates her for it. 'I didn't take the city. Semiramis and Onnes did. If she hadn't burned the acropolis and he hadn't brought down the gate, the Bactrians would have overpowered us.'

Nisat waves an impatient hand. 'Every battle your men win is your victory. When Ilu defeated the tribespeople of the Medes, whose victory was it? Yours.'

He watches as attendants come forward to pour wine. Their faces reflected in the cups make him think of his soldiers in Balkh, staring at him, their bodies covered with blood. 'We razed Balkh to the ground,' he says slowly. 'We burned the temples and impaled the men. And for what?'

Nisat stares at him as if he has lost his mind. 'Power is violence. In order to take it and exercise it, a king needs people who submit to him.'

He thinks back to Semiramis' words: *If your men rape them after killing their husbands and sons, do you really believe they can be loyal to the empire?* His mind wanders to Onnes' palace, beyond the royal road and the other governors' houses. He imagines Semiramis sitting on a couch, eating. The way she looks up through her dark lashes: fiercely, shamelessly, as if she could put a spell on him. He forces himself to stop the thoughts, or he will scream.

'Well, now that Balkh is taken, I won't "exercise my power" for a while,' he says.

'No,' Nisat agrees. 'You will think of other matters. Marriage, for a start.'

He puts down his cup. Her face is set, serious, and he can't help laughing. 'Whose? Mine?'

'Yours,' Nisat says. 'And Sosanê's.'

Sosanê says nothing, but he can see the faint blush on her cheeks. She is always so quiet – because she is stuck in her own world, or because she is always listening? Ninus can't tell. He hopes it is the latter: no one can survive in fantasies of dreams and wishes, not even a princess.

'She is a child,' Ninus says.

'No longer,' Nisat replies. 'She started to bleed last month.'

Ninus turns to his daughter. At Sosanê's age, Nisat had already been married for years. Ninus became a father when he was sixteen. He has been forced to grow up too soon. Ever since his brother decided to rebel and plunge the country into war, his life has been a raging river, flowing too quickly, bringing destruction wherever it goes. Now it strikes him, for the first time, that his daughter, too, has grown and that she is his legacy, his only heir.

'What do you think?' he asks her. 'Will you marry?'

'You are not married, Father,' Sosanê says simply. 'Think of your own marriage first.' They look at each other, then smile. Hers is a mischievous expression, which reminds him of Assur.

'Well then, Mother,' he says, 'it seems there is no escape for me this time.'

Nisat turns the wine cup in her hands. 'I know the crown wearies you, Ninus,' she says, 'but I will find a good match for you.' He waits for her to tell him that marriage is just another of his royal duties, but instead she says, 'As for Semiramis, do not trust her. She seduced Onnes, because no matter how strong he looks, deep down he is weak and easily charmed. Do not let her do the same to you.'

An image flashes before him: Semiramis waking in the healer's tent in Balkh, as his soldiers shouted orders of death outside. He had breathed deeply, the relief of seeing her alive accompanied by a sudden, surprising thought: *I could not bear to watch her die.*

'I doubt she wants to seduce me, Mother,' he says curtly.

Nisat's blue eyes burn into Ninus' face. 'Oh, Ninus,' she says. 'For someone so clever, sometimes you can be such a fool.'

*

He avoided her on the way back to Kalhu. Through the plains, green except for the burned villages they left smoking in their wake, he listened to the songs of victory his men sang and gazed at the gold and silver piled on the chariots. The days were cold and the nights colder, the soldiers' breath swirling. To cross the Zagros range, they followed the rivers that slithered between the mountains, but even down in the valleys their hands were chapped, and their faces stung by the wind. The Bactrian prisoners kept close to each other, moving in the shadows of the Assyrian chariots.

Every time they made camp to eat and rest, she was there. Always dirty and dishevelled, dust clinging to her tunic. In his mind, thoughts kept forming: his hand on her skin, scratching away the dirt, his lips kissing her bruises. He pushed them away.

Once, when the prisoners' songs filled the evening air and time stood briefly still, he felt her gaze on him across the fire. The mountains' peaks reached up into the clouds, and he let himself think that it was all a dream, that they were floating in a land between the earth and the heavens. When he finally looked back at her, her face was shining in the flames, her eyes round and large, like moons. She smiled at him, a brief, sad smile, then looked away.

*

He sends for her a week after they have returned from Balkh.

He orders his guards to leave and paces the small courtyard as he waits for her – the same courtyard where he once pressed his lips to Onnes'. His mind seems to be working of its own accord, concocting plans, each more outrageous than the last. He remembers something Sasi once told him: that the fatal moment is the one that comes before a mistake, when you know you could walk away but you won't.

Semiramis arrives dressed in purple, a necklace with suns of beaten gold gleaming against her collarbones. If she is curious, or confused, she doesn't show it. He expects her to say, 'You asked for me, my king,' as any other person would, but instead she looks behind him, at the columns that are covered with his writing from childhood.

'*The sun never leaves my heart, which surpasses a garden,*' she reads. His words in her mouth sound soft. It is as if she were tasting them, discovering bits of him as she reads. 'Did you write this?'

'I did.' He used to study here as a child, sitting on the floor with his back against the blue-painted walls.

'It is beautiful.'

She stares at him, waiting for him to say something more. He finds himself incapable of speaking – all he can see are her wide, beautiful eyes. He thinks about revealing what Onnes has told him, that she loves to read, but he doesn't want to mention his brother's name. Instead, he asks, 'Do you like poems?'

She smiles. 'Poems are special because they have a thousand hidden meanings in them. Words bend like truths.'

249

'Truths are unchanging.'

'Do you really believe that?'

The question takes him by surprise. He used to believe it. Now he isn't sure what he believes. 'Why did you choose the story of Gilgamesh and Enkidu?' he asks. 'In the camp at Balkh.'

Her expression doesn't waver. 'I thought you would like it, my king.'

'You want me to like you, then.'

'Doesn't everyone wish to please their king?'

He wonders what she is trying to tell him, what emotion she is hiding behind her words. Just like she said, *Words bend like truths.* 'No,' he says. Then, in spite of himself: 'Did you think about me and Onnes, as you told that story?'

She stares right at him. 'I did.' He waits, until she speaks again. 'It must have been hard for you when he married me.' Her voice is suddenly soft, like wind stirring water. 'It isn't easy to understand what Onnes feels, what he thinks, but I believe he cares about you more than he will ever care for me.'

No one has spoken to him like this before. It is a strange feeling, like needing something he hadn't known he wanted. He is quiet for a moment too long and she looks away from him. She starts pacing around the columns, crossing from light to shadow as if she were passing into different worlds.

'I can still feel the whispers of the spirits from Balkh,' she says. 'Can you?'

'Yes. It is always like this, after a campaign. All I see are the bodies of the men I killed, and I hear the voices of the ones I couldn't save.'

She stops in the long shadow of a column. The distance between them feels like nothing. So why can't he close it?

'Does it ever go away?' she asks.

'The mind is the last thing that heals.'

'What if it never does?'

'Then we must find a way to live with it.'

She laughs, a sound full of hurt. 'You are very wise.'

He shrugs, almost smiles. 'A lifetime of tutors and counsellors trying to teach me how to fight the world and bend it to my will.'

A shadow moves across her face. 'No one ever taught me anything.'

'And yet you are here.' *With me.*

'I taught myself as best I could.' She meets his gaze, dark and steady. He takes a step forward and brushes his fingers against her chest, where he knows her wound is. Then he stops, as if realizing what he is doing, but before he can move away, her hand is at his waist, around his scar. Pain cracks through him, but he does not flinch.

There is a challenge in her eyes, though whether aimed at him or herself he does not know. She presses her palm to his scar; his blood pulses under her hand. They stay still, caught in the silence, touching each other's wounds as if they could heal them.

The words slip from his mouth before he can stop them: 'Your face. I don't think I've ever seen anything as beautiful.'

She closes her eyes, bites her lip as if to drown the answer she wants to give. He remembers someone else, keeping silent as he opened his heart to him, in this very courtyard.

Above her head, his childhood writing reads like a warning: *My heart, don't act so stupidly. Why do you play the fool?*

Breathing deeply, she takes a step back. 'I must go,' she says. The air changes, as if a spell has broken. She fixes the sleeve of her dress and heads towards the door, then turns back to him. He is silent, trying to control the longing that courses through him like a raging river.

She studies his face, and he realizes she is waiting for him to speak. But the only words he can think of are wild flames in a forest: if he lets them loose, they will set the world on fire.

I want you to stay. I want you to tell me if you truly love Onnes. I want you to touch me. I want you to tell me your secrets. I want you. I want you.

Maybe she can hear his thoughts. Maybe she can't. 'I cannot stay, Ninus,' is all she says.

'I know.'

He watches her go, feeling as if she is carrying away a piece of him, towards the dawn that bleeds its golden light upon the city.

29.

Semiramis, a Traitor

She goes home, her heart aching for what she cannot have. It is a painful feeling. All her life she has longed for things that seemed too far from her to reach, but she could dream that she might, somehow, some day, achieve them. But this . . . It is madness, it is suicide: if she does not fight it, it would be like cutting her own throat.

Desire woven together with pain. She should have uprooted the feeling as soon as it started to form. But when did it start? When they hid together in Balkh? When he invited her and Onnes to dine in his apartments? When she saw him with Ilu in the training ground?

The night is ending, the gods lifting the veil that allows mortals to live undisturbed, for a few hours only. The palace is quiet. In her chambers, she removes her dress and rests her head against the wall.

Your face, Ninus said. *I've never seen anything as beautiful.*

She is reminded of the first time she spoke to Onnes, by the river in Mari. 'Do people tell you that you look like the goddess Ishtar?' he had asked, but his words were bait, for her to take and discover what he truly meant. Onnes' words are always made of darkness, feelings hidden behind a slab of coldness or half-spoken truths.

Ninus' face was open, ravenous. There is hunger in him, as if he is searching for another to fill him, to make him whole. She could see it then, a glimpse of something she couldn't see before. As a child, Onnes must have needed Ninus because being near him feels like being alive, all thoughts and feelings thrashing around like a windstorm. And Ninus needed Onnes because there is no greater peace from the torment of the mind than coldness, blankness.

She wonders if what happened between them was just a dream. Did she really walk away, or did she imagine it? Did she kiss him instead, just like she wanted to?

A betrayal isn't only a broken promise. It is also a word, a smile, a hand against the shoulder, skin against skin. It can be a thought, an obsession, a need.

A betrayal can be so many different things, which is why no one is exempt from it.

*

The city wakes, but the palace keeps sleeping. The leaves on the ceiling are luminous in the light of the lamps. The image of the goddess Ishtar on Semiramis' dagger glimmers, eyes blue like lapis lazuli. She can't look at it without hearing the sounds the Bactrian soldiers made when she sank it into their faces.

She had felt fierce when she was fighting, filled with rage and fire. But then, after the city had burned and everything had turned to ash, all the ruthlessness was gone. Only the cries remained, and the blackened faces, etched onto her mind, unwanted memories.

The portico is empty. She walks past it into Onnes' chambers. Her leopard sits at the opposite end of the room, staring at Semiramis warily. Onnes' breath catches, as if he were dreaming. But she knows he never dreams. When he sleeps, he travels to a place of stillness, where his mind stops spinning and his past stops haunting him.

She puts a hand to his cheek, imagines, for a moment, he is dead – dragged to the house of dust with all the souls he butchered. Sometimes she can hear him scream when he wakes, and the opium's effect has faded. She is already awake by his side, staring at the ceiling, too scared to close her eyes and see the nightmares that await her. He is part of them, those thoughts of death that refuse to leave her.

The leopard moves closer to the bed. *Close your eyes*, she seems to tell Semiramis. *I will protect you.*

Semiramis lies down. Despite all the anger, despite all the fear, she wraps her body around her husband's and tries to sleep.

*

When she wakes, Onnes is gone. She dresses and goes to find him. The royal road holds the warmth of the sun, but from the terraced gardens comes a fresh breeze. She walks past the Northwest Palace, dwarfed by its rich blue walls, until she reaches the temples.

The house of Ishtar is made of whispers. Semiramis finds her way to the chamber where vases pile up, rich with offerings to the goddess. Onnes is kneeling there, in the light that creeps through the arched doorway. Still and barely breathing, he looks like a gilded statue.

'Are you praying for redemption?' she asks.

He does not turn. His shoulders stiffen. 'No, there is no redemption. You were there with me, all of us were, and we have to carry the burden now.'

It is a conversation they have already had – and it always ends in a fight. She feels tired, hollowed out. 'What was it that carved out your heart?' she asks. 'Your mother? The war?'

He is quiet for such a long time that she thinks he has not heard her. But then he stands and turns to face her, moving away from the light. In the shadows, she can't see his expression, only the glint of his eyes.

'Sometimes I wish I was dead,' he says.

She is struck by the hopelessness in his voice. 'Don't say that,' she whispers.

Slowly, he lowers his head, lips hovering a breath from her shoulder. Then he buries his face in the hollow of her neck. She lets him, even if her anger hasn't faded. *Maybe it never will. Maybe I will never forgive him.*

She wonders if both of them have been irrevocably spoiled by war, and if they can ever go back to the people they were before they travelled to Balkh.

*

Nisat's gold necklace shines against the dark blue of her tunic. The clasp, Semiramis notices, is made of entwined dragons' heads. Sasi, Ilu, Sargon and the *bârû* all greet the queen as they enter. Sasi bows, Ilu kisses her hand and the *bârû* whispers in her ear before sitting to her left.

Ninus is nowhere to be seen. Nisat sits in his chair, chin high, as if challenging others to complain. Semiramis claims the place opposite her, close to the foot of the table, so she can study the men without being looked at. Next to her, Onnes sits with a cold, focused expression.

'I am told you fought well, my governor,' Sasi whispers with a smile that Onnes does not return. Then he winks at Semiramis, before turning his attention to the queen.

'There is much we need to discuss,' Nisat starts. 'The king isn't well, so I speak for him on all matters today.'

I don't think I've ever seen anything as beautiful. Ninus' words slip into Semiramis' head. She pushes them away, praying that his absence has nothing to do with her. As if hearing her thoughts, Nisat casts one disdainful look in her direction. Semiramis stares back until the queen turns away.

Ilu is speaking of the gold flowing from Balkh. With all they have taken, he says, they will build new statues and enrich the palaces with new bas-reliefs. Food is already coming from the provinces, as well as horses from the north, booty and tributes from the east, limestone and alabaster from the west. They have lost many soldiers at war, but they have gained a new labour force with the Bactrian men they have deported. They will get to work on the new fortresses north of Kalhu, heavily defended square citadels to keep the enemies of the north at bay.

'Good,' Nisat says. 'This will allow you to stop campaigning for a while. What else?'

Ilu swirls his beer cup round. 'There is the matter of our king's inheritance,' he says. 'He hasn't married yet.'

'The king has a daughter—' the *bârû* starts.

'No royal blood runs in her veins,' Ilu interrupts.

'My son's blood runs in her veins,' Nisat says sharply.

'Yes,' Ilu concedes. 'But legacy isn't the only reason to marry. A good marriage makes a good alliance.'

Semiramis shifts on her chair, noting the look that passes between the *turtanu* and the queen.

'Are you about to offer your daughter to my son again?' Nisat asks. Next to Ilu, Sargon smiles. The sick feeling that rises in Semiramis' chest has nothing to do with the wine.

'My daughter comes from the noble tribe of the Bit-Adini,' Ilu says. 'Uniting our families in marriage will mean uniting our king's lineage with my ancient Assyrian bloodline. It would send a message to all the lords and tribes who wish to empower themselves within the empire. Yes, we have expanded our borders, but let us show them that those who rule haven't changed.'

Nisat regards Ilu quietly. Then she turns to Sasi. 'Do you have an opinion on the matter, Spymaster? Of course you do,' she adds, before he can speak. 'And I am sure it will be something clever, as always.'

Sasi smiles. 'You flatter me, my queen.' He stops, a suspenseful pause, before speaking again. 'I have considered the matter carefully, and it seems to me that the best match for our king is the princess of Urartu.'

The *bârû* gasps. Semiramis forces her face to relax, aware that everyone in the council is exchanging glances. Ilu's grip tightens around his cup.

'Taria is Urartian,' Sasi continues, 'the key to the north. If we unite the reign of Assyria with Urartu, we eliminate our principal enemy, as well as securing the borders. The Urartian kingdom has not only survived but thrived despite being located in a dangerous, mountainous region. They are used to fighting their enemies to the north, so they can keep fighting them for us.'

There is a brief silence. Semiramis sees her hands are shaking, so she hides them under her fringed sleeves. She suddenly wishes that Marduk were here so that someone could object to this madness. It is Sargon who speaks. 'Taria is a hostage, and Urartu is an enemy,' he says. 'We do not make alliances with our enemies.'

'My lord, that is what an alliance is,' Sasi says. 'What is the point of an alliance with a friend?'

'A lesson in politics from a man without a cock.' Ilu laughs.

Sasi's smile does not falter. 'I try to compensate for my physical lacks with a clever brain. I am not sure everyone here has mastered that art.'

Ilu's mouth twists, but before he can smother Sasi, Nisat intervenes, 'Wise and selfless as always, Sasi. Let us think on it. And I'll bring your proposal to the king.'

And what does Taria have to say to this? Semiramis wonders, but the king's mother is standing, dismissing everyone. Ilu finishes his beer before leaving, a cohort of slaves hurrying behind him. Onnes goes after him, making for the training ground without a glance at Semiramis. She feels as if she is watching a play whose ending has been settled already, and she can do nothing to stop it.

As Sasi steps towards the door, she blocks his way. The eunuch smiles, unperturbed. 'You have been quiet, for someone who has just destroyed a city.' His eyes drop to her chest, where her wound is hidden under her dress. 'Tell me, what thoughts is your mind spinning?'

She goes back to the table, pouring beer for them both, biding her time. She could hide meanings in her words or cut straight to the point. She opts for the latter.

'Do you know what ails the king?' she asks.

Sasi doesn't speak. He cocks his head, a movement he often makes when people commit mistakes that he deems stupid, and Semiramis realizes she has asked the wrong question.

'I thought you might know,' he says. When she keeps quiet, he continues, 'The most interesting whisper reached me the other day. That you were in the king's apartments a few nights ago. I refused to believe it, of course. Such a thing would be madness.'

She almost strikes him. 'No need to play with words. You know I was there. The king called for me. Do you want to scold me, or betray me?'

He raises his brows innocently. 'I do not care for your private affairs. I gather information because that is my role as spymaster.'

'That is a lie.'

He smiles, like a mischievous child. 'Yes, it is. But you have heard the council. The king will marry the princess Taria.'

'Neither he nor Taria have agreed.'

'You are cleverer than this. You know how marriages work. They will marry, and that is why you must not be seen with the king, neither for your pleasure or interest nor for his.'

'That didn't sound like a suggestion.'

'Suggestion . . . order . . .' he shrugs. 'Take it as you will.'

'I thought you knew that I am not good at obeying orders.'

Sasi watches her sharply. 'You aren't. But I also believe you have a certain abhorrence of death and all things that might harm you. So I am confident that you will do what is most convenient for you.'

She thinks about all the times she ran towards risk when she was younger, simply to feel her heart racing, to convince herself she could tame even her greatest fears.

She puts her cup down. 'Do you think I'd be here, Spymaster, if I had done only what is most convenient for me?'

*

In the reception room, bowls have been cleaned and jars are lined against the wall, sealed with linen cloths. On the walls, deer are running straight into the wide nets that huntsmen have set for them. She caresses the contours of the biggest animal. There is an arrow in its leg; it makes her think of the spear thrust into Bel's face.

When she first came here, the palace gave her a sense of peace and power. She had liked every bas-relief, every alabaster panel, every stone figure protecting the rooms from angry spirits. Now all she sees is the violence that simmers beneath the surface of those images: the threatening eyes of the eagle-headed spirits, a soldier driving his sword into a bull's neck, foreign prisoners carrying their possessions in bundles across their shoulders.

'Mistress.'

She turns. Ribat's shadow is staring at her from a corner. 'What is it?'

He is looking at her strangely, as if there was a veil between them and he didn't know how to rip it away.

'Do you need herbs to sleep?' he asks.

'What makes you think I cannot sleep?' she asks, more sharply than she intends to.

'I hear you pacing. And you screamed in your sleep last night.'

Suddenly she is angry. 'That is because I saw my husband impale prisoners as if they weren't human beings, cut off their hands, then burn their bodies until even their souls were ashes.' Her hands are shaking again. She sinks her nails into the palms to stop it.

Ribat stays still. There is a flicker of light in his eyes, and for a moment he looks as if he is about to speak, but then he closes his mouth and draws the veil again, hiding his thoughts from her.

'I will bring you some herbs,' he says.

She nods, exhausted, but when he brings them to her, she does not take them. *I'd rather have the nightmares than the numbness.*

The gods hear her wish. When she falls asleep, her dreams are of tongues of fire, temples crumbling, and Onnes' hand on her shoulder as she screams into the burning air.

*

She wakes in the middle of the night to the sound of someone pacing. The leopard is biting her sleeve. The moon shines overhead, wearing the darkness of the night like a cloak. Onnes is roaming around the room.

She sits up, pushing the leopard away. Her throat is dry, and she gulps some water from a jar beside her bed.

'Onnes,' she says.

He doesn't reply, but when she looks at him more carefully, she sees that his eyes are wet. She stands quickly, unnerved. 'I will ask Ribat to bring you some opium.' She moves towards the door, but Onnes lunges and grabs her arm.

'I have to tell you something.' His grip is strong. 'I've done . . .' He stops. He seems to be hardly breathing. 'I have done something terrible.'

The leopard is growling. She sees the whites of Onnes' eyes, glass shards reflecting the light. 'It haunts me too,' she says, because he is scaring her, 'every night. But you said it is what war is about.'

His face is pale in the raw moonlight. 'I am not speaking of Balkh.' He lets her go and, before she can grasp what is happening, he slams his head into the wall. There is a dull, painful sound and when he looks back at her, his forehead is bleeding.

She stares at him. 'What have you done?'

Blood trickles down his forehead onto his cheeks. His eyes are dark and fathomless, and he looks as if he has come directly from the house of dust. 'I killed him.'

For a mad moment, she thinks he is speaking of Ninus.

'Who?' she croaks. 'Who did you kill?'

Then he tells her, and the paving drops from under her feet.

30.

Ribat, a Slave

He is summoned by Semiramis to her rooms, where she is sitting in an ivory chair by the window. Ana and Zamena are brushing her hair, which falls to her waist, dark and scented.

'Leave,' Semiramis orders them, when Ribat enters.

They are gone quickly, and the room grows quiet. There is something ominous about it. Ribat crosses the chamber and takes the ivory comb Ana has left on a stool. Slowly, he starts plaiting golden rings into Semiramis' hair.

She clears her throat. Her voice is strangely empty. 'When you came to me last night and I spoke about Onnes, you were about to tell me something.'

Ribat almost drops the comb. There is a beat. An intake of breath.

'There is no need to deny it,' she says. 'I could see it on your face.'

He wonders how she can read people's minds so easily. He decides that the safest course is to be quiet. She keeps talking: 'The first thing you told me when I arrived in this palace was that slaves were the eyes and ears of the city. If what you said is true, this is your moment to prove it. The moment to prove your loyalty.'

It seems to be a test, though Ribat doesn't know the right answer. If he does not tell her, he fails her. If he does, their future is threatened.

'You know what you must tell me,' she says, without turning. All he sees are her stiff shoulders, and her long hair in his hands. 'You must tell me Onnes' secret.'

Fear rushes in him, like wind. Is this a trick? Does she truly know? His hands keep plaiting her hair of their own accord. 'Secrets are like diseases,' he whispers. 'Once they are out, they keep spreading.'

She turns then, sets her dark eyes on him. 'Diseases can be contained.'

Only by eliminating the people who carry them. I have no intention of dying, have you?

'I need you to tell me the truth,' she says, and this time her tone tells him she will not ask again.

He thinks about his options, meticulously, like a merchant weighing his gold.

Then he reveals the memory that is buried inside him and was never meant to see the light.

*

The final year of the rebellion. The lower part of the citadel is burning. The traitor Assur-danin's army has made its way into the walls. Shamshi-Adad fights by the gate, leading his men with Onnes. Common women and children are taking all they can carry away from the narrow lanes at the foot of the walls and towards the palace. They beg the guards to let them pass, rocking their crying babies.

The sunlight burns, the wind scourging the skin. Slaves are meant to be hiding, but Ribat has left Onnes' palace because his mother is sick. Her fever is building, and she needs willow leaves that can only be found in two places: the healer's shop, down by the walls where soldiers are killing men like pigs, or in the Northwest Palace. Ribat crosses a square where the bodies of priests are scattered, arrows colouring the white tunics with splashes of crimson. A dog wanders, tail between its legs, paws soaked in a puddle of blood.

Ribat takes the side entrance to the palace. Quickly past the corridors of the domestic wing until he reaches a room filled with jars of herbal medicines. Someone has been here – pots have been broken, their contents spilled. He walks around frantically until he finds two small jugs of willow extract and shoves them into his tunic. Then he is running back the way he came, through rooms cast in semi-darkness. He enters the courtyard that connects the domestic wing to the palace banqueting suites and stops.

There is the sound of hurrying feet. From the opposite side of the courtyard, a man appears. He is wearing a pointed helmet and a short kilt – the guards' uniform. His arms are outstretched, his mouth open.

Before he can speak, a sword pierces his chest from behind. The guard falls, revealing a man behind him. Onnes.

Ribat throws himself into the closest room. He shouldn't be here – he must not be seen. This is a mistake he can't afford. He enters corridor after corridor until he finds himself in a wide bedroom, heart pounding so fast it sounds like a war drum. He looks around at the rich furniture – pure white ivories, couches covered with purple pillows. It takes him a moment to realize a man is lying on the large bed, eyes closed.

'Assur?' The voice is hoarse and deep. The king's. His forehead is slick with sweat: he also has the fever, the one that has been ravaging the city since before Assur's army attacked. The sickness that allowed Assur's army to attack. Why are there no guards protecting this place?

Ribat slides to the opposite side of the room, searching for an exit, then realizes that the only way out is through the door he came in. The king's eyes are still closed: he hasn't seen him. Ribat creeps into a wooden trunk, leaves the lid ajar to breathe. A row of smoking torches makes the room a furnace.

'Is that you, my son?' the king repeats.

A shadow fills the doorway, then Onnes' figure appears. He moves to the side of the bed, slowly. He should be by the gate with Shamshi-Adad, but there is something on his face, a shadow Ribat has never seen.

'Not Assur,' Onnes says, 'but I am your son.'

The king opens his eyes and turns his head to face him. He is wearing a white nightgown, yellow sweat stains all over it.

'Ninus sent you?' Shalmaneser asks.

'Didn't you hear what I said?' Onnes says. 'I am your son.'

The king coughs, sits up slowly, with effort. There is a jewelled dagger on the bed next to him. 'I know who you are, Onnes. Have you come to claim the throne? Because that would be a mistake.'

'I want no such thing.' His voice, always so empty, has something in it, a seed of emotion. 'I am here to talk about my mother.'

Shalmaneser laughs. Onnes stiffens. Ribat catches his breath. His legs are hurting, and his lungs are filling with hot, dry air.

'Your mother is dead because she was weak,' the king says. 'She expected to be treated like a queen but behaved like a whore. There is nothing else to know about her.'

Something passes over Onnes' face. 'Do not call her that.'

'Or what? Are you going to murder me? I already have a son who wishes me dead, and he will soon be here. Assur will complain about my decisions, as he always does because he is a child. Then I'll promise him he'll be king next, and the war will be over. But he won't kill me. His rebellion is a whim, a product of his never-ending stupidity.'

'Assur won't reach here,' Onnes says. 'Ninus' army is pushing him back. By the end of the day they'll be out of the city walls again, and they'll start their retreat.'

The king coughs again. 'You can't know that.'

'I can. Your son has made a pact with the Babylonian king. Babylon's forces are attacking Assur's army from the other side. They'll be crushed.'

'Ninus' idea?'

'Mine.'

'I see. Maybe you are my son after all.'

There is a moment of silence. Sounds of the war reach the citadel faintly, like the feeble fluttering of bat wings. With blood on his face, Onnes is an otherworldly creature.

'I didn't kill your mother,' Shalmaneser says. 'She did that to herself. But I understand that, as a son, you need someone to blame.'

'You should have killed me,' Onnes says.

'Yes. But Nisat convinced me that getting rid of you would mean enduring my son's hatred.'

'On that she was right.'

'Maybe I'll have you killed when this war is over.'

'You think anything's changed? Ninus would still hate you for ever.'

'He's not a child any more. People change.'

'But some feelings stay the same.'

Onnes' blade slashes the air. It stops at the hollow place at the king's throat. Waiting. Lingering. A moment when father and son lock eyes. Shalmaneser's wide open in shock. Onnes' burning with hatred.

'If you kill me, your life will be ruined.'

Onnes shakes his head. 'It is ruined already.'

The blade sinks into the soft skin. The body wriggles like an insect. A king's last breath. Onnes removes the dagger and cleans it, slowly, fastidiously. Sweat and blood all over him, and all he cares about is his weapon. When it is shiny enough, he lifts his head. The torches *paint his face orange. He lets out a shuddering breath, then leaves the room, away from the father he killed and back to the brother he betrayed.*

In the trunk, Ribat listens to his own laboured breathing. He waits and waits and waits. When everything is quiet, he slides out, without glancing at the dead body on the bed. The corridors feel like a tomb. He runs away, nothing more than a flying shadow, through every courtyard, down the steps of the palace, out of the Northwest walls. He runs and runs in the burning city until his feet are hurting and his lungs are raw.

*

Ribat stops speaking. The torches have gone out. Semiramis covers her face with her hands.

31.

A Marriage for a King

Onnes stays away from the palace for two days and nights, so she goes to the training ground at dawn, where she knows he will be alone.

He is throwing spears towards a target at the opposite end of the courtyard. The blades stab the wood with eerie precision. She wonders if he has been sleeping here, or in the Northwest Palace with the king. She isn't sure she wants to know the answer.

'Ninus doesn't know,' she says. She meant it as a question, but it sounds like a statement.

He turns, spear in hand. The bags under his eyes are deep and dark. 'No.'

'Why?' she asks. 'Why did you do it?'

His knuckles whiten around the spear. 'He is the reason my mother died. He made her feel like she was nothing.'

'He could have killed you too, but he kept you alive.'

'Am I supposed to feel grateful for that?'

No, I suppose not. 'Ninus killed Assur because of this,' she says, voice shaking.

'Assur needed to die, or we would never have won the war.'

'You've lied to Ninus, for all these years.'

'Do not speak to me about lying. You lied to me the very first time I met you.'

She did, but that lie was born of necessity. It was survival, or at least that was what she told herself. What is *this* lie? Where does it lead?

'He is your brother,' she says. 'Your king.'

'You seem suddenly to care a great deal about him.'

'He loves you *desperately*,' she cries, surprised by the pain in her own voice. 'And you don't.'

'What does it matter how I feel?'

'It *matters*,' she says, 'because you never feel anything for *anyone*.' Her pulse is beating furiously in her throat. He stares at her, saying nothing. She walks to him, grabs the spear from his hand and smashes it against his shoulder. The shaft breaks in two, but he doesn't flinch.

'Still feeling nothing?' she asks. Her voice is rising.

A drop of blood blossoms on his skin, then trails down his arm. He doesn't wipe it away. 'You are behaving like a child,' he says.

She hits his chest, punching the fading bruises he still carries from Balkh. 'Tell me how you feel,' she says. 'Tell me that you don't care for him.'

'You are disgracing yourself,' he says.

She hates the steadiness of his voice, the coldness. '*Tell me*.'

'Stop,' he warns her, 'before the soldiers arrive. Is this how you want them to see you?'

'I want to see you care about someone other than your *mother*,' she pants.

Something in his eyes lights up, as if his body has suddenly caught fire. He lashes out with his fist, striking her face. The courtyard goes black for a moment and, when she can see again, she is on the stone floor, tasting her own blood. It is pouring copiously across her mouth.

'I care,' he says. Slowly, he kneels in front of her. His eyes are wild with anger. Pain is burning in her face, but she feels a deep sense of satisfaction. It reminds her of the times Simmas used to hit her. Only now she has control over it. She smiles, enjoying the throbbing in her head.

'You are sick,' Onnes says.

'So are you,' she replies. But she has spoken to the air: he has already gone.

*

She stays in the courtyard for a long time. When the soldiers come to train, she crawls into one of the small, dark rooms, listening to the clang of iron against iron.

Once, after training with Onnes in the evening, she had taken his hand and said, 'Why don't we stay a bit longer?' They had lain down in the empty courtyard, waiting until the heavens filled with stars. Onnes listened while she identified the constellations that trace the path of the moon: 'the Snake', a creature with wings and a raven pecking at its tail; 'the Scorpion', whose claws were made of silver stars; 'the Lion', which burned brightest. She had felt something she had never known before then: peace. For a moment, she didn't crave anything but what she already had.

A lie, like all good memories are. She can see Onnes' face when he spat out the words, 'I care.' There was so much hurt in his eyes that if she cut him it would all bleed out. There is a wound in him that has become infected and turned into hatred.

She imagines him going back to Ninus' side after he had killed his father. 'Shalmaneser is dead,' Ninus would have said. 'Assur killed him.' And Onnes said nothing, let Ninus believe what he wanted to believe.

Cold anger is rising in her. It is the anger mortals feel when the people closest to them reveal themselves in a different light, starker, crueller. Now she sees Onnes for who he is, and she must take a side. Fall down with him, or find a way to keep her place.

*

The queen's household is crowded. The women are curiously eyeing Semiramis, faces bobbing out of rooms and corridors. She walks upstairs, making her way to the large room filled with braziers and dark tapestries.

Taria is seated on a chair, caressing the statuette of her goddess. She has grown fuller since the last time Semiramis saw her, and she has started painting her face in the Assyrian way: eyes and brows are lined with bronze kohl, which glows against her golden skin.

'I was wondering when you'd come to see me,' she says. '*The woman who burned down the acropolis of Balkh*. I thought you had forgotten about me.'

Semiramis steps forward, aware that, as she does so, the bruise on her face comes into the light. Taria's eyes fall on it, and she tilts her head, shocked.

'I am here to speak of the council's plans,' Semiramis says flatly. 'Surely you have heard about them.'

Taria's eyes do not leave her bruise. 'To marry me to the king? Yes, I have heard.'

'It would be a great honour,' Semiramis says, trying to see what Taria thinks of the match.

'One I did not ask for.'

'Would you rather marry the prince Marduk?' Semiramis can't help but ask.

Taria's face darkens, and she brings a hand to her belly, as if to steady herself. 'You once told me you'd never speak of this to anyone.'

Semiramis thinks of the happy, carefree days they spent together before Marduk ruined everything and she left for the war. 'And I've kept my promise.'

'What happened to your face?'

'I hit my husband until he hit me back.'

'Why?'

Because he is mad and a traitor, and now my whole life is threatened. 'It does not concern you.'

'I thought we were friends.'

'Are you still sleeping with Marduk?'

Taria turns to look at the tapestries. The embroidered mountains are pale against a stormy sky. 'No,' she says. 'Not any more.'

There is the sound of hurried steps and a slave comes into the room, carrying a large silver bucket. 'I brought a clean one, Princess.'

Taria's head snaps away from the tapestries. 'Take that away,' she hisses. The slave notices Semiramis, blushes, then runs out.

Semiramis watches her, her mind racing. A sudden thought occurs to her. She has never considered pregnancy as a possibility for Taria; she had just assumed the princess would be careful. *But Taria is highborn. She is used to having what she wants without thinking of the consequences.*

'You are pregnant,' she says.

Taria smiles bitterly, starts torturing the hem of her sleeve. 'It does not concern you.'

'You can't marry the king,' Semiramis says.

Taria lifts her painted eyebrows. '*You* want to marry him?'

'I already have a husband. What do you intend to do? Lie to the King of Assyria? Tell him that the child is his?'

'I don't see any other way out.'

Semiramis moves closer to her, lowers her voice. 'You could tell Ninus. He is kind and merciful. He would send you home.'

'*Merciful*,' Taria spits. 'Just like his mother? Like all the other Assyrians? Just like *you*, who destroyed a city of innocent people?'

Semiramis ignores her. 'You want to stay in the capital only because Marduk is here. Does he know about the child?'

'No.'

'Then you must not tell him.'

Taria scoffs. 'Do not use me as your political pawn. I have heard how you behave during the council meetings. You do everything in your power to turn things to your advantage.'

'Whatever is an advantage to me should be an advantage to you too.'

'Why? Because we are both women?' Taria snarls. 'You grew up with nothing. Your land is Eber-Nari, but you never speak of it as if it were your home. I had a life in Urartu, a family. You care nothing for those you've left behind, only for yourself.'

Semiramis ignores the sting in her heart. 'You know nothing about me.'

'Everyone says you are a riddle, but you are not so difficult to solve. You are just like the king's mother. You go where power is.' She suddenly stops, looks over Semiramis' shoulder, her face leaden.

Nisat is standing by the door, as if Taria's words had summoned her. Her hair isn't pinned, as it usually is, but falls down her back, streaked with silver. There are two slaves behind her, whom she dismisses with a flick of her hand. The room grows cold.

'You are quarrelling like children,' Nisat says, her lips thin with distaste. 'Unless you want my entire household to hear, you'd better put an end to this little scene.'

Taria turns her back to her, staring resolutely at the tapestries. Her shoulders are shaking, and, with her long, light hair cascading over her shoulders, she reminds Semiramis of the beautiful birds that are brought to the capital from the west, kept in cages before they are left in the gardens for visitors to look at.

'I will send someone to burn incense in this room,' Nisat adds. 'It smells of vomit.'

'I don't use incense to pray,' Taria says. 'It offends my gods.'

'I couldn't care less about your gods,' Nisat says. 'Come, Semiramis,' she speaks over her shoulder. 'Do not disturb the princess.'

Semiramis gives Taria one last look, then follows the king's mother. Out in the courtyard, the sun god Shamash rides his chariot high in the sky. The women who had gathered to eavesdrop disappear in a flutter of emerald dresses and perfumed sandals. Nisat walks into a quiet room, with bas-reliefs of lush plants and lionesses on the walls. Then she turns to face Semiramis.

'I thought it strange,' she starts, 'when Onnes first brought you to the capital. I had never seen him taken with a woman. And yet, to bring you here, all the way from Eber-Nari . . .' She tails off, her eyes on the bruise on Semiramis' face. To Semiramis' surprise, she reaches out and touches it, her fingers pressing into the skin. It stings, but Semiramis doesn't draw away. 'But now I see that you and Onnes are perfectly matched,' Nisat continues. 'Neither of you has any regard for your safety. You would throw away your lives as if they were nothing.'

'On the contrary, my queen,' Semiramis says, 'I wouldn't throw my life away for anything.'

Nisat lets her hand drop. 'Then why do you wish to upset the prince Marduk?'

She knows, Semiramis thinks. They look at each other for a moment.

'If she is pregnant, she cannot marry Ninus,' Semiramis says.

Nisat walks to the long table in the middle of the room, pours some wine for herself. 'If you speak of this to anyone, I will have you killed.'

It is the first time Nisat has openly threatened her, and Semiramis can't help but laugh. 'That is your plan? To contain the secret, while you keep Taria locked in your palace? And then what?'

'And *then* she can marry my son. The alliance still stands.'

'You think she will give up her child?'

'She will have no choice.'

Semiramis steadies herself against the table. The room they are in is beautiful, walls painted red, green and gold, light pouring from the courtyard into every corner. For a moment, she imagines growing up here, in a place so heavenly that one forgets it is also a cage. 'Your plan won't work,' she says.

Nisat's mouth tightens. 'Perhaps you have a better one.'

'I do. Send Taria back to the north. If she remains here, Babylon and Urartu might form an alliance.'

Nisat looks at her as if Semiramis has lost all reason. 'There is nothing more foolish than setting a hostage free.'

'There is nothing more foolish than thinking Taria won't do any-thing to keep her child. She might tell Marduk or, worse, the king.'

'You have no children, what do you know of being a mother?'

Nothing, as everyone has been eager to remind me from the moment I was born. 'I had little time to sleep with my husband while we were away at war.'

'A war you are so keen to remind everyone that *you* have won.'

'I hope they remember. I surely won't forget what I have seen.'

Nisat is quiet for a long time. When she speaks again, her face has grown darker, harder to read. 'You are ambitious, Semiramis, and I respect that, but we must all sacrifice something. What are you willing to sacrifice for power?'

The answer is easy. 'Anything,' Semiramis says. 'But what you see as power, I see as safety.'

Nisat snorts. 'Power and safety are opposites. The more powerful you are, the less safe you become.'

Semiramis shakes her head. 'You speak like that because you have never been a nobody, my queen. But when you are nothing, when no one is willing to serve you and protect you and die for you, that is when you are most vulnerable. No one is safe in this world. I'd much rather have power, and the means to protect myself, than rot in anonymity.'

Nisat's eyes on her feel like a dark wave, building and building before it breaks. Finally, she says, 'I see now why Onnes likes you so much. But he is a man, and men are easier to swindle. Now leave me. Leave and do not come back to my palace.'

*

Onnes is reading inventories in his chambers. Semiramis goes to him, lays her fingers against his cheek. The rage has drained from his face and left it white, bloodless.

'No one else can know,' she says.

'Why?' he asks. 'Because you would risk losing all the power you have so carefully gained?'

'Because it would destroy him.'

He holds her gaze, and she sees the torches reflected in it, flames of orange light. *Say something*, she thinks. *Give me a reason to stay.* But he says nothing, so she walks away.

She finds Ninus in the gardens, among the blooming tamarisk trees. He is speaking with two courtiers she has often seen in the Northwest Palace. They lean towards him, as if they could drink his light, feast on his attention.

Semiramis clears her throat. Ninus turns. The look he gives her is of hope and wariness. He dismisses the courtiers with a flick of his hand. They wait in silence, until their steps have faded, and they are left alone.

She is the one who breaks the silence. 'The gardens are beautiful today.'

'It is the month of blossoming and of love,' Ninus says, with a strange expression. 'They are always at their best.'

The trees around them are murmuring, a soothing sound.

'I imagine you have heard that I am soon to be married,' he says.

'Yes,' she says, glad that he has brought it up first.

'My mother suggested that I send Taria back to Urartu.'

'That sounds clever,' she says, in the most expressionless voice she can muster.

'I am not so sure. If I marry Taria, the war with the north ceases.' His face has taken on the cold look that Semiramis knows he reserves for the council meetings. Something stirs in her chest.

'Is that what you want, my king?' she asks.

His jaw tightens. She should leave now, go back to her palace and stop asking questions. But she seems not to know how.

'No, I do not want to marry the princess of Urartu,' Ninus says.

'Why?'

He turns so that they are facing each other. Her bruise is fading, though his eyes linger on it. She feels a lurch of intimacy: there is no one but them and the sun god, watching them from above.

'You know why.'

Yes, but I want you to say it.

'I am not free to do as I please,' he says. 'Each decision I make is part of a web that has been woven by countless others. To try to wriggle out of it would cause calamity.'

'You are the king. You can choose among countless women. There is no one else in the kingdom who can claim such a privilege.'

He laughs joylessly. 'Having a claim on all things is not such a privilege as you would think.'

'It is better than having a claim on nothing.'

The trees stir slightly with the breeze. Their branches drip with fruit, framing Ninus' face. It is serious, bright-eyed. She thinks of the poems written on the columns in his courtyard: his heart like a garden, blooming as the sun pours light on it.

Quietly, so quietly, he says, 'I can't stop thinking about you.'

She takes a step forward and her hand brushes his. The touch of a feather, of lips grazing the skin. She is so close to him that she can see how his black hair shines, his long, dark lashes, the curve of his jaw. His breathing stutters. She can feel it against her cheek.

Voices rise into the air. They spring away from each other. A group of courtiers appears from behind the rows of pomegranate trees, their voices rich with laughter. They stop when they see Ninus, bow deeply. Ninus casts one look at them, then at Semiramis.

He walks away, graceful and beautiful, a god in the gardens of Heaven. She is left alone, her skin cold with his absence.

32.

Semiramis, a Seductress

For days, she does not see him. There are no council meetings, and she avoids the training ground: if Onnes is there, and Ninus with him, what is she supposed to do? Look at her husband's brother? Tell him of Onnes' betrayal? Her heart feels raw inside her chest and her skin crawls with anger: towards Onnes, towards Ninus, towards herself.

On the seventh day – the last day of the month of love – Onnes is sent to deal with a rebellion south of the city of Ashur. He leaves at dawn, when she has just fallen asleep. When she wakes again, he is gone.

*

'The spymaster is leaving the capital too,' Ribat tells her in the evening. They are in her room, she sprawled on her couch, him smoothing the wrinkles out of the bright carpets that cover the floor. 'The king has sent him to bargain with Egyptian merchants for the sale of lapis lazuli.'

She says nothing, letting the words sink in. The room smells of sweet date wine, which she has drunk throughout the day, restless. The sound of the leopard eating a bird comes to her from the portico. Ribat stands to leave, but she stops him. 'Stay,' she says. If she sleeps alone, she will go mad. She can feel the nightmares waiting in the corner of her mind, ready to attack her when her guard slips.

'Yes, Mistress,' Ribat says. He puts her sandals away and blows out the lamps.

The evening light – warm and blue – comes from the portico. A breeze carries the scents of tamarisk and chamomile from the gardens. Ribat sits on the carpet; Semiramis curls up at the end of the bed. She imagines sinking into the sculpted waves on the walls, diving into the sea. She would find her mother and ask her if love truly is a curse, if it is worth dying for such a fleeting feeling.

She turns to Ribat. 'What do you do when you want something you know you can't have?'

The answer comes to him easily. 'Every good thing comes with bad consequences. I think of those consequences.'

She rolls onto her back and looks at the ceiling. In her mind, she draws a list of consequences.

If she goes to Ninus, Onnes will leave her.

If she goes to Ninus, Ninus might change his mind and reject her.

If she goes to Ninus, Sasi might find out.

If she goes to Ninus, she will be punished.

If she goes to Ninus, she will be killed.

If she goes to Ninus, she will become like her mother, a woman who can't govern her feelings and destroys everything around her.

She goes on for a long time, until she falls asleep, drawing comfort from Ribat's presence and his quiet breathing.

*

At dawn Ana comes into her room, holding a small lamp in front of her. She blinks when she sees Ribat curled up at the foot of the large bed.

'Mistress,' she says, 'the spymaster is in the courtyard.'

Ribat springs up, face flushed with embarrassment. Semiramis slips into a silver dress, wondering what Sasi wants at this hour.

In the courtyard, she pours two cups of beer. Sasi is waiting in a corner, his pale fingers crossed under his long-fringed shawl. 'Did I wake you?' he asks placidly.

She hands him a cup. 'You did.'

He sips, unfazed. The light of dawn creeps in, pale and tired. 'I thought you had left the capital,' she says.

'I am about to. I won't be away for more than a day, luckily. The Egyptians aren't easy to bargain with. They think the world owes everything to the Empire of the Nile.'

'Just like the Assyrians,' she comments, making him chuckle. 'Shouldn't you be preparing, then?'

'I am prepared,' he says. '*Always* prepared. But I am worried about you. After our last conversation at the council meeting . . .'

That makes her smile. 'I didn't know you could be worried about anyone.'

'You know I am fond of you. The two of us . . . we are allies, aren't we?'

She raises an eyebrow. 'As much as I like and respect you, an ally's greatest quality is loyalty, which I do not think you are capable of.'

He smiles, amused. 'You are wrong. An ally's greatest gift is honesty, which friends and lovers can never give, caught as they are in their webs of commitment and fealty.'

As always, he is right. 'You need not worry about me,' she says.

The smile disappears from his face. 'I do not know what happened between you and Ninus, but I need you to be cautious. You cannot afford such a mistake. You come from nothing, just like me, and you must not forget it, no matter how powerful you have become. Every day you must remind yourself of where you came from, so that you remember that no human is, in fact, untouchable.'

She stares at him. 'The king is untouchable.'

'You aren't the king.' His tone is, surprisingly, annoyed. Something has changed in him, and she tries to understand what it is. *He has bet on me and now believes I am failing him.*

She thinks about Ninus. Then she wonders how much the respect of the eunuch is worth. She takes a deep breath and says, 'I will not fail you.'

*

When Sasi leaves, the palace feels like a cage.

She walks through each room, feeling the silence, the stillness. Servants tiptoe around her. She sends them all away – to wash by the river, to buy food at the market, she does not care. Her head is pounding, and the walls seem to close in on her as she moves. Her leopard glares at her from the shadows. A sickly light creeps over the floor, trying to snatch the hem of her dress. She moves away, panic rising, choked by a sense of hopelessness. This is how lost souls must feel, when they are plagued by evil spirits.

In the bathroom, she tries to clear her mind. Her fingers find the scar on her chest, thin and fading between her ribs. Death and fire quickly take over. She sees two girls trying to drag their mother to safety, a temple whose walls burn her hands, a man who falls from the sky, like a wingless bird.

She doesn't realize she has fallen asleep until she wakes in the darkness. In her chest, a sharp stab of pain. She looks around, heart beating urgently in her throat. The shadows are unfamiliar, ashy and colourless, like the house of dust. She tries to dodge them, but they are everywhere. She can feel the ice on her arms where they grip her, see their sunken white eyes. She is buried alive in this hell.

Death has caught me.
It lurks in my bedroom, and everywhere I look,
Everywhere I turn, there is only death.

Her hands find the stone walls, and she drags herself out of the bathroom. Pale lamplight floods the courtyard. Evening is already creeping in – she must have slept for hours.

Her breathing slows. Shadows start gaining clearer contours. The palace is silent, empty. Hands shaking, she wears a long dress and hurries outside before the dead can haunt her again.

*

The guards let her into the king's quarters without blinking. There is only one lamp burning in Ninus' reception room – the room where he, Semiramis and Onnes once dined together. It throws dancing shadows on the tapestries. When Ninus arrives, he is still in his royal attire.

'You should be sleeping,' he says.

'I need better company than my dreams.'

He nods, as if he understands. He draws her to one of the couches, pours date beer into cups that shine feebly. He takes the couch opposite hers. The cuffs around his wrists are inlaid with stones that protrude like large, bright blue eyes. Even in this room, she feels she is watched.

'You were trying to stay away,' Ninus says. 'I went back to the gardens, but you weren't there.'

She looks at the darkness that creeps around the corners of the room. 'I know. I am afraid.' The words slip out before she can stop them. She has never spoken them aloud, not once in her life, not even when she was a child. If she doesn't admit fear, she forces it to go away. But there is no fighting this feeling: it claws at her from everywhere.

'I thought you weren't afraid of anything,' Ninus says.

'You don't know much about me.'

He says nothing, just watches her as if she were a story he wants to press into his mind, to commit to memory, word by word. He has been watching her like this ever since Balkh. She can hear soft voices from somewhere deep within the palace, the drip of water from the baths.

'You said you don't want to marry the princess of Urartu,' she says.

'Yes, that is what I said.'

'I don't want you to marry her.'

They look at each other. He smooths his black hair with his hand – he would look like a god if his hair weren't so messy – as he makes up his mind. She realizes she has made up hers already.

Think of the consequences, Ribat had told her, and here she is, thinking of every single consequence, yet unable to leave. But there are some who simply want, and some who burn with desire.

They stand in unison, as if tied by a cord. Her heartbeat is a song as she crosses the distance between them. A single step, or a thousand – she does not know. The lamp flickers and dies, leaving the room to the shadows. But with him, the fear is gone. He buries his hands in her hair. His eyes are so dark they are almost black.

Is this the point of no return? she wonders.

He looks at her as if to say, *Yes, this is it*, and touches his lips to hers.

Who is guilty of no sin against his god?
Which is he who kept a commandment for ever?
All human beings harbour sin.

From the Assyrian poem, 'Who Has Not Sinned?'

33.

Ninus, King of the World, King of Assyria

When he was thirteen, he asked his mother about love.

'How do you love Father? How do you know?'

She was sitting in an ivory chair, her hair brushed and loose on her back. It was autumn, and from her palace he could see the gardens, trees amber like the gems on Nisat's fingers.

She gave him a contemptuous look. 'Do not be as stupid as to think I, or you, have the luxury of loving someone. I was given to your grandfather in marriage and then I married your father when Ashur-nasirpal died. That's the end of it.'

'Maybe it will be different for me.'

'You may be king one day. You will have the power to choose any woman you like. When anyone has too much, he can't desire anything. Or he ends up wanting the few things he cannot have.'

He wished she were different sometimes. Truth can be overpowering, yet Nisat served it to him, mouthful by mouthful, until he felt like he was choking.

*

The council room is dark. Trickles of light flow from the courtyards. The prince Marduk is tapping his fingers on the table. It took Ninus' men a while to find him, and when they did, he was in a tavern in the lower part of the citadel, drinking with two lyre players.

He bows when Ninus enters but doesn't stand. 'I was enjoying my day,' he says, with a faint smile, 'until you interrupted me.'

'You can find better company,' Ninus says, taking his carved chair.

'Than whores? I doubt it.' He seems paler than usual, except for the dark smudges beneath his eyes.

'You didn't attend the last council meetings,' Ninus points out, eager to move the conversation away from taverns and brothels.

Marduk makes himself comfortable, stretching into his chair. 'I have been receiving envoys from Babylon. My brother has been wounded in a lion hunt. The healers have been treating him, but he is dying.'

Ninus watches him. He has heard that Marduk and his older brother were close, though the prince's face is calm, amused even.

'I am sorry,' Ninus says. 'When he dies, I assume you become the heir to Babylon?'

'There are always things to gain from such a loss,' Marduk replies. 'Especially for second sons such as ourselves.'

Ninus doesn't like the comparison. 'I grieved for my brother.'

'I am sure you did,' Marduk says. There is a clear, mocking edge to his voice. 'And I will grieve for mine.'

Ninus thinks about Assur's throat bursting open on his blade as he killed him, about the way he sat holding his dead brother's body until his arms were drenched with his blood. He wipes away the memories, focuses on Marduk.

'Will you travel back to Babylon?' he asks, careful. If Marduk leaves, the pact between Assyria and Babylon will be threatened.

'My father wants me to. But I would rather stay longer. There are . . . matters I must attend to.'

Ninus doesn't need to ask what matters those are. Women to sleep with, surely. Boys to torment in the training ground. Brothels to visit. 'I am glad to hear it,' he says. 'Does that mean you will attend the next meetings?'

'I will try. Unless that priest keeps sharing his calamitous premonitions. I can't stand him. Or the eunuch.'

'Nothing of the sort,' Ninus assures him, with a sour smile. 'All the council discusses lately is the woman I should marry.'

Marduk raises his eyebrows, deeply amused by the prospect. 'And who would that be?'

'Currently the preferred candidate is the princess of Urartu.'

The amusement is wiped out of Marduk's face. His eyes gleam dangerously. 'You will marry Taria?'

'I may have to.'

'But you don't want to.' To Ninus' amazement, Marduk throws back his head and laughs. The sound echoes on the walls, as if the sculpted warriors were laughing with him. 'Of course you don't. Is she too high-born for you? Her blood too pure?'

Ninus stiffens. He feels as he used to in the training ground, when noblemen's sons were readying themselves to taunt him. But then Marduk surprises him.

'I see the way you look at your brother's wife,' he says. 'She is charming, surely, but she comes from the lowest of places. And yet you desire her. There is no need to deny it,' he says, when Ninus opens his mouth. 'What surprises me is that you, until very recently, were in love with her husband.'

Ninus' blood runs cold. He is unnerved by Marduk's perception. 'I didn't take you for a man who listens to rumours.'

'Do you deny it?'

'Onnes is a man.'

'So? Haven't you slept with men before? But, then, it all aligns. Onnes is a bastard, so you could say he is also low-born, like Semiramis.' He tilts his head, studies Ninus' face. 'One can tell a lot about a man from the people he obsesses over. It tells you something about what he lacks.'

Ninus wishes he could just stand and leave the room. But gone are the days when he would run away from confrontation. 'And what do you lack, for desiring Taria?' he asks. 'I thought Babylonians considered Urartians savages.'

Marduk laughs. 'We do. Which is why, if you form an alliance with the savages of the north, my father will break the pact with Assyria and crush you.'

Ninus stands. He starts pacing the room, brushing his fingers against the walls. The more the prince speaks, the more he reminds him of Assur. A man in love with himself, who thinks the world owes him everything. Ninus has spent his life wondering what that might feel like.

'We met, you and I, years ago. Do you remember?' he asks. 'It was the commemoration of the peace between our kingdoms. Our fathers bowed to each other, and a group of sculptors worked on a carved relief that witnessed their meeting. You and your brother must have been thirteen and fifteen, Assur and I a little younger.'

'I remember,' Marduk says. 'You blamed Assur for dropping the royal mace.'

The shame that accompanies the memory washes over Ninus. But he forces himself to smile: the cold, deceptive expression he has learned from his mother. 'If Assur were here, he would attack you for disrespecting the king. But I am not my brother.'

'No, you aren't. You are a different kind of king: weak, ruled by women and corrupt appetites. It is a wonder Assyria hasn't been buried in the dirt yet.'

'Do you think your insults can harm me? I have listened to them throughout my life. I have listened and endured, and now I am king.'

They look at each other. Once, their fathers would have been speaking in this very room, two kings who taught their sons courage and cruelty. Ninus shrugs their presence off his shoulders. 'I won't keep you any longer,' he says coldly. 'You have whores to go back to, after all.'

Marduk stands, tosses down his wine. His hand rests on the handle of his blade, poised. There is something snake-like about him, shimmering blue scales and hard, cold eyes.

Ninus watches him slide to the door. 'And I am afraid you are right about Taria,' he says to Marduk's back. 'She is too high-born for me.'

*

He summons the princess to the throne room. It rained in the night, and the palace smells damp, despite the incense burning in every corridor. Out of the corner of his eye, he sees two slaves bringing bowls of perfumes in a feeble attempt to chase away evil spirits.

Taria arrives in a wide, dark tunic embroidered with bull's heads. She bows to him stiffly. For a moment, he imagines sinking his hands into her golden hair, bringing his lips to her neck. He feels nothing.

'My council wishes that I marry you. You must know that by now,' he says.

She looks at him, as if she is waiting for him to say what he was meant to say when he summoned her. But he has never been good at cutting straight to the heart.

284

'A union between our kingdoms would be favourable,' he continues, 'but I do not believe we need a marriage to form an alliance.'

She lifts her eyebrows, a genuine expression, which surprises Ninus. He is too used to a court of men and women who play tricks and hide their true meanings. *That is how I must look to other people.*

'Are you saying you don't wish to marry me, my king?' she asks.

'Your father is gone,' he says. 'Your brother rules now. If I were to send you back to Urartu, would he cease the war with Assyria?'

'It is Assyria that wages war against Urartu.'

'Alliances should be based on trust,' Ninus points out.

There is a flash in her grey eyes. 'I do not believe my brother would stop the incursions, but I will do my best to convince him, if you do not keep me hostage any longer.'

'Good,' he says. 'Then I will send you back to the mountains. To your home.'

Taria smiles. The gesture is jarring against her sharp features, like a seed of green blooming in the desert. 'You are a good king. Nothing like your father or your mother. I do not know how you survived in such a cruel place.'

The heat is growing unbearable and the perfumes sickening. Ninus dismisses her. He doesn't tell her that he is not doing this for her but, rather, for himself. She doesn't need to know that.

*

'Do you want me to read something to you?'

It is night. He is sitting at the foot of his daughter's bed, his hands filled with tablets he took from the library of the Northwest Palace.

Sosanê shakes her head. 'I read all the time when I am alone. I wish we would talk more.'

'What do you want to talk about?'

'We can start with what you came to tell me.' He opens his mouth, but she is faster: 'Whenever you come here, you always have some request to make, or news to give.'

Ninus feels a sudden flash of shame. He puts away the tablets. 'You are right,' he says. 'I came here to discuss your marriage.'

She nods wisely, as if she had expected it all along. 'I thought we said you'd marry first, Father.'

'We did, didn't we?'

285

Sosanê straightens. He studies her little face. There must be pieces of her mother in Sosanê's features, though Ninus can't even remember what the scribe girl looked like.

'I am fifteen,' Sosanê says. 'I know it is time for me to marry.'

'But you are scared,' he says.

She caresses the harpy that sits on the table by her bed. A gift from Assur, when she was little. 'My mother died giving birth,' Sosanê says. 'And she wasn't even married. If I marry, I will have to produce heirs . . . Grandmother lost five babies, did she not?'

He cannot argue with her. Her honesty, as always, is startling, but also strangely comforting. 'She did. But marriage can be a good thing too. An escape from solitude.'

'I do not mind the solitude. I thought you, of everyone, would understand.'

Her face is grave. He cups his hand around it. 'You can't be lonely for an entire lifetime.'

'Loneliness and solitude aren't the same thing.'

He smiles. 'No, they aren't.' Her expression mirrors his, like water. He lets his hand fall. 'If I marry, will you marry too?'

A moment passes. She looks down, hands clasped in her lap. 'Yes. But we will need to find the right husband.'

'Oh, I've already thought of that.'

Her head lifts. Hopeful, intrigued. 'Is he clever?'

He laughs, amused that, out of all the things she could ask, this is what she cares about. 'He is the best there is. Now let us speak of something else.'

She nods and asks him to tell her about Balkh. He lies down and tells her about the men who climbed trees and carved them with secret symbols, the impregnable city and the fire that destroyed it. She listens as if they were the greatest of stories, as if he were a poet, making magic with his blood-stained words.

*

His informants have told him that Onnes is back from Ashur, so he goes to find him on the training ground, when the shadows are long and most of the soldiers have gone.

He is standing in a corner, polishing his sword. He glances up when Ninus walks to him.

'Brother,' Ninus says. 'I wish to speak with you.'

Onnes puts away the sword. There is a fresh cut on his cheek, a thin red line. 'We crushed the rebellion south of Ashur and took some prisoners,' he says. 'I thought you'd like to talk to them. They are chained in one of the courtyards of the Northwest Palace.'

'I will talk to them, yes.' Ninus takes a breath, preparing himself for the fall.

But then Onnes moves aside. Semiramis is standing behind him, by the giant *lamassu* statue at the entrance of the yard. Her hair is plaited back, and she is wearing a simple tunic for training. She bows to Ninus, her face wary. Onnes goes to stand by her side. With his thumb, he traces her lower lip, then kisses her. Ninus feels sick. The courtyard shifts, turns darker, colourless.

Semiramis doesn't move. Onnes takes up his sword again. 'What did you wish to speak to me about?' he asks Ninus.

Across from him, Semiramis bites the inside of her lip. Ninus remembers the taste of her skin. 'Another time,' he replies.

Another time.

*

He orders all his guards away from his private apartments, stationing them in the anteroom that connects the throne room to the inner courtyard. He asks two of his most trusted slaves to call for Semiramis, then goes to wait for her in the East Suites, where walls are covered with images of his father and grandfather holding gifts to Ishtar and Shamash. Here, the king must come to pour offerings to the gods and to receive their blessing, but Ninus knows he won't be blessed for what he has done, so he walks past the bas-reliefs to the baths. The room is dim and low-ceilinged. He removes his clothes and steps into one of the tubs. The water is cool against his skin. He scrubs himself with a brush, then rests his head against the wall. When he hears voices coming from the anteroom, he stands, wrapping a towel around his waist, and walks back into the prayer rooms.

She is standing in the shadow of his father's bas-relief. 'Shouldn't you wear a dress, in this holy room?' she asks, though it doesn't seem that his nakedness troubles her. Her long plait is uncoiled down her back, reaching to her waist.

'What difference does a room make?' he asks. 'The gods always watch over us.'

She looks away from him, and he knows he has said the wrong thing. She must be thinking that the gods saw them the last time she was here.

'I didn't think you would come,' he says.

'Neither did I.' There is an edge to her voice.

'What made you change your mind?'

'I was angry. And I felt guilty.'

He draws closer to her and takes her plait, wrapping it around his hand. It makes him think of the blackest nights, when darkness hides the moon and stars. They are quiet for a while, each waiting for the other to close the distance between them. He savours the silence of the two of them, alone, in this godly room.

'I can't come back here,' she finally says. 'I'll lose everything if I do.'

'What if you didn't?'

'You are quick with promises.'

'You don't trust my promises?'

'Onnes said you don't want people, once you've had them.'

Is that why he never let me have him? he wonders. Instead, he says, 'I had you, and I still want you.'

The lamplight wakes fires in her eyes. She walks past him to the baths. He follows her. The sacred trees that line the walls are blurred with the heat. But her face is clear, closer and closer to his. He can see the way the steam curls the shorter strands of hair around her ears, the wetness of her eyelashes. She puts a hand on his chest to stop him taking another step. He feels as if she is holding his heart in her palm.

'My mother fell in love with a man who made promises to her,' she whispers. 'Then he left her, and she killed herself.'

He can't tell whether she is speaking to him or to herself. 'Have you fallen in love with me, then?'

To answer him, she removes her dress and rests her back against the painted trees.

*

What is love? Now, years later, he understands.

Love is the willingness to lose oneself, to enter a dark room without knowing what dangers lie inside, to be held by someone even if she could slit your throat.

He writes each sign on a tablet, pressing the stylus into the clay as one presses a knife into the skin.

34.

Ribat, a Slave

Ribat and the leopard are waiting for Semiramis in the reception room. The animal stretches out on the carpet, her black and bronze spots barely visible in the light of the torch. Outside, the clouds have gone, and the moonlight feels as close as skin. Ribat is restless – it is not the first time Semiramis has disappeared. He is thinking that maybe he should slide out of the palace and look for her, when she enters the room.

She moves silently, a creature underwater, slipping between the waves. Her black kohl is smudged. The leopard rises, suddenly alert. Ignoring them both, Semiramis sits on a palm-wood stool and her head sinks into her hands.

Ribat watches her, unsure what to say. 'Onnes is back from Ashur. He is sleeping,' he says, because this feels like something that may comfort her.

'I have made a mistake,' she says, into her hands.

He didn't expect this response. 'You want me to correct it?'

She lifts her head. 'You are the most loyal person I know.'

He looks at her uncomfortably. Maybe she has taken some of Onnes' drugs, he reasons. She doesn't look well.

'You can't,' she says. 'No one can.'

He doesn't like her tone: he has never heard her speak like that before. 'I would do anything for you.'

She shakes her head. 'It's not enough.'

The words hurt him. How can it not be enough? What can mortals want, more than loyalty and love? He looks at the pink light of dawn slowly cleaning away the grey of night. He wonders if there is a way to show her that it is, in fact, enough.

*

One should be careful what one wishes for. Slaves most of all.

The citadel looks empty. The yellow-brick houses seem to sway in the heat. It is the hottest day of the season, which means Shamash must be angry. Ribat walks in the shade of the palm trees, careful not to draw the god's attention. Even with his sandals on, he can feel the warmth of the stones underfoot. In the market, flies buzz around slices of meat. Soldiers stand still in the heat, their copper armour like fish scales under the sun. Ribat tries to think of something that might cheer Semiramis. A new dagger, perhaps? A bracelet of lions' heads?

He enters the alleys that lead to the shop, then notices some water spilled on the road. He stops, considering whether to walk around it or turn back – it is a bad omen – when he feels something sharp poking him in the ribs. Before he can turn, a hood is pulled over his head. The scream dies in his throat. Everything is dark and he can barely breathe with the rough fabric against his mouth. Two pairs of hands grab his arms and start dragging him in the direction he came from. His heart beats wildly as he stumbles forward. Through the dark fabric all he can hear are the whispers of other people, making space for him, avoiding contact with him as if he were tainted.

*

When the hood is pulled off his head, he is in a small, dark place. There are jars of varying sizes around him. The two men who caught him aren't dressed as guards but, to his astonishment, as slaves. *That is why I didn't notice them.* They are much bigger than Ribat, neck and arms thick with muscles. They move aside to reveal a woman standing in a corner: the king's mother. She is holding a lamp, which casts a red, dangerous light on her face. Ribat feels his courage fracture, followed by a bright wave of fury.

'Are you the slave called Ribat?' she demands.

There is no point in lying, since the identity disc around his neck clearly states who he is. 'Yes, my queen,' he says. He spits out the

291

words through gritted teeth. If she hears the hatred in them, she does not speak of it.

'Do you serve the governor Onnes?' Her features are drawn as a scribe draws his signs onto a tablet: sharp, pointed lines. Even her eyes have no softness in them.

Ribat feels light-headed, whether from the heat, the rage or the fear, he does not know. 'I have served him all my life. And now my mistress too.'

'And do you follow your mistress everywhere?'

'Not everywhere.' Danger is approaching as fast as a scorpion. He searches for the place of courage inside himself, the place that allows him to disappear if he needs to.

'Tell me one of her secrets,' she demands.

Which one? he thinks. *There are so many.* 'I cannot, my queen.'

She smiles coldly. The most unpleasant sensation overwhelms him, as if she were slicing his head with a cool blade and looking inside his skull. 'I will be more specific then. Where was Semiramis last night?'

Drops of sweat are forming on the nape of his neck. 'In her rooms, sleeping.'

She shakes her head. Her headdress glints feebly in the lamplight. 'My slaves saw her leave this palace, at dawn. Did she come to the Northwest Palace and try to seduce the king?'

That is what she was doing, Ribat thinks madly. *That is where she was.* 'That would be much beneath my mistress, my queen.'

She stares at him for so long he feels as if she is swallowing him. 'Would it still be beneath her if I ordered my men to whip you?'

Slowly, one of her men unrolls a long leather whip. Ribat looks away. He feels nauseous. He considers pleading, then remembers that the slave who pleads is always considered guilty.

'Yes, my queen.' His voice is steady, steel. He takes a sick pleasure from it. He will not show his fear.

The man takes a step forward and suddenly Ribat thinks that his mother might have died in one of these rooms. Maybe her spirit is still here.

'Do what you have to, but keep him conscious,' the queen says. 'I want an answer.'

Give me your courage, Mother, he thinks. *Give me your strength.*
The whip slashes the air like an angry snake. For a moment, the

room goes white and all he can think of is a proverb: *Your worthiness is the result of chance*. He repeats it like a prayer, his silent scream to the heavens.

*

He is dumped in front of the gate of Semiramis' palace. Somehow, he pulls himself up. The guards let him through. He drags himself through the main courtyard and into the reception room. Blood is dripping down his legs. His whole body is burning.

'Gods,' Ana's voice whispers. 'What happened?' She does not wait for an answer but quickly pours water into a cup for him. 'We need wine,' she says, 'and you must come downstairs—'

'Leave us, Ana,' Semiramis orders. Ribat looks up. Though his sight is blurred, he can see her standing at the entrance to the reception room.

To Ribat's surprise, Ana replies sharply, 'His wounds must be treated, or else—'

'I will treat them,' Semiramis says curtly.

When Ana lets go of him, he stumbles. Her feet disappear, and Semiramis' sandals come into focus. 'She must like you very much,' she says, 'to try to defy my orders.'

He doesn't reply. He is in a lot of pain. She is removing his tunic, and it feels as if the fabric is dragging away pieces of his skin.

'It is bad,' she says. 'But there will be no infection. I'll make sure of that.' She is grinding garlic and pomegranates. Her hands move expertly as she opens jars of cedar oil and strips clean pieces of linen. He is aware that he is half naked in her presence, and that they are in the reception room, where Onnes might appear at any moment.

'When my father beat me,' Semiramis says, 'I would treat the wounds myself. My brother was better at it, but I was too proud to ask for help.'

He knows it is costing her much to say this, but he can't listen properly. All his efforts are concentrated on being awake. She makes him drink a mouthful of wine – her fingers briefly touch his lips – then pours the rest on his back. He does his best not to scream.

'Who cut you?' she asks.

'The king's mother,' he manages. 'She wanted to know if you slept with the king.'

Semiramis doesn't reply and, for a long time, he thinks she hasn't heard. His eyes are closed, and the wine is doing its work. He can feel a soft cloth being wrapped around his back, and wonders if they are still in the reception room or if he has been moved to Semiramis' bed. He doesn't want to be put to sleep, but he can't seem to fight the exhaustion.

'You can't stay here,' Semiramis says. 'I must send you away.'

Contours are losing shape, and the smell of pomegranate juice is overwhelming. *At least I can't smell my blood*, he thinks, before losing consciousness.

*

He wakes to the silence of the portico. The leopard is sitting, her paws resting on his feet. Semiramis is reading a tablet, which she puts down when she sees that he has opened his eyes. They are seated in the shade, on two couches of plaited reeds. On the table there are clean clothes, a jug of wine and a bowl of water.

'What did you tell the king's mother?' Semiramis demands.

'That her accusation was vile.'

She nods. 'Yes. I expect I wouldn't be here otherwise.'

He takes the jug of wine and drinks. She watches him and says nothing.

'Is it true?' he asks.

Her mouth twists into a sad smile. 'Truth and lies are closer than you think. Often, what one man believes to be true, another deems outrageously false.'

She has started to speak like the eunuch and the courtiers from the Northwest Palace. Ribat doesn't like it. The wine in his cup will always be wine, no matter what people believe. And the cuts on his back may heal, but no lie will change that he was whipped.

'If I tell you the queen's accusation is a lie,' she says, 'you may not believe me. If I tell you it is the truth, you may resent me.'

He feels for the bandages wrapped around his chest and shoulders. Semiramis must have changed them while he was unconscious. He imagines her fingers pressing into his back, wiping away his blood. Then he looks at the leopard settled at his feet. If she had been with him, she would have ripped the queen's arm. The thought gives him some comfort.

'I went to the Nabu temple this morning,' Semiramis says, standing and walking to the edge of the portico, 'to speak to the priest who teaches the scribes.'

His back burns. He drinks more wine.

'He is in need of new apprentices,' she continues. 'And I told him I had one in mind.'

He almost drops the jug. Semiramis is looking at him, so he straightens, trying not to wince. 'He told me that the training will be rigorous,' she says, 'but I said you already know all the signs and read better than a priest. He wasn't pleased but said he'd take you.'

He keeps quiet. He isn't sure what he is hearing, and how he is meant to respond.

'You aren't safe here. Somehow Nisat has learned that you are the one I trust most, and she has used you to attack me. If you stay here, it may happen again.'

The one I trust most, she said, but Ribat has barely acknowledged it. His mind is focused on something else, something he cannot quite believe. 'Does this mean . . .?'

'You will be a scribe,' she says.

He feels as if he is going to fall, so he grips the armrest with all his might. His mind refuses the word. It must be a lie, an illusion, a trick. He is not breathing. He is afraid that, if he does, the illusion will shatter.

'A scribe,' he repeats.

'Yes, a *free* scribe,' she says again, her dark eyes fastened on his.

He is breathing now, yet the portico is still the same: Semiramis is still standing, and her words are in the air, a promise, a portent. His chest is swelling and he doesn't think he will be able to stop it.

Is this how one's life changes? Is this how a man stops being owned? Hope, joy, ambition, everything he has never allowed himself to feel are bursting inside him.

'I can never repay you,' he says. His voice is raw, the taste of salt on his tongue.

She shakes her head. 'You owe me nothing. Not all of us are made for the dust. Those who are destined to rise will rise one way or another.'

His cheeks are wet, and it takes him a long time to understand they are wet *with tears*. All his life, he has never cried. He didn't know it could be such a sweet feeling.

There is one thing he must do before he leaves.

Zamena is in the slaves' room, cleaning her arms with a wet cloth. Ribat watches her for a moment before stepping forward: she looks as ancient as a tree that has grown in the darkness.

'Was it you?' he asks. 'Did you sell my mother to the queen?'

Her head snaps up.

'You were the only one who knew what she had seen, except me. So you told the king's mother and she poisoned her.'

The trembling of her hands betrays her. She has never been able to hide her fears like Ribat. He guesses he should be grateful to her: if he hadn't seen her and all the others be punished for being too transparent, he would never have learned.

'Do not speak of the queen,' Zamena says. 'She has ears everywhere.'

There are only you and me now, he wants to say, but instead he says, 'My mother was your friend. She trusted you.'

Zamena shakes her head. 'Trust is fickle.'

Maybe for you it is. But not for me. He removes his identity disc and leaves it on his pallet.

Zamena walks to him, alarmed. 'What are you doing?'

'Leaving,' he says. 'Semiramis freed me.'

Zamena opens her mouth and closes it. Then, a glimmer of fear. 'You are going to punish me.'

He has thought about it. He has imagined beating her blue, telling Semiramis a lie to make Zamena pay. But now that he is here, he can't bring himself to do it. 'My mother wouldn't have wanted it. She did not want me to become the kind of person you are.'

Zamena's eyes fill with tears. He turns his back on her and the darkness of the servants' room and walks upstairs, where the day is warm and bathed in light.

*

He glances at the palace one last time before leaving. The bricks gleam green and golden under the sun. In the portico upstairs, a woman appears. Ana is looking at him, her face small against the giant columns.

Once, when Semiramis and Onnes were away in Balkh, he and Ana were sleeping side by side, and he had told her what his mother used to say about mortals being birds with different wings. Ana had touched his back, her hand cold against his skin, and joked, 'I see no wings here.' He had kissed her and thought, *Look closer. Check my shadow.*

The sky is such a pure gold it hurts to look straight at it.

To Assyrians, there are kings, there are noblemen, and then there is everybody else: nothing in that hierarchy can ever change. But, then, isn't it true that nature keeps shifting? Doesn't the sun shine, then disappear into the earth? Don't flowers bloom, before withering? Nothing can last for ever.

The heroes and the wise men, like the new moon, have their waxing and waning, The Epic of Gilgamesh says.

As for slaves, Ribat considers, they can die, or they can rise.

35.

Ninus, King of the World, King of Assyria

The gods must be enjoying their joke: to make him fall for his brother's wife. Even more than that: to make him fall for the wife of the man he has been in love with for as long as he can remember.

He learned long ago that he cannot tame his desires: he must have what he wants, even if he destroys everything in its wake. He simply cannot give up. And why should he? Life can be dark and miserable, and when he finds another who gives him a taste of happiness, how is he supposed to let that go?

Some believe he should let go little by little, until he finds someone else.

Ninus believes he can't.

*

Sometimes, when faced with what seems like an impossible decision, he asks himself what his father would do.

He remembers a story Shalmaneser told him many years ago. They were in the king's bedroom, just the two of them. The lamps were lit, small fires scalding the feet of the figures on the walls.

'Why did the gods create humans?' Shalmaneser had asked. It was a big question, to which Ninus had no answer. 'Your mother wants you to read too many stories,' Shalmaneser continued, 'but only one story counts.'

And so he told him.

When the universe was created, the gods Anu, Enlil and Ea divided it among themselves: Anu took the heavens, Enlil the earth, Ea the water depths.

Enlil, who was the cruellest, forced a large group of lesser gods to dig the courses for the rivers Tigris and Euphrates. Night and day they worked until, exhausted, they decided to rebel against this harsh servitude and lay siege to Enlil's house. The ruling gods answered: they met and asked the rebels to identify a leader. When the rebels stuck together, refusing to name one of their own, Enlil suggested that Anu create a new world order. Anu was clever and decided that a new race, the human race, would be created to assume the work of the gods. It was Ea who accomplished this task, mixing the blood of one of the slain rebels with clay. One after another, humans sprang out of the earth, like grain. In their blood they carried the ghost of a lesser god, and in their hands the prayers for those who had created them and wanted them to suffer in their place.

That was the only story Shalmaneser ever told Ninus.

For a long time, Ninus didn't understand why his father would choose such a myth. It was proof that humans were made to suffer, that they were born of nothing more than a god's whim.

But now he remembers how Shalmaneser spoke, how he used to sit on his throne, or fight on the training ground, the blood-like crimson of his clothes, his crown as gold as the searing summer sun. He took what he wanted as if it had always belonged to him.

His father didn't think himself human. He thought himself a god.

*

The guards in front of Onnes' palace let him through without a word. He orders his own men to stay outside and enters with his heart threatening to tear its way out of his chest.

The main courtyard is empty. Onnes appears after a moment, hair wet from his bath, a thin tunic hanging open on his chest. 'I wasn't expecting you,' he says.

'Is Semiramis here?' Ninus asks.

Onnes shakes his head. His earring shines feebly in the lamplight. A movement in the corner of Ninus' eye: a leopard, slinking around the balcony that overlooks the courtyard. It looks at him with golden, unsettling eyes.

'Let us speak somewhere private,' Ninus says.

Onnes nods, leads the way to his apartments. In the wide bedroom, a single torch is burning. Wine has already been brought and poured into two rich cups. Next to them, a necklace with suns of beaten gold that Ninus has often seen Semiramis wear.

'I imagine you want to discuss Babylon,' Onnes says, stripping off his vest.

Ninus watches his back, the muscles and scars. He knows how Onnes got each and every one: a fight with Assur in the training ground when they were fourteen, a beating by Ilu, a lion's scratch in the arena during a hunt, an arrow wound during the civil war. Now those memories seem to belong to another person, another world.

'I am not here to talk about Babylon,' he says.

'What, then?' Onnes asks, choosing from the dresses piled on a stool – one crimson, with silver pendants, a pale woollen one, a black simpler one.

Does he really not know? Has he not seen? 'Marriage,' Ninus says.

Onnes slips into the crimson tunic. 'Is the prospect of marrying the princess of Urartu such a weight?'

'I sent Taria away, back to the north. She will leave in the morning.'

Onnes raises an eyebrow. 'That was unexpected.' He goes to the table, pours the wine. When Ninus takes the cup, their fingers briefly touch. 'So, Taria is gone. What now?'

'Sosanê is ready for marriage,' Ninus says. 'I spoke to her.'

Onnes doesn't seem confused by the change of tack. He is used to Ninus' wandering thoughts. He sits on the couch, waiting for Ninus to continue.

'She is clever,' Ninus says, 'and more beautiful now than she used to be as a child. She tells good stories, but mostly, she likes to listen to others. That is her gift, I think.'

Still, Onnes doesn't speak.

'What do you think of her?' Ninus asks. He can't help but remember when Onnes asked him what he thought of Semiramis in the months before they left for Balkh.

Onnes shrugs. 'She is like you. And that is a good thing.'

Ninus takes a sip of wine. The taste is metallic. 'I am glad you think so. For she should have the best.'

Outside, evening sets on the city, like a veil. The priests start chanting to the moon god, and distant torches glow amber. Onnes is frowning, and Ninus looks away from him.

'I have been thinking about the traps the gods set for us,' he says. 'How they make us think that our path is one, when actually it is another.' He can't look at Onnes as he speaks, but he is aware of his shadow, touching his own. 'I used to feel wronged by my feelings for you. I couldn't understand why I desired someone I couldn't have. I don't bind myself to others easily, so I think it was easier with you, because we were already bound.'

'What are you trying to say?' Onnes asks.

Ninus turns and their eyes meet across the room. He knows that what he says next will expose his heart, and he can do nothing to stop it. 'I think you should marry my daughter.'

Onnes' face is flat. 'I am already married. To Semiramis.'

Ninus hears it: the low note of warning. It is a subtle change in his voice, the same Onnes used before he smashed someone's face on the training ground. Ninus does not care: it is too late to go back now.

'If you marry Sosanê,' he says. 'I will take care of Semiramis. I won't leave her without a husband.'

There is silence, during which Ninus feels a deep, dreadful shame – a crushing feeling. Then Onnes moves quickly. He rises and takes Ninus' face, opening his mouth with his. Ninus feels the heat from Onnes' body, his hand on his neck. It is an angry grip, as if Onnes wants to hurt him.

When they break apart, Ninus' head is pounding. Onnes is staring at him as if he was seeing him for the first time. 'You want to be with Semiramis.' He speaks each word slowly, carving them into the air.

Ninus doesn't reply. He doesn't need to.

'I thought you hated her.'

Because you haven't been paying attention, as always.

Onnes laughs. For one mad, fleeting moment, Ninus thinks he will hit him, or kiss him again. But instead he speaks in his coldest voice: 'You should leave, my king. You are not thinking clearly.'

Suddenly Ninus hates him. *You do not give orders to me*, he wants to say, but if there is one thing his father has taught him it is that any man who expects to be treated as a king can be no fearsome ruler.

So in spite of himself, in spite of everything he wants and feels, he leaves.

*

A secret doesn't last more than a heartbeat in the citadel.

His guards announce Sasi's visit when Kalhu has already gone to sleep. The eunuch enters the room with a dark shawl wrapped around his shoulders, like a mourning woman. The torches have burned out, so Ninus lights a small lamp.

'I am sorry for the late hour, my king,' Sasi starts, 'but I heard a rumour, just after the evening meal.'

'A rumour so troubling it couldn't wait until morning?'

'I was hoping you could tell me that.'

Ninus watches him. 'Did my mother send you?'

'No, my king,' Sasi says, surprised. The expression seems genuine. 'Though, if what I hear is true, she will come to you soon enough.'

Ninus looks at the lamp, flame moving in the darkness like a cat's tongue. He wonders where Sasi was when his informants came to him, feeding him news and gossip, as a bird feeds its chick.

The silence stretches. Ninus sets his eyes back on him. 'You wouldn't betray me, would you?'

'I am loyal to the power of the crown, always.'

'Loyal to *me*, you mean.'

'Of course.'

'Good,' Ninus says. 'Because I know Ilu isn't. He would plunge a dagger into my heart if my mother asked him to.'

Sasi looks at him with a worried expression. 'My king, your mother would never wish for such a thing.'

He snorts. 'You hold my mother in very high regard.'

Sasi doesn't contradict him. 'She loves you,' is all he says.

'And what is her love worth? She loved Assur and still she let me murder him.'

Sasi's smooth face creases, if only slightly. 'The queen has spent her life preparing you to rule, teaching you to make wise decisions.'

'Isn't it wise to marry for love?'

Understanding dawns on Sasi's face. His eyes open wide, as if to say, *It is true, then.* But he composes himself quickly. 'No, my king, that is never wise.'

'Let the rumour spread,' Ninus spits out. 'Let it fly like the whispers that bring you pieces from others' lives. I do not care.' His fingers close around the lamp. The room is cast into utter darkness. He hears Sasi's light steps move away, to the door, into the corridor, out of the king's apartments.

*

His mother bursts into the throne room before the first supplicants can beg for an audience.

It is past dawn, but the sky is still black, as if day refuses to break. She walks to the throne dais, thunder in her eyes.

'Everyone, out,' she orders. When the guards linger, she speaks again, her voice savage. 'I said *out*!'

Ninus sits back, waiting. He hasn't slept, and his head hurts. 'You look as if you are about to murder me, Mother,' he says, when they are alone.

She crosses the room and is before him in a moment, fingers shaking as if she wanted to choke him. 'Have you gone mad?'

He almost laughs. 'As a matter of fact, I have.'

'Don't speak to me like that!' she snaps. Her face is red. He has never seen her like this, wild, dishevelled.

'Didn't you once tell me that kings should speak as they wish?'

'It was I who made you so!' she hisses. 'Just as I made your father before you.'

'You cannot expect to put a man on a throne, then to control him.'

Lightning burns in her eyes and she lifts her arm. He grabs her wrist, stops her hand in mid-air. 'Do *not* touch me.'

She stumbles back. Behind her, the bas-relief of Ashurnasirpal and Shalmaneser frames her figure, as if the three of them were scolding Ninus.

'You *are* mad,' she says.

'I am doing what you did with my father,' he says. 'You wanted him and made sure to have him, even if he wasn't yours to claim.'

She shakes her head. 'I loved your father. He could be cruel, but he was a match for me. I've never found another man who could challenge me like he did. But let me be honest with you. You are no match for Semiramis. She would destroy you.'

Ninus remembers his father walking to him with his hand raised when he was a child. He struck his face, and when Ninus could see again, his mother was at the edge of his vision, silently contemplating the scene. He had thought she was too scared to intervene, but he also knew, deep down, that his mother wasn't scared of anything.

'What do you know about love?' he asks.

She stares at him, face as cold as stone. Standing there, armoured in gold and silver, she is as beautiful and angry as the greatest gods. 'There is a prophecy that foretells your death at the hands of a woman,' she says. 'It was spoken by the *bârû* after you killed Assur. It says that the king destined for joy and grief shall die young and forgotten, at the hands of his own madness, to the gain of his wife.'

A moment passes, when he tries to work out if she is lying to him. Her gaze does not waver. Under her eyes, her skin is blue and shadowed.

'Leave, Mother,' he orders.

She doesn't move. 'I spent my life trying to protect you,' she says, 'but no one can save you from yourself.' She turns, and when she reaches the door, she stops. 'And you are wrong, Ninus. I know love. I have loved you, more than anything in this world, from the moment you were born.' Then she leaves.

36.

Semiramis, a Witch

Semiramis goes to the Ishtar temple in the morning. It is a sweltering day, light pouring into the courtyards, like honey. She rests her head against the shrine of the goddess, trying to think about anything that isn't Ninus. It is impossible. Ever since she kissed him, it is as if the form of her own mind has changed, and now, like a piece of clay under a stylus, it is shaped with his words, his secrets, his promises. She cannot tell where his writing ends and hers begins.

She doesn't know for how long she stays like that, forehead against the goddess's feet. When she finally lifts her head, Taria is standing a few feet from her, hair trailing down her back and gilded by the sun.

'I didn't think you'd be the kind of woman who prays in temples,' she says, with a half-smile.

Semiramis stands. 'And what kind of woman do you think I am? Everyone in Kalhu seems to have a different opinion on the matter.'

'One who doesn't wait for gods to fulfil her wishes.'

A priest lights sticks of cedar and cypress to sweeten the air. When he starts praying, his whispers fill the courtyard.

'You were right about Marduk,' Taria says. 'He does not love me.'

'Men like him can't love anyone but themselves.'

Taria nods, bringing her hands to her belly. Her body is already changing, and soon she won't be able to hide it. The first time Semiramis saw her, she felt a strange pang of jealousy. *If I only had the status and power this woman has, I would know how to use it.* But now she knows that Taria has been in a different kind of cage all along, and that she has found her own means of escaping it.

'I am going home,' Taria says. 'A chariot is waiting for me by the gate.'

The words jar her. *If Taria is going home, who will marry Ninus?* 'And what has the king asked for in return?'

'That Urartu stops attacking the Assyrian borders.'

'That isn't an easy promise to keep.'

'No, but he decided to trust me.'

'Because he doesn't know you are pregnant with his enemy.'

'You haven't told him. I need to thank you for that.' Then, to Semiramis' surprise, she moves closer, brings her lips to her ear. 'Be careful,' she whispers. 'When Nisat came back to her palace last night, she was angry. She screamed your name once. I heard her.'

The shuffling of feet announces the arrival of the goddess's attendants. Something coils in Semiramis' chest. Taria takes a step back, bows. 'I will not see you again, but I know you will do great things. Remember that glory and danger often taste the same. All they leave behind is bitterness.' As she walks away from the courtyard, her plaited hair sways like a hundred wheat spikes.

The sun god Shamash starts riding in the sky, chasing away all shadows. Semiramis watches priests and attendants move, careful to avoid the sunlight as they check the corners of the courtyard for evil spirits. Somewhere deep within the temple, a wild cat howls. It is a sign of peril, an omen of grief.

Semiramis hurries out of the goddess's house. A warm wind lifts her hair, like a spirit's breath.

*

Sasi bursts into the council room as Semiramis is pouring beer from an alabaster jug. His steps are hurried and his expression unpleasant, as if he has swallowed a bite of rotten food. She puts down the jug.

'What is it?'

Sasi glides towards her and, to her surprise, grabs her arm. His hand is cold and pale. 'Where is your husband?'

She frowns. 'I do not know. He will be here in a moment, I suppose.'

'Something displeasing happened last night,' he says. He looks over her shoulder, checking that no one is listening. 'The king sent Taria home.'

'Yes, I know.'

306

His grip grows tighter. 'Then he visited your husband to propose two marriages. One, between Onnes and Sosanê. The other, between you and him.'

He has spoken so softly that, for a moment, she thinks she has misheard. Around her, the sculpted warriors seem to sway.

'Surely you knew this was coming,' Sasi insists.

She winces at the sharpness of his tone. 'I didn't.'

Impatience flares in his eyes. 'It would be unhelpful to lie to me.'

She shakes him away. 'Who else knows about this?'

'I went to the king last night,' he admits. 'And I have been called by the queen this morning. She believes you have bewitched her son. Ilu arrived as I left, so I expect he'll know too. It is only a matter of time before everyone else does.'

A hand is squeezing her lungs: she thinks she will faint. 'Did you deny the queen's accusation?'

'This is no longer an accusation. This is a fact. And I don't know how you will talk your way out of it.'

Dear gods, she thinks. *What is happening?* She opens her mouth to say something – she isn't sure what – but Sasi shakes his head. Nisat enters the room with Ilu, both taking their usual places. Ninus appears, eyes red as if he hasn't slept in days. As the *bârû* and the prince Marduk follow him inside, Sasi sits, wordlessly, and Semiramis does the same. It takes all her power not to stumble.

Onnes is the last to walk in. His face is blank, revealing nothing, but the muscles of his shoulders are clenched, as if he is ready to unsheathe his sword and cut their treacherous throats.

A moment of silence, when Nisat's mouth twitches and Ninus glances at Semiramis.

Then, Marduk speaks with a provocative smile: 'Whose marriage are we discussing today?'

Attendants come forward, bringing tablets and seals. Sasi looks down, a faint blush on his cheeks. Semiramis wants to leave, but her feet feel anchored to the floor.

'No one's,' Ninus replies sharply. His jaw is set, his face determined. 'The *bârû* has been studying the flight of birds. He should share it with us.'

The *bârû* bows, stands. 'That, and the patterns formed by oil spreading over water, my king.'

'Is that an omen of war?' Marduk says. 'Please enlighten us.'

The *bârû* ignores him. His throat rasps as he shares his observations. Ilu and Nisat exchange a glance. Semiramis' pulse leaps. Though they know of Ninus' proposal, no one mentions it. They behave as if the secret wasn't in the room, creeping around them like a poisonous vine.

*

She walks with Onnes back to their palace without speaking. Overhead, the sky seems sliced in half: blue and grey where the clouds float low, pale and golden higher, closer to the gods. She feels untethered from the earth, as if she were watching the scene from above.

Here comes the consequence, she thinks.

Here comes my fall.

Onnes takes the stairs that lead to his apartments. She follows. In the portico, she stands at a safe distance from him as he sits on one of the couches. Even in this, he and Ninus are opposite, she can't help but think: Ninus always lounges on chairs, while Onnes sits up straight and stiff, as if ready to spring to his feet and fight. She watches the dagger he wears at his waist.

'I didn't know Ninus would ask this of you,' she says.

He draws the blade from his belt and puts it down next to him on the couch. 'And how do you know now?'

'Sasi.'

'Of course.' He stares at her, as if waiting for her to continue. A trick of his: to wait in silence, until the other is compelled to speak. But she has long learned to deal with it. She remains quiet until he inhales deeply.

'I know you have been angry with me,' he says, 'because you saw me torture those prisoners. Because I told you what I did to my father. But seducing Ninus is not the right way to take your revenge.'

Blood rises to her cheeks. 'You think I would do something like that for *revenge*?'

His gaze doesn't waver. 'Revenge or power. The only two things that motivate you. What else is there? Love? You have grown up without it, so you can't feel or understand it. As for Ninus, his love is like a fire. It grows quickly and brightly, and just as quickly it burns out.'

'You think I don't love you?' she asks, voice hoarse.

'I don't care what you feel. We are discussing what you want.'

'I am your wife.'

'That is not an answer.'

'What are you asking me?'

His knuckles are white on the couch's arm. 'You know what I am asking. I am asking if you betrayed me.'

Down in the Nabu temple, the priests start chanting. The sound reaches the portico like an eerie warning.

'What would you do if I had?'

'I'd have to kill you,' he says. The words are calm, but she can feel their heat, like burning coals scorching her skin.

He reaches out and takes his dagger. She stares at him, disbelieving. 'Are you going to stab me?' But he is on his feet, turning his back to her, walking away. She follows him. '*You think, after all I have been through, that I am scared of you?*'

He turns. The light in his eyes is murderous. 'I'm sure you aren't. But you should be.' Then he stalks out of the portico.

*

Onnes' moods vary wildly. Sometimes he avoids Semiramis for entire days and goes assiduously to visit the healer in the citadel, as Ana tells her; at others he haunts her like an angry spirit, making cold remarks about her and Ninus.

'So did you do it? Did you really sleep with a man who used to dream about your husband?'

'Do you know that Ninus despises women? Except his mother, of course.'

'Can you imagine what Nisat would do, if *you* married her son?'

He is cruel to the guards, terrorizes the servants, and once orders Ana to sleep in bed with him. When Semiramis enters the room and sees her slave's body wrapped around her husband's, he stares at her in the darkness as if to say: *Go on, say something.* She doesn't.

In the council room, he is barely awake, his eyes emptied by the opium.

On the training ground, he challenges the strongest soldiers, humiliates them when they are defeated.

One day, Sargon decides to taunt him. 'My father says your wife slept with the king,' he says. 'Will she leave you now, just like your mother did?'

Onnes walks to him, calmly, in front of the eyes of training men and officials. Sargon flashes his spear out, but Onnes takes the blade in his hands and yanks it out of Sargon's grip. Then his palms close around Sargon's neck, bleeding all down his tunic. It takes five men, including Ilu, to push him away. When they finally do, Sargon lies on the ground, clutching his throat like a drowning man.

That night, Onnes creeps into Semiramis' bed, shaking all over, as if a fever has taken hold of him. 'I have taken some herbs that the healer gave me,' he says. 'I can't feel my heart.'

She puts a hand to his chest. The beating is barely perceptible, like a bird flapping its wings tiredly. But she says, 'It is there. I promise.'

He buries his face in her neck, while his body throbs against her shoulder. She holds him until the herbs' effect fades and Ana comes to blow out the lamps.

*

In the terraced gardens, nobles and governors eat on carved chairs and couches, while dark-haired attendants fan them with fly-whisks. The feast is loud. Women are tuning their harps, their hair covered by light shawls adorned with pendants of rubies and sapphires.

Semiramis drinks alone, shielded by palm trees and the columns of the pavilion. She watches Ninus as slaves pour him wine and bring platters of spiced meat. A few steps from him, under the bright branches of the tamarisk trees, Ilu's daughter glances at him, hopeful. Feeling Semiramis' eyes on him, Ninus lifts his head. He stands, goes to her.

'We can't talk here,' she says.

His eyes don't leave her face. 'There is nothing they can say that hasn't been said already.'

She guides him past the blooming trees and painted columns, deeper into the gardens. The branches dance around them. The fading sunlight falls across his face.

'I have called for you, but you have not come,' he says.

'I can't leave Onnes.'

'He won't speak to me.'

She shields her eyes with a hand. 'You shouldn't have asked him.'

'Would you rather watch me as I marry Ilu's daughter, make her my queen?'

She shakes her head. She can see them in her mind, Ninus embracing her, lying by her side at night. The thought is torture, but all she can say is: 'Onnes is unravelling.'

Ninus snorts. 'He never unravels. He has built walls too high and thick around himself.'

'The walls are crumbling.'

His hand grazes her skin. His fingers trace her jaw, find her lip and rest there, a moment only.

'I made my decision, Semiramis,' he says. 'It is time you made yours.'

She closes her eyes and remembers how he looked at her in the baths of the Northwest Palace. The warm scent that rose from his skin as he came closer and closer to her. His fingers on her skin were smoother than she had imagined, except for a couple of old, faded scars. So often in those first months in Kalhu she had wondered what it would feel like to touch him, and there he was, touching her. It was magical but, like all magic, brief and slippery, impossible to seize and keep.

When she opens her eyes again, he has gone back to his feast. Ilu's daughter sits on the couch opposite his, smiling as he speaks. The wine is sour on Semiramis' tongue.

You cannot afford such a mistake, Sasi had told her, before she slept with Ninus. The words ring in her head like an echo that refuses to fade. Even when she closes her eyes, and sinks into unconsciousness, they haunt her.

*

Back in his palace, Onnes has called for a diviner. The *bârû* is sitting in the courtyard, holding a thick sheepskin, watching him warily. Semiramis stops at the entrance, careful not to make a sound.

'Did you bring the liver of your sacrificial lamb?' she hears Onnes ask. The priest nods. 'Read it for me then.'

Slowly, the *bârû* unwraps the sheepskin. Inside, the dark red organ, glossy and wet. He places it on a table and touches different parts of it, muttering words: 'well-being', 'strength', 'yoke'. It goes on for a long time. When he finally stands, his fingertips are glowing crimson.

'My governor,' he says, 'the signs are clear.'

'What is it?' Onnes asks.

'Nothing speaks of our future more than the liver of a beast that has been sacrificed to the gods,' the priest says. 'It is our mirror of Heaven. And what I see here is that a death will happen soon.'

Semiramis flinches. The priest's hands are shaking, but she is focused on her husband. Onnes is nodding. He nods as if he already knew what the priest was going to say.

37.

Onnes' Secret

Ninus calls a council meeting when the month of Ishtar has reached its peak. The heat refuses to fade. It is a cloud that envelops the city, suffocating its inhabitants.

The room sparks with tension. Everyone takes their seats. There are dark smudges beneath Onnes' eyes. Semiramis heard him scream in his sleep last night, then wander restlessly through the rooms of the palace.

'My men reported to you from the borders, Ilu,' Ninus starts. 'Tell me everything.'

'Troubling news,' Ilu says. 'There have been rumours of an attack from Babylon . . . and Urartu.'

'Urartu?' Ninus says angrily.

'The princess Taria has been reunited with her brother,' Sasi intervenes, 'who seems to believe her return to their capital will now allow him to attack us without consequence. But these are rumours, nothing more,' he adds hastily.

'And Babylon?' Ninus asks. His fists are clenched, his knuckles white.

'The prince Marduk is gone,' the spymaster announces. 'He escaped from the city.'

'Escaped?' Nisat says, with a voice so sharp it could carve Sasi's tongue out.

'Yes, escaped,' Sasi repeats.

Semiramis stares at him, speechless. She isn't the only one: the *bârû* looks shocked, and Ninus seems torn between stabbing Sasi and leaving the room.

'There is something else,' Ilu says slowly. 'Marduk's brother has died. By the time the prince reaches the city, he will be the heir to the throne.'

They all sit quietly for a moment. Bright flecks are shining in Ninus' eyes.

'Is there no hope of a new treaty with Babylon?' Semiramis asks.

'As long as the king lives, there is hope,' Nisat says, staring at her, 'but we must pray that Urartu and Babylon do not conspire against us together.'

'My king,' Sasi starts softly, 'there are whispers that Marduk intends to gather an army close to the stronghold of Dur. He is speaking to some Aramean tribes at this very moment. He wants them to join him.'

'Does he have enough men to attack us?' Ninus asks.

'With the tribes, yes,' Ilu replies, 'but our men have been training hard. We can ready them to defend the city and select the strongest to deal with the Babylonians in case of open war. I'll alert the other governors. Onnes must send envoys to Eber-Nari straight away, to call for more men.'

They turn to Onnes, waiting for him to speak. His face is impenetrable. 'If Babylon attacks from the south and Urartu from the north, we lack the numbers to hold them back.' His voice is so cold that the entire room is chilled.

'Onnes,' Sasi warns.

Onnes continues, unperturbed: 'Of course we all know this madness is your fault, *my king*. The others are just too afraid to say it aloud. Even Assur would have handled the situation better. Your brother would never have let our hostages escape.'

There is a brief, stunned silence. Ninus is staring at Onnes as if he were stabbing him. Semiramis can see the smallest twitch in her husband's eye.

'Speak like that again,' Nisat hisses, 'and the king will have you whipped.'

Onnes pushes his chair back. 'No, he won't.'

Then, to everyone's shock, he strides out, leaving an ominous, sickening silence behind him.

*

When Semiramis goes back to the palace, Onnes isn't there. She roams every room, every courtyard and terrace. Her guards look at her as if she is mad. 'Where is he?' she demands. 'Where has Onnes gone?'

'He was seen in the gardens,' one of them says. 'With the king.'

She runs out of the palace to the wide road that takes her to the ziggurat. The sky is filled with menacing clouds, black and blue like bruises. Guards and slaves seem not to notice her: they are too busy shielding the orchards from the incoming storm. The trees are green and dark, the earth reeking of mud. The water in the canals is glittering, like a blade. She flies up the stone steps until she reaches the pavilion, stumbling in her long dress.

She sees Ninus first, standing by a large tamarisk tree. The branches above him, usually heavy with bright pink flowers, are now washed away in the grey light. He is silent, looking away as Onnes speaks to him. Semiramis hurries forward, hiding behind a large column to see her husband better. There is something wrong in the way Onnes stands, as if he were holding a burning brand to his skin.

Ninus holds up a hand, silences him. 'You mustn't speak of my brother in the council meetings,' he says, voice shaking. 'You mustn't speak of him at all.'

'Your anger towards him is misplaced. Always has been,' Onnes says.

Semiramis presses her hand against the cold column to steady herself. The diviner's words are swirling in her mind, making her nauseous.

'Assur rebelled against my father and *murdered* him while our armies were fighting at the gate,' Ninus spits.

'He never openly admitted it, did he?' Onnes asks. 'When you spoke to him before executing him, he never told you he killed Shalmaneser.'

Ninus keeps quiet. Onnes continues, relentless: 'He felt responsible, because he started the war, and eventually he would have had to murder his father. But he didn't.'

'Assur killed Shalmaneser,' Ninus says slowly. 'That is why I executed him.'

'He didn't.' Onnes shakes his head. 'I did.'

Nothing moves on Ninus' face. The world seems to have come to a halt. Semiramis feels as if she is standing on the brink of a precipice, looking down into the darkness. *I need to turn back. I need to stop this.* But Ninus is looking at his brother with the face of someone who has drunk a cup of wine, only to find he has swallowed poison.

'I do not believe you,' he says.

Onnes grabs his arm. There is something mad on his face. 'Do you want to know what he said to me before he died? He said, "Maybe you are my son after all." Only when faced with death did he acknowledge me. All my life, he shunned me and my mother, called her a whore, used her feelings to wipe his feet. She meant nothing to him. I meant nothing to him.'

Ninus looks sick. 'You killed him.'

Onnes opens his mouth, but the words are drowned. Ninus grabs him and bangs his head against a column. Onnes stumbles back, hair bloodied. Ninus pushes him down, on his knees. He punches his face, one, two, three times, and each time Onnes stares back at him, daring him to hit him once more.

'Kill me,' he says, and his voice sounds strangled. 'What are you waiting for?'

Ninus' hand closes around the handle of his sword. 'It was you,' he says, and this time his voice breaks, as if he finally believes it.

Semiramis cannot look any longer. She runs forward, feet slipping on the muddy ground. 'Ninus,' she says. He turns to her. The anger is like a fire on his face. 'Don't do this.'

It is hard to tell if he is truly seeing her. And it does not matter. He spits on the ground and unsheathes his sword. Onnes closes his eyes. The blade cuts into his temple, and Semiramis' heart stops. A moment of death, a moment of darkness. Then Ninus makes a sound like choking and throws away the sword. He walks past Semiramis and the pavilion, past the tamarisk trees and the sodden orchards.

Onnes' eyes are shining. 'YOU CAN'T EVEN AVENGE YOUR OWN FATHER!' he shouts. 'YOU CAN'T EVEN DO JUSTICE LIKE A KING!'

Rain starts falling. The gardens fill with the smell of rot.

*

'You shouldn't have told him,' Semiramis says.

Onnes is a dark figure in the portico. His hair is wet, blood and raindrops flowing down his face. He doesn't speak, doesn't move. She pulled him up and dragged him through the gardens, as the rain fell harder, blurring everything around them. Now the palace is empty, all the guards stationed outside.

'Onnes,' she tries again.

'He should have killed me,' he says. 'It was his duty to do so. But he is a coward.'

The cut on his temple is swelling. She looks at him. Death has always been a constant for him, a dream that haunts him even when he is awake. The death of their mothers, which had once seemed to Semiramis a rope that bound them together, had never bound them at all: for her, her mother's fate has always been something to dread and avoid, and it was that fear, the determination never to end up like her, that brought her here. But to Onnes, his mother has been a curse he can't escape, a destiny he is both repelled by and attracted to.

'Ninus loves you,' she says.

He shudders. With his bronze eyes, he is like one of those weathered statues that grow dark and green under the rain. 'Most of my life has been grey,' he says, 'uncoloured, as if there was a veil between me and the world. I couldn't feel things as others did. I couldn't care. Everything always faded, everything quiet. There are only a few moments that ripped open the veil. When I pushed the blade into my father's throat. When you came to my tent that day in Mari and lied about your father. I remember your face was battered and I had the terrible impulse to hurt you. But it also made me feel alive.' A shiver down her spine, yet she keeps still, yet he keeps talking. 'You saw me for who I was. You see it even now. Ninus doesn't. We've known each other all our lives, but he can't see anyone for who they truly are. When he loves someone, he sees only beauty, warmth and depth. Cruelty, vanity, weakness . . . when it comes to the truth, he becomes blind.' He wipes his face with the palm of his hand. Hair is plastered to his wound, strands like black worms against the bloody gash. 'Because he is a coward.'

The wind grows stronger, colder. The flame of the torch splutters, then dies.

Semiramis rests her face against his shoulder. Despite everything he has done, Onnes is still the man who saved her from her life in Mari. She wants to believe she can save him too.

38.

Madness Breeds Madness

Onnes

Onnes wakes from his dead man's sleep plagued by nightmares. His pillow is stained with the blood from his temple. Spirits are everywhere. His men, who died for him in Balkh, are sitting in every corner, reproachful, blood blooming from their wounds. And then there is his mother, as always, quiet by the bas-relief of the tree of life.

He stands and pulls on his tunic for training. His mother watches him. She is wearing the smooth emerald dress she once wore during feasts, and there is concern on her face.

'You shouldn't have told him,' she says.

He almost laughs as she echoes Semiramis' words. He wishes he could grab her and shout at her, but she is nothing more than air, as he has learned the countless times he tried to touch her.

'No, I shouldn't have,' he replies bitterly. 'I should have spent my life with regret spreading inside me instead.'

'He will forgive you,' she says softly. Her bracelets tinkle and, for a moment, they look real. He has a vision of her long arm dangling by the side of a large bed, as she lay, half asleep, after taking her drugs. He had nestled his head under her hand and felt her bracelets cool his cheek.

'I don't deserve his forgiveness,' he says.

'You are too hard on yourself, my love.'

'You can't tell me what to feel!' he snaps. 'You abandoned me!'

It is a conversation they have had many times. She keeps watching him, waiting for him to say more.

'I hate you,' he says quietly.

She smiles sadly at him, then disappears.

*

The training ground is baking in the sun. Soldiers are fighting with iron swords in close range. They stop practising when they see Onnes. He sends them all away. If they stay, he will hurt them. When they are gone, he goes to stand in the shadows and touches his palm to an iron spearhead. He imagines it sinking into his skin.

'Don't hurt yourself,' Nisat's voice says.

He turns. She is standing in the courtyard, her golden headdress shimmering in the heat. Her eyes, her most striking feature, are like a warning. Ninus has the same eyes, Egyptian blue, though not as dark as hers. Her eye colour is the same as the carbon black mixed with the blue pigment that is painted on the bas-reliefs of the palace.

'You would only enjoy it, if I did,' he says.

'You don't know what I enjoy,' she replies sharply.

'That is because you never allowed me to be close to you.'

'You are the son of the woman who wanted to take everything from me. What did you expect? You were already treated much better than any other bastard son of my husband.'

He doesn't know what to say. She walks to him and takes the spear from his hands. The gesture is almost maternal; it breaks something inside him.

She puts the spear next to all the others, then passes a hand over her face. There is something vulnerable in her eyes, which confounds Onnes. 'I have lost one son already,' she says. 'I can't lose another. Ninus has gone mad. You must speak to him.'

'I am afraid he doesn't listen to me any more.'

'He always did what you told him,' she says. 'Always.' It is clear the words leave a bad taste in her mouth. She is looking at him as if he is the cause of her problems with her son. He probably is.

'Do you remember my mother?' he asks. The words tumble out of him.

She looks as if he has slapped her. 'Of course I do.'

'I can't see her face any more. Even when I do, I think my memories are far from the truth.'

Nisat's expression is icy. She won't give him any pity, Onnes knows. But it isn't pity he wants. 'She lived in my palace,' she says. 'And so did you, when you were little. She was beautiful.'

'Is that why Shalmaneser loved her?'

The ice melts, and her gaze grows hard and angry. 'He didn't. My husband didn't love anyone. And your mother was too kind to understand that.'

They look at each other, unnerved by the strange moment of honesty. He feels exhausted, his mouth filling with salt water.

'You are so much like her,' she says softly. 'She didn't understand that life is a fight, something you must win. She gave up too easily.' Her hand brushes his cheek. 'She was kind, but she was weak. And I am sorry you had to grow up knowing this.'

He can't see: his eyes are filling with tears. When they are dry again, Nisat is gone.

*

He lies down on the highest terrace of the hanging gardens and runs his fingers through the blades of grass. The world is quiet. He can still feel Nisat's hand on his cheek.

Ninus always did what you told him, she said. And that is true, but what about Onnes? Hasn't he fought for Ninus, trained with him, read with him? Didn't he let Ninus kiss him? Both of them have lived for the other, done everything the other wanted. Except for when Onnes killed Shalmaneser. But then, even if he acted for himself, he made Ninus king.

It is a strange thing to be willing to do anything for a person yet to betray him.

A gentle breeze reaches him. His mother joins him under the pavilion. Her hair is lighter, her eyes forgiving.

'Don't be afraid, my love,' she says.

Onnes wants to say he isn't afraid, hasn't been for a very long time. He wishes he were afraid, rather than feeling indifferent, the need of violence and hatred constantly surging through him. 'I miss you,' he whispers, and notices, to his horror, that his voice is pleading, like that of a child.

*

Ninus

Ninus punches the bas-reliefs of his room. The winged figures on the wall are already crimson and his knuckles are clotted with blood. His thoughts keep catching on each other, driving him mad.

Do you want to know what he said to me before he died?

He punches the wall again. His skin splits, but it isn't enough. He longs to hurt, to wreck, to kill. His body is so alight with hatred that he thinks he might catch fire. Without knowing what he is doing, he walks out of his apartments, across the central courtyard and past the narrow dark rooms until he finds himself on the terrace where Onnes and Semiramis' wedding feast had taken place. Sasi is standing there by himself. He looks so clean and calm that Ninus feels a sudden instinct to seize him by the neck and strangle him, smashing his head against the wall until his brains bleed out.

'My king,' Sasi starts, 'there are matters we should discuss—'

'You pride yourself on knowing everyone's secrets,' Ninus interrupts, voice shaking. 'Did you know that Onnes and I kissed, in this very palace?'

Sasi raises his eyebrows. His gaze lands on Ninus' hands. 'My king, you are bleeding.'

'That was before he was a traitor, of course,' Ninus continues, as if Sasi hasn't spoken. 'But I am sure you didn't know that either.'

Sasi's expression grows worried. 'Onnes is your governor and most trusted adviser.'

'Onnes is a traitor.'

Sasi holds his gaze, though Ninus can feel him calculating whether to call for help, or deal with his king alone. 'Go on,' he spits. 'Who will you report this to? My mother? Ilu? Semiramis?'

'My duty is to report secrets to you and you only—'

'*Then you have failed!*' Ninus shouts. 'You haven't told me the most important secret!'

For the first time since Ninus has known him, Sasi seems at a loss for words. He remains silent for a long moment. Then, slowly, he says, 'As much as it pains me to admit it, my king, I do not know what you are talking about.'

Ninus starts pacing the terrace. The painted columns seem to sway in the heat. 'Kings are tyrants,' he says. 'Everyone knows that. Our whole lives we are taught to worship heroes like Gilgamesh, even if they are cruel. *Because* they are cruel.'

Sasi follows him with his appalled stare. 'Not all heroes are cruel. Gilgamesh is arrogant, but Enkidu is humble. One is violent, the other peaceful.' He pauses, then adds, 'You don't have to be like all the other kings.'

Ninus stops pacing. They are standing at the opposite ends of the terrace now, their shadows stark in the setting sun.

'I am afraid it is too late to be good and forgiving,' Ninus says.

Sasi shakes his head. When he speaks, it is as if he is pulling the words from the deepest darkness. 'I do not know what happened, but there are a thousand solutions between punishment and forgiveness. You need not choose one or the other.'

Yes, I must.

*

Semiramis

Nisat enters Onnes' palace before Semiramis' guards have time to announce her. Onnes is gone, and Semiramis is sitting in the reception room as Ana carves small pieces of wood: a lion, a sphinx, a lotus flower. In the courtyard, the leopard is trying to catch the birds that fly past.

Nisat casts a disdainful look at Ana and sits on a carved chair as if it were her throne. Ana springs up, as fast as a fired arrow. From the courtyard Semiramis hears the shuffle of feet, a whisper, and then the growl of the leopard. She and Nisat survey each other across the table.

'Do you always let slaves sit beside you?' Nisat asks.

'Slaves are people,' Semiramis says, 'even if you and everyone else in this citadel refuse to see them as such.'

'Spare me the act of generosity,' Nisat replies. 'You are gentle with them only because you were once nobody.'

'If you want my help, this is not the way to get it.'

'Your help?' Nisat snorts. 'I am here because everyone in the Northwest Palace seems to have lost their reason.'

Semiramis sits, waiting. The torch above their heads casts red shadows on their faces.

'The gods granted my son beauty and brilliance,' Nisat says, 'but they burdened him with a restless heart. I can do nothing about it. I have tried. I do not know what you feel for him, and I do not care. But you can't marry him.' Her lips are blood red, her eyes as sharp as they have always been. And yet, Semiramis notices, her hands are shaking. *All of us are unravelling now.*

'Why?' she asks. 'Because, in your eyes, I will always be a commoner?'

Nisat slams her hands on the table. 'Because you are already married!'

'You married twice.'

'My first husband died. And unless you intend to murder Onnes, you are in a very different position.'

Semiramis takes a deep breath. 'What do you want me to do?'

Nisat waves a hand. 'Ninus can't help it. He is drawn by people he can't understand.' He speaks of his love as if it were an illness without a cure. 'So, you need to go to him. Tell him you don't love him, you despise him. Tell him that you wish to stay with Onnes. He will send you away, because he won't be able to bear having you in the capital. You will go back to Eber-Nari, and will have a palace built for you there. I will make sure of that. Onnes will travel back to the capital, but you will never set foot here again.'

The ground is shifting beneath Semiramis' feet, and she can do nothing to stop it. When Nisat speaks again, the words slash the air like whips.

'If you refuse, you will be executed for seducing a king while married to another man. Onnes will lose a wife, but he will remarry. He will keep floating while you rot in the house of dust. And, from what Sasi tells me, you are like a child, terrified of death.'

She lets the last words linger. Then she leaves.

*

Semiramis sits alone in the portico as the sky turns orange, then grey. Soon the god Sin will travel through the heavens, and under his stars the city will go to sleep, its people unaware of the secrets that burn behind palace doors. Once, she was one of them, and she had suffered, knowing that whatever happened to her was of no consequence to anyone else. She was alone. Now, what she chooses will have consequence over thousands. But every possible choice is wrong.

What Nisat said is true, but she doesn't know that, even if Semiramis stays with Onnes, her position is compromised, for the king now has learned the truth about her husband.

The shadows grow longer on the floor. The white light of the moon creeps over the walls. The spirits come out of their hiding places, whispering, *You are finally caught. This time, there is no escape.*

All her life, she has moved forward, leaving everything behind as she focused on what she wanted to achieve, relentless in her purpose, like the hero Gilgamesh in his quest for immortality.

But she can't leave Onnes behind. She remembers his face in her village the first time they spoke. He was a stranger, who looked and sounded as if he belonged with the gods, and she had felt more mortal than ever: from the other side of the river she could see him, and all his world behind him, but she could not cross. Then he had asked her to go with him and there it was: her chance. Most people are never offered one, and some of those who are, aren't brave enough to take it.

Her heart bleeds, for she knows what she must do. She will go to Ninus and tell him she is staying with Onnes. She will beg for Onnes' forgiveness and his exile. And she will try to build a new life.

And what of her love for Ninus? A prince reared on violence, who does his best to fight against it. The answer to the question is simple: she must live knowing that she had the man she wanted and that she can't have him again, except in memories, until the taste of him fades and she is left with nothing.

*

The Northwest Palace is bathing in the clear light of the moon. Inside, the bull statues glitter menacingly. The guards let her in. Semiramis crosses the quiet rooms and courtyards until she is in the king's apartments. She knows Ninus will be here, in his old father's room, even if it makes him feel heartbroken.

'You have made your decision,' he says. He is standing by the arched window that overlooks a portico. When he turns, his eyes are red, and his face looks ill.

Yes, she thinks. *Let us put an end to this.* She walks to him and puts a hand to his cheek. One last time, one last touch. He closes his storm-coloured eyes.

Then there is the quietest sound – a step, a breath – and Onnes is in the room. The lamps flicker. The cut on his head is hard and yellowish, blood-crusted, the skin swelling with infection. He is looking at Semiramis, his gaze slowly dismantling her. She lets her hand drop.

'It is true, then,' he says. 'You betrayed me.'

Ninus opens his eyes. His face changes, fills with pure, simmering hatred. 'Take one more step and I will kill you,' he rasps.

'You won't,' Onnes says. 'You can't.' He steps forward and unsheathes his sword. Ninus grabs his dagger, pushing Semiramis behind him. Onnes' breathing is ragged, but his grip on the sword is firm. *How long since he last took his opium?* Semiramis wonders. *And where are the guards?* But she has seen Onnes take down more than three soldiers by himself. She has seen him cut off men's heads as if they were wheat.

'Are you truly going to fight me?' For a moment, Onnes' expression softens. 'When have you ever won against me?'

Semiramis steps into his path, forcing her husband to look into her eyes. He shifts and the sword touches her chest. The blade cuts the fabric of her dress, finds her skin. She can feel the steady beat of her blood against the metal.

'Do it,' she says. She hears the calm in her voice, the determination, as if it didn't belong to her. 'I am not afraid.'

'Semiramis.' He says her name as he once did in a village of the province. As if she mattered, as if she were a goddess. 'I know you aren't.' He lowers the sword and steps back, stumbling. A moment of hope, before she hears Ninus say, 'No,' and she doesn't understand, because Onnes hasn't done anything.

They are all still. Then Onnes closes his eyes and says, 'I love you' – to her, to Ninus? He puts the sword against his own neck and presses the blade into the skin.

Blood comes like a river. There is a scream and Onnes falls to his knees, in a pool of crimson. The torches are shaking and the light is burning and Ninus is pressing his hand against his brother's neck, uselessly, hopelessly, as Onnes' life flows away from him.

39.

Ninus, King of the World, King of Assyria

Kings aren't meant to weep, but weep he does.

He clings to the body, even if life has long left his brother. He felt it, as he held him close, pulse by pulse, flowing away like a dying river. They had looked at each other, knowing it was for the last time. A heartbeat, then he knew he had lost him for ever.

*

In a tent that reeked of death, before Ninus cut Assur's throat, before he executed the wrong brother, Assur had looked at him with his amused stare – which Ninus had often deemed vacuous and stupid – and told him: 'Onnes has grown too cold, inscrutable. How can you trust a man when you don't know what he's thinking?'

And yet Ninus would have thrown himself into the fire for Onnes. Why?

Because, deep down, he liked not knowing what Onnes was thinking: it allowed Ninus to reinvent him, to make him different from what he actually was, to tell himself, *He loves me too*, when all Onnes offered were brief glances and selfish truths.

When Onnes told him he had killed their father, Ninus hated him. But then, under all that hate, under all the remorse, there was something else, as if Ninus had already known what Onnes had done. As if he wasn't surprised.

Ninus had seen him smash boys' faces in the training ground, cut slaves' backs with a whip, order countless soldiers to be impaled. And yet, in all those years, he always clung to his first memory of Onnes: a lonely, broken boy whom Ninus could save. Surrounded by people who wielded brutality as a weapon, he had thought he had found someone who could need and love him. But need and love aren't always the same thing. And Onnes never needed anyone. Yes, he was broken, yes, he was lonely, but he was strong and slippery and often cruel. And Ninus loved him, in spite of it all.

*

The body burns on a hill, noblemen and governors crowded around it. His mother tries to stand by his side, but he moves away. For years she despised Onnes with all her might and now he is gone and she finally got what she wanted. She always does.

Semiramis wears a long blue dress that flows behind her, like an ocean's wave. Ninus wants to speak to her, but she doesn't look at him. She doesn't look at anyone. She is like a shadow, perched at the top of the hill, with dark-lidded eyes and tears on her cheeks.

The fire crackles, the wind screams.

Ninus thinks about Onnes' expression before he said, 'I love you,' to the air between him and her, before he brought the sword to his neck.

He thinks about the face he made when they used to eat the opium together.

About the way he used to defend him when other children spoke ill of him.

About the first time he saw him, in the gardens. He was reading *Gilgamesh* that day. What did Gilgamesh say when Enkidu died?

The river rises, flows over its banks,
and carries us all away, like mayflies.
Floating downstream: they stare at the sun,
then all at once there is nothing.

40.

Semiramis, Born With No Name

She kneels with her hands on the cold ground, the shadows around her so deep she could sink into them. Under her, the earth is a shell, the underworld brimming with spirits, their hands tapping to reach her, to be dragged back to the world of the living.

She has prayed and she has pleaded, but no god has replied. Not even Nergal, god of death, who let Enkidu return to the earth after he died, opening the ground like a trapdoor so that his spirit floated up and reunited, for a brief, precious moment, with his lover.

She has prayed to Nergal to open the earth for Onnes, but she is a woman and Onnes a bastard son: the gods don't care about them.

She punches the pavement, as if she could crack it herself. Her leopard comes, licks her hands, presses to her side. Semiramis cries into her fur. The animal's pulse rises and falls, like all life, until it stops. And then what? An eternity of grief and coldness, inevitable, inescapable. She doesn't know how to bear this sorrow, this fear of death. It bursts inside her, seethes like a stormy sea. It is dread, but it is also anger, the crack of a heart, a deafening ache. And, above all, regret. *I failed him. I could not save him.*

'Do you love me?' she had asked Onnes once after Balkh.

'You want a kind of love I cannot give,' he had said.

He had thought his heart was rotted, too broken to be healed. From the moment he lost his mother, he longed for something he could never have. And that's every mortal's undoing: longing. *But despite knowing the ruin it brings, we can never stop wanting.*

Humans have only a single lifetime. How can they truly understand love? Those who believe they can are even more lost than the rest.

*

Sasi visits her at night. She lets him sit in the reception room, while Ana serves him beer and broth. He touches neither.

'You have played your game well,' he says.

'Except it isn't a game,' she says. She sounds as if she is choking. 'It's my *life*.'

'Onnes' life,' he corrects her. 'Which he lost.'

'Do you think that is what I wanted?' she snaps.

The lamp between them shakes with her shuddering breaths. She places her hands on the table to steady herself. 'I thought he was going to kill us.'

Sasi sighs. 'For years, I have seen many study Onnes for a glimpse of his thoughts. The king. You. Me, even. But, in the end, I believe all he truly concerned himself with was his own pain.'

She feels a wave of despair. 'What will happen to me?'

Maybe he knows, maybe he doesn't. Either way, he doesn't answer her. He sits in the darkened silence until she orders him to leave.

*

The answer comes to her at dawn. Five guards from the Northwest Palace burst into her courtyard. 'You are expected in the throne room,' they say. 'By order of the king's mother.'

She makes for her apartments to change, but the guards drag her outside. Ana hurries behind her as she leaves the palace, handing her a dark blue cloak, which she wraps around her shoulders, pinning it tight so that it covers her night tunic.

They walk past the obelisk under a paling, bloodless sky. The reckoning: the moment of unbearable stillness before the fall.

Once, when she was climbing the cliffs around Mari, her hands slipped, and she lost her balance. She twisted into the air then hit the earth, shocked when the ground did not bend for her. What had she done afterwards? She cannot remember.

330

In the throne room, Nisat, Ilu and Sasi are waiting for her. Ninus sits on his throne quietly and, for a moment, Semiramis thinks about the first time she saw him, right in this room. She had thought him beautiful, and he hadn't once looked at her. *Speak*, she pleads. *Help me*. But he keeps silent, looking as if something inside him has broken.

It is Nisat who speaks, her face a blade of iron. 'You know why you are here.'

Semiramis feels the coldness of her voice on the skin. It would cut her, if only she had any blood left to spill. 'I don't.'

Nisat moves closer to the throne. 'King Hammurabi created the code almost a thousand years ago. He claimed he had received the laws from the sun god Shamash himself. It changed everything for our people. It taught them that each crime has a punishment, that each act has a consequence. The code stripped everyone of their lies, and it gave us order. No one can act with impunity. No one can think himself above the code, high or low.'

'And yet Hammurabi thought himself above it,' Semiramis says. 'He thought himself a god.'

A flash in Nisat's eyes. 'Hammurabi was a king. The people called him "the brace that grasps wrongdoers", "the fear-inspiring ruler who gives the disobedient the death sentence". But you don't understand the laws of power, do you? You think you can play any game you want, and still come out of it unharmed.' They stare at each other, then Nisat turns to Sasi. 'Tell us, Spymaster, what is law 153 of the code?'

Sasi startles, as if surprised to be asked. Dutifully, he fixes the long sleeves of his dress, then recites, '*If a man's wife, for the sake of another, has caused her husband to be killed, that woman shall be impaled.*'

'Yes,' Nisat says. 'A death for a death.'

Ninus clenches his fist. Semiramis sees a storm in his eyes, but she doesn't wait for him or any of them to speak. She comes to stand in the torchlight, so her voice carries the length of the room.

'I was born with no name,' she says. 'When my mother gave birth to me, she didn't want me. She left me on a rock before drowning herself in a lake. I wasn't meant to survive, but survive I did. A travelling shepherd found me and claimed me as his own.'

She remembers now what she had done all those years ago, after she had fallen down the cliff in Mari. The same thing she always does: she had wiped her tears and climbed again.

'I've been beaten so many times I've lost count,' she says. 'I've been dragged in the mud and spat upon. I always stood up again.'

Ninus is staring at her. Sasi keeps still, but Semiramis sees the approval in his eyes, hears the thoughts in his head as clearly as if he were speaking them out loud: *You are doing well. Using your past to secure your future.*

'Then Onnes came to my village. He gave me a new life. I had wings and he was the wind that made me fly.' She looks at Ninus. There is lightning inside her, her heart like the sky during a storm. 'I did not cause Onnes' death. He brought it upon himself. The king was there. He saw it too.'

She takes a step forward. Ilu mirrors her movement, his fingers tight around the handle of his sword. She ignores him. Her eyes are fastened on Ninus.

'My king,' she says, 'you wanted me before, but I couldn't give myself to you, not fully. Now I am here.'

For a moment, everything in the room seems to fade. Ninus stands, his head framed by the lush tree carved behind him. When he speaks, his voice is so soft, it feels like a breeze.

'I will have you.'

*

In the ancient stories, the first gods to walk the earth were Anu and Ea. With Anu the heavens were born, and with Ea the abyss of waters upon which the world floats. Semiramis thinks this must be why sometimes the sky looks like a river, a blue current with stars like golden fish, and the river looks like the sky, dark and sacred, with secrets hidden at the bottom.

From the terrace of the Northwest Palace, she looks at the river, and Ninus looks at her. Everyone else has left, at his behest.

'Onnes is gone,' he says. She knows he needs to say it to believe it is true. 'Are you sure you want to do this?'

She turns to him. He is so close that she can almost feel his heart. 'I am sure.'

The gods watch them from the sky. She takes Ninus' face in her hands, and he kisses her.

*

She is crowned on the last day of summer. An early moon shines as the sun dives behind the mountains – a gift from the god Sin. Nobles, priests and governors crowd into the courtyards of the Northwest Palace to witness it.

She wears a long crimson dress and a golden mantle, her hair cascading down her back. Ninus places the crown on her head. The cold gems press against her forehead.

He asks her what her royal name will be, his voice echoing against the carved walls. He looks at her as he did when they were seated at the foot of the walls of Balkh. She had told him of her dream, how she feared she was shut out from the highest heavens, and he had said to her: *I believe you could find your way even into the halls of the gods.*

She glances at the crowd that stretches at their feet and says, 'Sammuramat.'

High heaven.

BOOK V

815–813 BC

Which of your husbands did you love for ever?
Which could satisfy your endless desires?
Let me remind you how they suffered,
How each one came to a bitter end.

From *The Epic of Gilgamesh*

41.

Semiramis, a Queen

In the throne room of the capital of the Assyrian Empire, a boy is singing. His voice is soft and sweet, the sound accompanied by his long-necked lute. He sings a tale of love and death, which he has already played countless times in the streets of Babylon. Now in front of him, on a dais carved with lions and sphinxes, are the King of Assyria and his new queen.

'In the city of Babylon,
the jewel hanging from the sky,
people whisper about the Assyrian king
who fell in love with his governor's bride.
Who knows if out of fear of his king
or out of passion for his wife
the husband went mad,
cut his throat and died?'

When he stops singing, the boy kneels, waiting for the verdict. The silence hums. At the foot of the dais, a leopard shifts. She is bored, annoyed by every new supplicant, and has already tried to snap off the arm of a Cretan merchant.

From his place close to the brazier, a sweet voice asks, 'Do you wish to have this man dragged away and whipped, my king?'

The boy looks up at the eunuch nervously. He clearly hadn't expected such a reaction: in the glowing streets of Babylon, the people loved the song so much that they sent him to sing in the mighty palaces, in front of the noblest men. He decides to appeal to the queen. 'Didn't my voice please the queen?' he tries.

Semiramis plays with a strand of black hair. She can feel Ninus' anger next to her, ready to lash out. His blood has drained from his face, and his fists are clenched. 'Take the boy away,' she orders.

'Perhaps the queen would like to hear another song,' the boy says tentatively.

'Or perhaps she would like to have your tongue,' Semiramis replies. Sasi giggles as the boy disappears from the throne room, terrified.

It is cold, despite the burning brazier at the centre. Semiramis is wearing a gold headdress made of rosettes woven together. From the door guarded by the giant winged bulls, they can see shadows moving on the paving, shifting nervously.

'How many more seek audience?' Ninus asks.

'The envoys from Egypt are waiting in the courtyard,' Sasi replies. 'They have brought gifts: monkeys, for our hanging gardens.'

'Who else?'

'Offerings of cattle from Eber-Nari, from the Bactrian women Semiramis sent there, my king.'

'Do they send the cattle only, or is there a woman too, to give her thanks?' Semiramis asks.

'There is a woman, my queen.'

'I will see her.'

Sasi nods. The courtiers by the door move aside, letting a woman enter. She has long black hair in simple plaits and a tunic the colour of butter. She looks at the leopard with a strange, reverential expression, then kneels.

'My queen,' she starts, 'I bring the gratitude of the people of Eber-Nari, and of those Bactrian prisoners you welcomed to the empire.' Her accent is foreign, though it has some of the cadences of Eber-Nari. She looks young, her features still those of a girl. Semiramis wonders why the Bactrians chose her to bring their thanks to the capital.

'Stand,' Semiramis says. 'Those women are no longer prisoners.'

'Yes, my queen. But we do not forget to whom we owe our freedom.'

You were free before we came to destroy your city, Semiramis wants to say. But how are kings and queens worshipped, if not through the gratitude of their subjects?

'Our gods forsook us in Balkh,' the black-haired girl continues. 'But we have found others in our new land. When we pray to them, we always whisper the name of the woman who is daughter of a goddess.'

'Daughter of a goddess,' Semiramis repeats.

Sasi steps closer to the dais, an enigmatic smile on his face. On his throne, Ninus shifts, almost imperceptibly.

'There were already rumours in Eber-Nari,' the girl says, 'of a child found by a shepherd and raised in a village before she married the governor. They say that the child was born in a lake, the daughter of a fish goddess by the name of Derceto.'

Her mother's name, like a blade being twisted in her belly. 'And the Bactrian women believe such rumours?' Semiramis asks.

'We saw you in battle, as fierce as the goddess Ishtar. You walked with men as if you were one of them. The people of Eber-Nari say it must be the same woman who grew up in their land, for her strength and beauty come from the divine blood running thick inside her.'

They treated me as if I were no one while I was there, and now that I rule an empire, they wish to worship me. But there is something familiar in the girl's face, a memory that refuses to be caught.

'We have met before,' Semiramis says.

The girl nods. 'We have, my queen, in the darkness of the battle. You tried to save me and my sister.'

The memory washes over her. Two girls clutching their mother's arm, refusing to let go. Semiramis had dragged them away, until an Assyrian soldier had come and killed one of them. 'I am sorry for your sister.'

The girl bows her head slightly. Her eyelashes are wet, but she does not wipe them.

'Thank you for reporting these rumours,' Semiramis says. 'And thank the Bactrian women for their offerings. Attendants will join you in the courtyard and take care of the cattle.'

The girl kneels again before taking her leave. For a long moment, the room grows quiet again. When Semiramis turns to Ninus, his expression is impenetrable. 'My mother was no goddess,' she says. 'She was a villager.'

'My queen,' Sasi intervenes, 'that isn't as interesting.'

She wants to ask him if he is responsible for some of the rumours, but this isn't the time, or place. The light of the courtyard trickles into the room. The leopard comes to stand at Semiramis' feet.

'Ninus,' Semiramis says. But he isn't looking at her.

'Send the next one in,' he orders.

*

Night blossoms like a flower, stars and clouds unfurling in the darkness. On the terrace of the Northwest Palace, a hundred small lamps are flickering: bright and golden, luring the dead. Ninus has ordered them lit day and night.

Semiramis joins him, the breeze soft on her skin. His eyes are closed, his face turned towards the river.

'You didn't say anything about the Bactrian woman,' she says softly.

'What is there to say?'

She reaches a hand to swipe at his curls, but he moves away. She looks at the fine bones of his face, the way he clenches his jaw. 'You are angry,' she says.

He waves an arm to encompass the view around them: the temples and the city walls, the fields and orchards. His empire, and hers. 'You enjoy all this.'

She can hear the accusation in his tone. 'And what if I do?'

She knows what he is thinking: if she enjoys power so much, perhaps she married him because of it, not because she loved him. But instead he asks, 'What more do you want? It is never enough for you.'

Only a few months they have been together, yet he understands her better than anyone ever has. She wants to give him the words he craves, to tell him, *It is enough*, but she cannot lie to him.

He turns away from her and looks at the dark sky gleaming like a moonlit river. 'He married you here,' he says. 'Do you know why?'

She shakes her head. Onnes is stitched on their lips, in their hearts. They do not speak his name, but they feel the constant ache, a cut that never heals.

'Neither do I.' He sighs. 'It was my favourite place, so it felt like a cruel joke. Maybe he did it on purpose.'

'Maybe he did it because he loved you.'

He turns back to her. 'Do you really believe that?'

'It does not matter what I believe. All that matters is that he's gone.' *And we have to accept it.*

'All my life, he was by my side. I don't know what to do now.'

She leans to him, lifts her hands to his dark hair, smoothing it out of his eyes. This time he doesn't draw away.

I would go to the underworld myself to bring him back, she thinks. But what good would that do? Sometimes you make a choice that you cannot unmake. Then you have to live with it.

*

She goes to Shalmaneser's palace when all the men have finished their training. Ilu is polishing an iron sword, careful not to spoil the inlaid gold on the blade. She has always noticed how he diminishes others by standing next to them, as if he drew his power from the comparison. But now she sees that, even when he is alone, power sits on him, on the folds of his robe, on his bronze skin, his smug half-smile. She remembers something Sasi once told her: 'Ilu is like a cockroach: he will outlive us all.'

It had made her laugh. 'You despise him.'

'On the contrary, I quite admire him. Most soldiers favour strength, rather than intelligence. Ilu is as strong as he looks and cleverer than he seems. A dangerous mix.'

Before she can step forward, Ilu turns, his eyes appraising her coldly. 'What are you doing here?'

'I came to train.'

'Alone?'

'With you.'

His mouth curves into an indolent smile. 'I am not sure that is a good idea.' Slowly, lazily, he runs his thumb over the edge of the sword. A drop of blood appears, grows until it falls to the ground. She wonders if the gesture is meant as a threat, or if he simply enjoys the feeling of pain before a confrontation.

'I know you spent a lot of time here with Onnes,' he says, 'when you first married him.'

She stares at him calmly. 'Surely not as much as you.'

He wipes his finger on the wall, leaving a crimson trail. 'This palace didn't exist when I was a boy,' he says. 'Shalmaneser had it built after he became king, and I supervised its construction with Dayyan-Assur. The three of us established the largest army the world had ever seen. Infantry, charioteers, mounted archers, fast horses, engineers and wagoners . . . They all came to train here. We lived and ate and fought here during the day. And at night, we brought our whores to these rooms.'

She tries to imagine them, lying down in the darkest corners of the palace, sharing women as if they were war spoils.

'Dayyan wasn't a handsome man,' Ilu says, 'but women liked him, because he wasn't cruel. Shalmaneser didn't even see them. He treated them as just another of his princely duties.'

Semiramis tilts her head. 'Was this before or after you started sleeping with his wife?'

His gaze snaps to hers. 'People have been killed for saying such things.'

'Do you deny it?'

'Why should I? Nisat and I are made for each other. We both see the world as it is, not as it should be. Do you know how many battles I have seen? How many men I have killed? I have seen enemies skewered like pigs on spikes, cut their throats as if they were sheep. Killing means nothing to me, or to her. Because we are strong. That is what a true Assyrian is.' He regards her with narrow, cunning eyes. 'But you are not like us. You shielded those women in Balkh. You free your slaves. You love Ninus, who is weak.'

'I do not want to be like you,' she says.

He frowns, as if he cannot imagine such a thing. To him, the world is made of fools and of people clever enough to understand that ruthlessness is the only way to power. *And he has lived this long, so maybe he is right. But I will take my chances.*

'I will come back tomorrow, when all the soldiers are gone,' she says. 'And I will train with you.'

'You can train with someone else.'

She unsheathes her dagger and presses it against her palm. The pain is slow and burning. Then she walks to the wall he marked with his blood and covers it with her own. 'You fight better than anyone else,' she says. 'I will train with you. And that is the queen's order, not a request.'

She does not bother to wait for his reply. She turns and leaves him alone in the room where he used to share whores with his king.

*

Incense is heavy in the air, its scent mixing with the aroma of wine. They dine in the inner courtyard of the palace, joined by Nisat and Sosanê. Their couches are draped with gold streamers, the table laid with spiced fish and cheese, mutton stewed in milk with onions and carrots. A cupbearer pours sweet wine, while a eunuch dressed in purple appears, a lyre in hand.

'Play us something,' Nisat orders. '"The Ballad of Former Heroes".'

Ninus lets out a mirthless laugh. He looks godly in his embroidered tasselled robe, though his eyes are haunted.

Nisat looks at him sharply. 'You used to love it. Come,' she calls to the eunuch. 'Sing.'

He bows and caresses the strings. '*Where are the great kings from former days now?*' he sings. '*They will not be born again.*'

Semiramis looks at the platters spread on the table. She has noticed that, whenever the king's mother dines with them, there are always more courses, more wine. *While the people starve in the provinces*, she thinks. The others are eating in silence, listening to the ballad, so she turns to Sosanê. 'If you could marry anyone in the world, who would it be?' she asks.

The girl startles, as if surprised to be addressed. 'Someone like Father, I suppose,' she says. 'Someone who likes to read.'

Ninus smiles, caresses her head.

'*These kings were superior to those, and others to them . . .*'

'I have heard that Ilu's younger son is a good man,' Semiramis continues. 'Strong and clever.' She can't help but remember how Sargon had looked at her in her first council meeting, the arrogance in his voice, the indolence in the way he moved. But Sasi has whispered a little secret in her ear, and now she wants to know if it is true.

Sosanê takes a bite of fish, intrigued. 'Did he fight in Balkh?'

'His brother did. He died bravely. I was there.'

'Grandmother says that bravery often breeds dullness,' Sosanê says.

Semiramis can't help but laugh. Ninus arches a brow. 'Bel may have been brave,' he says, 'but I doubt Sargon is. As a child he often hid behind his brother when he wanted to taunt me.'

'*Where is King Ashurnasirpal, the mightiest of them all?*
Where is King Shalmaneser, who went up to the heavens?'

Nisat's hair shines dark against her face. The gold flowers engraved on her headdress resemble the chamomile that blossoms in the gardens in spring. 'How thoughtful of Semiramis to mention Ilu's son,' she says. 'I have been thinking Sargon would be the perfect match for Sosanê.'

Is Sasi ever wrong? Semiramis thinks. Sosanê stops eating, shock in her wide eyes, and Ninus puts down his cup. 'You didn't consult me on this,' he says.

'I am telling you now,' Nisat says. 'And I have already consulted Ilu.'

Ninus snorts. 'So now you confide first in the man you sleep with, then in your son?'

'Just as you didn't confide in me when you decided to marry.'

'How far did a life without glamour transcend death?
Cast away unhappiness, forget the silence of death!'

The last notes shimmer in the air. The eunuch lingers in a corner, unsure what to do. Semiramis dismisses him with a flick of her hand. In the silence that follows, Ninus' voice is rough. 'You have been confiding in Ilu for years,' he says. 'What would Father say, if he knew you had betrayed him?'

Nisat sits back. Firelight gleams in the braziers behind her. 'Are you speaking of betrayal? Your father slept with countless women. Let us name some. The administrator from my palace, remember her? She used to let you sit by her side as she took care of buying, lending and borrowing. And at night, she would warm Shalmaneser's bed. The female scribe from my household? He fucked her too. She died by poisoning, poor thing. The high-ranking ladies who came from the provinces? He would have them. And let us not talk about the slave girls. Or Onnes' mother.'

Semiramis thinks Ninus will stand and smash something, but he is staring at his mother, silent.

'When men take noblewomen and slaves, it is their duty to do so,' Nisat says. 'When women pursue their pleasure, they are at fault.'

'You have always pursued your pleasure without caring for anyone else's opinion,' Ninus says bitterly.

'And you used to respect me for it. As a child you wished to be free of everyone's thoughts and expectations.'

He still wishes that. But the burden has grown too heavy, and his shoulders now carry mountains of regret.

344

Sosanê's hands are restless, torturing her sleeves, then the hem of her tunic.

'Onnes was like that too,' Ninus says. 'He never cared for anyone's thoughts.'

They all look at him – his wife, his daughter, his mother. Nisat reaches out and takes his hand in hers. 'You know he loved you.'

Ninus shakes his head. 'The gods punished him.'

'If it is true,' Nisat says, 'then you were punished too. What is the greater grief? To be gone, or to be left on earth when the one you love has joined the house of dust?'

Sosanê's eyes fill with tears. Semiramis watches Nisat's hand gripping Ninus'. *This is how Onnes must have felt*, she thinks, *as he grew up, motherless, watching a woman like Nisat willing to do anything to protect her son.*

The heavens grow darker, then fill with stars. The air that hangs around them doesn't stir. A night when the spirits rest.

*

When dinner is ended, Semiramis accompanies Sosanê back to the women's palace. There are tablets everywhere in the princess's room and, on the bed, two carved ivories: a harpy and the plaque of a lioness eating a man.

'May I?' Semiramis says, reaching for the plaque. Sosanê nods. Lotus and papyrus flowers are blossoming in the background, gold leaf and lapis lazuli. The man is lying back, knees drawn up as the lioness bites his neck. His curls are made of gilt-topped ivory pegs. It makes Semiramis think of Amon, her long-lost brother.

'My uncle Assur brought it here from the Phoenician cities,' Sosanê says. 'He would always bring me things, before the war.'

There is longing in the girl's voice, which surprises Semiramis. She has never heard anyone speak of Assur in such a way. 'Do you miss him?'

'I know he was cruel to others, but he was kind to me,' Sosanê says. 'I grieved when he died.'

'He betrayed your father,' Semiramis says.

Sosanê shrugs. 'We all betray the people we love.'

Semiramis walks to the window. Music and chatter float up to her. How many people has she betrayed? Her father, her brother, her

345

husband. Sacrifices that she made along the way, to be with the man she truly loved. And to claim a throne no one promised her.

'Is it true you saved all those women from Balkh?'

Semiramis turns. Sosanê is looking at her, and, for a moment, her expression is so like Ninus' that Semiramis can't help but smile. 'I didn't save them. They may be alive, but they lost their brothers and husbands. Some griefs cannot be forgotten.'

'But you freed them.'

'I did.'

'Why?'

'I was like them, once.'

'Not any more.' Sosanê smiles. The expression is strange on her face, for her eyes remain sad. She looks small in her wide room, and Semiramis imagines how lonely she must have felt growing up here, no mother and a father too young to care much for her.

Semiramis puts down the statuette. 'I will let you rest now.'

The girl watches her curiously, as if Semiramis were foreign writing, impossible to decipher. Semiramis thinks she will ask her to stay, but instead Sosanê says, 'You knew about Grandmother's plan to marry me to Sargon. That is why you brought it up.'

Semiramis feels her breath catch. She hides it with a smile. 'You are clever.'

'And you are brave. But I think that if you play too much with fire, you will be burned.' She bows her head slightly. 'Goodnight.'

*

Ninus is standing in the king's bedroom when she returns. The *lamassu* statues guard the door, their wings arranged into neat rows of feathers. Semiramis walks past them and pours a cup of wine.

'Sosanê is a special child,' she says. 'No one ever told me what happened to her mother.'

He sinks into a silver chair and brings his hand to his forehead, as if to ease a headache. 'She was a scribe.'

'From your mother's palace?'

He nods faintly.

'What happened to her?' she repeats.

He looks outside the window. The evening sky is clear, the moon god ready to spy on mortal lovers. 'She was the first girl I brought to my bed,' he says. 'I was sixteen.' He stops, and she waits for him to continue.

'I didn't want to, but Assur kept taunting me, he kept telling me to look for the pretty scribe who worked for our mother. He said to me, "She could recite *Gilgamesh* to you while you're inside her."' He shrugs. 'My brother always knew how to make me uncomfortable.

'So I went to the scribe. I spent the night with her, but I never asked her back to my bed. Then, a few months later, I was eating with Onnes and Assur, when Nisat came to find me. She told me the scribe had just given birth in the queen's household.'

The memory is drawn clear across his face, the surprise one feels when the consequences of one's actions are made clear.

'I still remember what Assur said. He said, "Don't tell me that now you have to marry a scribe." I hadn't thought of marriage, hadn't thought of anything. But my mother said she was dead. She had died giving birth, but the child lived.'

He looks at her. Usually, when he speaks of the past, his voice is hurt, and his eyes are shadowed. But now it is different.

'Would you have married her, if she had lived?' she asks.

He shakes his head. 'I remember . . . I felt relieved when she died. I thought I had escaped her somehow.'

She imagines the girl's scent on him, soft and common. Ninus' hands on her skin.

'And what would you feel if I died?' she asks.

His eyes meet hers. 'You can't die. You can't leave me.'

They stand looking at each other. So many times she has wondered if he truly loves her, or if he seduced her only because of Onnes. Now she glimpses the truth: Onnes didn't need her, while Ninus can't live without her. She wonders which of the two shows real love.

Ninus comes to her. She breathes in the small stretch of darkness between them. When he leans forward, her lips open, welcoming him. They drink each other in. She removes his tunic and finds his skin, the thick scar on his waist. He gasps as she touches him, clings to her, as if she is the air he needs to breathe. She lets him. It fills her with desire but something else too, something she never felt with Onnes: power.

*

347

The throne room is dark in the night, the green and gold of the painted walls glowing feebly. There are only two guards, standing by the door, staring blankly ahead of them, and a figure beside the wall carved with tribute bearers: Sasi.

'I was just thinking of you,' he says when she joins him.

'I wish I could say I am flattered.'

He almost laughs. They walk towards the dais, watch as light-footed attendants put out the last torches. When they are gone, Sasi turns to her. 'The king isn't well.'

'What do you expect? His brother died.'

'Bastard brother. Friend. Lover.'

She keeps quiet. He touches the bas-relief of a tribute absentmindedly. 'Aren't siblings the most fascinating thing? I was born alone so I am constantly curious when it comes to understanding how people are bound by blood. I find that, with brothers and sisters, with parents even, people are much more inclined to forgive, to be blind to weakness and flaws. Because family can't be chosen so you must make do with what you are given.'

'Are you trying to tell me something? If so, be clear.'

He fixes the long, dark sleeves of his tunic. 'If you had met Assur, the king's older brother, you would know exactly what I mean. He was headstrong and often dull, unwilling to listen to others. He lacked the talent, essential in my opinion, to handle people with grace. He thought the world would bend to him and his commands. But, for years, Ninus refused to see Assur's flaws.'

'Many Assyrians are like Assur.'

'Unfortunately, they are. But you are not like that. You never assume others will bend to you, never underestimate them. Yet Onnes did something you didn't expect. You underestimated him, and now you spend your time thinking of how you could change what is already done.'

She stares at him. It is as if he has opened her skull, looked at the thoughts that have been haunting her. 'How do you know what I feel?' she asks, more sharply than she intends. 'You have never cared for anyone.'

He hesitates, takes a slow breath. 'I had a lover once. He came from my city and was deported with me and many others. We were close. I had lost everything, but I had him, and he had me. A small joy, a small hope.'

She had always thought Sasi was born this way, as if he had crawled out of an alley already with a secret on his lips. But now she sees there was once a different Sasi, one with the same soft hair and features, but whose soul has long disappeared.

'When we arrived in the capital,' Sasi continues, 'Shalmaneser's men asked us what we wanted to become. Deportees are carefully chosen for their abilities, you see, and sent to regions where they can make the most of their talents. A loyal servant to the king, a slave, a prostitute, a shepherd – those were the options. I knew a life on the hills wouldn't suit me, for I was born in a city of merchants and traders, and I have no physical strength, only the tricks of the mind. I didn't wish to sell my body, because I had seen what happens to the hearts of those who do. As for a slave, does anyone want to become one?

'So there was my choice. A loyal servant. But loyalty was a gift they offered to me, not the other way around, so I had to give something in return. They cut me, down there, so that if I ever rose too high I would still be harmless. I thought my lover would choose the same fate. I thought we would be together. But when he saw the pain and the terror, he couldn't bear it. He chose a different life, which took him away from me.'

Semiramis searches for a hint of pain on his face, but there is only coldness. It is unsettling.

'I grieved for him,' Sasi says, 'but what did I gain from such grief? Nothing. So I forgot about him. If he couldn't follow me, he wasn't meant to be with me.'

It is something Semiramis has told herself many times, when she left Mari and her brother behind, then again in the long, painful days after Onnes' death. If you don't run fast enough, the past will come and grab you. But now she has left too many behind, and they all reach out to her with desperate hands.

Sasi fixes a dark plait behind her ear. 'I've shed my past, like snake-skin. To survive, I was reborn. You must do the same.'

For a moment, she wants to cry into his shoulder, to let herself fall and see if he is willing to catch her. But she cannot afford to stumble, and Sasi has never caught anyone but himself.

'I know you won't believe me,' she says, 'but I loved him.'

Sasi's smile has no comfort in it. 'Oh, I believe you. But do you think that, in our world, love can ever be a strength?'

349

In the deep of the night, Semiramis wakes, feeling watched. She keeps still, barely breathing, waiting for the feeling to go away. It doesn't. When she opens her eyes, Onnes is standing by the bed. His bronze hair is faded, and his neck is covered with blood.

'Go away,' she whispers.

He doesn't, so she turns her back on him. Beside her, Ninus' sleep is restless. His eyelids flutter, his hands shake. She wonders, for the hundredth time, if he, too, is aware that Onnes' shadow lives beside them, watching them as they grieve, rule, make love.

And, if he is, for how long he will be able to bear it.

42.

Ninus, King of the World, King of Assyria

Ninus walks in the gardens, under a pale, shy light. The plants around him must be rich and blooming but the colours are faded in his eyes. The world has taken a different shape since Onnes' death: greyer, hazier.

It is spring, the first spring he has lived without his brother. Once, when Onnes was woven so intimately into the tapestry of his life, the idea of time moving forward without him would have been unfathomable. Now he has to accept it, though he can barely make sense of it.

> *You were the axe at my side,*
> *The knife in my sheath,*
> *the shield I carried . . .*
> *Weren't we to remain inseparable, you and I?*

He follows a lotus flower as it floats in the water of the canal. His hands shake slightly. All his life, he craved answers that Onnes never gave him. What Onnes thought of him the first time they met. Why he wanted to become Ninus' friend. What he felt when Ninus kissed him. Why they never talked about Shalmaneser. How he managed to keep silent as Ninus executed Assur, who was innocent.

Onnes was part of him, yet there was so much of him that Ninus couldn't understand. *But we are strangers to ourselves. There are parts of us we will never fully grasp.*

The rage comes back, savage. It is like a punch in the gut. He grabs his dagger and throws it against a column. It clatters to the ground, startling a flock of songbirds. They fly towards the sky, away from this city of madness. Ninus watches them. All the rage that is lodged in his body was meant to pour out and drown Onnes. But now Onnes is gone and Ninus has no choice but to keep the feeling inside himself, until he is the one who is drowned.

*

He summons the council on the terrace. The sky is cobalt blue, the buildings glittering under it. It is hot, and a few flies stir around them. A slave waves them away with a whisk.

'What news from Babylon?' he asks.

'The king lives,' Ilu says.

'As long as he does, his army won't attack us in the open,' Semiramis comments, touching the bright rings on her fingers. Ninus remembers how dirty her hands were the first time he met her, dust and mud under her fingernails. Now they are more and more like Nisat's, covered with rings and precious stones. *Love and duty*, Ninus had once told Onnes. *Every one of us must choose.* And his choice has dragged them into the darkness.

Sasi shifts in his chair. 'I have heard that he has fallen ill. Poison, my spies say.'

Ninus turns to him. 'Would Marduk poison his father?'

No one answers. They all know he would. Ninus glances at Semiramis, but she doesn't look back. 'The army Marduk wanted to gather at Dur,' she says. 'What of it?'

'It is already there,' Ilu replies. 'But they won't make a move against us unless the king commands it.'

'Good,' Ninus says, though there is nothing good about it. 'Keep me informed on the health of the king, Spymaster. What of Urartu?'

'Urartu has attacked our northern borders,' Ilu says. 'Villages have been raided and burned.'

'We let Taria go back to her home unharmed,' Nisat seethes. 'She can't repay us like this.'

'Is her child born?' Ninus asks.

Semiramis told him, and it was a moment of relief: he refused to marry the princess and that, at least, is one thing he has done right.

'It seems so,' Sasi says. 'A son.'

'Send an envoy to the north, then,' Ninus says. 'Remind the princess of Urartu what we did for her. And ask her about the health of her child, the bastard son of Marduk. If she isn't our ally, she is our enemy.'

Nisat smiles. 'Is that meant to be a threat?'

Yes, Mother, he thinks. *Didn't you teach me that kings do not understand kindness? You were right, and I, as always, was slow to learn. But I have learned.*

*

He leaves his guards outside the women's palace and enters his mother's chambers unannounced, to find her sitting by the window, a string of emeralds at her throat.

'Ninus,' she says calmly, as if she was expecting him. 'You did well on the council today.'

He takes the couch opposite her, pours some wine. The heat of the day has faded, and now a soft, sweet breeze is dancing around the palace.

'I should have murdered that traitor Marduk when I had the chance,' he says.

'We will be rid of him soon,' Nisat says. 'He needs to be eliminated, I agree.'

Ninus swirls his wine. He almost hopes Marduk will raise his madman's army, so Ninus can crush him. Lately there is a surge of violence in him that he does not know how to tame: his heart has grown rotten, as if he poisoned himself on anger.

Nisat reads his mind. 'You couldn't defeat him,' she says. 'He is stronger than you.'

He raises his cup to her. 'Thank you for believing in him so unwaveringly.'

'I believe in you,' she says, emptying her own cup in a mouthful. 'But your . . .' she searches for a word '. . . fervency is a weakness.'

'My fervency,' he repeats.

'It must be kept under control. We can all see that you are grieving, and it is time to move on. Onnes was your friend and governor, not your husband.'

He slams the cup on the table between them. Suddenly he is sick of it all, the lies, the threats. 'No, Mother,' he says. 'He was not only my friend. He was my half-brother, my greatest ally and confidant.'

She waves a hand, trying to dismiss his words. He keeps talking: 'You know it, but you have always pretended not to see. What did you think? That if you turned away, I would too?'

She stands, as if she can't bear to be near him. 'What I think,' she says slowly, 'is that you weep and grieve, but you do not see how the real world is. Have you ever paused to compare what you have with what a common man has? You were made from the blood of gods and mortals. You have been given a throne and men to rule over. And to the common man? Crumbs. He takes the leftovers of what you eat. You have worn yourself out through ceaseless, futile complaining and what have you achieved, but to bring yourself closer to death with all your suffering?'

He almost laughs. 'Have you been reading *Gilgamesh*, Mother?' he mocks. 'I didn't know you could be so poetic.'

She closes the distance between them and grips his wrist, burying her rings in his flesh. 'Show me your strength,' she snarls. 'Or I will put someone else on the throne.'

He doesn't draw away. It is freeing, this rage, these words that feel like blows. He rearranges his face and looks at her with the expression his father wore when she went too far. His words, when he speaks them, have a touch of madness. 'I will do nothing of the sort. I earned that crown after shedding the blood of my brother, and now I will keep it until the day I die.'

*

Ilu's palace is not far from where Onnes' was, though it is much grander. Torches are mounted on columns, and the floor is made of glazed terracotta tiles with images of Assyrian nobles toasting the king. Ninus crosses the main courtyard and passes the stone winged lions that protect the entrance to the apartments.

Ilu is in the portico, where couches are set. His feet are bare, dark against the eastern rugs that cover the floor. 'The King of the Universe, in my own palace,' he says when he sees Ninus. 'What an honour.' He gestures to the slaves standing by the walls to bring food and drinks, and they disappear into the corridors.

'Where is Sargon?' Ninus asks, as he sits.

'In the training ground, taunting some weaker soldiers, as he usually does.'

Ninus does not miss the hint of pride in Ilu's voice. He looks at the beer in front of him, then takes a sip.

Ilu does the same. 'You used to read in this portico while my sons played with Assur, do you remember?'

He remembers, though those memories feel so far from him now that he wonders if they ever really belonged to him. 'You didn't like me much then,' Ninus says.

'I didn't. But I was wrong. I underestimated you.'

'Just like everyone else.'

Ilu laughs again. 'Yes, just like everyone else.'

A small procession of slaves appears, carrying platters with heaps of bright grapes and pomegranates. Ilu waits until they have gone away, then asks, 'I imagine you are in need of counsel?'

Ninus watches him for a moment. He has aged a little since Balkh, but his eyes are still bright, his hands large and firm. Ninus once saw him kill a man with a blow to the head: his fist was so strong that the skull cracked open, like an egg. Ilu is watching him too, and Ninus wonders what he is thinking. He decides to cut to the chase.

'I know of your plot to marry your son to my daughter,' he says.

Ilu raises his eyebrows, sits back. Ninus enjoys seeing the glimmer of surprise on his face. 'I plotted nothing,' Ilu says.

'You didn't tell me of your plan and conspired with my mother. So we can call it a plot.'

Ilu sighs, makes himself more comfortable on the couch. 'Do you know why I underestimated you? Because you were a sweet child. Everyone beat you – your father, your bastard brothers, Assur – and you never fought back. I thought, Here is the most foolish boy who ever lived. He won't last.'

'You used to beat me too.'

'I had to. You were a boy and had to become a man.'

Ninus can't keep the sarcasm out of his voice: 'And am I a man now?'

'You are more than that,' Ilu says, raising his cup as if in a toast. 'You are a king. All the power is in your hands.'

Ninus doesn't drink. He looks at the giant stone creatures standing guard to the portico and wonders what his father thought of Ilu decorating his own palace so lavishly. 'And what about your power?' he asks.

Ilu frowns, as if he wasn't expecting such a question. 'I fought for it,' he says, caressing the lions carved into the arms of his couch. 'I campaigned for your father for years, then again for you. I eliminated your opponents. I sat in endless council meetings, listening to priests and eunuchs share their tedious insights. I have done all of it to better my family interests. Your father respected me for it. Why can't you do the same?'

'I can't respect you,' Ninus says calmly. 'You are heartless, manipulative and power-hungry. You humiliated me, beat Onnes whenever you could, slept with my mother.' He pauses, stares into Ilu's eyes. 'But I know what you have done for me. You helped me win the war against Assur, you fought for me in Balkh, and you have been a father to me, more than Shalmaneser ever was. Not a good one, of course, but still.'

Ilu is watching him, poised, unsure where Ninus is going. Then, quickly, Ninus grabs his sword and stabs the armrest of Ilu's couch. The blade sinks into the lion's head between Ilu's fingers. Ilu doesn't move. They stare at each other, barely breathing.

'You have come to threaten me, then,' Ilu says. There is the hint of a smile on his face, a mad glitter in his eyes.

Ninus shifts the dagger slightly, so that the metal presses against Ilu's thumb. 'Your son can marry Sosanê. A wedding will be good for us. And it is time our houses are joined.' A drop of blood appears on Ilu's hand. 'But if you plot with my mother again, I will kill you and your family, then give your position to someone else.'

Ilu's face is glowing like a fire's heart. Slowly, he rises from his couch. Then, to Ninus' surprise, he kneels. His lips brush Ninus' fingers.

'I am loyal to you, my king,' Ilu says. 'You will not rid yourself of me just yet.'

*

Ninus finds Semiramis in the prayer room, sitting on the floor at the feet of his father's bas-relief. A sandstorm is rising, and everyone is taking refuge in the painted rooms. He goes to her and rests his head on her lap. A handful of dust reaches the room, hiding at the foot of the winged bulls. Ninus watches it dance.

West of the river Euphrates, towards Eber-Nari, the sand takes the form of copper arrows, setting the arid land on fire. In Egypt it can drown cities, murdering people like a plague. In the myth of Gilgamesh, Enkidu is formed from the dust by the great mother goddess Aruru, before Gilgamesh falls in love with him. *And before Gilgamesh loses him for ever.*

'I have told Ilu I accept his proposal,' Ninus says. 'Sosanê will marry his son.'

He can feel her stiffening, her hands moving away from his cheek. 'Ilu and Nisat want to make sure their heir is in line to the throne, rather than mine,' she says.

'What they want doesn't matter. You'll carry a child sooner than Sosanê will.'

'And if I don't?'

He doesn't answer. He sits up and brushes the sand from her chest. For a moment, her face is as naked as he has ever seen it, before she hides it again.

'You didn't want a child with Onnes,' he says quietly. 'Did you?'

She looks away from him, at the sand moving in the shadows. 'Sometimes I think children are a weakness.'

'How can legacy be a weakness?'

She covers her face with her hands. Her hair falls around her shoulders. He thinks that both of them have been drowning but, rather than fight the storm together, they've lost each other at sea.

'My father was a person, and I am another,' he says. 'Just like you and your mother. If you love someone, could you ever give her away? I don't think so.'

She turns her palms upwards, as if to catch his words. When she looks at him, her expression is fierce and shameless, the face he first fell in love with.

'Onnes once said that when you love someone, you see only the good in them,' she says.

'Is that such a bad thing?'

'No,' she says. 'It isn't.'

Her lips find his. For a moment, all thoughts stop clawing at his head. All is calm, all is still. When they break apart, there is a strange light in her eyes. The thoughts return and, with them, a sense of distrust. Semiramis never shows anything but what she wants to reveal. And how does he know that what he sees is true?

357

Loving her sometimes feels like looking at the sun, feeling the warmth on his skin, but never being able to see its true shape, for it is too blinding.

*

He brings his daughter to Ilu's palace as the god Shamash rides his chariot beyond the mountains. The moon god Sin takes his place in the sky, and Ninus is glad that Sosanê is marrying under his merciful eyes.

Sargon is standing tall and slim, under the bas-reliefs that showcase his father's glory. He veils Sosanê's head and says, 'She is my wife,' as the ceremony demands.

Nisat puts a hand on her granddaughter's shoulder and says, 'May this be the beginning of a fruitful union between our families!' Her eyes meet Ilu's and she smiles her most satisfied, and dangerous, smile.

Ninus shifts so that his lips are close to Sargon's ear. 'Hurt my daughter,' he says, 'and I will carve out your eyes and feed them to the dogs.'

*

Despite the darkness of the sky, Ilu's palace is a blaze of light, lamps and torches burning in every corner. Attendants pour sweet red wine into golden cups, as musicians caress the strings of their harps. Ninus watches as courtiers crowd around Sargon and Sosanê, each more eager to bathe in their light. They look splendid, Sosanê in a rich green dress and a diadem of coloured stones, Sargon in a crimson tunic with roaring lions embroidered on it.

'Such a selfless act,' a high voice behind Ninus says, 'to give your daughter in marriage to Sargon.'

Ninus turns. Sasi's eyes are bright. His fingernails are painted green – a Babylonian custom. He looks strangely out of place in Ilu's palace, like a fish out of water.

'I don't expect you, of all people, to understand it,' Ninus says.

Sasi bows slightly. 'You misjudge me, my king.'

'I'm sure many people do.'

'Yes. But not your wife.'

Ninus thinks about all the times he has seen Sasi slip into the royal quarters to speak to Semiramis, the two of them close in the large, shadowed courtyards. 'I imagine the two of you have much in common,' he says.

This amuses Sasi. 'A difficult past, I'd say.'

'And unbridled ambition.'

Sasi chuckles, looks at the musicians plucking the strings of their harps. Ilu and his wife are sitting close to them, on the finest couches. On Ilu's right Nisat is smiling indulgently as noblemen compliment the jewels around her wrists.

When Sasi turns back to Ninus, his face is lit and his voice a whisper. 'I bring good news,' he says. 'Urartu has stopped attacking our borders.'

'Our threats have worked,' Ninus says.

'Yes.' Sasi nods. 'In my experience, they always do. You did well, my king. I dare say that after so much war, peace is finally upon us.' He bows and slides away.

A line of slaves passes, heads bowed to make sure their eyes do not meet the king's. Ninus moves further into the shadows, resting his back against the carved soldiers. Once, Onnes was his safe place during these feasts. They would sit together on the couches and drink sweet wine until the edges of things grew blurred and dream-like. *But Onnes betrayed you.*

Now he has Semiramis. He looks for her across the courtyard. As if hearing his thoughts, she turns, hair swaying around her shoulders. They do not say anything, just look at each other.

What are you thinking about? he wonders. *How will you betray me?*

43.

Semiramis, Destined for Greatness

The summer heat fades, and autumn fills the city with the smells of incense and cedar-wood.

She is in the training ground when it happens. Shalmaneser's palace is empty, but she likes to be there at sunrise, before Ilu, to test new swords and spears. As she wields an iron dagger, she stumbles and loses her footing. She falls and, as she hits the ground, her stomach lurches and she nearly heaves. She gulps down the sickness, then panics and thinks she has been poisoned.

She bends forward, retches until her throat hurts. *Is that all?* she thinks, as the vomit spreads at her feet. She pulls herself up and straightens against the wall. Then she notices the sky, which is growing red as the sun rises.

'The red sunrise is an omen of childbirth,' Ribat once told her. 'It is for children who battle to be born, but whose future is destined for glory.'

She looks at the sky, heart beating fast. Everything is blurring around her, contours fading as weapons and bas-reliefs lose their shape.

She storms out of the training ground and meets her guards outside. When she is safely back in the Northwest Palace, she orders every courtier away from the royal quarters and hides in the baths, sitting in water so warm it is as if touched by the god Shamash himself. Her blood is beating, an urgent rhythm.

She touches her belly. It is still smooth and taut from all her training. But she can feel something inside her, a seed and a sudden certainty. *I am with child.*

Slowly, she blows out the lamps and curls in the water. *Goddess,* she prays to Ishtar, *let this not be the end of me.*

*

When the poets sing of time, they depict it as something that keeps moving forward, like a leaf carried by a stream, flowing with the current: the present, constantly unfolding towards the future. But sometimes, the leaf becomes stuck in the river – a trunk, a twig obstructing its path – and in those brief moments the past catches up.

That night, as she sleeps half wrapped in perfumed sheets, she dreams of her mother. She is in a strange temple, where statues of a foreign goddess are cold and beautiful, and the paving is stained with blood. 'Don't you want to hold your child?' a voice asks, but there is no one to answer her, and the words echo against the walls, until they fill the temple with loneliness.

Semiramis wakes to the sound of a baby screaming, and it takes her a moment to understand that the screaming comes from the dream, and that the bedroom is silent.

She sits up. Moonlight streams through the windows, turning the room to silver. She rises and walks barefoot to the portico, where her leopard is resting. The air is cool, and the leaves of the palm trees are singing. She wonders if her mother felt as she feels now, when she discovered she was pregnant: love and fear wrapped together. If it was Semiramis' birth that tore Derceto from her lover and made her mad.

When she goes back to the bedroom, the contours of Ninus' body appear in the darkness. He is lying in bed. Even in sleep, his face is raw with grief. She sits by his side, feeling the soft pulse of his heart. *I should tell him,* she thinks. *He should know.* She imagines his face intent as she speaks, and then . . . What would come then? Fear? Happiness? Relief?

'Ninus,' she whispers. 'Ninus.'

But there is no answer, so she keeps the words to herself.

*

The envoy bursts into the throne room at dawn. He is covered with sweat, and pants like a wild animal. Ninus and Semiramis watch him as a courtier hurries to give him some water. The envoy drinks greedily, then kneels.

'Rise,' Ninus orders. 'You bring news from Babylon.'

The envoy obeys. 'Yes, my king. The king is dead. His son Marduk has taken the throne. He declares war on Assyria.'

Ninus doesn't flinch, but Semiramis sees his hand grip the arm of his throne. 'How many men?' he asks.

'Fifteen thousand,' the envoy replies. 'But more are coming. He has allied forces of Chaldeans, Elamites and Arameans currently gathering in Babylon.'

'Leave us,' Ninus orders.

The envoy nods. His steps feebly echo off the walls, until the room fades to silence. At the foot of the throne dais, Ilu and Nisat exchange a glance. For a long moment, no one speaks.

Then Ninus stands. 'The Elamites and Arameans were wronged by my father. And now they are ready to repay us.'

'How many men have we?' Semiramis asks.

'Sixteen thousand that we can spare,' Ilu replies. 'But with the allied forces from the tribes, Marduk will have more.'

'Those tribes are gathering in Babylon,' Semiramis points out. 'Marduk's army is in Dur.'

'Yes,' Ninus says. He walks down his throne dais and starts pacing the room. 'We must crush the revolt before the tribes can join Marduk.'

Nisat's eyes follow him. Her voice, usually so sharp and controlled, is urgent. 'This is what Marduk wants. He wants you to go to him.'

'You think it's a trap?' Ninus asks.

'He would already have attacked us otherwise.'

'Your mother is right,' Semiramis says. 'Let us stay here, strengthen our defences. There are other cities between Babylon and Kalhu. To get here, Marduk will have to conquer all the others first.'

Ninus stops pacing. His eyes are filled with spite. 'You think I will sit here waiting for him to destroy half of my empire?'

'A king goes into battle,' Ilu agrees. 'He doesn't wait for his enemies to come to him. He meets them in the open.'

'Marduk is king too,' Semiramis says. 'And he is waiting.'

'Let Marduk tire first,' Nisat says. 'Then we can strike.'

Ninus keeps silent. Then a look passes over his face, and Semiramis knows they have made a mistake. He turns to Ilu. 'Prepare our army. Gather the new iron weapons we have been forging. Ask the governors for as many men as they can send. The sooner they can send them, the better.'

'Where are they sending them?' Ilu asks. 'Here?'

'No,' Ninus says. 'To Dur.'

*

In the lower part of the citadel, her guards lead her to a door that isn't decorated – no carved lions or palm trees, no protective spirits.

'He is here, my queen,' they say.

'Stay,' she orders, then pulls the mantle away from her head and slips inside.

The room is bright and cool. On the walls, a single bas-relief: an eagle, perched on a tree, with a snake wound about its trunk. Semiramis watches it curiously.

'The symbol of my city, Tyre,' Sasi's voice says. He appears dressed in a dark tunic, his skin glistening, as if he has just bathed in oil.

'Your city is Kalhu now,' Semiramis points out.

'Of course,' he says, with a chuckle. 'Come, let us talk somewhere more private.' She wants to say that there is no one around, but then follows him into a small internal courtyard, where columns with bases in the form of sphinxes surround two palm-wood stools. Neither sits.

'You want to tell me why you've come all this way to my humble house?' Sasi asks.

'You missed an envoy in the throne room this morning,' she says. 'Marduk is king.'

'And ready to attack us.' Sasi nods. 'Yes, I have heard.'

'Ninus wants to fight. He wants to meet Marduk's forces at Dur.'

There is thin, dark paint around Sasi's eyes, giving the impression that he is startled. 'If you want my opinion on war tactics, in which I am obviously not well versed, I'd say our best hope is to hide behind the walls of Kalhu, close the gates, and let them come to us.'

'Yes,' she says. 'That is what I believe too. But it is also true that, if we close the gates, the common people will starve.'

'And if they go to war, they will die. Which is the better option?'

Smoke curls from the incense burning in a bronze bowl. She can feel Sasi's mind spinning as his eyes dart and skitter, checking that no one is listening.

'Ninus is strong,' he says. 'Stronger than others believe him to be. But he has some inconvenient ideas about justice and loyalty.'

She hardly suppresses a bitter laugh. 'And I don't?'

'You are different. Like Onnes was.' The name between them, rotting in the air. 'You don't shy away from the world's necessities. You would do what needs to be done to keep the empire safe and strong.'

She looks into his face. 'Are you saying I'd be a better ruler than my husband?'

A gust of wind makes the palm fronds shake. He inclines his head. 'I remain your ally and servant. And, as such, I try to speak the truth when I can.'

'Until a better ruler comes along,' she says.

He looks back at her, understands what she is asking him. 'If it is my loyalty you want, you should know that you have it.'

She wonders if he once said the same things to Onnes. Words are fickle in his mouth, jewels beautiful but cheap. She turns and makes for the main room. Then a thought occurs to her. 'Ninus doesn't like you, you know.'

Behind her, she can feel Sasi smile. 'Of course he doesn't. I am the eunuch, the spymaster, the one who brings havoc to people's lives with nothing more than a whisper. Who would like such a man?'

*

As soon as she is back in the Northwest Palace, the nausea returns. Her eyes water, her stomach churns. She hurries to her apartments, where Ana appears, hurries to tie back her hair, to clean the spatter from her dress. Semiramis sits on a couch, looking at the blurred shapes around her.

She has barely managed to pull herself upright when Ninus walks inside. He is so caught up in his thoughts, he almost doesn't see her. His body is tense, his eyes deathly.

'We leave tomorrow,' he says, more to himself than to Semiramis.

'So soon?' Her throat hurts, and she clears it. 'You haven't enough men.'

'We attack before Marduk's joined forces can reach Dur from Babylon. Our men from the provinces will come in a day or two.'

She wants to say, *Ninus, I am pregnant*, but he looks like a ghost.

He leans his head against her shoulder and stays there for a moment. She sinks her hand into his hair, whispers, 'Don't go.'

He pulls away, as if she had slapped him. 'The empire is watching,' he says. 'If I don't go into battle against Marduk, my men will sense weakness.'

'If you die, you are weak. If you live, you aren't.'

'Of course you speak like that.'

Like what? she wants to ask, but instead she says, 'If Onnes were here, he would tell you the same thing.'

He turns to her. 'Onnes is dead,' he says flatly.

'Do you want to join him? Because if you go to war with Marduk, that is what will happen.'

He shakes his head, looks away from her. 'I don't even know if you love me any more.'

For a moment, she is shocked. She stares at him, but he doesn't look back. 'Listen to yourself,' she says. 'You are mad.'

'So are you. You think I don't see your face when people whisper about the queen with divine blood in her veins? The woman destined for greatness?' She hates the spite in his voice, the challenge. 'This is what power does to you. You tell yourself, I want more, more, more, and then suddenly you have too much, and the gods punish you for it.'

Her anger is rising, and she can do nothing to tame it. 'Are you condemning me for my desire? My ambition? Onnes never—'

'*You betrayed Onnes!*' he shouts. 'With me!'

She stands, takes a step away from him. 'Every day I think of what we did. I wish I could take it back, I truly do. But one can't live one's life with nothing but regrets.'

The words have no effect on him. She can see that his face is locked, and that his grief is ravenous, eating him alive. 'You speak of regrets?' he asks. 'I've lived with regrets ever since I killed my brother. Regret is etched onto my skin. It flows in my blood with my anger and my weakness.' Each word is sharp, a butcher's knife cutting meat. 'I regret that I ever laid eyes on you. I regret that I told Onnes I wanted you. I regret that I let myself be seduced by you.'

'*Seduced?*' Her skin aches, as if he has ripped it from her body. '*You* wanted me. You would stop at nothing to have me. Because you can't imagine a life in which you don't get what you want!'

He raises his arm, and she prepares for the blow, but then he clenches his fist and punches his own chest instead. She sees the tension in his neck, the shame in his face. 'Neither can you.' His voice is burning, shaking with rage.

'I am your queen, Ninus,' she says. 'And you are my king.'

He doesn't look at her. 'Yes, but I am afraid we want different things. We are not the same people we were.' Then he is walking away, his steps heavy and angry as he strides down the corridor and disappears into the growing shadows.

*

She wakes in her large bed, alone. For a moment she looks at the ceiling, wrapped in the silence of the room. Then she remembers. She seizes her armour, runs out of the domestic quarters. Sasi is standing by the entrance to the central courtyard, dwarfed by the giant stone creatures.

'My queen,' he says, 'I must urge you to be reasonable.'

'You will lead the council while I am gone,' she orders. She tries to step around him, but he moves to stand in her way.

'If you leave now, the city will be left to the vultures,' he says. She doesn't like his tone – it is the same soothing voice he uses whenever he wants to manipulate noblemen and courtiers.

'Move aside,' she orders.

He doesn't. 'If you and Ninus die, who will take the throne then?'

'You said you were loyal to me.'

'Loyalty is not insanity.'

She grabs his arm. There is no patience in her, no reason. 'You told me the prophecy before I went to Balkh, do you remember?' she asks. *The king destined for joy and grief shall make Assyria bleed with his brother's blood. He shall die young and forgotten, at the hands of his own madness.'*

Sasi seems barely to breathe. She continues, voice strained, 'We thought the prophecy referred to Assur, but Onnes was the brother Ninus was destined to kill. And now he is growing mad and reckless, and he will die, if I do nothing to stop it.'

Sasi stares at her. Slowly, he uncurls her fingers from his wrist. 'Forgive me, my queen, but you think you hold a power you do not have. No man can come between the gods and their wishes.'

'You underestimate me, Spymaster,' she says coldly. 'Now move aside or I will cut you down.'

This time, he moves. She storms past him, shouting for her guards to prepare a chariot. As she walks out of the Northwest Palace, she thinks, *No man has done the things I have done.*

44.

The Battle of the
Two Kings

City of Dur (Babylonian Royal Residence)

Ninus

The rain falls in showers, turning the ground into cold, wet mud. Ninus looks at the forces gathered outside Dur. It is the wet season, the one priests always bless and cherish, but now, as the earth grows soft under the horses' hoofs, Ninus thinks the rain is more of a curse.

There is the sound of splashing in the wet mud, and their main scout appears. 'Marduk's foreign tribes from Babylon are coming. They are too many for us to attack.'

'How long before they are here?' Ninus asks.

'At the end of the day, my king.'

We won't be able to tell when the day ends if the rain keeps coming. 'That leaves us no choice,' he says. 'We take Dur before they arrive.'

'If we attack now,' Ilu says, 'they will surround us from all sides.'

There is an ominous beat, and the earth starts shaking, as if it couldn't control the pounding of its heart. Ninus looks at Ilu through the thick layer of rain. 'It doesn't make a difference whether we attack or not. Can't you hear the drums? *They* are attacking *us*.'

*

They ride past the tents of the Assyrian army into the open battle. Horses fly past them, faces blurring by. The tribes of the Elamites and Kassites are easy to recognize: they wear no pointed helmets, no heavy armour. *They are right*, Ninus thinks. *We need to be as light as possible.* He jumps down from his chariot, ignoring the cries of protest from his guards, and strips off his armour. His boots sink into the mud. A horse with no rider gallops towards him. He dodges it. Mud splashes on his face and he has to remove his helmet to see more clearly.

A cloud of arrows rains from the sky. The men fall to their knees in unison, covering their heads. When Ninus looks up again, he sees Ilu, smashing the face of an Elamite. When another soldier tries to attack him, Ilu throws his axe at him. The blow is so strong it shatters the bones of the soldier's face.

Hills are oceans of mud. The Assyrian cavalry is charging against the tribes, but the horses keep slipping on ground already streaked with blood. Ninus' guards have disappeared. A soldier sees him, aims the spear at his heart. Ninus lunges, throwing himself against him. They fall together, and he feels for a weapon to stab him, but there is no need. The fall has broken the soldier's neck.

He moves among bodies buried so deep in the mud that only their eyes and teeth are visible. When he gets to the river, the water is red, corpses floating on it. The ground is even more slippery here. He almost falls down the bank, grabs the leg of a dead horse to keep his balance.

'Push the tribes to the rivers!' he screams to his men. 'Push them into the water!' The thunder and battle cries are so loud he doesn't know if anyone can hear him. But then Ilu is standing above him, higher on the riverbank – there is an arrow shaft in his shoulder, but he seems not to care. He pulls Ninus up, safely away from the rushing water.

'If the tribes are cornered by the riverbank, they will drown,' Ninus says.

Ilu grabs the arrow shaft and pulls it out of his skin with a grunt. 'Let us drown them, then. But you get away from here or you will drown with them.'

Ninus stares at the blood spurting out of Ilu's shoulder. It shoots out with each heartbeat, a chilling rhythm. Ilu grabs his arm. 'Did you hear me? *Get away from here!*'

Ninus clings to the wet earth, climbing away from the roaring waters as Ilu keeps shouting orders. Iron flashes at his cheek. He plunges his sword into the belly of an Elamite soldier, whose intestines spill onto the ground. A chariot flies past him, raising a wave of mud. Ninus is trying to wipe it off his face – he can barely see – when a man runs at him. Half blindly, Ninus wrenches a spear from the body next to him to defend himself. The blade sinks into the man's chest. Ninus watches him fall, life fading from the soldier's eyes.

Another, Ninus thinks, moving forward. He slashes his sword, listening to the grunts as he hits his mark. He wades through mud and gore, feeling like a butcher as he cuts the world to pieces. The hundreds of wounded around him beg for help. *What difference does it make, if you travel to the house of dust?* he thinks. *We are already in hell.*

Ilu, his father, his mother, his brother, all his life they have pushed him and now this is what he is: a man who kills to wash his soul clean.

He screams at the sky: '*Are you watching? Can you see me now? I've become what you all wanted me to become. My heart has blackened and only feeds on violence.*'

*

Marduk

At the base of Dur's high blue walls, Marduk watches his men drown in the river. They trudge through bodies in a useless attempt to keep afloat, before the muddy waters swallow them.

Marduk can't tell if he is winning or losing: it is a massacre on both sides. The guards around him keep killing the Assyrians who advance, relentless, in his direction. For a people who fear death more than anything else, they walk into its jaws without flinching.

When he was a boy, his father would tell him stories of the god Nergal, the destroying flame, the bringer of death. Nergal deals out hunger and devastation in the world of the living, and in the realm of the dead, he becomes king by threatening to cut off the head of the queen Ereshkigal. 'He is the greatest, the bravest,' Marduk's father said. And Marduk believed him.

What is the purpose of a ruler, if not to bring others to dust? How do you show power, if you do not crush the world? He cuts off an enemy's head, laughing when he sees the shock in his victim's eyes. He watches them coming at him, hoping to bring down the King of Babylon. He takes pleasure in showing them that they are fools.

He tightens his grip on the hilt of his sword, preparing for another fight, when the guard in front of him falls to his knees – an Assyrian has sliced his head in half. The soldier looks as if he has swum into the mud and wields a sword soaked in the blood of his enemies. One by one, he cuts down Marduk's guards.

Marduk watches him with a smile. He thrills, as always when he is about to kill a worthy opponent.

Then the soldier faces him, and Marduk recognizes him with a jolt: Ninus.

He aims his sword at the last of Marduk's guards, slitting his throat. The soldier falls and Ninus kicks him away with his boot.

Now there are only two kings, staring at each other.

'If you want to win,' Ninus says, breathless, 'you will have to kill me.'

Marduk smiles, predatorial. 'Good. That is exactly why I have come.'

45.

Semiramis, a Murderess

She rides south following the silver shape of the river. Ten men accompany her: her guards from the Northwest Palace. They pass the city of Ashur and the stone fortresses built on the banks of the Tigris. From there, the plains grow greener as they approach Babylonian territory. They ride hard, stopping only once when the horses are exhausted. When they cross the Diyala, one of the rivers that feed into the Tigris, rain starts falling.

Dur is north of Babylon: a walled city close to where the two rivers meet. As they ride nearer, they can hear the cries of the wounded lacerating the air, and see the smoke rising from the tents. They spur their horses.

A man meets them at the edge of the camp, one of Ilu's. His pointed helmet is spattered with mud.

'Tell me what happened,' Semiramis orders.

'Shamshi-Adad has destroyed the Babylon forces, my queen,' he says, voice shaking. 'Dur has fallen.'

'What happened?' Semiramis demands again. The rain is blurring everything. She struggles to see clearly.

'The king Marduk brought the foreign tribes from Babylon. They ambushed our army.' He hesitates, then says, 'The king has been wounded.'

She spurs her horse on before the soldier can say more. The others follow. The river flows on their right, carrying corpses south. 'Shouting River', the Diyala is called, and now its waters roar like thunder. The horses' hoofs splash in puddles; the wounded and the captors' voices blend like a desperate song.

When she storms into the king's tent, Ilu is sitting on a pallet, panting. A healer is bent over him, easing an arrow point from his forearm.

She walks past him, to a stretcher where Ninus lies, barely conscious. There are two healers and a priest around him, passing herbs and ointments, whispering, praying. Their tunics are spattered with Ninus' blood. She swallows as she looks at Ninus' chest, holding down the rising sickness. She can barely see the size of the wound because there is mud, mud everywhere, which the healers are trying to clean away without doing further damage. Ninus makes a terrible sound, and Semiramis moves forward to push the healers away.

A hand grabs her and pulls her back. Ilu. His face is livid as he grits his teeth. She looks at the swollen skin of his arm.

'He is delirious,' he spits out. 'Marduk almost killed him.'

The anger in her chest is like a beast ready to be set loose. 'Where is he?' she demands. 'Where is Marduk?'

'In the prisoners' tent. We are bringing him back to Kalhu.'

Semiramis walks away with her fingers tight on the handle of her dagger. *Oh yes, you will bring him to Kalhu. But first, I am going to make him pay. I am going to paint the city of Dur with Marduk's blood.*

*

The prisoners' tent is thick with the smell of sweat. Marduk is standing, alone, hands tied to a post. Though covered with dried mud, he doesn't seem wounded. He laughs when he sees her.

'Here is the bitch from Mari,' he says. 'Come to keep me company?'

She covers the distance between them and strikes him. His head flies sideways. When he turns back to her, blood is dripping from his nose.

'I am queen now,' she says.

He laughs again. 'Have you come to take me back to Kalhu? I hated that place, and all the people in it. Liars, madmen, murderers. But, still, better there than here, sitting in the mud with a rope around my chest.'

'You won't be a hostage for much longer.'

'Good.'

'You won't be a hostage because you will be dead.'

373

The smile drops from his face. He stares at her for a long moment. 'You can't kill me,' he says slowly. 'If I die, you lose any hope of a new treaty with Babylon.'

'As long as you live, Babylon will belong to a Babylonian ruler. If you die, the throne is empty.'

He snorts. 'And who will take it? Ninus? He will die soon. I would have killed him, if Ilu hadn't intervened. For a man who used to beat him, he still protects him as a father would.'

She almost strikes him again. 'Ninus will not die.'

Marduk's eyes gleam like black gemstones. '*You* want to take the throne. Just say it.'

'And if I do?'

'You can keep climbing, Semiramis. It will not change what you are.'

And what is that? A whore? A murderess? She grabs the handle of her dagger. 'You have been given too much. Now you must learn what it means to lose everything.'

The rope is tight against his waist. He stares at her, challenge in his eyes. Even tied and painted in mud, he looks as he did the first time she saw him: a man who doesn't know fear. And yet, when she brings her blade to his chest, she can feel his heart betraying him.

A crimson gash flowers where she sinks the blade. He makes a choked sound, then drops into the mud, his body hanging from the ropes, like a puppet.

She looks at him before retrieving her dagger. He isn't so different from the other soldiers strewn across the camp. But, then, what poets say about the house of dust is true: in death, there are no kings.

46.

Ribat, a Scribe

In the Nabu temple, Ribat is pressing his stylus into a drying clay tablet. He does so with slow, precise movements, imagining he is uncovering secret seeds, making them spring from the tablet like trees.

Outside the streets are flooded, the courtyards dark and wet from the rain. He has almost finished with his story when there is a call from the temple. The scribes' heads shoot up in unison.

A soldier walks into the school, drenched, ignoring the old tutor's outraged expression. He is wearing cuffs with precious stones around his wrists, which tell Ribat he comes from the Northwest Palace. To everyone's surprise, he says, 'I am looking for the scribe called Ribat.'

Ribat stands, putting down his tablet to hide the sudden trembling of his hands.

The soldier's eyes narrow, considering him. 'Are you the scribe who was a slave?'

'Yes,' Ribat says. 'I am the scribe who was a slave to the queen.'

The soldier nods. 'She demands your presence. She is waiting for you in the Northwest Palace.'

The other scribes stare at him. Ribat hurries to follow the guard. They cross the wide courtyards and make their way out of the temple. The rain soaks his tunic as they walk past the governors' houses onto the royal road. The clouds are low, hiding even the Northwest Palace.

They hurry inside, past the entrance to the domestic wing. In the wide courtyard, there is a strange silence, except for the pattering of the rain, and the strong smell of incense. The guard leads Ribat into a long, narrow corridor. At the end, he stops. 'The queen is inside,' he says.

Ribat enters. It takes his eyes a moment to adjust.

The room is chaos. Slaves are running around, breathless, hands filled with bloody rags. A priest is murmuring prayers to the goddess Gula. The place is dark, heavy with the metallic scent of blood. He can see the eunuch in a corner, whispering in the ears of a healer, and the king's mother examining some amulets the attendants are showing her. Under her royal headdress her face is very pale, her lips pursed. The scars on Ribat's back start itching.

Semiramis is standing by a couch. Her trousers are caked with mud and her skin glistens with sweat. He goes to stand behind her.

'My queen,' he says. 'I am here.'

She looks over her shoulder. Her hair falls down her waist, undressed, unkempt. Her eyes are brimming with tears, though none fall on her cheeks. Behind her, a bare-chested figure is lying on a long couch covered with soft pillows. Ribat walks closer.

The king's breath comes in muffled, painful pants. His eyes are closed, and his skin is pale, like that of a corpse. Two healers are cleaning a large wound on his chest. A sword cut: the blade has pierced his skin deeply, and Ribat can see inside as blood spurts out. The parted skin makes him think of the gaping mouth of a fish.

'Is he—' he starts, but Semiramis grabs his arm.

'He is alive, but he won't wake,' she says. As she speaks, her eyes flicker wildly to the other people in the room. 'If I leave this room, someone will take the throne. I don't trust any of them. And what if someone wants him dead?' There is something mad in her eyes, something fearful in the way she grips his wrist. 'You once said you'd do anything for me, do you remember? You must stay here. Make sure no one hurts him.'

A slave girl brings more incense to mask the stench of blood. More lamps are lit, until the room is ablaze, a nightmare of sickness and fire.

'Promise you will keep him alive,' Semiramis says. 'Promise.'

The words come easily to Ribat's lips. 'I promise.'

*

Healers come and go. They wash the king's wound with wine, then burn it to avoid infection. Courtiers whisper and hurry around, ready to rearrange the kingdom, to take sides.

He can smell fear – the room is drenched in it. He is kneeling by the couch, his hands cupped around a small jug that contains willow tree extract, the best to treat fever, pain and inflammation. He gives it to the king every hour: it keeps his temperature down, and the pain at bay. The healer once explained to Ribat that, no matter how well a wound is treated, if a patient's fever climbs too high, he will die.

He remembers giving the remedy to his mother when she was sick, the last year of the war. She was on the brink of death, but the willow bark brought her back to life.

From a corner of the room, a diviner says, 'The fever is in his very bones. This must be the work of the gods.'

'And by your hands it will be undone!' Semiramis hisses. She is pacing the room, her fists clenched, her shoulders shaking.

The evening is full of spirits. They stir, breathe across the courtyard. They peer at the body on the couch from the cracks of the paving, prowl around him, impatient.

Time passes strangely, rushing past, so that soon it is night, and the rain stops pattering. Ribat feels like he is trapped in another world, hovering between the living and the dead.

When he looks up again, Semiramis is gone, and so is the king's mother. Only a few frightened faces float in the lamplight: a priest, the healers, a shaking attendant.

The king clears his throat, whispers something. Ribat moves closer to catch the words. He wants the willow extract. Ribat looks at the sky and, yes, it is time to give it to him. He glances around. The other servants have gone to fetch fresh water. The healers are arranging their scalpels.

Ribat tightens his grip around the willow jug. He hesitates for a moment, thinking about the absurdity of the situation: a king's life in the hands of a former slave.

The sky grows darker. The gods blot out the moon. The king calls again. His voice is feeble – only Ribat hears it. He uncorks the jug when suddenly the king opens his pale blue eyes. Ribat shifts back. It is as if the king's mother is staring at him. He has never noticed how alike they are before.

The king's mother. He stares and stares.

Slowly, he reaches out and touches the king's wrist. It is almost a dare, to see if some god falls from the sky and punishes him. No one comes. The skin burns under his hand.

377

For a long moment, he doesn't move. He doesn't seem to be able to.

He thinks about Semiramis, her fierce expression as she said, *Promise.*

Then he imagines his mother, poisoned in a small, hidden room of the Northwest Palace, with no one to mourn her.

The king gasps and thrashes. Ribat puts the medicine back into the folds of his tunic, then leaves the room.

47.

What the Gods See

Semiramis sits in the throne room. Her head hurts from lack of sleep and her heart sits in her chest, like a stone. In front of her, two men are bowing by the brazier, their tunics embroidered with the lion of Babylon.

'We bring news from Babylon, Queen.'

Ilu comes out of the shadows into the light of the brazier. His wounded arm is stiff, and a bruise is darkening on his temple. 'Your king is dead. Who sends you?'

The envoys lift their heads and take a step towards the throne dais. 'Our city is bleeding. The Elamites, Arameans and Chaldeans are putting their claims forward. They plan to seize every noble and murder them so that their own leaders can take the throne.'

'So the noble families of the city sent you,' Semiramis says.

'Yes.'

'And what do the noblemen want?'

'They ask for Assyria's military support against the tribes until they can find a new king,' the envoys say.

Just as I had hoped, Semiramis thinks.

'Our king's ancestors plundered Babylon when the Babylonian king attacked Assyria,' she says. 'Then Assyria ruled over your city through a succession of puppet kings. Is that what you want my husband to do now?' She knows that, if the decision is taken by the noblemen of the city, commoners won't resent an Assyrian ruler on the Babylonian throne.

Ilu lifts his eyebrows. She gives him a significant look and, from the way he turns back to the messengers, she knows he has understood. 'Answer her,' he commands.

'Order is always preferable to chaos,' one of the messengers says. 'If the tribes take power in Babylon, our people are lost.'

'If the noblemen of Babylon swear allegiance to Assyria, we will help you,' Semiramis says. 'We will be allies once more, as we were before Marduk came to power. Babylon protected Assyria from a civil war, and now we will come to your aid. Assyria will take the Babylon throne and hold it . . .' she lingers over the next words '. . . until a worthy successor comes forward.'

The messengers kneel, push their foreheads against the floor. 'Thank you, Queen.'

'Leave,' she orders. 'Bring the king's decision to Babylon.'

They hurry out of the long room, their shadows stark against the stone walls. The brazier crackles. Cold winds come from the large entrances, bending the flames of the torches.

'*The king's decision?*' Ilu asks scornfully.

'No,' she says calmly. 'My decision.'

Ilu climbs the steps of the dais so that he is level with her. 'You killed Marduk. If the tribes come for us, it is because of you.'

She waves a hand. 'The tribes won't come. This is the end of Babylon. Their kingdom falls, but a new one is born. We will take control of the south.'

'Marduk was the son of kings,' Ilu spits. 'He may have been our enemy, but you disrespected his power, his position.'

She stares into his eyes. 'You think because I am common-born, and a woman, I cannot touch a king?'

Ilu takes a step closer and, for a moment, she thinks he will hit her. Then a courtier comes forward, his steps hurried on the stone floor.

'The Chaldean tribes send their tributes, my queen, in the hope of winning your support as they claim the throne of Babylon.'

Ilu turns to him, his face a mask of stone. 'They are a little late for that.'

'They bring slaves, ivory, gold and carnelian,' the courtier continues, 'as well as new beasts for our gardens—'

'Out.' A voice cuts across him.

It takes Semiramis a moment to understand it is Sasi who has spoken. He is standing by the entrance, a pale cloak wrapped around his shoulders. Guards and courtiers obey. Semiramis stands, heart hammering her chest. Next to her, Ilu is so still he seems not to be breathing.

'My queen,' Sasi says. 'The king is dying.'

*

They cross the palace as fast as they can. Outside, a procession has started – lamenters are praying to the goddess Gula. Semiramis quickens her pace. She can hear Ilu and Sasi whispering but not what they are saying. Terror is cutting through her like a spear.

The king has been moved into the bedroom. Nisat is standing by the door like a guard dog. The ritual healer is speaking to her in hushed tones, touching the green and blue amulets hanging on the wall. 'The gods must be punishing an offence the king has committed, or the fever would have disappeared.'

'MY SON IS KING,' Nisat shouts. 'HE IS A GOD. If you can't heal him, you are a traitor. If he dies, you will not survive either, do you hear me?'

The healer hurries back to the table where his herbs are laid out. Nisat scratches her cheeks until she draws blood. Ilu watches her, horrified. *He is afraid of her*, Semiramis thinks. *He has never seen her like this.*

She looks frantically for Ribat, but he is nowhere to be seen. She crosses the room and kneels by the side of the bed, taking Ninus' hand in hers. It is as hot as burning coal. He is mumbling in pain, and his eyes are unfocused. On the other side of the bed, Sosanê is staring at her father, gripping the ivory harpy with her small fingers.

'His fever has been building,' Sosanê whispers.

'The willow bark?' Semiramis asks.

'There isn't any.'

Where is Ribat? she thinks. *Where?*

'IS ANYONE CAPABLE OF SERVING THEIR KING?' Nisat shouts. Her face is purple, her headdress abandoned on a stool.

A diviner takes a step forward. 'The gods often signal their displeasure by sending signs in the physical world—'

'Take him away,' Nisat says to the guard in a voice that could slice stone. 'Whip him.'

Silence. The guards hesitate: no one touches the messengers of the gods. Sasi takes a careful step forward. 'May I suggest—'

'I said, *whip him*,' Nisat repeats. 'Take this man away from my son.'

As if he heard her, Ninus stirs. Sweat sticks his hair to his forehead. Semiramis wipes it away.

'Ninus,' she says. She is barely aware of the diviner, pleading desperately as the guards drag him away. Nisat and Ilu are arguing. Sasi slips away from the room.

Semiramis soaks some clean cloth in cold water and straps it to Ninus' forehead. His skin burns her fingers. 'Listen to me,' she says softly. 'You are going to have a son. I am pregnant.'

He lifts his head, barely, and his dark hair parts. He opens his eyes and looks straight at her. 'I didn't want to hurt you,' he says.

She feels something tear inside. 'You didn't.'

'My mother told me a prophecy . . .' He coughs and blood spatters the sheets. Sosanê moves back as if burned. Semiramis squeezes his hand. 'Prophecies mean nothing,' she says. 'You are the king.'

'I think I'm going.' The breath rasps in his throat. 'I'm joining my brothers in the house of dust.'

You can't go. You can't leave me. What of my child? What of our promises? Of everything we sacrificed to be together?

A tear trickles down his cheek, onto his neck. A breath of wind reaches the room. It must be Onnes' spirit, trying to take his brother away. Sosanê is sobbing quietly. Nisat has joined her next to the bed, wailing.

'I don't want to be a coward,' Ninus says and now his voice is strangled, a trickle of red coming from his mouth.

'You are not a coward,' Semiramis whispers. 'You are the bravest man I have ever known.'

His eyes grow wide, unfocused. His breath is rasping, slowly fading.

'Please don't leave me,' she says, but her voice is so faint, and his hand is growing cold.

He is going, she thinks. *He is really going.* The darkness is thick and there are tears in her eyes and through them she sees his face, small in her lap.

This is what gods see when they look down from the sky, she thinks, *at men who live and suffer and die, and yet do nothing to save them.*

48.

Semiramis, a Widow

The body remains on the bed. Semiramis kneels by its side. With a wet cloth, she washes the blood and sweat from the skin. There is no one else – she has sent them all away. And away they went, as fast as they could: they think this room is cursed, now that two kings have died in it.

Soon, they will come back. They will want to see their king, to touch their lips to his hands, to mourn him. But he is hers, and no one else's.

They defied the sky to be together, and now the gods have punished them. Or was it Onnes, his angry spirit, tormenting them? She looks at Ninus' face, cold as stone, pale as the winter sun. *Even in death, you had to join him*, she thinks. *You couldn't bear to be apart from him.*

In the old village of Mari, by the wall that still bears the old frescos of men and goddesses, she once asked her father why her mother had died.

'The gods give as the gods take,' Simmas had said. 'Our lives are never what we think they will be.'

His words had felt like a riddle then, but now she understands. No matter how hard she tries to guide the course of her life, she can't control the fate of those around her. She can try, she can fight but, in the end, they will come to dust.

*

Nisat enters the room when the first stars appear. The night is silent – the city doesn't know the king is dead yet. Semiramis look at her husband's mother, standing by the door with her hair unbound. Their eyes meet over the body.

'You are a plague,' Nisat says. 'You bring destruction wherever you go.'

'I did everything I could to save him.'

'Get away from my son,' Nisat spits out.

Semiramis doesn't move. 'I won't leave him.'

'*He is dead!* Dead because of you!'

Tears burn in Semiramis' eyes. Nisat spits her words like poison. 'Mourn him all you wish. I want you gone from the city before dawn. Tomorrow, I will announce his death to the people. My granddaughter will take the throne with Ilu's son. If you are still in Kalhu, they will execute you. I will watch as they skin you alive, tie your hands and throw you into the river, where you will rot, like your mother before you.'

'I am pregnant,' Semiramis says.

Nisat stares at her for a moment. Then she walks around the bed and strikes Semiramis, hard. The rings cut her cheekbone.

'You lie,' Nisat says.

Semiramis' face is throbbing. 'Why would I?'

'Because you always do.' Then she vanishes, swallowed by the blackness of the corridor.

Semiramis kneels by Ninus' side again. She rests her head on his chest, tastes the salt of her tears. The stars fade, dawn comes, and still she doesn't leave him.

*

When Nisat comes back, her face is pale, as if blood was drained out of her. 'Are you really carrying my son's child?' she asks.

'Yes.' Semiramis' voice cracks for lack of use. Her hand has grown cold in Ninus'.

Nisat sits on a couch at the opposite end of the room. She is silent for a long time. The anger has faded from her face, and now there is only grief.

'Shalmaneser couldn't believe that he was his, at first,' she says. 'But I knew he was mine. The cleverest child you ever saw. He could read before he could walk. He remembered everything you told him. He always listened in a way that made you feel seen.'

Semiramis doesn't speak. She can see the memories floating on Nisat's face and she wants to grab them. She wants to hold them, taste them, breathe them. 'You are lucky,' she says. 'You had a lifetime with him.'

Nisat watches her for a long moment. Then she closes her eyes and remembers.

She remembers sleeping with Shalmaneser, her first husband's son. She was meant to be mourning – Ashurnasirpal had just died – but she could not afford to spend time grieving: she had to defend her future. So, she had gone to her stepson's chamber and held him as he prayed for his dead father. When he had finished, he had asked her: 'What do I need to do now?' And she had told him.

She remembers Shalmaneser's hands as they bruised her skin the first time they slept together. *It means my son will grow strong too*, she told herself. Her children, growing inside her, as she whispered, 'You are sons of a king.'

She remembers when Ninus asked her what love is. His eyes were like the ocean, and she had kissed his forehead, cupped a hand around his cheek. *This is love*, she wanted to tell him, but gave him another answer instead, one that would make him stronger.

She remembers when she had seen Onnes with her sons for the first time. 'A new friend,' Ninus had said, looking at the boy as if he were a god. She had looked at Onnes' face and seen, painted on it, the features of the woman who used to sleep in her husband's bed. And so she had hated him.

She remembers Ninus bringing her the news of Shalmaneser's death. He had held her as she shook, and comforted her, as she had done with him a hundred times. 'Promise you will avenge him,' she had said, even though she knew the cost to him of what she was asking. But Ninus was loyal, and willing to do anything for those he loved. He had looked her in the eye and said, 'I promise, Mother.'

*

Nothing can bring back the dead. Nothing but memories. So Semiramis listens to Nisat as she speaks of Ninus, and she can see him as a child, as a young man, as a king.

385

When Nisat stops speaking, the night birds are singing. She looks at Semiramis with eyes so like her son's. 'When the sun rises, I will announce his death to the people.'

Semiramis casts one last look at Ninus. He is gone, but she is still here. She will finish what she has started. She lifts her head to meet Nisat's and says, 'A boy will always come before a girl to inherit the throne. If the child I am carrying is a son, he will be king.'

Nisat looks at her. 'Do you think I will allow it?'

'I think you will. Because if you don't, the throne will go to Sosanê, and we both know she is not strong enough to hold it, so all the power will be in Sargon's hands. In *Ilu's hands*, the man who has served you for years, who has done your bidding, but who has always wanted the throne for his own family. And I don't think you will sit and let him take it.' *Because if he does, what will become of you?*

A vein pulses at Nisat's throat. 'If I don't, I shall watch *you* sit on the throne that belonged to my son.'

Semiramis ignores her. 'I am going to do what you should have done when your first husband died. I do not believe that you didn't resent having to work through him, having to operate in the shadows, fighting to make others listen to you.'

'Of course I resented it. But there was no other way.'

'There is always another way,' Semiramis says. *I do not want to live in service to men. I do not want my fate to depend on anyone but myself.*

A sliver of light appears at the window, cutting the room in two. Nisat kneels by Ninus' side and kisses his forehead. Then she turns to Semiramis. Her eyes are rimmed with red. 'You want too much from this world. And you leave everything burning in the wake of your desire.'

*

They come to take Ninus' body. Sasi finds her in one of the smaller courtyards – where Ninus once called for her, and she first realized he wanted her.

'I grieve for your loss, my queen,' Sasi says. 'Assyria will never have such a king again.'

'His son will be king,' she says, touching her hand to her belly.

He stares at the curve of her abdomen. There is shock, then hope, on his face. 'And if it is a girl?'

'Girl or boy, it does not matter. I will rule first, and, when my child has grown, he will rule next.'

He is silent. She knows he is thinking of the prophecy: *He shall die young and forgotten, to the gain of his wife.* Her own prophecy is etched onto her heart, driving her towards her future: *The woman arrayed in purple and gold, with a cup in her hand full of lust and faults, will be as great as Babylon, the glowing city that reigns over the kings of the earth.* She had thought it spoke of a goddess, but now she knows it is her own future the diviner saw, all those years ago in Mari.

She steps closer to Sasi. 'Do I have your support?'

He doesn't kneel, but his eyes hold fires. 'Now and always.'

I will make a lasting name for myself,
I will stamp my fame on men's minds for ever.

From *The Epic of Gilgamesh*

49.

Semiramis, Queen of the World, Queen of Babylon, Queen of Assyria

Semiramis stands on the terrace of the Northwest Palace, her leopard sprawled at her feet. Moonlight streams over the city, silvering its roofs and streets, its temples and squares. A faint breeze blows from the river. It makes her shiver, but she does not cover herself. She is barefoot on the marble floor, her nightdress thin and pale. Down by the walls, distant torches glow orange and golden as the guards stand sentry by the stone spirits. A lamp glimmers, faint as a star. Semiramis imagines Sasi gliding down an alley towards his house, his heart heavy with the burden of new secrets. It reminds her of a girl who used to sneak out of her village when the shadows came, who wandered the hills longing for freedom and a better life.

'Semiramis?'

Sosanê stands in a dark blue nightrobe, sandals at her feet. Her eyes are red and puffy with tears, though she holds herself like a princess.

'Come,' Semiramis says. 'Watch the sunrise with me.'

Sosanê obeys, coming to stand by her side. 'My father used to come here, looking for peace. He could never find it.'

'Maybe he will find it in the house of dust. With Onnes.'

Sosanê shakes her head. 'Some souls are always destined to wander.' She looks at Semiramis, and it seems that she is not speaking of Ninus. 'Will you take the throne?' she asks.

'I will.'

Sosanê nods. 'I do not want it. It dragged my father into the dust.'

'Will you come with me and tell the council?'

Sosanê says nothing. Semiramis takes her hand and holds it. The sky turns brighter as the sun comes up. The fields and hills glow as they wake, and the blue-brick buildings come alive as their carved creatures fall into the light. The palm trees in the gardens stir, shaking away the cloak of night. The leopard rises and comes between the two women, as the sun pours its light over the arena beyond the walls.

They watch the city while it wakes and sings. A day of change, though Kalhu doesn't know it yet.

A golden dawn.

A fallen king.

A rising queen.

*

Her servants are dressing her when she hears shouts at the door. A voice, hissing, menacing, and the unsheathing of a blade.

'Let him in,' she orders. She is seated in an ivory chair by the open window, two women kneeling behind her, plaiting her black hair. She is clean and scented, and wears a robe that falls in a moon-like pool at her feet.

Ilu walks inside. He approaches her with his hand on the hilt of his sword, then notices the guards stationed in the shadows of the room and the leopard lying on a couch. He stops, chest heaving.

'Have you come to kill me?' Semiramis asks. The women remain kneeling, eyes fixed on the floor, as if willing themselves to disappear.

'I hear that you are with child,' Ilu says.

'Yes. Ninus' child.'

'I wouldn't be so sure. You must fuck hundreds of men.'

The servants gasp, shocked. The guards take a step forward. Semiramis holds out a hand to stop them. 'Not nearly as many as the women you have had,' she says, standing. Then, to the women, 'Continue. I am not dressed yet.'

They look at her as if she is mad, but then rise and continue plaiting her hair, putting rings of chiselled gold into her ears. Ilu's body is as sharp and tense as the blade in his hands.

'Should we speak of those women? The ones you sleep with?' Semiramis asks. *Should we speak of Nisat?*

'You are an evil, lustful woman,' Ilu says. His fist clenches and unclenches around the hilt of the sword. She can tell that he is calculating his options, realizing that he cannot strike her down, not when there are guards and a leopard, not when she has said aloud that she is carrying the king's child. And she can see the rage that this knowledge brings to him, a man who is used to dealing death to those who oppose him.

The servants put a tall crown enriched with gold flowers on her head. 'If you want to harm me,' she says calmly, 'this is the time. You will not get a better chance.'

He shakes his head. 'I will fight you as long as I live.'

'You will not live for ever.'

He looks at her, stunned. Suddenly he is so close that she can feel his breath on her face, his blade against her belly –

– but a shadow leaps between them and Ilu stumbles back, grunting. The leopard's mouth is closed around his arm. Ilu lets go of his sword, and the leopard takes her place at Semiramis' side, causing the women to scatter. Blood drips onto the stone floor in an eerie rhythm.

Semiramis watches him. *Strike me and I will strike back. I will strike your family. I will strike your son. There'll be nothing left of you.*

'You threaten me,' Ilu says.

'All men are mortals,' she says. 'Or do you think yourself a god?'

'I should have killed you as soon as you stepped into this city.'

'Maybe you should have. But if you oppose me now, I will tell everyone your secret. What will they do to you when they learn you have been sleeping with a former queen? Will they follow a traitor, who stabbed his own king in the back?'

The guards' faces are stone. At the edge of the room, the servants shift uneasily. Ilu shakes his head, then barks a laugh, as if he cannot believe her words. He walks away without picking up his sword, leaving a crimson trail behind him.

'Take it to him,' Semiramis orders the guards. 'He will need it when he comes to serve me.' He has not knelt to her, but it doesn't matter. She has shown him her power, and now he can decide if she is worth fighting for. Or if he'd rather join the forgotten ones in the house of dust.

She summons courtiers and governors to the gardens.

Guards are stationed at the foot of the stairs. Nisat, Sasi, the *bârû*, Sargon and Sosanê come to the pavilion and take their places on the glowing couches. From here, they can see as far as the city walls and the river. Sasi has ordered his informants to start spreading the news of Ninus' death and Semiramis imagines them sliding along every street, whispering in the common people's ears.

She stands, her leopard on a long leash. 'When Ninus took the throne after crushing his brother's rebellion, all he wanted was to stabilize the empire. He succeeded, but he did much more than that. With every upheaval crushed and the victory in Bactria, he showed the world that Assyria is destined for glory.'

'Ninus is dead,' Sargon says. 'He leaves no heirs, except his daughter, my wife.'

'You are wrong,' Semiramis says. 'Ninus leaves a boy, your future king. I carry him now as I speak.'

Everyone grows silent. The world has never been so still. The city basks in the sun, as if caught in a dream. Semiramis waits until everyone is watching her, then says, 'Until my son comes of age, I will sit on the throne.'

Sargon is the first to speak, as Semiramis knew he would be. 'My father will not let you do this,' he says.

'Your father is in his palace right now, blood pouring from his arm where my leopard bit his flesh.'

Sargon opens his mouth, closes it. His eyes don't leave Semiramis' face. She waits, giving time to the others to object. No one does.

'I have called you here with plans for our great empire,' she says. 'We will continue the military campaigns, which I will lead myself, with Ilu and Sargon at my side. We will expand the borders and build a secure nation for my son. We will build cities and strongholds, aqueducts and roads, canals and bridges. We will start with Babylon. The city needs embankments to hold back the river from flooding it. I want you to gather the most skilled artisans you can find. They will build palaces as glorious as the ones Ashurnasirpal built in Kalhu. Our buildings will be among the wonders of the world, our temples with no equals in size or beauty.'

Birds start chirping in the trees. The sky is as clear as water.

Sasi takes a step forward and says, 'Sammuramat. Queen of the World, Queen of Babylon, Queen of Assyria.'

A ray of golden sun floods the pavilion and, in unison, men and women bow as Semiramis stands in the light.

*

At night the eunuch comes to join her in her apartments, his eyes heavily lined, his bright tunic sweeping the floor.

'Ilu will support you, and so will Nisat,' he says. 'She knows that if she backs Sosanê's claim against your own, she will have to kill your son, and she would never do that. Besides, Sosanê does not want the throne, so Sargon has no choice but to follow you.'

'Good,' she says. 'Is there more?'

He nods. 'My informants delivered. They came back with the first secrets of their own. The people already tell the most fascinating tales about your ascent to the throne. Some say you convinced your husband to give you power for five days, to see how well you could manage it. When he agreed, you had him executed and seized the crown for yourself.'

He watches her face. She casts her gaze towards the dark blue night.

'Others say you are selecting lovers from among the most handsome men in the army. That you plan to sleep with them and have them executed at the first morning light.'

She can't help but think about her prophecy. 'A cup full of lusts and faults,' she says, with a faint smile.

'What cup is this?' he asks, puzzled.

She turns back to look at him. 'My cup,' she says. 'My empire.'

*

The death of a king shakes the earth to its core. He spans the gulf between earth and Heaven, so when he dies, he disturbs the established order of things. The rains don't come, the plants wither and, for a while, the earth isn't fruitful. Semiramis is glad for it. The people of Kalhu will see this as proof that Ninus was a true king, as close to the gods as a king can be.

They bury him in the precinct of the palace, under a sky the colour of fire. The tomb is plain, the stone pale. Over it, Semiramis orders

395

the men to erect a large mound, so high that it will be visible from far away, when travellers ride on the plain along the river. Everyone will pray to Ninus, the king who was loved by the gods.

A dove appears, flying over the mound and up towards the heavens. Others join it and soon it is the largest flock Semiramis has ever seen, the birds like white clouds carrying Ninus' spirit into the sky.

For a moment, the world glimmers, bright and vivid, and she sees the future she has lost, unfolding in front of her eyes, like a painted bas-relief:

She and Ninus together, ruling an empire that stretched to the glittering sea in the west, and to the endless deserts in the south. Their children, reading and playing, fighting and taming lions. A life of love, despite all the scars and all the anger: how many souls can say they have been so lucky?

And the other future, the one that never really belonged to her: the life in which she stayed with Onnes, gave up Ninus and promised her soul to the man who saved her but couldn't love anyone because he was consumed with suffering.

Past lives that slipped through her fingers, no matter how hard she tried to hold on to them.

The sky turns darker, bleeding for its king. Semiramis casts one last look at the tomb, then walks away. The wind follows her, the spirits of the dead whispering. She doesn't fear them.

She knows that they will meet again in the house of dust:

the common woman who became queen,

the governor she married,

and the king who loved them both.

Epilogue

Ribat watches Semiramis take the throne as the flowers blossom on the trees. She sits in a golden chair, which ten servants bear on their shoulders as they advance towards the temple of Ishtar. The priests order the sacrifices to begin, and the people acclaim their new ruler, shouting her name again and again: Sammuramat, High Heaven.

She is dressed in purple, with gold-embroidered sleeves and a gown that flows behind her as if she were a water goddess. Ribat imagines tracing the pale scars hidden under it: the one on her chest, between the ribs, the faded ones on her back and arms, the loss in her heart, and the fear of being forgotten that is part of her every breath.

He thinks: This is what it means to be born in the dust and reach for the heavens.

To be as bright and dangerous as the burning sun.

To make a life out of nothing.

*

Spring is ending, and summer is coming with its long, burning days.

The eunuch walks into the school one evening when the fading light paints the city blue. Scribes quickly disappear at the sight of him. Through the large windows, boys are playing, reciting proverbs to a tall priest. Ribat wipes his hands on a piece of cloth, hiding his surprise. He bows slightly as Sasi studies his face, a faint smile on his lips.

'You are still alive,' the eunuch says. 'And no longer a slave.'

'And you are still a spymaster.'

Sasi chuckles. 'You almost say it as if it were a curse.'

'Did the queen send you?' Ribat asks, careful to empty his voice of any hope. He hasn't spoken to her since that terrible day in the king's chambers, when he ran away from the palace, his heart bleeding and his mind praying for forgiveness.

'I came of my own accord.' There is a slight shift in his voice, and Ribat stands still, waiting. He can *taste* danger, as he used to when he was a slave.

'Our king died a horrible death,' Sasi says, after a long silence. 'A wound, festering inside him. He fought Marduk bravely yet it was the fever that killed him. Can you imagine? Thrashing in your own bed, hopeless, without even knowing that you're going to have a son.'

Ribat says nothing. Images float in his mind: the king's unfocused eyes, his feverish skin.

'You were there, I remember,' Sasi continues. 'You were administering the willow bark to him.'

His heart is hammering his chest. He keeps staring into Sasi's eyes, his face emotionless.

'And yet,' Sasi says, 'when I told this to the queen, she dismissed me. She ordered me never to speak of it again. Whatever happened, she protected you. Why?'

Ribat chooses his words carefully. 'The queen knows I am devoted to her.'

There is something grim in Sasi's quiet laugh. 'That is how obses- sion blinds. It makes one think one is the only person in another's world. But our greatest mistake is to think that obsession comes with loyalty. It doesn't. Our king was obsessed with Onnes, yet he betrayed him. You are obsessed with our queen, yet you betrayed her.'

'I did not betray her,' Ribat says. The words ring in the room, false like off-key notes.

'She gave birth this morning,' Sasi says. 'I thought you would want to know.'

Ribat's heart aches. 'She did?'

'A boy. Ninyas, she has called him.'

Once, Ribat would have been next to Semiramis as she gave birth. Now there is this eunuch, who has replaced him. Ribat hates him. But Sasi is walking away, and Ribat can't help himself.

'What will you do when she tires of you?' he asks. 'When her heart turns elsewhere?'

Sasi stops. When he turns again, the sun is in his face, and for a moment he seems to have no features. 'I will change, of course. I will be a different man, the one she will need. That is the secret to survival: to keep transforming into something else. The heart of a lion, the skill of a snake, the wings of a bird – such a slippery creature can never be caught.'

'Anyone can be caught,' Ribat says.

'Perhaps,' Sasi concedes. 'But if what you say is true, then you can be caught too.'

Ribat watches him go, his blue dress fading in the evening light. Scribes and priests scatter around him, letting him pass.

I was born a slave, Ribat thinks. *I have spent every waking moment observing the people around me. I can be a scribe, I can be a noble-man, I can be a courtier. But, most of all, I can be nothing. I can disappear. I am not sure you have that gift, Spymaster.*

*

She comes to the temple wearing a turquoise dress and bracelets with lions' heads around her wrists. She looks godly, unreachable, as if the very air around her is burning, and he will catch fire by walking into it.

He kneels, forehead pressed against the floor. 'My queen,' he says.

For a long time, there is silence. When she finally speaks, her words are cold, as if spoken by a statue. 'What is done is done,' she says. 'And yet sometimes we are fools, wishing we could change the past.'

He looks up at her. Slowly, he stands. 'I didn't understand, at first,' she says, 'but then, one day, Sasi told me that years ago a group of slaves was poisoned for seeing Nisat and Ilu together. I imagine your mother was among them, wasn't she?'

His eyes sting. His skin is aching, as if her gaze was burning him.

'I don't know how or when you found out,' she continues. 'Maybe you've always known.'

The king was already dying, Ribat wants to say, but what good would the lie do? He did it to avenge his mother, and he will not take back his action.

'I never wanted to hurt you,' he says. He wishes he could explain that he *had* to make a choice, that he, unlike her, cannot leave his past behind. But all he can think is, *I love you.*

'You betrayed me,' she says.

The pain in his chest is too strong to bear. He thinks he will die from it. Then, to his surprise, she covers the distance between them and touches his shoulder. He doesn't move, for he fears she'd step back. She stays there as if she can't leave him either.

'You have done everything for me,' she says. 'I will never forget that. But I don't know how I can forgive you.'

It is the last thing she says to him before she walks away. He stays still until the echo of her steps has faded and the sky has filled with a thousand watchful stars.

*

At dawn, the shadows are still, the school empty. Ribat walks between the tables, looks at the tablets around him. He can almost hear them humming, as if they are waiting for him to unlock their secrets: endless deeds of kings and governors, exploits of great men, their fathers and their sons.

There are no women carved into the clay. When Ribat had first noticed it, he had gone to the priest and asked why. The man had looked at Ribat with a curious expression. 'The echoes of most lives are destined to fade with the passing of time,' he had said. 'And slaves and women fade before everyone else.'

Ribat did not like his answer. Didn't Semiramis teach him to challenge the order of things? He has learned to read from the scar on his mother's back and now he holds a stylus in his hand.

Outside the window, the head of the sun appears, while the pale moon slowly vanishes. Ribat is sure it is an omen. Empires shine before they drown in the darkness.

Yes, he thinks, there will be a time when the empire will fall, and another will rise in its stead. But the clay filled with stories will last for ever.

He grips his stylus and starts writing.

Thus the queen Semiramis,
also known as Sammuramat,
the only female ruler of the mighty empire of Assyria,
the most renowned of all women of whom we have any record,
rose from a lowly fortune to the greatest fame.

Author's note

In the ninth century BC, one woman ruled an empire stretching from the Mediterranean coast in Syria to present-day western Iran. Her name was Sammuramat, meaning 'high heaven'. The Greeks called her Semiramis.

Sammuramat is the only Assyrian woman who succeeded in imposing her personality on history. According to historical sources, she ruled for five years after her husband died and before her son came of age. Her rise to power coincided with a critical moment for the empire: her husband, Shamshi-Adad the Fifth, was the grandson of one of the greatest rulers of Assyria, Ashurnasirpal the Second, who made the ancient Kalhu capital and expanded the empire with a level of cruelty he made no attempt to hide. For two generations the empire remained stable, until Shamshi-Adad's brother plunged it into civil war. By the time Shamshi-Adad died, Assyria was financially and politically weakened, and it was left to Sammuramat to restore stability.

History might not speak much of Sammuramat but, after her death, myth made sure that her name echoed through the generations. In the fifth century BC, historian Herodotus wrote about her, using the Greek form of her name, but our main source for the mythical life of this warrior queen is Diodorus Siculus (90–30 BCE). In his monumental work *Bibliotheca Historica*, Diodorus offers a detailed narrative of a clever and beautiful woman, who rose from humble beginnings to rule one of the biggest empires in the world. I have included much of Diodorus' myth in the novel, in one form or another. According to the historian's tale, Semiramis was born in present-day Syria, daughter of a goddess named Derceto and a handsome young man who was devoted to the Greek Aphrodite. Derceto killed her lover and threw herself into a lake, but the baby Semiramis survived. She was cared for by doves, until a shepherd found her. When she came of age, the governor of Syria – 'his name was Onnes, and he stood first among the members of the king's council', Diodorus writes – was struck by her beauty, married her and took her with him to the capital.

A few years later, when he was sent on a campaign to the faraway land of Bactria, Semiramis followed him and came up with the winning strategy to make the city surrender. After the battle, the king – Ninus – fell for her. Here, as Diodorus tells us, tragedy ensued:

> *The king, marvelling at the ability of the woman and becoming infatuated with her, tried to persuade her husband to yield her to him of his own accord, offering in return to give him his own daughter Sosanê to wife. And Onnes, partly out of fear of the king's threats and partly out of his passion for his wife, fell into a frenzy and madness and killed himself. Such then, were the circumstances whereby Semiramis attained the position of queen.*

Shamshi-Adad the Fifth's father and grandfather were kings who established a reputation for all time. Ashurnasirpal especially flagged his cruelty on various inscriptions: '*I had a column built at the city gate and I flayed all the leaders who had rebelled, and I covered the column with their skins. Some I impaled on stakes and others I bound to stakes around it.*' (In the novel I have mentioned this scene when Onnes and Semiramis speak after the Balkh attack.)

This brutality, which is so shocking to us, was the norm for the Assyrian Empire. Their callous and ruthless character is shown on the bas-reliefs that have survived, on which we see people flayed alive, impaled on stakes and having their heads cut off. Many other ancient civilizations were responsible for similar brutal acts, but the Assyrians revelled in it. By depicting these acts in graphic detail in their art, they celebrated their conquests and showed what would happen to those who opposed them: the purpose was propagandistic.

Lord Byron wrote that the Assyrians went after their neighbours like a 'wolf in the fold … his cohorts gleaming with purple and gold'. Assyrian King Sennacherib had his writers describe how he defeated the Elamites: 'I cut their throats like sheep … My prancing steeds plunged into their welling blood as into a river; the wheels of battle chariots were bespattered with blood and filth. I filled the plain with corpses of their warriors like herbage.' These are some of the lines that inspired the scene of the Balkh attack in my novel.

While the battle of Balkh is narrated by Diodorus Siculus, the battle of Dur was a real historical event. After enjoying a relatively peaceful period, during the last years of Shamshi-Adad's reign the new king of Babylon turned against Assyria in 814 BC. Shamshi-Adad besieged Marduk's army at the city of Dur-Papsukkal, destroyed the joint forces of Babylonian, Elamite, Aramean and Chaldean troops, captured the king, Marduk, and plundered the country.

The more I researched the world of ancient Mesopotamia, the more I asked myself, What impact did this brutality have on those who exercised it and those who endured it? Because of the constant campaigns and shows of atrocity, Assyrian warriors might have suffered from what we know as post-traumatic stress disorder. Texts from the period tell us how an Assyrian king's mind 'changed', meaning he was disturbed, or suffering from PTSD. I relied heavily on this to explore the mental state of Ninus, Onnes and Semiramis after the Balkh campaign.

While their empire was renowned for its cruelty, the Assyrians' culture was dazzlingly rich. Western civilization originated from the land between the rivers Tigris and Euphrates, where writing was first invented, where Hammurabi created the first legal code, and where the oldest story in the world was written, a thousand years before *The Iliad*, *The Odyssey* and the Bible: *The Epic of Gilgamesh*.

Gilgamesh is a story about the love between two brothers, and what happens when one of them dies. The most extraordinary thing about it is its exploration of grief and longing for immortality, two themes that are also the beating heart of my novel. The relationship between Ninus and Onnes is heavily inspired by the one between Gilgamesh and his friend and brother, Enkidu: the first great friendship in literature, a thousand years before Achilles and Patroclus.

I wrote *Babylonia* as the inexorable journey of its main characters towards death, their desperate efforts to avoid it and reach for the highest heavens, and their quest to learn how to deal with love in the face of grief.

Many of the characters of my novel were real people, though their portrayal comes from my own interpretation of historical sources. The character of Ilu is based on the real-life *turtanu* Shamshi-Ilu, one of the strongest political and military figures of the Neo-Assyrian Empire. Dayyan-Assur was the *turtanu* to whom Shalmaneser gave control of his army and it was he who provoked Assur-danin into opening the civil war.

Nisat is the first Neo-Assyrian queen recorded in history. Her real name was Mullissu-mukkanisat-Ninua and she was the daughter of King Ashurnasirpal's great cupbearer. She married two kings: Ashurnasirpal first, then Ashurnasirpal's son, Shalmaneser.

The character of Sasi is invented, but many governors and state officials were eunuchs.

Of the prisoners Assyrians took from their campaigns, the rebels were killed, while the rest of the population was usually left alive. The victors tended to deport and resettle them elsewhere, but the practice, over time, changed the heart of the empire.

Finally, Urartu was a powerful kingdom that emerged in eastern Anatolia, centred around Lake Van. For years, it threatened the military dominance of Assyria. The character of Taria comes from my research into this fascinating and forgotten culture.

While the main beats of the novel are taken from mythical and historical sources, much of it is a figment of my imagination, though I have done extensive research to make the story as true to its historical, cultural and political backdrop as possible. Many of the scenes – the lion hunt, Ninus' memory of the garden celebrations with his father and the head of a defeated enemy, the treatment of prisoners after Balkh – are based on Assyrian art.

The poems, proverbs and myths in the novel are lines from Mesopotamian literature, and are taken either from *Gilgamesh*, or *Before the Muses*, an anthology of Akkadian literature. The only poems that are mine are the prophecies that foresee Ninus' death and Semiramis' rise to power. The latter is inspired by the identification of Semiramis as 'Babylon', which comes from the Christian tradition. There are many references to Babylon in the Bible, both historical and allegorical. Babylon the Great, also known as the 'Whore of Babylon', refers to both a symbolic female figure and a place of lust and evil, as mentioned in the Bible's Book of Revelation: 'Babylon the Great, the Mother of Harlots and Abominations of the Earth, the great city which reigneth over the kings of the earth'. In his nineteenth-century book *The Two Babylons*, Christian minister Alexander Hislop named Semiramis 'the Whore of Babylon'.

The depiction of Semiramis as a lustful, sinful figure prevailed for centuries in the literary tradition, from Petrarch and Boccaccio to

Rossini and Voltaire. In his *Inferno*, Dante puts Semiramis in the Circle of Lust, next to Helen, Dido and Cleopatra: 'to sensual vices she was so abandoned, that lustful she made licit in her law, to remove the blame to which she had been led'.

Finally, Ribat. While I was fascinated by the dynamics between powerful characters in the novel, I felt my portrait of ancient Mesopotamia wouldn't be complete without a glimpse into the lives of those who had no power. At first I hadn't planned to write chapters from Ribat's perspective, but one day his voice came to me so vividly that I couldn't ignore him. His presence transformed the trajectory of the story, and I love the parallel between Onnes' and Ninus' fall from the highest heavens on the one side, and Semiramis' and Ribat's rise from the dust on the other.

As I mentioned before, the historian Diodorus drew on earlier authors to write the myth of Semiramis, such as Ctesias of Cnidus, who, for his part, must have drawn on even earlier sources. Thus the ending of my book came to life. Whoever formulated the myth of Semiramis must have revered the queen to ensure that her name reverberated through history. And I love the idea that it might have been a scribe and a former slave who first told her story.